—

HEMLOCK LAKE

HEMLOCK LAKE

CAROLYN J. ROSE

FIVE STAR
A part of Gale, Cengage Learning

GALE
CENGAGE Learning·

Detroit • New York • San Francisco • New Haven, Conn • Waterville, Maine • London

GALE
CENGAGE Learning

LIBRARY OF CONGRESS CATALOGING-IN-PUBLICATION DATA

Rose, Carolyn J.
    Hemlock Lake / Carolyn J. Rose. — 1st ed.
      p. cm.
    ISBN-13: 978-1-59414-884-2 (hardcover)
    ISBN-10: 1-59414-884-8 (hardcover)
      1. Murder—Investigation—Fiction. 2. Catskill Mountains (N.Y.)—Fiction. I. Title.
    PS3618.O7829H46 2010
    813'.6—dc22   2010008534

First Edition. First Printing: July 2010.
Published in 2010 in conjunction with Tekno Books and Ed Gorman.

Printed in the United States of America
1 2 3 4 5 6 7 14 13 12 11 10

This book is dedicated to the memory of my parents, Malcolm Rose and Elizabeth Louise Busch Rose, members of the Greatest Generation.

AUTHOR'S NOTE

This book is a work of fiction. Ashokan County, New York, is an imaginary place, as are all of its residents and all of the landmarks and geographical features within it, including Hemlock Lake.

ACKNOWLEDGMENTS

Many thanks to my husband for all of his support. And thanks to my brother, Lorin Rose, and to Fire Marshal David Lynam for details about guns, bombs, arson, and firefighting. Any errors or mistakes are mine, not theirs.

Chapter 1
October

Fists clenched, I watched the medical examiner's van wallow along the rutted gravel driveway. With a flicker of brake lights, it turned onto the patched asphalt road that circled Hemlock Lake as Sheriff Clement North laid a weathered hand on my shoulder. I flinched and drove my fingernails into my palms.

"Phil can take care of the rest of this, Dan." North's voice was muted, his words tentative. "Why don't you go on—"

"Home?" I laughed bitterly as the van disappeared beyond a stand of white birches. Yellow leaves fluttered in its wake, drifting through dusty October air. "Is that what you were going to say? That I should go home?"

North's fingers flexed. "No. Why don't you ride back to the office with me? Someone will bring your cruiser along later. I called the chaplain. He'll notify your father."

"No." I shrugged his hand away and walked to the edge of the porch, my heels thudding on the thick oak planks. "I can handle this."

"I know you can handle it, Dan. I'm not questioning your ability. But it would be better if you—"

"No." I turned on him, glimpsing my pain, dark and knotted, reflected in his eyes. "This is my responsibility. My duty."

I trudged down the broad steps and along the path toward the rippling indigo water. "It's all paperwork from here on out, anyway," I called over my shoulder. "Just like any other accident, any other suicide."

North didn't answer, didn't state the obvious—this time there had been no need to check the bodies for identification, this time I wouldn't search for next of kin.

The names I'd write at the top of the reports would be Nathaniel Justice Stone and Susanna Elizabeth Chase Stone.

My brother.

My wife.

CHAPTER 2
APRIL

"I called you in because I'm looking for fresh ideas on a case," Sheriff North said. "We have damn little to go on."

I tore my gaze from the tiny buds on the gnarled maple tree outside the window. Spring had come to my wasteland. Each pale leaf and bright blossom seemed to mock my misery. Swallowing long-simmering rage, I watched the sheriff deal six sheets of paper and an equal number of envelopes onto the dog-eared green blotter staking its claim between stacks of worn file folders.

"It's not much." North shrugged. "Wasn't a decent fingerprint once we ruled out the construction chief who opened them. And with the way the system operates now—centralized—all we know is the general area they were mailed from. Used to be easier when every little post office had its own mark."

I fingered a piece of three-ring binder paper speckled with words sliced from a newspaper and stiff with yellowing globs of dried glue. "You build. We'll burn."

"They cut up an Albany newspaper for that one," the sheriff said. "The type matches. But I'm thinking these threats could be linked to eco-terrorists. Like that case out on Long Island."

I nodded. I'd read about a group claiming responsibility for explosive devices set in a number of luxury homes under construction. The group had declared it an effort to stop urban sprawl, halt overdevelopment, and preserve farmland. Perhaps they'd decided the Catskills needed saving next. I glanced at the other papers: "Stop construction or we will. Preserve, don't pillage. You put it up, we'll burn it down. Don't desecrate this land." My fingers curled as I read the final note. "Don't destroy Hemlock Lake."

Images of my father's house and the two bodies I'd found inside rose in my mind. I forced words past my teeth. "Hemlock Lake?"

"Yep." North leaned back, his worn leather swivel chair creaking, and packed shreds of honey-colored tobacco into his pipe. "Some developer bought a parcel of land across the lake and up aways from your father's place. He's putting up ten luxury homes." Rocking forward, he set the pipe on the corner of the desk and shuffled the letters together. "I thought you could go up there, sort of on a part-time basis, and—"

"No." The thud of sodden earth against Susanna's coffin filled my ears. I would never return to the lake. "No."

The sheriff's chair rolled against the credenza behind his desk with a dull clunk as he stood and ambled to the map of Ashokan County that covered an entire wall. He splayed mottled fingers across the green-gray mass representing mountains and the blue vein of a stream swelling out of Dark Moon Hollow and feeding Hemlock Lake. "With your dad in that nursing home now, his place probably needs a lick of paint or a few shingles. While you're making repairs, you can nose around, see if anybody's seen or heard anything connected to the letters or the other incidents."

I felt a twinge of curiosity, couldn't tamp it down. "Other incidents?"

"Vandalism. Minor theft. Graffiti." He tapped a file folder at the top of one heap. "Here's the file. Look it over. I'll clear you to start on this next week."

I dug my fingers into the scarred oak armrests of the visitor's chair. "Is that an order?"

He hitched at his pants and scratched a bristling eyebrow with a thumbnail. "Well, no, Dan, it's not an order. But you're the best man for this job. You grew up around Hemlock Lake; you know what it's like. They've got cable TV and their calendars show they're in the new century just like all the rest of us, but they've still got one foot in the past. Deep in the past. They keep themselves apart, take care of their own. Hell, for all I know, it's not tree-huggers behind this, it's someone local."

Someone local. I fought to keep my face still, to show no sign of interest.

North slapped the file folders. "I sent an investigator up there twice. Waste of manpower. Nobody saw anything. Nobody knew anything. People up there wouldn't give an outsider a glass of water if his teeth were on fire."

I rose from my chair. He'd drawn an accurate sketch and given me a way out. "What good would I do? I'm not an investigator. I'm a patrol sergeant." I liked it that way, preferred space and stretches of solitude. I didn't want an office and walls around me—especially now.

North waved me back into my seat, slumped into his own, lifted the pipe, and tamped more tobacco into the bowl. "You've had some training." He dug a pack of matches from his pocket, struck one, and touched it to the tobacco. "I'm betting you'll pick up on something." He puffed, cheeks reddening.

A cloud of apple-scented smoke swirled around him. I blinked away the image of that black van carrying Nat and Susanna through falling leaves as sunset bloodied the lake.

"And face it Dan, you haven't been yourself since the, uh . . ." He paused, chewing at the corners of his mustache. "Not that anyone expected you to bounce right back. You went through more hell in one day than any man deserves in an entire lifetime. And then to have your father go down with a stroke . . ." He shook his head. "But we're comin' up on May. It's been almost

15

seven months. You don't eat enough to keep a bird alive; you're in that cruiser all night, every night." He puffed at the pipe again, cursed and set it aside. "And damn it, you're not calling for backup when you should. It's just a matter of time before you get hurt. Or hurt someone else." He leaned closer, narrowed his eyes. "I can't have that."

Red anger clogged my throat, distorting my voice. "That won't happen."

He held out his hands, palms up. I recognized the gesture from a dozen other discussions. It meant he had no choice, was only doing his job. "Sometimes you can't carry the weight alone. I'd hate to have to order you to take time off and get counseling, but I will if . . ." He shrugged, leaving it there.

Muscles knotted at the hinges of my jaw and around my eyes. No one would trespass in my mind, dissect my pain.

The sheriff fingered his pipe again. "I'd appreciate it if you'd look into this. As a favor to me."

I stood and slung the chair into a bookcase crammed with grimy regulation manuals dating back to the Nixon administration. Two appreciation plaques teetered, then fell from the top shelf. Glass splintered and skittered across the pitted green linoleum. "Assign me to jail duty. Put me on a desk. Fire my ass if you want. I'll never go to Hemlock Lake again if I live to be a hundred."

A wintry smile crossed the sheriff's face. "Maybe you'll live that long, son. But maybe you won't make it through next week. Those two ghosts have a hell of a hold on you. Better lay them to rest before they drag you into a grave beside them."

I didn't feel it then, but he'd set the hook.

My mind played the idea like a fisherman plays a rainbow trout, watching it arc into the sunlight, then plunge beneath the dark surface to run out line and leap again. Like Ahab, whose hunt for the white whale became a fatal obsession, my unconscious mind became consumed by the vision of returning to the lake where Susanna drowned. Trembling and sweating, I'd rise from uneasy sleep and swear I'd never do it. But each long day, as I prowled the house Susanna and I had shared, the vision loomed larger.

The length of Ashokan County lay between that house and Hemlock Lake. The distance had been the condition of my return from Arizona, where I'd stayed on after college, determined that my family's past wouldn't be a prologue to my future, determined to forge my own identity in welcome anonymity. I'd changed a tire for Susanna on a snowy Flagstaff night and proposed before spring. Three years ago, when we learned my mother had breast cancer, Susanna insisted I return to New York. I was the son my mother had been closest to, she'd argued, the son born while my father flew missions over Vietnam, the child my mother had clung to for solace when he'd volunteered for a second tour of duty. Nat, who'd come later, had been raised with a less cautious maternal hand. My father, home by then with medals and grim memories, had crafted Nat in his own image while making it clear I lacked the raw material for him to do the same with me.

I'd gotten on with the sheriff's department, and Susanna found work as a legal secretary. I'd had six months of awkward visits with my mother before she'd slipped permanently into morphine-laced sleep. I'd started to pack before the funeral flowers wilted. But Susanna had argued that my father and Nat needed our help. "Someone has to stop Nat from cleaning truck parts in the dishwasher. Someone has to keep your dad from getting scurvy eating venison stew and oyster crackers three times a day. You owe it to your mother to visit whenever you can, to help them through their grief."

I knew far too well that family custom was to project strength and spurn assistance—there would be no displays of grief, no sharing of emotions—but I'd felt obligated to let her make her sacrifice and I'd loved her enough to go along. When I drew a duty rotation that put me on patrol Friday and Saturday evenings, Susanna had gone without me. She'd loved the shadowed mountains, clean air, and bright water.

On her thirtieth birthday, the lake killed her.

"Damn it, Susanna!" I punched the pillow that had been hers. "Why did you take the boat out in the dark? How could you have been so reckless with our lives?"

Her death had set off a chain reaction of misery: Nat, dead by his own hand; my father, struck down by the loss of his steadfast son, drifting toward death; me, clinging blindly to routine through hollow days, waiting for—what?

I pressed the pillow to my face and breathed in the faint and elusive scent of Susanna's skin and hair. Pain, they say, forces you to change. But pain had only made me tighten my grip on the essence of what I'd lost. Since the night Susanna died, I'd altered nothing in this three-bedroom ranch house—not her towel in the bathroom or the sheets on our bed. I slept on the sofa, showered at the gym, and ate in my car or at the counter of any derelict diner where I could rely on a surly owner never to ask how I was doing.

I flung the pillow aside and turned to the silver-framed photograph of the smiling woman tossing a bouquet of yellow roses toward a thicket of grasping hands. If I abandoned this house, this shrine to her memory, what would I feel? If I accepted the loss of love, what remained?

"Nothing."

I examined the word. It was both confining and freeing. Nothing. No attachments, no one to care for me and no one to care about. Neither less, nor more, than what I had now.

I felt lightheaded, but calm, as if I'd stopped spinning in

place at a crossroads, adjusted my balance, and chose a highway. The highway to Hemlock Lake.

I slid Susanna's smile into a drawer. I would return to the lodge, and I would strip it of every memento, leave the ghosts no earthly anchors, and drive them from the earth, from me.

Seizing the phone, I dialed the sheriff's private line and left a message. Then I dismantled my shrine to Susanna. Like an advancing army scorches earth and burns bridges behind it, I made certain return was not an option. I tossed clothing, jewelry, shoes, and hair clips into boxes, and trucked everything to a shelter for battered women.

That weekend I sold our furniture, stored the books in which I'd sought refuge and found none, and handed the house keys to a blade-faced woman who warned me I'd lose a month's rent for failing to give proper notice.

I told her money couldn't buy back the past.

CHAPTER 3

I glanced up at the curtained windows of the lodge, half expecting to see a face appear, hear footsteps as Susanna hurried to greet me. Tears burned the corners of my eyes, and I squeezed the lids shut. No time for that.

Snagging a gallon jug of water from the back of the SUV, I tugged off a section of graying latticework and duck-walked under the porch to the pump. I poured in enough water to prime it, threw the switch, and listened as it gargled and sputtered to life and began filling the reservoir tank on the uphill side of the house.

"Nothing to it," I coached myself as I replaced the drain plug Ronny Miller had removed last fall. I tightened it as far as I could, reminding myself to check it later to see if it needed more persuasion from a wrench. Lifting the dripping boughs of a young hemlock, I crunched through a crust of dirty snow and moldering leaves to the far corner of the stone foundation. A blackened metal rod thrust itself from the ground, a warped and rusted wheel at the top, level with my knees. I wrapped my hands around the wheel and threw my weight against it.

"Unggh."

It shuddered but didn't budge. Months of paint-peeling winds, temperatures below freezing, and the range of precipitation a Catskill winter delivers had riveted the metal in place. I kicked aside a clump of leaves sodden with the acid scent of decay, anchored my feet, and strained until a wire of pain hummed between my ears.

Tires ground along the gravel of the driveway and someone gunned a big engine twice, then shut it down. A door slammed and feet stomped to the front walk. "Dan! My man! Where are you?"

I didn't answer. Kneeling, I shoved at the wheel. Bright lights pinged off the black wall rising before my eyes.

"Hey, bud." Ronny shouldered aside the budding canes of an aged lilac bush and slapped my back. "How you doing? I saw you drive by. Glad you're here. Real glad." His gaze slid to the wheel. "Shit, man, did I turn that too hard? Let me take a shot."

"I can get—"

"Not as thin and mangy as you've gotten." He laughed and planted his thigh against my shoulder, pushing me aside. "Let me at it."

I stood, shrugged, and backed off, feeling powerless despite my hundred and eighty pounds, my six feet and an inch. Self-sufficiency was the Stone family legacy, passed on even before I'd learned to cobble words into complete sentences. But from a lifetime of experience I knew it would be pointless and self-defeating to argue with Ronny. Like spitting into the wind.

He rolled massive shoulders, rubbed his hands together, and tilted the bill of his cap back for a better look. I glanced at the words stitched in screaming yellow on the black cloth: "One Mean Mother." Ronny was either your best friend or the person you'd least like to find yourself on the wrong side of. Looking at him, I thought of the way Cassius described Caesar in Shakespeare's play. Beside Ronny, we were all "petty men," all "underlings," especially here in the constricted world of Hemlock Lake.

His wiry red beard scratched against the collar of his flannel shirt as he bent, gripped the wheel, and leaned into it. "Son of a—" It turned with a dull grating shriek, then knocked and chattered as water gushed into the pipes. Through the double-paned glass of the window above my head I heard a faucet gasp, then belch out explosions of trapped air.

"Better let that run a good long while. Get your pipes and the reservoir cleared out." Ronny stood with a grunt, wiped his hands on the back pockets of his bib overalls, and grasped my hand. "Goddamn, it's good to see you again, bud. We'd begun to wonder if you were ever coming back. Willie Dean even thought you might sell this place to some damn outlander." His laugh dulled some of the edge on that last comment, but left plenty of steel.

I didn't betray myself. No point in testing the slogan on his hat. Ronny's family went back as far as my own at Hemlock Lake—six generations quarrying, fishing, hunting, and trying to plow a straight furrow among stones thrust up by soil-splitting frost. "Thou shalt not sell your land to an outsider" was the first commandment up here, far ahead of admonitions about murder and adultery. He released my hand and torpedoed through a welter of downed limbs and whip-like saplings to the front of the house.

Protecting my eyes from recoiling branches, I followed, as I had almost from the time I'd taken my first steps.

"Sure missed your brother this winter," he said as we climbed the shallow stone steps to the porch. "The best number-two man I ever had on the darts team."

"Yeah. Nat always had a good—" I choked on the word "aim," remembering the bullet he'd put in his brain.

Ronny clamped a hand on my shoulder. "How's your father doing?"

I stepped out of his grip, rejecting sympathy. "He's holding on, Ronny. That's all they'll say." Shading my eyes, I stared at the shards of red shale littering the rim of the lake, then looked across the rippling water to a stand of shivering white birches and the slope-shouldered mountains looming beyond. Platoons of pine and hemlock marched along the ridges among greening stands of oak and maple. Intersecting stone walls outlined rock-strewn pastures; young trees crouched inside their perimeters like advance scouts surveying the terrain.

"You taking a leave?" Ronny broke the silence.

"No."

His eyes narrowed. "Here for the fishing?"

I considered my options, realized I had only the truth. Lying to Ronny about my mission would close doors I'd never pry open again. "The sheriff wants me to look into the trouble at the construction site."

Ronny's mouth tightened. Pivoting on the heel of a scuffed work boot, he strode across the porch. "Let's check those faucets."

I hung back, fingering the key ring in my pocket. I'd envisioned myself walking through the lodge alone, touching each familiar piece of furniture, greeting the ghosts in my own way, in my own time. "You've done enough already."

"Nothing's too much for a buddy. Open the door. We're burning daylight."

I gave up the fight, unlocked the door, and trailed him across the high-ceiling living room, past a fireplace so large you could park a motorcycle inside, and into the kitchen. As he had in the other rooms, my great-grandfather had paneled it with thick slabs of knotty pine. Smoke, grease, and time had stained the walls the color of caramel syrup, and beads of amber pitch bled from the knotholes. Water gushed into the stainless steel double sink my father had added. I noticed that rust spewed by the first surge had spattered the pale blue countertop and the white ceramic tile beneath a window framed by red-checked café curtains my mother had sewn the winter before she died. Had she found the bright color comforting? I'd never asked. I'd never know.

"Running clear now." Ronny shut off the faucets. "I'll turn on the propane for the stove and get the refrigerator up and working. You check the rest."

Whistling the chorus of "Sweet Home Alabama," he didn't wait to see if I obeyed his order. He plunged the plug into its socket, then embraced the refrigerator and waltzed it back to the wall.

I crossed the living room again and opened the worn wine-colored velvet drapes that my grandmother had saved an entire year to buy, then took the stairs to the loft two at a time and entered the half bath wedged between the two small knotty-pine-paneled bedrooms where Nat and I had spent our child-hood. After my mother died, he appropriated the downstairs guest room. Susanna and I had squeezed into my old room, a space she called "cozy."

Trying not to see her comb and toothbrush at the edge of the sink, I thumbed back the handles on the faucets and flushed the toilet. Brown water swirled in the bowl, gurgled away. I watched the bowl fill, flushed it again, and returned to the main floor.

My father's room, overlooking the lake, was just as he'd left it when he'd taken off on an elk-spotting trip to Colorado two days before Susanna's accident. As I turned the faucets in the bathroom, I noticed he'd left behind his safety razor. Fingering the cross-hatched metal handle, I remembered how I'd watched him whip lather with the shaving brush, the wooden handle tinking against the sides of the mug, spicy scent filling the room. Standing on a chair and squinting into the mottled mirror, I'd mimicked the way he'd crimp his lips before he spread the froth on his cheeks and chin. Times long gone. I nudged the razor from the edge of the sink, heard it clatter into the lopsided wooden wastebasket I'd made in shop class my freshman year. An attendant shaved my father now. Mondays and Thursdays.

I picked my way over musty braided rugs along the hall to the main bathroom where water spattered sharply against a mildewed plastic shower curtain. Tweaking it aside, I shoved in the shower knob, and then moved on to the sink and toilet.

I had no intention of going into Nat's bedroom but, like a man hypnotized, I shuffled to the door, jerked it open, and flipped the light switch. A rectangle of dusty oak flooring, paler than the rest, marked the place where the bed had stood until I'd hauled it outside and set fire to it. I tasted gun oil at the back of my mouth, swallowed, and closed my eyes. The image of my brother's body and the blood-soaked mattress burned through the lids.

"You about done?" Ronny called from the kitchen.

I opened my eyes, half expecting to see the vast, throbbing pain that filled my chest and head. "Yeah." Closing the door, I leaned against it, breathing hard, overwhelmed by the job ahead of me, by the relentless avalanche of the remaining days of my life.

Ronny said something else, but I heard only a muffled echo. I suspected he was crouched alongside the stove, checking the couplings on the gas line, or perhaps peering into the oven to see if the ignition system worked. Back in high school, teachers had told Ronny's parents he was "a natural leader with strong mechanical aptitude, but not scholastically inclined." A nice way to say "not on the fast track toward college." Not that he'd cared. He could rebuild a carburetor in his sleep, chop cordwood with a beer in one hand, out-wrestle a writhing fire hose, and shoot a squirrel through the eye at a hundred yards. I'd checked the curriculum at college. None of those subjects had been listed. Despite my father's derision, I'd majored in English, finding it a luxury to read as much as I wanted. But six years into teaching kids who didn't share my enthusiasm, in the wake of a jaw-clenching Thanksgiving visit when I'd refused to shoot a four-point buck drinking at the lake, I'd gone into law enforcement to prove I was as much of a man as Nat. My father hadn't seemed to notice. But when the decision put me on the highway where I'd met Susanna, his opinion ceased to matter quite as much.

"What?" I started toward the kitchen. "I didn't hear you."

"Did you run into any problems?" Ronny asked.

"No." I caught a glint of sunlight off the glass eyeballs in the head of the twelve-point buck mounted over the fireplace. My grandfather had put a bullet in its heart the year before my parents married. As a child, I'd often wondered if the stag had heard the shot, if he'd leaped to greet death on his own terms, or simply bent his knees to it. "How's the stove look?"

"In good shape for a piece of shit." Ronny laughed. "A regular rodent condominium. I'd get some traps first thing. And get it cleaned out. Ask Louisa Marie. She'll find somebody who don't mind dealing with a few mouse turds."

"I'll take care of it myself."

"I'll call her in a bit." He rambled on as if I'd said nothing. "Get her right on it." He shut the oven and dusted off his knees. "That'll save time. She never answers the damn phone, and you probably won't be going over there until later to get groceries. You know." He winked broadly. "Beer. And ale. And such."

"Last time I looked, Lou Marie didn't carry ale. Or such."

"That's the truth. Variety ain't the spice of her life."

"I guess you won't mind the brew I brought along."

"Does a fox lust after chicken?" He smiled, white teeth gleaming between his beard and mustache. "Out in your rig?"

I nodded, and he shoved past me. Once again I trailed behind, itching with irrational irritation, telling myself I'd intended to go outside anyway and it didn't matter who went first. But it mattered to Ronny. He was the alpha male and I had three choices: fight him, follow him, or leave.

I'd fought him once, when we were ten. I'd lost. After that I'd followed until I got old enough to leave. But now I was back.

By the time I got outside, he'd found the cooler, pulled two bottles of microbrew ale from the ice, and twisted off the caps. He handed me one and poured half of his down his throat. "Aaahhh!" He wiped his mouth on the back of a hand dense with freckles, scars, and red-gold hair. "That's fine stuff, bud, real smooth brew." He took another deep swallow and nodded toward the other side of the lake. "What kind of trouble they having over there?"

I suspected he was playing dumb, that he knew more than I did about the spray paint, slashed tires, and stolen supplies. "Graffiti. Vandalism. Threatening letters." I rolled the cold bottle between my hands, wondering why I'd bought ale when I preferred something that brought numbness more quickly. Had I unconsciously stocked it as an offering?

Ronny shrugged. "Could be kids. You know how we were back then."

"We didn't threaten arson if I recall correctly."

He arched his eyebrows, swallowed the rest of his brew, set the bottle on the hood, and fished another from the cooler. "So you gotta protect those assholes? No matter that they're ruining your home?"

"My job is to enforce the law."

"The law sucks."

He glared at me. I drank a little ale, felt it bite at my tongue, and remembered his sense of duty, as strong as my own. "If there's a fire up there, one that they can't handle themselves, you'll respond, won't you?"

He hesitated, then threw back his shoulders. "Shit, yes. But you know the fire department is all volunteer 'cept me."

I nodded.

"Well, I could haul ass to an inferno and find I'm on my lonesome. It's not something they'd put to a vote, you understand, but those guys ain't paid a dime. If they don't show, I might as well get some marshmallows and a long stick."

"The guys will come if they get the call, Ronny." *Because they'll have to face you if they don't,* I thought. *And every one of them would rather go up against a wall of flame.* "They'll come."

"Don't be so sure. That there is different. That ain't just one little house on a parcel that was sold off to a son or daughter, or someone's good buddy." He leveled his index finger toward the development across the lake, then aimed it at me. "That's rape. In-your-face rape."

"Times change, Ronny. I don't like it any more than you do." I set my ale beside his empty bottle on the hood. "It's a damn shame, but Tom Andersen talked about selling that land for years before he died and it passed to his nephew. Anyone who wanted to keep it the way it was could have made an offer on it. No one did."

"For a million dollars? You think I've got that kind of cash? You think anyone around here has?" He hurled his bottle against a tree, and then kicked the front fender on his rust-eaten pickup truck. "You don't give a shit about Hemlock Lake. You never did." He climbed into his truck, fired the engine, and backed up, tires spewing a flume of gravel.

Nice work, Dan, I thought. *You not only closed all the doors in Hemlock Lake, you locked them, too.*

The truck braked, rattled back down the driveway, and nosed in beside me. "Hey!" Ronny chewed at his mustache for a few seconds, then nodded and spit into the gravel. "You had some firefighter training, didn't you?"

"Some." Ronny might make amends, but he'd never admit he'd been wrong. I forced a smile. "Like you always said, it's not that tough. You just pour the wet stuff on the red stuff."

He studied me, then nodded slowly and grinned. "All right then. I'll get you a pager and some gear tomorrow." He smacked the truck into reverse again. "If the almanac's right, it'll be dry as a temperance convention around here this summer."

As the roar of his truck faded, I raised the bottle and filled my dry mouth. The lodge hulked in the thin sunlight, its shadow stretching toward me. The ghosts were waiting.

CHAPTER 4

Like a broken puppet, Susanna tumbled along the rippling black skin of the lake, the tow rope tight around her neck, her mouth open in a soundless scream. I leaped from the dock. Hung in the air. Drifted to the water. I swam toward her, my arms churning the chill water to white froth as I labored along the path blazed by the rising moon. The harder I swam, the more the distance between us grew.

Then Nat brought the boat to a shuddering stop. Susanna splashed beneath the surface.

Kicking off his shoes, Nat knifed into the water.

I flailed harder, raising my head to drag in air. I tried to scream, felt myself gag on the cry, choking on silence.

Nat's head rose. I saw him suck air, hump his back, dive again. Thrusting my arms forward, I pulled with all my strength. Water filled my ears and mouth. I turned my head and saw Susanna's wakeboard. It glittered in the cold moonlight. I slammed my fists against it.

Nat surfaced, dove again. My hands clawed the water, my lungs labored. Too late. Too late.

A ripping crash of thunder jolted me awake.

"Nat! Save her!" I heard the scream and opened my eyes as I realized the words were mine. A jagged bolt of lightning tore the clouds above the lake. My nostrils filled with the smell of ozone, and I shuddered and gasped for breath. Rain dripped from the hemlock boughs above me, dropping onto my face, seeping into my pillow and the patch of moss where I'd laid my sleeping bag when I'd retreated from the lodge.

After Ronny left, I'd found a dozen mousetraps in the garage, baited them with half-rancid peanut butter I'd scooped from a jar in the pantry, and set them around the kitchen. I'd brought in wood and built a fire, swept pine needles and twigs from the porch, and ate cold spaghetti from a can. Later, I'd boxed up the few things Susanna had kept in my old room: jeans, T-shirts, sweaters, and shoes. I stashed the boxes under the house, hauled my things in, wiped at the worst of the dust with a towel, and made up the bed. Sipping bourbon, I'd read for a while from a dog-eared copy of *Huckleberry Finn,* but the room under the eaves seemed to shrink each minute. When my chest felt so tight I could barely breath, I'd retreated downstairs to the sofa, stretched out under a quilt pieced by a great aunt, and closed my eyes, hoping for sleep.

My unconscious mind wouldn't allow it.

My ears had strained for muffled muttering, for shuffling footsteps in the hall. My nose had tingled with the fragrance of Susanna's gardenia perfume, the buttery scent of suntan lotion on her skin. My eyes had strafed the darkness, searching for a wisp of movement, a familiar shape. Sometime after midnight, I'd gone to the kitchen for more bourbon and caught the aroma of the cinnamon buns my mother had baked on winter mornings and the garlic-laden game stews Nat and my father had cooked nearly every Sunday. When the scent of the oil they'd used to clean the assortment of guns in the rack beside the fireplace pervaded the living room, I'd bolted.

Now a gust of wind shook the hemlock above me, filling my eyes with rain. Gathering the sodden bag and pillow, my shoes and gun, I ran toward the light I'd left burning beside the front door. I fished a wool blanket from the cedar chest in the corner of the living room, wrapped it around me, and settled in the porch swing to wait out the storm. The scent of mothballs cleared my sinuses and scattered the last remnants of the dream—my first dream about Susanna's final moments. I closed my eyes, willing the vision to return, to see her one more time, even if only to see her die. Nothing came.

I opened my eyes to see lightning slash the gray dawn sky. In two seconds thunder boomed around me, echoes rumbling down the slopes like huge boulders, crashing into the hollows. A sheet of rain swept across the dock and pounded the roof. The gutters, packed with leaves, filled and overflowed, hanging a curtain of dirty water between me and the lake. I stretched out on the swing, wondering, if I were to sleep again, if the dream would return, wondering how much more my imagination would create. Would I see Nat bring Susanna's body to the surface? Would I see him carry her into the lodge, load the rifle, and dial my number? Would I hear the words he'd left on my answering machine? "It's Nat. Susanna's dead. Forgive me." And would I see him lie down on the bed, jam the barrel into his mouth, and pull the trigger?

Lightning flashed beyond the mountains. I counted to ten before I heard a low grumble of thunder among the distant ridges. The storm was moving off. I felt drained and impotent, angry that my dream self hadn't been stronger and faster, guilty because I hadn't been here to stop them.

Mary Louise Van Valkenberg shoved a lopsided cardboard carton toward me across the scuffed gray counter that separated the post office lobby from her work space. "I've really missed your brother these past few months, Dan. Nathaniel was a spark plug. Always something fascinating running through his mind and always willing to share it." Her brown eyes grew misty. "And of course your dad is a wonderful man; it's such a shame about the stroke. I wish I could get down to see him more often."

I nodded, feeling the comparison, thinking that I wasn't the kind of person who shared my thoughts easily. I eyed the carton with dismay. Junk mail, catalogs, and circulars. More things to sort and throw away, to suck up my time.

She brushed back a tangle of graying curls and straightened the collar of her crisp blouse. I caught the faint scent of roses as she pursed small pink lips. "Anyway, I saved the mail all winter, and transferred box number six to your name. I didn't want to call and bother you about such a trivial thing. Your family has had that box since they put up this building back before World War Two. Would be a shame to see it go to somebody else."

She said the last as if that box was a priceless family heirloom and glanced around at gray plastered walls and a bulletin board layered with curling official notices and shiny pictures of commemorative stamps. Then she laid a hand on the carton. "It's mostly magazines and circulars. I sent the important stuff on to your dad's lawyer."

She paused and gave me a twinkling smile, and I guessed she'd done that without benefit of official forms. Mary Lou knew all the regulations, but often pointed out that rules were made by bureaucrats a long way from Hemlock Lake. Unlike her twin sister, Mary Lou never argued outright with authority. She bided her time and then did what she'd intended all along.

"Thanks. Is there some form I should fill out for the box?"

She flicked her hand. "Don't worry about that now. It's not like you're leaving tomorrow." She leaned closer, her gaze slewing toward the door that divided the post office from the general store her sister ran. "And some folks aren't too happy about that."

"So I've noticed." When I'd stopped at the cramped diner tacked onto the side of Stub Wilson's service station, his wife, Marcella, had scowled as she poured me a cup of scorched black coffee. Stub didn't want to mess with credit cards, she'd told me, her glance slithering away from mine, so I'd have to pay cash for my gas and food. I'd had a feeling the policy was a new one, enacted in reaction to my assignment. But I'd decided not to inquire whether Ronny, for example, also had to pay cash. I hadn't lingered over my coffee and took only two bites of the cold Danish that Marcella snatched from beside the microwave oven and plunked on a paper plate but didn't offer to heat. The mystery filling tasted like recycled motor oil smelled.

I'd intended to head to the construction site after a quick stop at the post office, but I'd forgotten about the pace of life at Hemlock Lake.

"It doesn't upset me, though." Once again Mary Lou put her plump hand on the carton. "I've always been fond of you, Dan. Ever since you were a tiny little thing and I used to babysit you."

I hoped she wouldn't launch into a detailed description of the contents of the diapers she'd changed and the baby powder she'd sprinkled on my butt.

She twinkled a smile. "Don't worry, I'm not going to relive that. I just wanted you to know I've got rules I have to follow, too. How much I like or dislike someone has nothing to do with the level of service I'm obligated to offer." She sighed. "But you know how it is up here. These folks realize time doesn't stand still, but they fight that notion tooth and nail, more so now that we just turned a new century. You've seen those rock piles, haven't you?"

"One. Near Bobcat Hollow." I'd spotted it on my way to the store. Set beneath a stand of young maples, the stack of carefully balanced rounded stones seemed to lean toward the lake like a water witcher's wand. The cairn looked as if a single touch could topple it, and yet, when I'd laid my hand on the topmost rock, the column hadn't trembled. I'd retrieved my camera and photographed it from several angles, thinking of sculptors like Michelangelo who seemed to sense the yearning inside a block of stone, chip at it, and find its soul.

"Well, you'll see more if you keep your eyes open. Seems like there's a new one almost every other day lately. I'm worried about what they mean, but Ronny thinks it could be kids building them. Or maybe somebody with a warped sense of humor—like Willie Dean." She shook her head. "Except Willie Dean's not that coordinated. And somebody would have seen him for sure."

"Yeah," I said. Scrawny and slow at his studies, Willie Dean Denton had been voted the clown of the graduating class two years ahead of mine. He liked practical jokes of the whoopee-cushion variety, and played the same ones, over and over, crowing with delight. He might build a rock pile, but only if it was part of a scheme to get a laugh. And Mary Lou was right; he wouldn't do a very good job of it.

"Do you think it's outsiders, some of those environmentalists or anarchists?"

"I don't know," I said. "That's what I hope to find out. Maybe just by being here for a few weeks I can head off trouble. Besides, the lodge needs a lot of painting, patching, and cleaning. There are things to pack up, sort out."

"Death leaves a lot of loose ends. Especially when it comes all of a sudden." She patted my hand and gave me another misty smile. "Well, you'd best get along." She glanced toward the far end of the building. "If I were you, I'd get your groceries while you're here. Don't wait 'til later, otherwise you'll put Louisa Marie's nose out of joint. And don't let her send Denny Balmer's daughter over to clean for you. That child is bone-lazy. She couldn't spot dirt if you piled it on top of a hundred-dollar bill."

I pulled the carton into my arms. "I'll bear that in mind." I shoved open the dividing door and stepped into Lou Marie's domain. I'd intended to put my shopping trip off, but there was no point in antagonizing someone as quick to anger as Lou Marie.

The door swung shut behind me and I glanced around. Floor-to-ceiling shelves crammed with everything from cocktail onions to kitty litter staggered across the room, defining narrow aisles. I set the carton beside the outside door and hooked one of six red baskets stacked in a wobbling metal rack.

"Might have known you'd stop in to see her first." Louisa Marie Van Valkenberg looked up from the book resting on the worn red linoleum counter, her words dripping acid. With her angular body, straight brown hair, and sharp nose, she was the physical opposite of her fraternal twin. Years of waiting for love or resolution had eaten away at a once-warm and generous personality, eroding it to a bitter core.

"Good morning, Louisa Marie." I gave her a tight-lipped smile and a quickly improvised lie. "No offense intended. I thought it made sense to pick up the mail first, so my milk wouldn't go sour if I got hung up next door."

Lou Marie sniffed and shot a vicious glance toward the post office. "She doesn't know when to shut up, does she? Just goes on and on 'til the cows home, and then talks their ears off after they get in the barn."

I didn't defend Mary Lou. I knew better.

"I'll bet she told you to tell me not to get Donna Balmer in to clean your place, didn't she?"

"Well . . ."

"I knew it!" A bony fist thudded on the countertop, making the cash register jingle. "She never gives me any credit. Thinks she got all the brains in the family." Lou Marie raised her voice and bellowed at the dividing door. "Well you can tell her I've got someone twenty times better. And then you can tell her to keep her big butt out of my business."

An outsider's reaction might be to suggest Lou Marie pass that advice on herself. But an outsider wouldn't know that Lou Marie had stopped speaking to her twin after deciding that Mary Lou had deliberately destroyed letters from Jefferson Longyear, letters that explained why he hadn't returned to Hemlock Lake after the fall of Vietnam. Mary Lou vehemently denied her sister's charges, saying she'd never tamper with the mail and pointing out that even the Marine Corps didn't know what had become of Jefferson after he'd walked away from a veterans' hospital in San Francisco. But none of that mattered to Lou Marie. She'd started a silent civil war that raged in this building and in the house the sisters split down the middle when their mother passed away. Unwilling to leave her sister, and unable to enjoy the happiness she'd found with Pete Whistler, Mary Lou had broken her engagement. Now the sisters marched in lockstep to the slow cadence of Louisa Marie's misery and Mary Lou's blameless guilt.

"How fresh is the bread?" I poked at a loaf of rye.

"Yesterday. And don't go smushing it all. Take the first loaf in line on the shelf. Same with the milk." She straightened shoulders that turned up into knobs of bone, making it look like she'd stuck an old wooden coat hanger upside down inside her black sweater.

"Yes ma'am." Saluting, I took a loaf, stepped around the corner of a shelf, and made my way toward the cooler, picking up a couple of cans of chili, jars of mustard, mayonnaise, pickles, and a box of crackers as I went.

"Don't sass me, Dan Stone." Her black high-tops squeaked behind me on the pitted linoleum. "You may be the long arm of the law, but I still remember when you wore nothing but short pants."

I slid open the glass door, plucked a carton of milk from one shelf and a six-pack of cola from another, and moved on toward the vegetable case.

"It's fifteen miles to the next store, Dan Stone. That's a long way to go when you run out of sugar or sandwich meat."

I turned into the threat, stood my ground, and looked into her chilly brown eyes. This was about more than a flippant tone of voice. "No sass intended, Lou Marie."

She curled her lower lip over her teeth and bit down on it, holding my gaze. "Just so you know." She squeaked off, moving with the jerky motions of a crow approaching a piece of carrion on the highway.

I know, I thought, *your life stopped when Jefferson didn't come back. You're bitter and resentful and unhappy and it's a good day when you can take it out on someone besides your sister. I know you think you've cornered the market on heartache. And I know you see a bulls-eye on my back.*

I said nothing as I loaded a wilting head of lettuce, two shriveling tomatoes, a red onion, and a cucumber into the basket and topped it with a half pound of bacon, a dozen eggs, and a can of coffee. I looked at the price label stuck to the bottom of that can. A thirty-mile round trip might be more bargain than punishment.

"That it?" Lou Marie yanked items from the basket with her left hand, pounding the buttons and smacking the handle of an antique adding machine with her right.

I glanced around, and then hooked a bag of potato chips from the rack behind me. "And these."

She hit the total button, yanked the handle a final time, and tore the paper strip from the adding machine. "Thirty-nine-seventy-three."

I reached for my wallet, then decided to play out the scene, let her use the lines I was sure she'd memorized and practiced. "Just put it on the tab and I'll pay you at the end of the month."

"No. No tabs. Cash only."

"How about a check?" I baited her.

"No. No checks."

Pretending disbelief, I opened my wallet. "You're not getting forged checks in here, are you? I'd be happy to look into it if that's the case. Or is it just the usual problem, insufficient funds?"

"Neither!" She tossed her head and her eyes hooked mine. "It's just your checks I'm not taking, Dan Stone. As long as you're helping those sons of bitches who took over Tom Andersen's place, there's no reason I should go out of my way to help you. And you're gonna find there are a lot of people up here who feel exactly the same way."

CHAPTER 5

Welcome home, I thought. Zipping my down vest against a probing wind and a spatter of rain, I stowed the groceries and mail in the back and started the engine. The windshield wipers streaked along the glass, pointing toward the road leading to the construction site, then drawing away. What was my hurry? I wasn't punching a time clock and I was getting a fraction of my regular pay, the deal I'd asked for because I wasn't a qualified investigator, and because the lodge would consume my days. Unless I was called to help with an accident or emergency situation, my assignment consisted of checking on the construction site, looking into any problems, and making myself visible. With that in mind, I decided to survey the community before I scoped out the development.

I rolled past the small white Methodist church with its squatty steeple, past the one-room schoolhouse where no student had sat for nearly forty years, and along the two short residential streets that looped off the main road. I noticed a fresh coat of paint on one house, a new roof on another, and a bird bath I hadn't seen before centered in the yard of a third. Change in Hemlock Lake came with the speed of an uphill snail race on a sun-soaked July day. As a child, I'd chafed against the disgust in my grandfather's voice when he'd cursed "cheap modern conveniences" and pointed with pride to homes without frills like central heating or garage door openers. I hadn't seen the glory in doing without by choice.

Circling back, I spotted curtains twitched aside as I passed and saw drivers cock their heads and squint; the phone lines would be humming all afternoon. I rolled by the post office again and cruised along the west side of the lake toward the construction site. The forces of erosion had flattened and peeled away more rock on this shore; the land sloped languidly to the water and nudged under it. The shoreline was scalloped into small bays and coves, and the road wound close beside them. Across the lake, on the eastern shore, a glacier had clawed the earth like an angry cat. Short, narrow pleats crimped rock ledges and the terrain writhed and fell sharply to the water, with only an occasional rounded inlet or slim spit of land like the one on which the lodge squatted.

Studying the difference, I could see why Tom Andersen's nephew got such a high price for the farm where Tom once tended a few cows, kept a flock of chickens, and grew enormous apples. I remembered how Ronny and I would climb the stone wall at the upper end of the orchard and slither on knees and elbows through the grass to our favorite tree. Bent and gnarled, its tired branches sagged under the weight of dark red apples fat with juice. We'd scramble up the trunk, seize two apples apiece, jump to the ground, and run like hell.

In all our years of thievery, Tom never pursued us. If he noticed at all, he probably shrugged, muttered "boys will be boys," and went back to his work. But we pretended he stood armed with a shotgun, pretended he'd pepper our hides for stealing forbidden fruit. Nothing had ever tasted as sweet as those apples and Tom's purple grapes that burst with sugar on our tongues.

I slowed as I passed Willie Dean Denton's bait and boat repair shop. Several boats rocked beside the dock, waiting for serious summer fishermen to launch their assault against bass and trout, but the windows of the shop were dark. Willie Dean, I expected, was off working one of the many odd jobs that kept him going, maybe helping Ronny saw lumber, or tilling someone's yard. A man without a mortgage could make a pretty good living at this and that, once he covered his property and school taxes. If he didn't join the others and refuse to accept checks and credit cards, Willie Dean seemed to be in a good position to make money off the newcomers and the boats they'd surely buy.

I goosed the gas and flicked the wiper control down a notch as the rain softened to a persistent mist. I'd catch up to Willie Dean later and ask him about the rock piles. I wouldn't get a straight answer—Willie Dean fed on the annoyance of others, so a conversation was merely a series of jabs—but I felt sure I'd know if he lied. Willie Dean's laughter tightened and sharpened when he departed from the truth.

Speeding up, I rocked through a couple of turns, along the edge of a thick stand of white pine, and past the stone wall that marked the end of Willie Dean's property and the start of what had been Tom Andersen's. I wondered if the orchard would be in bloom, if I'd see haloes of white around the ancient trees. I leaned into the last turn.

The sight hit me like a blow to the gut. "Son of a bitch!" I stood on the brake and clutch. Ronny's comment about rape hadn't been an exaggeration. The orchard and grape arbors were gone. Tom's house and barn had been leveled. The fieldstone walls and fireplace had been razed, the rocks dumped into a heap near the road. Bulldozers had ripped his pasture into an open wound from which rusty mud oozed toward barricades of hay and plastic sheeting erected to keep runoff from the lake. No lilacs would bloom in Tom's dooryard this year; spring would bring nothing but weeds from this blasted earth.

I sat for a long minute, then turned up Tom's old driveway toward a battered silver trailer with patches of white paint on its sides that hunkered beside stacks of gray cinder blocks. Two pickup trucks, one a mud-coated faded green and the other a bright and gleaming metallic red, nosed up against the trailer.

A short man with a blue cap and green plaid shirt stuck his head out the door as I turned off the engine and unbuckled my seat belt. He gestured to someone else and a second man, taller, thinner, and wearing a black windbreaker and jeans, emerged and jumped to the ground.

He closed the distance as I swung off the seat. "What can we do for you?" There was nothing friendly in his voice, just a challenge.

I unzipped my vest and showed him my badge. "Sergeant Dan Stone."

He squinted at it, glanced back at the trailer, and squared up to me, his face bunched like a baby's fist. "We didn't call you." It was half statement of fact, half complaint, as if he thought I intended to charge for my time.

"I know that, sir." I used the last word out of habit, used it like I would if I were talking to a belligerent driver caught doing twenty over the limit, or someone who'd threatened to call the sheriff and have my job. I slid my wallet from my hip pocket, drew out a card, and offered it to him. "I'm here to look into the problems you're having."

His face unclenched; he took the cardboard rectangle and squinted again.

"Are you in charge here, sir?"

"Yeah." He jammed the card into his breast pocket.

I bet he'd been a real hit with Louisa Marie. I waited, keeping my expression neutral, watching his face bunch again, then relax. His eyes remained tight.

"Lee Fosmark." He stuck a hand toward me and I took it, noticing his fingernails had been bitten to the quick and that he gripped my fingers too hard and held on too long. Worried, I decided, maybe even frightened.

"I'm the contractor," he continued, nodding toward the trailer and the blue-capped man who'd been watching from the doorway. "That's Marvin DeFazio, the developer. He's nervous as hell about those letters we got. And the spray paint on the trailer. And the spikes in the road that flattened his tires. And those piles of rocks." He gestured toward the edge of the bulldozed area. "Someone builds them at night. We knock 'em down as fast as they pop up."

He glanced back at DeFazio, and then walked up the slope toward the first homesite. I followed. "What he's really worried about is his profit margin if you want the truth. And how he's going to make his alimony payments. But don't get him started on that or you'll be here all day." Fosmark sighed. "I'm hoping he'll go back to Albany soon so I can get some work done."

I surveyed the vacant site, then checked my watch and scanned the sodden hillside. Just after ten. Too early for the crew to be taking a lunch break. "You don't have much going on today."

"Nah," he agreed and studied the sky. "Called the guys early this morning and told them to take the day off. Hoped the rain would let up and those trenches would dry out after the downpour last night and we could start on the foundations." He pointed to the stacks of cinder blocks. "But it ain't happening. I tell Marvin it's always slow starting in the spring. Make the crews struggle in the mud now and they'll hold it against you later. But he just sees the bottom line." Fosmark laughed maliciously and winked at me. "And the big number on that check he has to write every month. His ex took him to the cleaners after she found him with that little chippy, but no way will Marvin admit he's to blame. Anyway, give us a few weeks and you'll see real progress."

Progress? I remembered Tom Andersen's apple orchard and wondered where the deer would graze this autumn, wondered what had become of that ten-point buck I'd seen two years ago silhouetted against a moon the color of a Christmas orange. I took a long breath before I spoke. "I wanted you to know I'll be here if there's any trouble. More graffiti. Anything. You can reach me through that top number on the card. Any time. Just ask the dispatcher to page me." I turned toward my rig and he trailed along.

"You're staying up here? Renting a room somewhere? They told me everything was booked through October." His mocking tone made it clear he knew he'd been lied to. "That's why I brought in this palatial trailer. I guess the natives miraculously found some room at the inn when they saw your badge."

"No." I brushed rain from my vest and reached for the door handle. "I'm at my father's place, across the lake."

That was a mistake. His face bunched again and he backed away. "You're a local?" He made it sound like I had leprosy.

I jerked the door open. "Not for years. I'm assigned here." I got behind the wheel. "For a few weeks. That's all."

He pulled my card out of his pocket, studied it, and put it away again. "All I mean is, it seemed like we didn't get much more than lip service when the others came out."

I looked down into his narrow brown eyes and kept my voice even. "I'll come if you call and I'll investigate your complaints. If I find the people responsible, I'll arrest them and do my best to see that they're prosecuted. No matter who they are." I slammed the door, turned the key and shifted into reverse. Gunning the engine, I spun the wheels, spraying mud on the shiny pickup. Take that for the apple trees you bulldozed, for the grapes you uprooted, for Tom's house with its stone chimney and oak floors and glass doorknobs and the cold cellar where he'd piled cabbages as big as basketballs.

Feeling a little better, I skidded onto the asphalt and turned toward the north end of the lake. The paved road didn't encompass the lake; it stopped a few hundred yards past the last house, where state forest land fanned up the mountainside from Dark Moon Hollow. Old logging roads zigzagged through that forest, crossed the stream, and intersected the asphalt on the east side below the lodge. A heavy chain and a sign were intended to keep motorized traffic out, but longtime residents often bushwhacked around the posts that supported the chain to cut off a few miles. I decided to do the same.

I passed the last house on the west side of the lake, noticed the shutters were pulled back, and wondered if the Brocktons had returned from whichever southern town they'd wintered in this year. A small silver car squatted beside the house—not a luxury model like the Brocktons drove. Slowing, I noticed the hedge had been trimmed and a ladder and window-cleaning supplies lay on the porch. No burglar would wash the windows. They must have hired a caretaker. And about time. William and Angela were in their eighties and plagued by arthritis and rheumatism, but the retired teachers turned watercolor artists clung to their independence like lichens to weathered rock. I guessed their daughter, who'd married money in Saratoga, had put her foot down.

The mist became a relentless rain, the sky darkened, and I sped up. I thought about dragging in more firewood to take the chill off the lodge and draw the musty scent of the house up the chimney. The tires hissed on the narrowing pavement and I fishtailed on a drift of pine needles where the road snaked around a rocky outcropping and settled into the final soft curve before it ended.

I didn't see the dark gray truck coming toward me until the driver hit his lights.

I took my foot off the gas and eased to the right, expecting that he'd swing over onto his shoulder, making room to pass. He didn't. He moved to his left and flashed his high beams.

Somebody playing chicken? Somebody in a high-riding truck with a giant push bumper on the front?

I blinked. *Nat's truck.*

The SUV slid onto the soggy shoulder. Gripping the wheel hard, I felt the tires wallow in soupy mud beneath a thin layer of gravel.

The truck's driver arrowed toward me, turning on the spotlights mounted on top of the cab.

"What the hell?" I jerked the wheel left, tore loose from the mud, and slid across the pavement to the opposite shoulder. Branches ripped at the side mirror and gravel rattled against the undercarriage as the left wheels bit.

The truck changed its course and roared toward me again, horn blaring.

"Who are you?"

The gap narrowed and I saw a black ski mask covering the driver's face.

"Who the hell are you?"

I twisted the wheel right, downshifted, goosed the gas, and rocketed across the pavement again. The spotlights half-blinded me as I shot through the beams. I heard a tearing crunch as his bumper raked my taillight and felt the wheel shudder in my grip.

I braked hard. The tires lost traction and I skidded onto the shoulder. The ground gave way beneath the right wheels. Afraid I'd roll, I went with the skid, sliding hub deep into a stand of whip-like brush beside the lake and jolting to a mud-sucking stop. The truck thundered off.

"Son of a bitch!" I pounded the wheel, a dull backbeat for the rhythm of my ragged breath and thudding heart. Looking over my shoulder, I watched the truck disappear around the curve. Nat's truck. No mistake. But it couldn't be. Ronny had sold it in December. The money had gone into my father's account. I wiped cold sweat from my forehead and took the gun from the glove compartment.

Holding the cold metal connected me to reality. My breathing slowed and I leaned back, unbuckled my seat belt, and considered my options. None of them included using my cell phone. For one thing, I doubted the call would go through. Reception in this crevice among the mountains was spotty at best. But if I got the dispatcher and asked for a wrecker, she'd call the nearest service station operator—Stub Wilson. If Stub hadn't warmed to the idea of me being here, he'd take his sweet time coming and charge me triple the going rate. And, if I called for assistance, I'd violate the Stone family code of honor, the words that would be gilded onto our coat of arms, if we had one: "Be proud. Be strong. Never ask for help."

I sighed and reached for the door handle. Those were lonely words. Doing it yourself built character—that's what my father and grandfather always told me. Would there come a point where I'd built all the character I needed?

I set the thought aside. I could get out of this on my own. I had a hatchet in the back. I'd cut some brush and put it under the wheels. It would be muddy work, but nothing I hadn't done before.

I opened the door, trudged to the rear, and fitted the key in the latch. Then I heard an engine revving up. Pivoting, I saw Nat's truck roar out of the curve and speed toward me.

CHAPTER 6

I clutched at my revolver as the truck bore down on me and realized I'd need more stopping power. I scrambled for the shotgun on the back seat and fitted the stock against my shoulder. Try to take out a tire, or go for the windshield?

Windshield, I decided. Let the son of a bitch pick shot from his face for a week. Icy sweat trickled down my sides. If he had a face. If he wasn't a ghost.

I raised the barrel a few inches, tightened my finger on the trigger, and braced my legs, squinting against the spotlights, waiting until I saw his eyes inside the cutouts of that mask.

The truck's tires squealed as his brakes locked. He skidded toward me, arcing sideways. His rear wheels bit into the opposite shoulder and the front end slewed around. He grappled with the wheel, eyes wide, arms stiff. Brush snapped and I heard a tire go with a sharp whoomph. The truck plowed into an ancient oak with a grinding crash.

I crossed the road in four long bounds, tore open the passenger door, and leveled the shotgun at the driver's chest. "Get your hands up. Now!"

He turned, brown eyes staring past me, hands resting on the wheel.

"Now! Get out of the truck now and get down on the ground!"

He whistled. A tuneless series of notes.

A normal person would have been on the ground begging me

not to shoot. My hands shook. I'd read about sociopaths, people who knew little fear, for whom authority was a joke, whose actions couldn't be predicted. The barrel wobbled. "You're in enough trouble already. Don't add resisting arrest."

The eyes focused on me, blinked twice.

I took two steps back. "On the ground! Now!" Why the hell didn't he move? My gut cramped and I swallowed bile. Did he want me to shoot?

Laughter erupted from behind the mask. "Jeez, Dan," he whined. "My clothes will get all muddy if I get down there."

Relief flooded my mind, washed down the back of my neck; my legs trembled from the aftershock of an adrenaline charge. "Willie Dean?"

"Yeah." He pulled off the ski mask, revealing his pock-marked face and oily hair standing in tufts. "Got you good, didn't I? Saw you coming and stuck on the ski mask I had behind the seat since last winter. Scared the shit out of you, didn't I?" Chortling, he pointed a grimy finger and sang an old Bob Marley tune, "I Shot the Sheriff." Only he substituted "got" for "shot."

Anger replaced relief, pounding behind my eyes. I raised the gun again, remembering all the other times Willie Dean had "got" me—the time he glued the pages of my history book together, the day he'd stolen my clothing from my gym locker, and the time he melted my scholastic honors pin with a welding torch. I wanted to club him with the shotgun, but I gritted my teeth and swallowed the acid taste of rage. By striking him I would have broken one of the unwritten laws of Hemlock Lake—tolerate Willie Dean's jokes on you, so you're allowed to enjoy his jokes on others. "I'd say we got each other. My rig's stuck, but you'll need some serious body work."

His laughter choked to a stop. He leaned out the window and studied the mutilated bumper. "You're right. Whooeee, Priscilla's gonna fry my guts and make me eat them without ketchup. She was madder than a rabid fox when I emptied out our savings account and bought this truck out from under the guy Ronny planned to sell it to. She'd been saving for a new roof and a deck." He patted the door. "Well, I guess we'd better call and have someone pull us out. That's assuming you've got one of those fancy little phones."

"I do, but I won't need any help. I can get out by myself."

"Dan, Dan, Dan." He climbed out of the passenger door and waded on bowed legs through crumpled brush. "When you gonna learn that it's easier to let the other guy do the work?" He slapped a hand on my back between the shoulder blades and steered me across the road. "Besides, everyone loves it when I screw up. They'll still be laughing about this come Christmas."

And I'll be part of the joke, I thought as I stowed the shotgun and retrieved the cell phone. The incompetent who couldn't recognize one of Willie Dean's gags. But on the positive side, maybe folks would figure I was too dumb to catch my pants on a nail, let alone catch the person who'd sent the threatening letters and vandalized the construction site. And being "got" by Willie Dean might make me one of them.

"Ain't that the cutest little thingy." Willie Dean snatched the cell phone from my hand. "I've got lures bigger than this." He turned it in his stubby fingers, then flipped it open and laboriously punched in a series of numbers. To my surprise, the call went through, and I heard a tinny ring as I surveyed the front bumper.

"You're footing the bill for getting us out," I told him.

"Won't be one." He grinned. "Ronny? This here's Willie Dean." He paused and shook the phone. "Can you hear me okay? I got some static on this end. Yeah? Okay then, how you be, boy? I'm calling 'cause I got myself into a little predicament down here at the end of the lake past the Brocktons'. Yeah, you got it, another day, another mess. That's me."

I snorted at the hayseed act Willie Dean had perfected as a child. It was designed both to keep bullies at bay and keep teachers from expecting him to do more than sit in the back of the room, make smart-aleck remarks, and toss spit wads. A few years ago I'd asked Nat if Willie Dean ever dropped the hick routine when he was among friends. Nat considered for a few minutes and said he doubted that Willie Dean thought he had any friends. Nat had trained his steady gaze on me and said he guessed Willie Dean's act was like old wallpaper, or pride—almost impossible to peel off.

"Well, you see I just finished tuning up the truck and I came down to the end of the road to get up some speed and kind of blow out the pipes and . . ." Willie Dean's voice droned on in a mix of apologetic laughter and subservient whining. He reminded me of a puppy flipping onto his back, revealing his neck and soft belly to a bigger dog. Then he snapped the phone shut and shuffled around to look at my tires. "He'll be along in a bit. Shouldn't take him but a few minutes to get you out."

"Great," I grunted, knowing that getting out would come after a lecture on how to drive these roads and how I should have known that was Willie Dean behind the mask. I clenched my jaw until my back teeth ached.

Willie Dean clapped me on the shoulder and tucked the phone into the pocket of my vest. "I told him it was my fault. You know me, always fooling around. But I never mean any harm, do I?"

The hell you don't, I thought. But I didn't answer because I didn't know for sure. Over the years we'd all assumed he was basically harmless. Just like that puppy, he pissed on everything and no one expected otherwise. I shrugged off his hand, removed the phone, and put it in the glove box. Not responding wasn't as satisfying as clubbing him with the shotgun, but it was all I had.

"Shoulda realized you wouldn't be in the mood for a little fun," Willie Dean told my back. "After all that's happened with your family. And I'm sorry about that, but hell, when I saw you come around that turn everything else just went out of my mind. I thought, 'Willie Dean, let's see if old Dan the man will play a little game of chicken.' That's all it was, honest."

I made one second of eye contact, nodded, and walked over to examine the damage to his truck, my anger turning to disgust. He trundled along behind me, corduroy pants whiffling.

"Anyway, I know some aren't, but I'm tickled pink that the law's here. It's not that I like the idea of all them homes going up on Tom's land, but that's the way it is. We can't change what's been done, so we might as well make the best of it. And I know it will be good for my business."

I squatted beside the ruptured tire, fingering the rim to see if it had been bent. Willie Dean shifted from foot to foot, his shoes making soft squishing sounds in the mud.

"And to tell you the truth, Dan, I'm getting real worried about those weird rock piles and there's that guy hiding in the woods and—"

I looked up. "What guy in the woods?"

"Well, that's the big question, ain't it? Nobody knows who he is. Or even if he is. About a week ago Priscilla was coming back from visiting her mother when she picked up somebody in her headlights not far from the post office. He walked kind of hunched over, and jumped into the ditch when she got close, like he was trying to hide something, or planning to jump her if she stopped to see what was going on. But she floored it. Told me it had to be one of them carjackers you hear about. Except who'd come all the way up here to steal a car?"

When I didn't answer, Willie Dean said, "Well, I went out

and took a look, but it was raining up a real toad-floater that night, so there weren't any tracks. And it being that time of the month, I figured Priscilla had one of them attacks of nerves she's prone to. Having been married, you must know the words to that tune."

He paused to wink broadly. I felt a ripple of revulsion in my gut.

"Anyway, not long after that, Stub heard something digging in his garbage buckets. He got his gun and turned the outside light on, but it took off. Probably a bear."

"Yeah," I agreed, drawn into the story now that it involved someone besides Willie Dean and Priscilla. "It was a hard winter. I doubt there's much to eat up on the ridges."

"That's what I thought, too. Most likely a bear Priscilla saw, too, and a bear that made off with the old bread Marcella set outside the back door meaning to put it in the bird feeder. But yesterday I noticed someone had been messing with the lock on the pop cooler on my dock."

"Probably the same bear." I stood and wiped my hands on my thighs. "Maybe you got a can of soda leaking and he sniffed it out." I remembered a local legend. A dozen years ago, when Willie Dean took over the business from his uncle, he'd tried to cut corners. "Are you keeping bait in that cooler again?"

"No, just pop and beer and—" Willie Dean slapped his thigh and chortled. "Hee, hee, hee. I forgot about that. Nearly gave that guy from the health department an infarction when he pulled out that bottle of minnows. I told him I only needed one cooler because I had a system. The caps with the X's on them were bait and the others were pop. How hard is that to understand?"

I grinned in spite of myself. Stories like this illustrated another reason why Willie Dean was tolerated. He could always be counted on make the rest of us look smart.

"That tight ass shut me down for a week, and I had to scrub that cooler with bleach twice. On hot days I swear the pop smells like chlorine." He shook his head in disgust. "But anyway, weren't no bear tried to get in there unless bears can use hammers. I found one lying on the dock."

Was this linked to the construction site vandalism? "What did you do with it?"

"Hell, I tossed it somewhere." He rubbed at his head. "No, wait, I used it this morning to knock together a couple of planter boxes for Priscilla to put out on the front porch. Nice hammer. Old, but it's got good balance."

So much for that piece of evidence. "What about the cooler? Did you touch that?"

"Why sure, Dan, I had to check that padlock, didn't I? He'd taken a couple good whacks and tried to pry loose the hasp. I bent it back and then—oh, I get it." He roared with laughter. "I screwed up your evidence."

If there was any. If he hadn't done it himself to make me think there was someone lurking around here making trouble, someone who could take the blame for anything that happened, a convenient ghost to lead me on a wild-goose chase all summer. I wondered again how smart Willie Dean really was.

"Here comes Ronny." Willie Dean pointed at a truck barreling along the lake road about half a mile away. "He's got Stub's wrecker."

Ronny tapped the horn as he came around the bend, nodded as he rolled past, then turned the tow truck and parked it a few feet from my rear bumper. "Good afternoon, ladies," he said with a snort as he played out cable. "Having a little social hour out here? A clandestine rendezvous?"

I looked away, clamping my teeth. Willie Dean cackled like a chicken on meth. "Ronny, you are a hoot and a half."

Ronny bent and hitched the cable. "Yeah, well I wish I had

time to hang out and entertain you, Willie Dean, but I got a lot on my plate today and this kind of shit chaps my rear."

Willie Dean smothered a laugh as Ronny straightened and leveled his finger at me. "Get in and put her in neutral. Take off the emergency brake."

I stiffened, but did as I was told without pointing out that I knew better than to set the brake on a vehicle about to be towed. The wrecker rumbled forward; the SUV came out of the mud with a thick slurping sound and lurched onto the road.

Willie Dean scuttled over to remove the cable while Ronny and I checked the tires and fenders. The only damage appeared to be the taillight.

"You're good to go," Ronny told me.

"I'll stay and help you get Willie Dean's truck out," I offered.

"No need, bud. I'm sure you've got more important things to do." Ronny stomped toward the truck.

"Yeah, go on, Dan," Willie Dean muttered. "Sorry I'm such a horse's ass."

"Are you?" I climbed in and turned the key.

He raised his eyebrows as if he'd never thought about it before. "Well, I'm sorry if I scared you."

"That's my fault, not yours." I backed around and drove off, mud splattering from the wheels and pinging under the fenders. Getting stuck on the shoulder had made me think twice about taking the old logging road, so I stuck to the asphalt—thirteen miles of it. I kept it under forty and slowed even more when I passed the cairns near the construction site and the ditch near the post office where Priscilla had seen the mystery man.

The fictional mystery man, I told myself as I pulled up beside the lodge, retrieved my gun from the back seat and opened the hatch to find the collision had scattered my groceries. "Damn you, Willie Dean." I stuffed items back into their bags, set the gun on top, and climbed the steps to the front porch. The screen door, warped and in need of paint, sagged open. I kneed it aside and spotted the two-inch gap between the heavy Dutch door and the jamb.

I'd locked that door when I left.

I flattened myself against the side of the house, easing the sacks to the log bench beside the door, and gripping my gun. Crouching, I leaned forward and peered into the living room. Empty. I strained my ears and heard a faint scraping from the kitchen.

Step by cautious step I eased myself along the living room wall, my gaze sweeping the hallway and darting to the loft. Checking for a second intruder.

The scraping gave way to the sound of running water, and I heard a cabinet slam and the tired squeak of the refrigerator door as it opened. The water stopped and I heard metal scrape metal.

I gripped the gun with both hands and spun into the doorway. "Get your hands up."

The figure lifting a bucket of water from the sink yelped and threw the pail at me.

CHAPTER 7

Scalding water cascaded over my head. The bucket slammed against my right elbow. Crazy pain shot up my arm. My fingers spasmed and the gun clattered to the floor.

"Stay where you are!" I threw myself down, scrabbling for the revolver.

"Don't shoot, Sergeant," a woman's voice pleaded. "You already scared me half to death."

Wrapping my fingers around the gun butt, I rolled onto my back and looked up into eyes reddish-brown—the shade of a fox's fur at sunset—flecked with gold and green. Springy tendrils of cinnamon-colored hair curled around a smiling face. She raised her hands, and I noticed how pale her palms were compared to the dusky skin on her arms.

"Who are you?"

"Camille Chancellor." Her voice had a whispery texture, like fingernails on velvet, and she spoke those two words as if they would explain everything, not only about the past few seconds, but about her entire life.

I got to my feet and rubbed my elbow. "What are you doing here?"

She laughed, a rippling rainbow of notes. "I was attempting to clean this hellhole of a kitchen when you came through the door like a gunslinging Wyatt Earp."

"I'd planned to clean it myself." I set the gun on the table. When you added this encounter to the losing game of chicken with Willie Dean Denton, I'd be the source of all laughter at Hemlock Lake for the rest of the year.

"That's what Louisa Marie told me." She stuck out a hand and lowered the other. "I'll accept your apology if you'll excuse me for giving you a shower." Her voice was stronger now, thick and sweet, like warm syrup.

"You're excused." I clasped her damp hand, realizing she was taller than I'd thought—about five-eleven, I guessed. "How did you get in?"

"Louisa Marie got the spare key from Ronny." She bent to pick the bucket from the floor, her faded gray sweatpants molding to the strong muscles of her flanks, her spine and shoulder blades outlined beneath her T-shirt.

I fumed silently at the assumption that I didn't need to be consulted when Ronny or Lou Marie gave orders. "How'd you get here? I didn't see a car."

She stepped to the kitchen door and pointed across the living room toward the lake and a green and blue canoe bobbing beside the dock. "I found that in the Brocktons' garage. I didn't think they'd mind, and it was probably quicker than driving."

"So you're staying at their place?"

"Working at their place." She set the bucket in the sink. "Their daughter hired me to clean before they get back from Texas, and to cook and keep the house through the summer. If they approve."

I studied her neatly trimmed nails, strong shoulders, and eyes that needed no makeup to define them. "Why wouldn't they?"

Her eyes widened, her full lips twitched and opened on a deep laugh. "Do you have a vision problem, Sergeant Stone? Did you not notice my skin isn't the color of everyone else's up here?"

I felt myself flush. Of course I'd noticed. Her skin was like strong coffee thick with fresh cream, polished walnut shell, pumpkin pie rich with nutmeg and ginger.

She seized a handful of her hair. "And look at this."

I spotted a few strands of white in her grip. Salt and cinnamon, I thought. Or sugar and cinnamon.

"Kinks like this are because my ancestors got here courtesy of a slave trader."

"Sorry," I mumbled. The word was both inadequate and presumptuous.

"Hey." She patted her hair back into place. "That's ancient history. Not your fault."

"Sorry," I mumbled again. The word was all I had. For the first time in my life I wished I'd inherited what my grandmother called "the gift of gab," the ability to turn thoughts into words and fling them easily to others, bat them back and forth like a game of verbal badminton. But Nat had gotten that gift.

"Go ahead and feel guilty if you want. Gives me an edge." She laughed again and retrieved a mop that leaned against the wall beside the refrigerator.

I reached for it. "I can finish up."

"No, I have my orders from Ronny and Louisa Marie." She didn't look at me as she sopped up puddles of water. "Those two expect to be obeyed. Besides, I've seen how most men clean kitchens. And bathrooms. Believe me, I wouldn't be able to sleep at night thinking about all that rogue bacteria. But if you insist, you can get what I splashed into the living room. Use those paper towels." She nodded toward a roll on top of the refrigerator.

I did as she asked, then changed into a dry shirt, retrieved my sacks of groceries, and set them on the counter. Leaning against the doorjamb, I watched her as she knelt, scrubbing the linoleum with a brown-bristled brush. "I got the refrigerator and stove washed out before you burst in," she told me. "This linoleum looks worse than it is. After I scrub it, I'll put on a couple of coats of wax. It appears no one has done that for a long time."

Probably not since before my mother died three years ago, I thought. Dad and Nat wouldn't have cared how dull and scuffed it had become. And Susanna, well, Susanna might have noticed, but she would have been seduced by sunny days, rippling water, falling leaves, snowy trails. Being a responsible older child, I'd always felt obligated to do the chores before I could enjoy myself. Sometimes it seemed I'd had more chores than enjoyment.

"I said," Camille rattled the brush against the bucket and brought me back to the present, "first we'll have lunch. The sight of that refrigerator took the edge off my appetite, but now it's back."

I nodded at the sacks of groceries. "I've got the makings of BLTs."

Camille washed her hands and peered into the first sack. "I've seen better-looking lettuce in the bottom of a garbage can. You must not be on Louisa Marie's list of favorites."

"Who is?"

I thought that was a rhetorical question, but she answered it. "The Brocktons." She grinned. "That means she's willing to tolerate me. As long as I know my place and stay in it." She snatched the lettuce from the top of the bag and tossed it over her shoulder into the sink. It landed with a dull clang. Surveying the tomatoes, she shook her head sadly. "She keeps the best stuff in the back. For her pets. Tell you what. You make coffee and toast some of that bread, and I'll share my lunch: vegetable soup and a hunk of cherry pie." She pointed her chin at a plastic container and foil-wrapped package on the table in the breakfast nook. "I'll factor feeding you onto what I'll charge for cleaning."

"What if I don't like the soup and pie?" I'd intended my

words to be light and flippant, but they sounded peevish.

She smiled as if she hadn't noticed. "You will."

I did. The soup was thick with barley, potatoes, carrots, beans, and tomatoes, and flavored with pungent spices I couldn't identify. The pie was both tart and sweet, contained in crust that dissolved against the roof of my mouth with a burst of butter and salt.

"If this isn't a fluke and you cook like this all the time," I told her, "the Brocktons won't care if you're green with purple spots and your ancestors came from Mars. Not that I think they'd give a damn anyway. They're not that type."

She studied me for a moment and sighed. "We're all 'that type' about something." She pressed the tines of her fork down on the last crumbs of crust on her plate. "Some of us just hide it better than others." She raised her eyes and stared at me. "And if you say you aren't, that makes you either a liar or a man who's never thought about it." She licked crust from the fork, then picked up our plates and carried them to the dishwasher. "Think before you speak. And don't say you're sorry. You've worn that out."

I brought the soup bowls and silverware to the counter. Oddly, I didn't feel like I'd been chastised, more like I'd been challenged. My silence didn't feel strained.

She glanced at the clock on the wall over the refrigerator. "Wow. Four, already. I could use a hand with the cabinets if I'm going to finish up and get back across the lake before dark." She rinsed the bowls, slid them into the rack, and closed the dishwasher. "Would you mind sorting through things and putting them back after I've scrubbed down the shelves?"

I took another clumsy stab at humor. "If you think I can do that without leaving too many rogue bacteria behind."

She narrowed those fox-like eyes at me, but then rewarded me with another burst of musical laughter. "I'll give you one chance. Don't blow it. Find me a stepladder and we'll start with the top shelves."

I unearthed a red metal chair with fold-down steps from the back of the pantry. The paint was scarred and the rubber pads on the steps had frayed. The chair had been my grandmother's. She'd stood, as she put it, "in the shadow of five feet," and used the chair every day to retrieve dishes, hang curtains, and place preserves on their proper shelves.

"Perfect." Camille grinned. "Who designed this kitchen? A basketball player?"

"My grandfather." I unfolded the steps. "He liked high ceilings but hated wasted space."

She climbed the steps and surveyed the cobwebbed recesses of the top shelf. "Someone else hated waste, too. There are enough jelly glasses up here to set yourself up in business when the strawberries get ripe." She held a few out for me to look at. "Want to keep them?"

"Should I?"

She turned one over in her hands. "These are pretty old. If they're still good, maybe you can hold a yard sale later in the summer. Or you can give them away. Mary Lou probably knows someone who can use them. Either way, there's no point in washing them. Find a box or a bag and we'll pack them up."

I nodded, found I was glad to have the decision delayed, and dug a couple of bags from the pantry. As I unfolded them, I realized that I'd need a lot more. The closets were packed with pieces of the past I'd have to examine, sort, and pass on to a yard sale or the dump or the burning barrel out behind the house. Stripping the lodge down to its essentials, like fate had stripped my life, would mean hundreds of tiny decisions. And, as I considered each relic, the ghosts of my mother, my grandmother and grandfather, Nat, and Susanna would sit in judgment. And before too long my father's ghost would join them. My chest compressed and I struggled to drag breath in.

"This is a beautiful house." Camille clinked another quartet of dusty jars into formation on the counter. "And the lake is lovely. Mary Lou told me you grew up here. That you and Ronny were good friends when you were boys."

Her voice rose at the end of the last sentence, giving a hint of a question, prompting me. I took two quick breaths and filled in the blank. "But I went away to college and never came back here to live. That's the rest of the story you've heard, right? That I got 'too big for my britches.' That I exiled myself from this paradise on earth." I clanked jars into the first bag.

Her eyes tightened as she handed down four more glasses. "People who don't appreciate what they've got annoy the hell out of me, Dan Stone. You had a family around you when you were growing up, people who cared, a place in the community."

She didn't say it, but the implication was that she'd had none of that. I felt a desperate need to make her see that what looked like perfection wasn't. "And I had a long list of expectations about what I'd be and do because of who I was." I snatched the jars from her hands and tumbled them into the bag, not caring if they shattered. "Hundreds of eyes watching all the time, hundreds of ears listening. Everyone ready to report to my father if I strayed outside the lines drawn for me the day I was born."

I was surprised, not by the bitterness in my voice, but that I was sharing this burden with a stranger. "If I hadn't left, I would have suffocated. And if I hadn't come back—" I bit down on my tongue, tasted the coppery flavor of blood. I wouldn't talk about Susanna. I filled the sack, carried it into the pantry, and loaded another.

I felt Camille studying me, but she said nothing. I imagined she was reviewing every morsel she'd heard about Nat, Susanna, and my father. I wondered what opinions she'd formed, decided I wouldn't ask. I lugged a kitchen chair to a cabinet on the other side of the stove, stepped up, and cleared pepper and salt shakers, chipped mugs, mismatched wine glasses, and plastic cups. I thrust them all into sacks and moved to the next shelf, pawing through stacks of plates and saucers.

Camille gathered up a spray bottle of cleaning solution and a handful of paper towels and went to work on the shelves. "Forgive me if I upset you." Her voice was so low I barely heard it.

"It's okay." I slammed a stack of dishes into a sack, heard a sharp crack.

"No, it's not." She climbed down from the chair and stood in front of me. "How you feel is how you feel. Just because I wish my own childhood had been better gives me no right to . . . well, I'm sorry, that's all."

"It's okay." I picked up the sack and stowed it in the pantry. "Sometimes I feel like one of those butterflies pinned to a piece of cardboard inside a display case. I'm alive. I can see where I'd like to fly to. But I can't escape without dragging the pins and cardboard with me." I leaned on the counter, feeling weak, as if I'd vomited words like so much bad meat, purging myself.

She was quiet for a minute. "You can go to the other side of the globe. But the past is right up here." She touched her forehead. "All it takes is the right word, a slant of the sun, or the sight of your face in the mirror, and you're right back again." She seized the paper towels and went back to work.

I nodded, watching the muscles ripple in her back as she scrubbed the shelves I'd cleared. My mother would have admired her intensity.

"I wonder why it is that some of us stay and some of us go." She tossed down a filthy wad of paper towels and I ripped more from the roll and handed them to her. "Why some of us can't wait to get out and others can't imagine ever living anywhere else. I don't mean me." She stuck her head into the cabinet, shielding her face. "My mother and I moved because we had to, but you had a choice."

Had I? I shook my head. Staying had never been an option.

"Maybe that's why there's so much tension here."

I shook off my thoughts. "I don't follow you."

"You should." She smiled. "It's exactly what you said."

"What I said?"

"That everyone knew who you were, they had set ideas about what they expected from you, and certain controls on your behavior to ensure you wouldn't stray too far from those expectations." She climbed down and tossed the dirty towels in the waste basket. "That was safe for you, and for them. But those new homes will upset the balance. They'll be filled with people who will see everyone here with new eyes and judge everyone by different criteria."

I saw her face reflected in the dark window above the sink and realized the sun had set. She'd wanted to paddle home before dark.

"It's forced change," she said. "It's like someone coming in with a great big scissors and cutting the social fabric of this community, slicing the threads that hold it together." She turned to look at me. "No one can be sure of their place. They're afraid. And—"

The strident wail of the fire siren snapped our heads toward the town at the tip of the lake.

CHAPTER 8

"Fire!"

On the run, I started for the door, but then skidded to a stop. "How will you get home?"

She arched her brows. "In the canoe, of course."

An image of Nat and Susanna flashed through my brain. "You can't. It's dark. Wait until I come back and I'll drive you."

The siren blared.

"I'll be fine, Sergeant Stone," she insisted. "You might be gone for hours. I'll finish the shelves and put down a coat of wax while you're not here to tromp through it. I left the porch light on to guide me. And the moon is full."

That hadn't saved Susanna. "The lake is dangerous at night."

"I know." Her eyes softened for a second. "But I'm very careful." She turned to the sink and a can of scouring powder. "And I'm a strong swimmer."

The siren screamed. I raised my voice above it. "Strong swimmers drown, too."

The siren faded and in the silence that followed, I saw her spine stiffen. She pursed her lips and shook her head. "I appreciate your concern." She stretched out her hand and touched my shoulder. "I'll wear my life jacket." She flicked her fingers at me. "I'll lock up when I leave. And I'll flip on the upstairs lights at the Brocktons' so you know I made it."

The siren blasted again.

Gripping my arm, she hustled me to the door. "Go! They

might need you."

They didn't.

When I located the fire scene at Willie Dean's dock, Ronny and the others were huddled in a tight semicircle, passing a bottle of whiskey and watching a puny wooden boat burn to the waterline. Reflected flames bronzed the dark water. Ripples hissed as they sucked at the fire.

"Total loss," Ronny told me. "Wasn't worth trying to put it out. Hardly even worth sounding the alarm except for the practice."

"Good thing Willie Dean had some common sense for once and cut the rope before the fire spread to the dock," Stub Wilson commented. "Otherwise we woulda had to get sweaty."

"And we all know how much you hate that," Willie Dean jeered at the garage mechanic. "That's why you got you such an elite white-collar job."

"Beats herding bait." Stub took a deep swig and offered the bottle to me. I shook my head and he passed it on to Evan Bonesteel, a slight man whose gray-blond hair glinted in the firelight.

"How did it start?" I directed the question at Willie Dean, but it was Ronny who answered.

"Arson," he said as if there could be no doubt. "Motor was in the shed. Nothing to cause spontaneous combustion." He cocked his head toward Willie Dean. "Or so he says."

"That's the truth," Willie Dean said. "I keep those boats clean and neat. You know I do. My business depends on it."

A spray of sparks burst from the boat as the stern slumped into the water. I watched it for a few seconds, noting that the flames seemed to have taken hold everywhere, as if someone had sloshed gasoline over the seats, along the sides, and into the bottom, let it soak in, then tossed a match. Any one of the men standing around me could have done it, just as they could have assessed the value of the boat at a glance. "That's your oldest boat, isn't it, Willie Dean?"

In the dim light, I couldn't read his physical reaction, but his verbal defense was clear. "Yeah. And what of it? You thinkin' I lit it?"

"Hell no," Ronny answered. "You'd probably screw it up. Burn the dock, instead."

The others laughed, Freeman Keefe so hard he spit whiskey into the lake.

"Don't be wasting that whiskey," Stub told him as he snatched the bottle. "That's for sipping, not spitting."

"I didn't start the damn fire. Come here, I'll show you." Willie Dean stomped along the dock to the gravel parking lot on the bank. "Look." In the dying light from the sinking boat he pointed at something on the ground. "See that. It's one of them rock piles. Another one. Not the one I kicked down this morning. I seen this one as I ran over from the house."

With the others trailing behind, Ronny and I walked to the cairn and I squatted to study it. Seven or eight slabs of rock had been piled in order of size, with the smallest on top.

"It's a warning, that's what it is," Willie Dean insisted. "A sign. Telling me something bad was gonna happen."

Ronny snorted. "There are plenty of other rock piles around the lake. I've got one practically in my front yard and nothing bad's happened."

"Yeah," Stub agreed. "Only problems have been over at the development."

"Well, maybe this fire's the first that's going to happen somewhere else," Willie Dean said. "Maybe it's got something to do with the moon being full."

"If I was an arsonist, I'd prefer a new moon," Evan Bonesteel said.

"Me, too," Stub said. "And I wouldn't waste my accelerant

on a leaky old boat. You've been watching too much crap on satellite TV, Willie Dean."

"Don't kick this rock pile over like you did the other," I told Willie Dean as I stood. "I'll want to get a couple of pictures of it in the morning."

A final tongue of flame licked the bow of the boat, then it sank with a harsh whisper of steam and only the lights from the bait shop and the rising moon lit the lake. I imagined Camille paddling in its path, and remembered my dream self laboring toward Susanna. I crossed my arms and slapped my shoulders. "Think someone can winch up what's left in the morning so we can take a look at it?"

"Hardly worth the trouble," Ronny muttered. "Anyone can tell that fire was set deliberately."

The others nodded. I could almost hear them thinking I couldn't tell arson from asparagus. "That's true." I fought to keep the irritation out of my voice. I shouldn't have to justify my decision, shouldn't have to prove myself, but that came with claiming a place in this territory. "But I'd like to get some pictures and the fire investigator may want some samples. You know how they are about procedure." I shrugged the blame off my back. "They'll have me send in a couple of square yards of paperwork. Stuff that will get stuck in some file drawer without anyone ever looking at it." I sighed, conveying that I was a grunt like them. "Of course the county will pay whoever pulls it up. But if you don't have the equipment, or you just don't want—"

"I didn't say that," Ronny interrupted. "I just said it wasn't worth the effort. But if that's what needs to be done, Stub and I will do it first thing."

"I'll help," Willie Dean said.

Ronny snorted and slung an arm around my shoulder, drawing me toward the line of vehicles parked on the gravel. "Nothing more to see here. Why don't you come on over and have some dinner? Lisa was stuffing pork chops when we got the call."

I stiffened, slowing as the others passed. A few minutes ago I'd been an idiot, now I was a dinner guest. The transition wasn't easy on the ego. "I need to get back." Camille might still be at the lodge. I'd drive her home. Keep her off the water.

"Back to what?" He tightened his grip. "It can't compete with one of Lisa's dinners, I guarantee you that."

I opened my mouth to tell him about Camille, but stopped, my stomach squirming when I realized that might bring a round of guffaws and side-eyed winks. My skin crawled. Was I trying to protect her or myself? *She'll be okay,* I told myself. *You can't keep everyone off the lake.*

Ronny dug a finger into the soft spot below my collar bone, testing me as he had when we'd been kids. When I didn't flinch, he released the pressure. "No, you come on home with me, bud. Lisa and the kids would love to see you."

I shrugged, giving in. I was hungry and, according to Camille's analysis, the food I'd purchased from Louisa Marie would give me indigestion, or worse. "Okay. But shouldn't you call?"

He slapped my back. "No need. Lisa cooks plenty." He pointed to the fire truck. "Let's get and leave Stub room to turn that beast around."

I followed Ronny up the sloping apron of gravel, climbed into my rig, and trailed him past the store and post office, then north to the gravel road that led into Bobcat Hollow. Glancing across the lake, I thought I saw a flicker of light. I convinced myself it came from the Brockton house and then turned my attention to the glowing windows in the added-onto house where Ronny had been born and raised.

He and Lisa had shared it with Ronny's parents until Lisa gave birth to Justin. Then Rachel, displaying uncommon insight, announced that she and Buck would move out to "give the kids some space." With the help of much of the community, Ronny built his parents a compact ranch-style home a quarter of a mile farther up the hollow. Close enough to keep an eye on things, Buck had said. And for two years, until his heart quit pumping, he did just that, dropping in several times a day to offer advice that Lisa didn't need, but accepted graciously.

Bobcat Creek sparkled under the rising moon that lit the long meadow below the house and glazed the dew on the lawn around it. I parked beside a row of sprouting rose bushes and followed Ronny through tidy living and dining rooms filled with potted plants, paintings, and shelves stuffed with whimsical creatures made from acorns, walnuts, rocks, and twigs. Lisa scavenged the woods for materials and sold the creations at craft fairs. "Look what the cat drug in," Ronny yelled as he crossed into the kitchen.

Lisa turned from the stove and greeted me with a long hug and a short kiss delivered to the point of my jaw. "Dan! It's so good to see you." She backed off to arms' length, peering at my face as I studied her in return. A few more worry lines bracketed her chestnut-brown eyes, and her caramel hair seemed to have lost some of its sheen, but Lisa Miller was as trim as she'd been when she led the cheers on the sidelines while Ronny led the team on the gridiron. "How are you doing?"

"He's doing fine, Lisa." Ronny cadged two beers from the refrigerator and folded my fingers around one. "We're going to the den. How long 'til dinner's ready?" He started down the hall without waiting for an answer.

Lisa's lips twitched into a tight line. "Just a few minutes, Ronny," she called over my shoulder.

"Good. I could eat a buzzard if you plucked and boiled it." His voice rumbled back to us over the sudden blare of a television. "Damn. Come on in here, bud, the Yankees are burying the Mariners."

I glanced toward the den and back to Lisa. "Sorry to intrude like this, but Ronny said you wouldn't mind. Can I help with anything?"

"No. But thanks for asking." She smiled again. "I think you're the only man who ever has." She squeezed my hand. "And I don't mind an extra person for dinner. Not when it's you. I'm so sorry for what you've had to go through these last few months." Her eyes misted over and she blinked.

The tears took me back to the November afternoon twenty years before, when I'd driven her home after Ronny had been carried from the field with an ankle injury and hauled off to see a doctor. Hands knotted in the short skirt of her cheerleading uniform, she'd told me she admired my determination to get good grades so I'd have my pick of colleges in the spring. She wished she could do the same, she said, but with watching her little brothers and sisters, and cheerleading practice, there wasn't much time to study. There also wasn't any money for college.

I'd glared at the run-down farmhouse with its packed-earth yard and muttered something about loans and grants. She'd given me a wistful smile as she slid out of my father's old truck. "I guess," she'd said. "But Ronny wants to get married the day after graduation. He's got our lives all planned out."

"Get in here, bud, and watch the replay," Ronny bellowed. "You won't believe this."

I shook off the memory, spun toward the den, then caught myself and looked back at Lisa.

"Go on. Get in there." She rubbed her eyes and turned to pull a plate from the cabinet.

"Okay." I twisted the cap off my beer, tossed it into a trash can beside the refrigerator, and carried the bottle to the den. The room was a shrine to the fish, birds, and animals that had given their lives to demonstrate Ronny's skill with rod and gun. Dozens of glass eyes reflected the flickering picture on the television, which sat like an altar before a hump-backed plaid sofa and the green vinyl recliner patched with silver tape in which Ronny sprawled.

"Damn. You just missed a great play." He waved me to the sofa and swallowed beer. "I can't remember, you a Yankee fan, bud?"

Shoving a stack of sports magazines aside, I thought about my options. I didn't watch much baseball and didn't have a favorite team. As a rule I pulled for the underdog, but admitting that would probably launch Ronny into a lecture on the differences between winners and losers—one of his favorite topics. I surveyed gun parts, fly-tying equipment, and a snarl of fishing line on the coffee table before me while I groped for a follow-up remark. "Sure. Think they'll go all the way?"

"No doubt." Ronny drained his beer and set the bottle on top of an old safe he used to store boxes of ammunition. I leaned to set mine on the coffee table, and then hesitated, wiping the bottom of the bottle on my sleeve. "Don't worry about leaving a ring, bud. The furniture's wrecked already. And Lisa's not allowed in here. Every man has to have a place where he can kick back in peace." He shucked off his work boots and snatched at a set of darts stuck into the left armrest of the recliner. "First one to miss gets the next beer." He tossed half the darts onto the table between us.

I looked around for a dart board. "Miss what?"

"Him." Ronny took aim at the dusty head of a moose mounted on the wall above the television. The dart flew from his fingers and lodged in the nose. "Your turn. Rules are you gotta stay in your seat."

I fingered a dart, admiring the green and blue butterfly on the flights and testing the weight and balance. Should I miss deliberately? Or should I take my best shot? Should I pander to Ronny's need to win and listen to him gloat, or try to outdo him and suffer the consequences? My hand took over. The dart soared, struck between the eyes, quivered, and held.

"Lucky shot." Ronny's voice held a bushel of disbelief. He selected a dart, cocked his arm, and sailed it into a spot just below the moose's left ear.

I lifted a dart with a rainbow pattern on the flights, fingered it gently, leaned forward, and let it glide in beside the first one.

Ronny looked at me from the corners of his eyes. "You been holding out on me, Dan?"

"No." I sipped at my beer, hiding both my face and the lie. "That was another lucky shot." All the long days since Susanna's death, I'd found release by aiming things at targets: bullets, rocks, darts—it didn't matter. That hadn't carved away any of my anger, but it had improved my aim.

Ronny studied a dart, then stuck it back into the armrest and examined another. "You're not trying to hustle me, are you?"

"For a beer?"

He squinted and scrutinized another dart. We both knew this wasn't about who'd get the beer. And it wasn't about who could hit the moose head. It was, as Camille probably would realize instantly, about weaving a thread of my own into Hemlock Lake's social fabric, about whether I would accept the role I'd played since childhood as Ronny's sidekick, or whether I'd write a new script. If I lost this game, everything would remain the same. But if I won, we'd enter uncharted territory. I'd also sabotage my chance of being accepted back into the community. Maybe that was what I wanted—to be able to get the hell out as fast as I could.

I picked up a third dart and bounced it on my palm. Ronny checked the flights on his—black with blue lightning bolts—then cocked his arm.

"Dinner's ready!" Lisa called from the kitchen.

Ronny's dart hand, level with his ear, didn't move. I watched his chest rise and fall, then made my decision and set my dart on the table. "I'm hungry. Let's finish this later."

Ronny's lips twitched into a smile and he pegged the dart into the moose's upper lip. "Quitter."

"Yeah," I acknowledged, "but I'd rather get it while it's hot, than hang around in here smelling your socks." I pried myself from the sofa, and he yanked the recliner's handle, lurched to his feet, and followed.

"I'll slaughter you after dinner."

"Sure," I said, following the aroma of sage to the dining room.

"It's not much," Lisa apologized as she set a plate of thick pork chops beside a mounded bowl of steaming mashed potatoes.

I thought of the shriveling lettuce and tomatoes back at the lodge. "It looks wonderful. Especially those candied carrots." I pointed at an oval bowl of glistening orange discs. "Are those like the ones Ronny's mom used to make?"

Lisa smiled. "Sort of. She gave me the recipe, but I have to admit I've tampered with it over the years."

I leaned over the bowl, inhaling. "What did you put in them?"

"Ginger," Lisa chuckled. "And brandy."

"Waste of good liquor if you ask me." Ronny snagged the chair at the head of the table. "All the alcohol's cooked out of it."

"I don't use much," Lisa said, defending her creation. "Besides, I get tired of doing things the same way every time." She turned away from Ronny's narrowing eyes and bustled from the room. "I'll get the kids."

I stood still, feeling the tension, wishing for a valid excuse to leave.

"Sit there." Ronny aimed his fork at the chair to his right, then speared a chop. I sat. He passed the platter to me, glopped a pile of potatoes onto his own plate, and surveyed the table. "Guess there's no gravy tonight." He set the potato bowl beside my plate and reached for the butter. "Getting so you can't depend on anything. Go on. Dish up."

I took a chop and scooped up potatoes redolent with garlic. "I can live without gravy."

"Whether you can live without it isn't the point. My mother always had gravy on the table. Still does when we eat there on Sundays." Ronny slid carrots onto his plate. "Pass me those green beans."

Lisa returned with Justin and Julie as I handed over the bowl. Justin, already looming over Lisa at sixteen, merely nodded as he took the chair across the table from me, but Julie, a fourteen-year-old replica of her mother, flung her arms around my neck and kissed my cheek. "Uncle Dan!"

I hugged her back, remembering that she'd granted me the title when she was too young to understand the framework of families, pleased that she still thought of me as related. "And we're having my favorite carrots, too!" She dropped into the chair next to mine. "I want a big helping. And no beans."

"You'll eat your beans." Ronny handed the bowl to me.

"But Dad—"

"Beans are good for you." Lisa set a plate of white bread between Ronny and Justin. "They're full of vitamins and minerals. How about you just eat ten of them. Okay?"

"Okay." Julie ladled carrots, and I counted ten beans onto her plate, conscious of the simmering look Ronny shot at Lisa. Again, I wanted to bolt, but to do that would acknowledge I'd detected the rift. Having already made a decision to allow Ronny to save face, I stuck to it and looked across the table at Justin. He pared the bone away from his chop, put the meat on a slice of white bread, spread on a layer of mashed potatoes and butter, topped the pile with another slice of bread, and took a huge bite.

"Reminds me of me." Ronny slapped his son on his back. "If he keeps eating and growing, he'll break those old football records of mine. Won't you, son?"

Justin swallowed. "I'm sure gonna try this year." He studied my arms and shoulders. "Did you set any records, Dan?"

"Just for being sacked," Ronny said with a laugh. "Dan used to spend more time on the ground than he did upright."

"Really?" Julie slipped a bean onto the edge of my plate. I speared it, swallowed the evidence, and forced myself to smile.

"No," Lisa said, defending me. "Dan was a fine quarterback. One of the best the school ever had."

"Shows you how lame those other quarterbacks were, don't it?" Ronny guffawed and forked up a second pork chop. "And they were prone to reading the playbook, too." He guffawed again. "Dan, he'd be walking around with Shakespeare or some poetry book instead. Our last season, he got so many mud and grass stains on his uniform the team lobbied to change the school colors to brown and green."

"That's not true." Lisa flushed. "Dan got an award and everything."

"Everybody got an award," I told her, seeing a way to deflect the conversation and ease the tension. "But your dad got the biggest trophy." I turned to Julie. "And he married the prettiest girl in the school."

Julie smiled the way girls do when they still believe in fairy tales and handsome princes. She whisked a bean into her napkin. "And then he had to help granddaddy in the sawmill and the quarry, so he had to give up his college scholarship."

I blinked but didn't correct her. Ronny's grades had been far short of the mark. And his skill as a tight end not quite enough to tip the balance. He'd never gotten a scholarship offer. Oh, he'd gotten a call all right. From someone claiming to be a big-school coach. But that coach turned out to be Willie Dean play-ing a gag that earned him two black eyes and a broken wrist. Ronny had been the only person who'd ever taken revenge on Willie Dean and, to his credit, Willie Dean had claimed he got the injuries falling out of a tree. He'd never crowed about his joke, and as far as I knew, Lisa and I were the only ones who shared the truth. So Ronny hadn't discovered how he'd handle the jump to a larger puddle with bigger frogs. By staying, he'd preserved the glory days. I didn't fault him for that, and I didn't envy his job or his life. I envied only his sense of belonging and certainty. And I envied his marriage, flawed though it might be.

"If I get a scholarship, I'm going to college," Justin an-nounced. He piled up another pork chop sandwich, his eyes on his father. "But I'll go pro as soon as I can and make good money and build a house up at the top of the ridge where I can see the whole lake."

Julie reached for the bowl of carrots and scraped the rest onto her plate. "I'm going to college, too," she told me. "I want to be a teacher. But I'm not coming back. I'm going to live far, far away. Like you did, Uncle Dan. Maybe in San Francisco or Arizona. Or Paris or London or Hawaii or Rome."

Ronny set his knife and fork down and studied Julie, his mouth tight. For the first time I realized he might envy me, that it might have been fear, not contentment that held him here.

"And maybe I'll join the Peace Corps," Julie prattled on. "Go to Africa or India, or, or just any place." She spread her arms. "There's the whole world. Everybody's always saying Hemlock Lake is the greatest place on earth, but how do they know? Nobody here ever goes much of anyplace." She popped a carrot in her mouth and smiled at me. "I wish I was older and out of school. I'd pack my things and leave right now."

Ronny turned bitter eyes on me. "Only fools leave Hemlock Lake."

Or maybe, I thought, *only fools return.*

CHAPTER 9

Susanna's limp hands seemed to wave as I swam toward her, my arms like lead. Nat dove from the boat, then sliced the water like a razor. I plowed on, lungs laboring, fiery. Nat surfaced and dove again He didn't see me. I thrashed, water pulling at my clothing, bearing me down, down. Something heavy struck my shoulder. A ball. Brown. Elongated. I clutched it and lifted my knees, running, churning black water that gave way to a grid of muddy green and white. My feet touched it. I ran, breath whistling through my teeth. Ronny appeared in front of me, grinned and side-stepped. A helmeted figure in red and gray slammed me to the ground. My face scraped the chalk mark. The ball squirted from my hands. End over end, it bounced away.

I woke, damp with sweat, wedged deep into my sleeping bag in a fetal position. For a moment I lay tense, waiting for the team to pile on, for the referee's whistle, for Ronny's derisive laughter. Nothing. I sat up, brushed pine needles from my hair, and sucked in damp morning air. Peering across the lake, I saw Camille's canoe resting high on a scrap of beach near the Brockton house. I glanced at my watch. Nearly eight. I wondered if she was awake and what she would have for breakfast.

I skipped the shower, put on the clothes I'd worn yesterday, brewed a pot of overpriced coffee in the sparkling kitchen, and took a mug along with me to Willie Dean's dock. I found him at the top of the gravel parking lot, semaphoring his arms. Ronny and Stub paid no attention to his directions as they dragged the boat from the water with the tow truck's winch.

"Hey, look who decided to get out of bed and join us." Stub leaned out of the driver's window and spat the chewed-off end of a small cigar onto the ground. Striking a match on his thumbnail, he fired up, drew in a long breath, then puffed out a cloud as acrid as burning cowhide. Keeping my distance, I watched the charred bow emerge.

"How'd you get a line on it?"

"We tied Willie Dean to a rope and trolled for it," Stub said with a snort.

Smiling, I looked toward Willie Dean, whose clothing and hair appeared dry. "Exactly what I would have done." I moved to the rear of the truck where Ronny monitored the line, jaw clenched, ropes of tendon tight along his neck.

"Good morning."

He nodded, his gaze on the dripping bow.

"Thanks again for dinner. Tell Lisa those were the best pork chops I've ever had."

He nodded again but said nothing. I found a spot on the dock where the cell phone would work, got through to the fire investigator, and asked him if he wanted to come up and take a look. He laughed and said he had too many other irons in the fire. Then he laughed again and told me to take some pictures, hack out a section where the damage seemed the greatest, and send it along. I retrieved the camera and a knife and followed his instructions, knowing accelerants like gasoline, kerosene, or paint thinner, were stashed in almost every garage in Hemlock Lake. Stub and Ronny, leaning against the side of the tow truck, smirked. Willie Dean followed me, asking every few minutes if I thought we'd catch the arsonist. I didn't bother to answer. I suspected one of these three men had set the blaze, either as a joke or a test. If it was a joke, I couldn't see the punch line. If it was a test, I knew they'd already given me a failing grade.

Self-consciously, I walked along the dock, feeling it bob

beneath my feet, and located the cleat where the boat had been tied. Kneeling, I studied thick planks bleached a soft gray by years of weather, and then peered over the edge.

"What are you doin' now?" Willie Dean asked.

"Looking for something like this." I pointed to a short streak on the rough edge of a plank.

He squatted beside me, squinting as a hank of hair fell over his face. "What izzit?"

I lay down on the dock a few feet from the mark, leaned out over the water, turned the camera backward, and clicked off two shots. Then I ran a finger along the mark. "A strike mark. From your garden variety kitchen match." The kind some of the men at Hemlock Lake tucked into their shirt pockets each morning to light cigars or cigarettes, use for toothpicks, or just chew on.

I didn't say that the mark didn't mean a thing—except that the arsonist hadn't used a book match or a lighter. With Willie Dean trailing, I stood, walked over to the stone cairn and took a series of photographs, both wide and tight. The jagged edges of the red shale slabs pointed off in random directions. A long and slender slab, which I hadn't noticed in the dark, propped the bottom rocks in place. "Where's the one you kicked over?"

"Up there." He led me past Ronny and Stub, who shook their heads and smiled, to a cluster of rounded stones in the short grass at the edge of the gravel. I counted nine, one the size of a ten-pound sack of flour, the rest smaller. I took a picture. "How high were they piled?"

"About to my knees." Willie Dean gestured. "Maybe higher."

"Anything propping them up? Sticks? Wire? Other stones?"

"Nah."

I knelt and examined the rocks, wondering how they'd been balanced and who had hauled them here. They weren't shale or slate or bluestone like you'd find in the local quarries and in outcroppings around the lake and on its shores. These were what some would call river rock or fieldstone, smoothed by centuries of water, ice, and wind. I turned one over and saw a patch of green-gray lichen splayed across it. That meant the rock had been exposed to the air. I guessed it had come from a wall or a pasture, not from the stream. Wall, I decided. There was no soil in the crevices, no darker area to indicate that part of it had been buried until recently.

"What do you see?" Willie Dean bent over me, his breath thick with fried onions and scorched coffee.

I pulled away, stood, dusted off my knees, and headed for the tow truck. I handed Stub one of my cards. "Make out a bill for your time and send it to the sheriff at that address." I didn't tell him that some clerk would send back an official form for him to fill out and that he wouldn't get his money for months.

Fueled by coffee and a fried pie I bought from Lou Marie at the grocery store (*Don't poke them all, Dan Stone, just take the one off the top, and I'll thank you to give me exact change this morning; I'm not going to waste my ones on anybody who spends less than ten dollars.*) I made a complete circuit of the lake, taking photographs of each of the cairns and making notes about them. They were all similar to the cairn Willie Dean had kicked down—all built of rounded stones, balanced with such precision that each structure appeared as if the slightest breeze would tumble it. I counted fourteen standing and another ten that had been kicked down. Nine had been built from fieldstone, the others, all on the north end of the lake, had been created from stones pried from one of the creeks. Those stones were free of lichens and smoother than the others.

Only one, the cairn by Willie Dean's dock, had been constructed from slabs of shale. Was it the work of another artist, one who lacked the patience, talent, or time to select and balance rocks? Or had the cairn builder changed his style?

It was after one when I took two rolls of film and a chunk of burned boat to the post office and asked Mary Lou for a padded mailing envelope.

She eyed the film canisters and charred wood as I addressed the envelope. "Evidence?"

"I doubt it." I shoveled the stuff inside and sealed the flap.

She weighed the envelope, hit some keys on the postage meter, and ran off a sticker. "Three dollars and thirty-six cents." She nodded toward the open door to the grocery store and smiled. "Want to write me a check?"

I reached for my wallet, giving her a grim smile. Tomorrow I'd have to drive fifteen miles to the nearest branch bank and get a wad of bills. I'd buy a week's worth of groceries, too. "No, but I'll take a receipt so I can get reimbursed." Not that three dollars and change was worth filling out a form for, but there would be more expenses—gas, for example.

"You got it." She printed out the receipt and handed it to me. "What's your take on Willie Dean's conflagration? Think he did it himself?"

I hesitated, searching for a polite way to say "no comment."

"Because that's what everyone else thinks," she went on. "At least, everyone who's been through here this morning."

"Did they hazard any guesses about why?"

"Oh, sure. This was a regular hazard zone." She held up her hands, ticking reasons off on her fingers. "Because he thought he could collect some insurance and get a new boat. Because he wanted attention from the rest of us. Because he wanted to make it look like the person who's been threatening the development is after him, too. Because he was pissed off at Ronny and thought he'd create some paperwork for him over the fire. And my personal favorite, because he's as stupid as mud."

I nodded. "That about covers it."

"Then there are those who think that last reason rules him out entirely."

"That's possible."

"Anyway, I expect you have a lot more important things to think about, like getting the lodge back into shape. I hear you met Camille. Kind of made a splash with her, you might say." Mary Lou reached over the counter and patted my arm. "I don't think she told anyone else. Camille's not one to run her mouth, but you know how it is, Dan, people tell me all manner of things. Interesting woman, isn't she? Lived all over the place. And a hard worker, too. She'll help you whip things into shape. Just don't go throwing away anything until I get a look at it. There might be something I can use for the museum."

"The museum?" Hemlock Lake had a post office, grocery story, café, tavern, gas station, and bait shop. They'd all been present and accounted for this morning. There hadn't been a museum among them.

"I have to do something after I retire in two years. And that old one-room schoolhouse isn't in bad condition. I've had the roof patched a couple of times and I get in there now and again to air it out and beat back the cobwebs."

I remembered that Mary Lou's great-grandfather had wooed a schoolteacher and put up the building to win her. Three generations of Hemlock Lake youngsters learned to read and write in the tiny white school with the miniscule bell tower, until the school district centralized. When I started the first grade, I caught a bus outside the post office and bounced fifteen miles on a seat with less padding than you'd find under your average carpet. I tried to imagine what would go into display cases in a Hemlock Lake museum. Mary Lou filled in the blank.

"I've been collecting things for years: old tools and cooking utensils and some wonderful photographs, carvings, and cloth-ing. I've nearly filled our attic and cellar." She leaned over the counter and glanced toward the grocery store. "And don't you know that frosts Lou Marie. She says half that space is hers. Not that she uses it. Lives like a nun. Not even a picture in her bedroom." Mary Lou's face softened. "Except for the one of Jefferson on her bedside table. It's a shame she never got over that. But, anyway, when she gets all huffy and complains to someone else about it and they tell me, I just smile at them and say, 'Fine, tell her to throw out the stuff that's on her side and I'll call it Mary Lou's Museum instead of the Van Valkenberg Family Museum.' When that gets back to her, it really gets her goat."

A bell jangled on the door behind me, and I turned to see Evan Bonesteel's wife with a baby slung over her shoulder. Mary Lou patted my arm again. "I'll see you later, Dan. I've got to coo at Pattie's grandbaby. Don't throw out anything 'til I get a look at it."

"Right." I turned, smiling at Pattie Bonesteel, who studied me with obvious interest. "How you doing, Miz Bonesteel?"

Bonesteel men were notoriously stingy with their words, and they tended to marry women who also hoarded the language. I didn't wait for an answer.

As I pulled up in front of the lodge after a swing around the area, Camille came out on the porch with her hands in the air.

"I just finished the kitchen," she called as she bounded down the steps. She wore faded blue jeans and a lavender T-shirt with a smudge of dust on one sleeve. "You're down to dishes, glasses, and utensils that match, pots, pans, and bowls you might conceivably use, towels, potholders, and other necessities. Everything else is sacked up for Mary Lou to go through."

I paused, one foot on the ground, the other on the brake, pleased that I didn't have to deal with it, and angry for the same reason.

She seemed to read my thoughts. "See what happens when you move away? You start thinking you have a right to privacy. I saw Mary Lou early this morning and she gave me my marching orders about the museum."

I decided to go with the positive, slid out, and closed the door. "Yeah. Me, too."

"Anyway, I brought you a chicken pot pie for lunch, and oatmeal and cranberry cookies. Maybe after you eat we can get one of the bedrooms cleaned." She pointed to the sleeping bag I'd flung over the porch railing to air out. "So you don't have to rough it anymore."

I gazed toward the lake, avoiding her eyes. In all the cities I'd visited, I'd never felt as hemmed in by humanity as I did here. I wished that made me feel safe and cared for instead of annoyed. My anger built. "That's okay. I can—"

"Do it yourself," she finished with a laugh. "I know you can. But I've got time on my hands until the Brocktons get here at the end of the week."

"Thanks, but leave it. I can handle it." The words sounded harsh, and she took a step away, her brow furrowing. I stared at my shoes for a second, then at her darkening cheeks. "I don't mean to be rude. But I really would rather take care of it myself. In my own time."

"Okay." She turned and climbed the steps to the porch, speaking to the house more than to me. "I'll get my sweater and get out of your way. I didn't mean to be pushy."

"You're not. Not at all." I followed her across the porch and into the shadowed living room, groping for words that would soothe without inviting closeness. "It's just that . . ."

She tugged a thick green sweater over her head, her words muffled by the wool. "I know. You'd rather be alone someplace where everyone doesn't know your business." The sweater cleared her chin. "And now you've got a total stranger butting in. I can understand why you're angry at me."

"It's not you." I fumbled for words. It was like trying to describe what the itch of poison ivy feels like when scratching will only make it worse. "You're not butting in. I appreciate what you've done so far." Reaching for my wallet, I thumbed through the few remaining bills. "How much do I owe you? Can I write you a check? Because if you need cash, I may not have enough until—"

"You don't owe me anything." She tugged at the sweater's sleeves.

"Yes, I do." I pulled a number out of my head. "How about fifteen dollars an hour. Extra for the food, of course. How many hours were you here?"

She turned and stared, her eyes touched with frost. "Watch my lips. I don't want your money. I won't take it."

My anger flashed hotter. "You earned it, Camille. You did the work."

"It wasn't work. It was a favor."

I shook my head. "It was dirty, hard work. I'm obligated to pay you." *And a Stone always met his obligations.*

"Obligated? Well, I don't want that. I don't want to be an employee." She spat that word and pivoted toward the porch. "I wanted to be your friend."

She slammed the door behind her. I listened to the light thudding of her feet on the porch and then on the stone steps. In a few seconds, I heard only the hum of the refrigerator.

"Damn." I hurled my wallet against my grandfather's knotty pine paneling and slumped to the couch, thinking that Stone family tradition didn't allow much emotional space in which to establish a friendship.

CHAPTER 10

"I wanted to be your friend." The words stabbed into my brain. Like porcupine quills, they worked their way deeper, questions festering around them. Why would she want to be my friend? I had nothing to offer. Since Susanna's death, my soul was hollow.

For the next three weeks, I kept to myself as much as possible. I established a routine that included twice-a-day patrols around the lake, stops at the post office and grocery store, and regular inspections of the construction site. During that time the rain tapered off and workers laid several foundations, framed two of the homes, and hauled in a welter of supplies.

After two weeks, I called the lab to ask about the charred wood. A harried technician told me everyone was tied up on a couple of major murder cases that had finally come to trial. He promised to get to my evidence soon. When I pressed him, he said soon might be before Christmas. Neither of us laughed. I selected the best pictures of the cairns and tacked them to the perimeter of a bulletin board I'd hung in the kitchen. In the center I stapled a hand-drawn map of the area with dots representing each cairn and a date indicating when it had appeared or been noticed.

Five more rock cairns appeared during those weeks, two near the subdivision. I took pictures and notes and added them to the display. Twice I got calls about spray-painted warnings on lumber stacked at the subdivision, and once Freeman Keefe's wife, Alda, called to say someone had stolen some of Freeman's clothing off the line and pilfered a gallon of elderberry wine and a sack of potatoes from their cold cellar. I added those incidents to my list.

Sheriff North got a fresh anonymous letter each week. Two of them threatened my life, and he called to read them to me. "Call off Stone or he'll get hurt" and "The pig will get stuck if he sticks around." I told the sheriff I was staying.

I drove every road and knocked on every door, introducing or reintroducing myself, explaining my mission, and asking folks to help me by keeping their eyes and ears open. I marked the positions of all the houses, assigned a number to each one, then listed the occupants on index cards and noted their possible reasons for taking action to stop the development. For the few people I hadn't been acquainted with since childhood, I pried background information from Mary Lou.

When I had my census complete, I trimmed the list by eliminating the very young and the very old. I made a new list of likely suspects—those who'd been especially outspoken about their dislike for the development or my assignment, those who would be most affected by it, and those I knew so little about that I simply had to include.

When I finished, I had a short list that included Ronny, Stub, Willie Dean, Evan, Freeman, and Louisa Marie. After I read that a pair of teenagers had pleaded guilty to setting a fire at a school in the next county, I included Justin, Denny Balmer's son Peter, and three other youngsters. Some kids, I reasoned, couldn't understand consequences, believed they were bulletproof, or might think they were carrying out the wishes of their families. Finally, I put Camille's name beneath the others. I didn't want to, and I nearly argued myself out of it, but no one knew much about her. The job at the Brocktons' might be cover for her real mission.

Several times I caught glimpses of her paddling along the far shore, or driving the Brocktons' car, but she never acknowledged my wave. The first time she ignored me, I felt a flash of rage. I'd tried to explain, to apologize, but she hadn't listened. The next few times I waved more vigorously, vowing to freeze her out if she responded. She didn't. Rage became chagrin. The next time I saw her I looked away.

But she wasn't the only one brushing me off. One morning, as I drove past the ramshackle sawmill that had been his great grandfather's, I saw Ronny wrestling a log from his truck. I'd slowed, thinking I'd stop to help, but he'd waved me on. I floored the gas pedal. If he didn't want my help, he wouldn't get it. A corollary to the Stone family motto. Some night, when I'd had enough bourbon, I'd write down all the traditions. Maybe dig out Nat's wood-carving tools and make a plaque to hang over the fireplace. Lest I forget.

That same day I saw Ronny, I ran into Lisa at the post office. "Hey, Dan," she'd said with a smile. "When are you coming up for dinner again?"

Remembering the tension between them and the way Ronny had pilloried me, I'd searched my brain for a diplomatic answer.

Her eyes had probed mine, and then she'd sighed and laid a hand on my arm. "I know Ronny can be prickly. The truth is, he's never told Justin, or anyone, the real story about the scholarship. You could have blown him out of the water. But you didn't." She didn't have to tell me she was grateful, I could see it in her face. "Anyway, I keep telling him he needs to tell Justin the truth. But Ronny's . . . well, I guess he's afraid Justin won't respect him."

I'd nodded, trying to imagine what being afraid would feel like to a man who never acknowledged fear.

She'd leaned against the SUV, pushing up the sleeves of her sweater and turning her face to the sun. "Being a parent, you want to be perfect, to do everything right. But it's just not possible. All you can really do with kids is love them and hope that they love you, no matter who you are or what you haven't accomplished."

"I'm sure your kids love you. They're terrific. Julie's a sweetheart."

"Isn't she just." Lisa had laughed. "And as confident about her future as she can be. She'll see the world, I know she will." Lisa scuffed at a pebble on the asphalt apron in front of Mary Lou's domain. I wondered if she remembered that shred of conversation from twenty years before, the day she'd closed the door on her own dreams. "I sometimes think about how it would have been if Ronny had gone off to Ohio or Nebraska, if he'd feel differently about the way things are changing here."

"Maybe." I looked into eyes that stared beyond me into the land of never was and wondered how things would have turned out if she hadn't married Ronny, or hadn't been the kind of woman who stuck by her vows.

"Maybe not," she'd said. "Since Buck died, everybody in town depends on Ronny. He feels responsible, like he has to hold it all together. You know how he is."

"Yeah." I tried to keep my voice neutral. "I know how he is."

"We'll have you up to dinner again real soon."

I hadn't held my breath waiting for an invitation. In the evenings, when I wasn't making myself visible to the community, I raked leaves rank with the smell of decay from a hillside spring that fed a meandering brook and cut brush around the lodge. Sunlight flooded in, and too often I glanced across the glittering lake, searching for Camille. Flushing with humiliation, I turned to other tasks. I caulked chinks in the log walls and scraped and painted the trim around the outside of the windows with a ruddy-beige to cover the dirty white. I worked until my muscles shrieked in protest and, when it grew dark, I dragged a few boxes from seemingly endless rows in the attic and sipped bourbon while I sorted the contents.

Perhaps my mother and grandmother had hoped time would mend broken wooden toys or sew the eyes back on ragged teddy bears. Or maybe they'd believed the years would somehow miraculously roll back, and they'd be able to slip into skirts and dresses their thickening bodies had forced them to lay aside. The sharp smell of mothballs lingered inside the boxes, but moths and mice had been and gone, and there was little I could salvage for Mary Lou's museum except an old train set and a whittled rocking horse with only one ear and my great-grandfather's initials carved into its belly.

Twice I set aside things for myself—a set of alphabet blocks from which my mother had sworn I'd crafted sentences at age three, and a green ceramic bowl a great aunt had gotten as a wedding gift from the wife of a governor. The next night I put the bowl in a sack for Mary Lou and tossed the blocks into a box marked "Salvation Army." There was too much pain in the past. Better to be rid of it.

I cleaned the main downstairs bathroom, painted it bright yellow, bought a new shower curtain, towels and rug, fresh bottles of shampoo, bars of soap, deodorant, and disposable razors. I wiped dust from the living room bookcases, washed windows, vacuumed the furniture and damp-sponged the floor. With each swipe of the mop, I felt as if I were sterilizing the wounds of the past, pouring alcohol into cuts still deep, still raw.

Every night, body throbbing with fatigue, mind fuzzed with drink, I hauled my sleeping bag outside. And every night, no matter how I'd punished myself physically, or how much I drank, the dream claimed me. Every night I plunged into the lake, but my reaction time lengthened, my dream body moved ever more slowly. One night I merely stood on the dock, watching, knowing Nat's efforts were futile. The next day I drove myself harder.

Every other day I called the nursing home where my father lay like a netted fish, twitching and dying in his own slow time. I'd have the obligatory conversation about his condition. "About the same, Dan. I'm sorry. I wish I had better news." Then an aide would hold the phone next to his ear and I'd talk.

"Weather's been good, Dad," I'd say, raising my voice and spacing out the words. "I saw a fox by the spring yesterday evening and five deer at the lake this morning. There's been a bear around. He got into Pattie Bonesteel's bird feeder and tore up half the stones in their front walk looking for grubs. I think once the berry crops come on he'll move back up on the ridges, unless we get a drought. I didn't get any peas or onions in, but maybe I'll plant some sweet corn and cucumbers and tomatoes soon. When you come home we'll have an old-fashioned summer barbecue."

Whether we had the one-sided conversation on the phone, or whether I drove twenty miles to sit beside his bed, that was how I always ended it—that he'd come home and life would go on as it had when we still passed as some semblance of a family.

Late on a Wednesday afternoon, I started resetting all the stones in the walkway to the lake. I was scraping off moss when I heard the phone in the lodge. I vaulted up the steps to get it.

"Volunteer firefighter meeting tonight," Ronny stated before I could say hello. "Seven o'clock. Back room at the Shovel It Inn. Don't be late."

I wasn't surprised when he hung up before I could respond. That and the last-minute summons indicated my status in Hemlock Lake. As I showered, I thought about ignoring the call, or going to the tavern for a beer and avoiding the meeting, or showing up just long enough to drop off the box of gear he'd left for me at the post office. All counterproductive. I settled on arriving late, opening the outside door to the meeting room with no effort at silence, and rattling a folding chair along the ripped and dented linoleum before I sat. Willie Dean turned to grin at me, and Evan peered from the corners of his eyes, but the two dozen others didn't shift their attention from the front of the room where Ronny sat behind a battered table. Stub stood beside him, reading from a sheet of paper.

Stub lowered the paper to stare at me. "Like I was saying, the truck's in good shape for the shape it's in. But we've got to get a new timing chain and water pump soon or we'll have to push it to the next emergency. Ronny and I'll do the labor, but we're talking a good chunk of change for parts." He fluttered the paper with fingers stained brown from years of changing oil, rebuilding engines, and pumping gas. "I've got the exact costs right here if you want to look at them." He offered the sheet to Evan Bonesteel, who shook his head.

"We trust you, Stub," Willie Dean said as he turned and winked at me. I ignored him and surveyed the others, many of whom had tracked Willie Dean's motion and were now staring at me with a mix of curiosity and disinterest. I stared back. Staring is something cops get good at.

Stub coughed to get their attention, then smiled, thin lips stretching over uneven teeth. "All right then. I'll turn the meeting back over to our chief." He took the empty seat in the front row, folded the paper, and slid it into the pocket of a gray coverall with "Stub's Service" embroidered across the front.

"Thanks, Stub." Ronny unfolded himself from his chair. "Well, in case you didn't guess, the next order of business is fundraising. We've got a hundred and fourteen dollars in the kitty and not a dime coming in until the dance in October. Now some of you have talked about putting on a pancake breakfast, and I think that's a great plan. But here's another idea— fireworks."

"Fireworks?" Freeman Keefe scratched his head, riffling curling black hair shot with gray. "You want us to sell them little sparkling sticks and such?"

"No. We couldn't make but a few bucks that way." Ronny scoffed. "I'm thinking of a big sky show. Lots of color and explosions. Shoot 'em off the end of Willie Dean's dock, maybe. Set up chairs in his parking lot. Charge three bucks a head for folks to come down and watch. Sell popcorn and soda."

A low rumble of excitement swept through the room. To my amazement, Willie Dean was the one who spotted the gaping financial hole in the plan. "What's to stop folks from just parking down the road and watching for free? We gonna put up a big curtain or something? Hee, hee, hee." He tipped his chair back, puffing out his chest, enjoying his moment of glory. "Make 'em wear blindfolds if they don't pay?"

The skin on Ronny's cheekbones turned a mottled red, and I saw his fingers curl into fists. Willie Dean would suffer for his comments.

"We'll set up a roadblock by the dam." Stub popped from his chair. "Ronny thought of all that already." Stub, far more loyal and supportive, made a better sidekick than I ever had. "As for the others, folks who live around here, we'll just go down the line with a coffee can, tell them it's for a good cause, make them ashamed if they don't pitch in. We'll get the kids to ask for money. Nobody can say no to kids."

The volunteers nodded, Willie Dean hung his head, and Ronny's fingers flexed. He fixed narrowed eyes on me. "Anybody else got concerns?"

His body language made it clear he didn't want any other ideas. Unblinking, I stared at a spot to the right of his head, where two cracks in the plaster wall intertwined.

"All right, then, Stub and me will call around and see what we can arrange. Willie Dean, you'd best lay in some extra soda and chips. I'll talk to Merle out there at the bar about us serving beer."

"How about watermelon," Freeman Keefe suggested.

Ronny nodded. "Watermelon's not a bad idea. It's pretty cheap and we could sell it by the slice. Okay. I guess that wraps it up."

"How about barbecued chicken and pie," Willie Dean blurted. "And spaghetti."

Ronny and Stub looked at each other. "Spaghetti," Stub said. "Linguine or fettuccini?"

"Angel hair or them little bow ties?" Freeman laughed.

"Nah, Willie Dean's probably thinking of some of that ravioli stuff out of the can," someone in the front scoffed.

"Yeah, that's Willy Dean's idea of high cuisine," Ronny said.

"Puts the can on the table. Probably has napkins to match the label." Stub wiped his eyes as Willie Dean crossed his arms and deflated into a sulk.

I hated to be the one to defend his idea, but it was for the good of the community. Standing, I pushed back my folding chair with a sharp squeal and cleared my throat. "Willy Dean has hit on something that could bring in a lot of money."

"Spaghetti?" Stub widened his eyes and shared a laugh with Ronny. Willie Dean turned toward me and laughed too, aligning himself with his tormentors.

I surveyed the disbelieving faces and thought about just walking away. Then I decided to see how far I could get, how much I could loosen Ronny's grip. "Yeah, I know. It's hard to believe, but Willie Dean's onto something. Not the spaghetti part, but the bit about fried chicken and barbecue. Pie's good, too. You could advertise it as a country picnic supper by the lake."

"Who's gonna make all that shit?" Ronny rose to the challenge. "You?"

I waited for the guffaws to die away and shrugged. "I guess I could make some cookies. Maybe a cake or a salad." I played the sympathy card. "My mother used to make chocolate truffle cakes for Christmas presents. I imagine I could find the recipe."

A ripple of laughter lapped toward me, and I saw Ronny frown.

"Anyway," I continued, "you'd get as much of the food and drink donated as you could. Keep your costs down but jack ticket prices up." Freeman and Evan nodded. They liked that part. I picked a price out of the air. "Twenty dollars a head. Or more. Less for kids. Fireworks included. Beer and wine extra."

Freeman and Evan grinned, and Stub rubbed his chin, a sign he was considering the idea, even ready to jeopardize his sidekick status. But Ronny's fingers coiled again. "Twenty dollars? That's a lot of money for people around here."

The volunteers swung their heads toward me, waiting for me to return the volley. "People who contribute food or work to set things up won't pay. You can give anyone who lives around here a discount and make the big money off tourists and outsiders." I raised the idea like a football, showed Ronny I was ready to pass it to him. "You're running the show. You can make any rules you want."

Stub scratched his ear. "We could sure use the money."

"Yeah," Freeman agreed. "And I'd pay twenty dollars for a couple of slices of Pattie's peach pie." He turned to Evan. "Think you could get her to make up a dozen?"

"Might could. If you persuade Alda to make her potato salad and—"

"This is going to be a hell of a lot of work for someone," Ronny interrupted. "Lots of little details. None of us has the time to coordinate it all. Maybe it's best to keep it small this year."

The volunteers swiveled their heads in anticipation of my response. "You guys don't have to do all the work. Delegate.

There are others who've got the time and would probably enjoy helping out. Retired folks like the Brocktons. Some of your wives, maybe." I lofted the ball to Ronny, watched it hang in the air. "How about Lisa? She was terrific at organizing things back in high school."

"Yeah," Evan Bonesteel said. "Lisa would be great. She planned my daughter's wedding. Even had place card things for the tables so the relatives who weren't speaking didn't end up elbow to elbow."

"She's sure good with details," Freeman agreed.

"And you'd be right there for when she needed advice." I showed Ronny the field, open all the way to the goal line.

"How about it, Ronny?" Stub looked to his leader. The others stared at me. "Think we could get this thing off the ground?"

Ronny's eyes narrowed, but then he shrugged and hauled in the pass. "If you all can get your asses in gear, we could." The volunteers' heads swiveled toward the front of the room, and I heard a rumble of agreement. They'd go with him down the field, run interference, help him score.

"All right then, here's how we'll do it." Ronny seized a yellow pad and pencil from the table. Willie Dean gave me a thumbs-up signal. I ducked my head, hiding a smug smile. I had no doubt Ronny knew he'd been manipulated, but I suspected most of the volunteers had never seen it happen.

"If you're all agreed, I'll put Lisa in charge of getting the word out, making tickets, getting donations, setting the menu, and finding enough volunteer cooks to take care of it all. I'll call around about the fireworks. Willie Dean, you and Evan will see about getting tables and barbecue grills." Ronny made a note on his pad. "Freeman, you'll be in charge of some kind of decorations. Red, white, and blue kind of stuff. But don't spend any money if you don't have to. Stub, paper plates and plastic forks and such. The rest of you get your kids out and clean up the lakeshore. Get rid of all the litter and fishing lures and other crap. Do it next week, and do it again right before the picnic. And Dan, you've got the toughest job of all." A slow grin spread over his face. "You get us some of those mobile shitters, those portable outhouses or whatever you call 'em." The grin broadened. I'd challenged his authority, but he'd put me in my place.

"Yeah," Stub chimed in, "got to have some place to recycle all the beer."

The volunteers rotated in their seats, knowing I'd been insulted, wondering what I'd do. Turn down the assignment, and I'd be back on the outside. Accept it, and gates would swing open.

I shrugged and forced myself to smile. I knew the guy who handled that detail for the annual sheriff's department picnic. It would take one phone call to make the arrangements, and I'd never have to lay a hand on the contraptions myself. But Ronny didn't need to know that. "I'll take care of it."

A sigh whispered through the room. The volunteers turned back to Ronny, and I let my lips sag, erasing the smile.

"Okay. Any questions?" Ronny scanned the room. "No, then meeting adjourned. And don't forget, next Wednesday at six, practice drill."

I didn't wait for the others. Shoving open the door, I started for my SUV. Camille Chancellor leaned against the front fender. She wore running shoes and shiny purple pants, an oversized turquoise T-shirt, and a pink baseball cap. I felt my heart lighten and my breath quicken. I took a step toward her, but then reminded myself that I'd intended to ignore her and that she was on my list of suspects.

A tiny smile twitched at her lips. "I was out for a jog and that chip fell off my shoulder. May I buy you a drink, Sergeant?"

CHAPTER 11

I tried to remember if I'd ever let Susanna buy me a drink when we were dating. No, I was positive I hadn't, just as I was positive that she'd never offered. Susanna had been the kind of woman who expected men to open doors and pick up checks. I'd understood that, and understood the potent effect on my male ego. But Susanna was gone, and I wanted to learn more about this woman whose name was on my list of suspects. "How about I let you? I'm nearly out of cash and businesses around here won't take my checks."

"Good." She pushed off from the fender and walked to the front door of the tavern, pants shimmering in the slanting sunlight. "Will I get any arguments out of you if I spring for some pretzels, too?"

"None at all."

"Then let's go."

I strode ahead to open the door; old habits die hard. She rolled her eyes and strolled into the mellow darkness of the tavern.

The smell of frying onions and stale grease mingled with decades of beer spilled and mopped deep into the cracks of the oak-planked floor. Behind the bar, Merle McDaniel rubbed at the water spots on a glass. His wife, Shirley, wiped the plastic sheet protecting a red and white checked table cloth on one of six unoccupied tables. From the jukebox beside the bar, Bonnie Raitt sang "Something to Talk About." I followed Camille to a table at the back and held her chair, earning another eye roll. I dropped into my own seat. I noticed Ronny and Stub come through the door from the back room, and I thought Camille and I might be fodder for a lot of conversations tonight. Small town. Small minds. Small talk.

"How you doin'?" Shirley slapped a couple of menus in front of us and pushed a wave of gray-blond hair back behind her right ear as her gaze slid over Camille. "Thought I would have seen you in here before now, Dan."

I didn't mention I'd been uncertain of my welcome and had been doing my drinking alone. "I've had a lot to take care of, Shirl. How are you doing?" Behind her, Ronny and Stub hefted themselves onto stools at the bar, then spun halfway around, watching us.

"Tolerable. Merle's fighting the gout, and I'm fighting my gall bladder. We're a regular matched set of misery. What will you have?"

"Just beer for me. Whatever's on tap will be fine."

"And you?" Shirley turned to Camille, her body stiff. "I've seen you driving the Brocktons' car, but I never did get your name."

I knew that wasn't true. Shirley must have known Camille's name before she'd been in town ten minutes. Shirley was a conduit between Mary Lou and Louisa Marie; she got a double dose of daily gossip.

Camille apparently decided to ignore the negative vibes and stretched out her right hand. "Camille Chancellor. Pleased to meet you, Mrs. McDaniel. I've heard you make some amazing onion rings."

Shirley blushed, stared at the hand, then shook it quickly. "Well, pleased to meet you, too. I hear you're a gourmet cook."

"I'm not too shabby," Camille admitted, and then launched into what I suspected was a lie large enough to require its own zip code. "But I can't make an onion ring to save my life. If I get the batter to stay on, I get the grease too hot or not hot enough. May I have a large order? And a beer? The same as Sergeant Stone."

Shirley nodded, hollered at Merle to pull two drafts, and bustled toward the kitchen as Willie Dean sidled through the back door and pulled himself up on the stool beside Ronny's.

"One smart-ass comment about me sucking up," Camille whispered, "and I'll put all those mouse turds back in your stove."

"Consider me silent." Camille's honesty and acceptance amazed me. I wouldn't have put myself in a situation where I stood out like she did. Then I realized that I'd done just that. I bit back an ironic laugh and watched Camille's eyes widen as she studied the decor. Racks of antlers and arching rainbow trout studded the wall, and smaller taxidermied critters dangled from the rafters: squirrels, raccoons, bats, even a couple of rattlesnakes.

I grinned as she shuddered at an owl with a chipmunk in its mouth. "Homey, isn't it? Appetizing, too. Did you know that Merle's hobby is taxidermy?" I whispered as he approached with the beers.

"You're lying," she said softly, as Merle trudged away again. "Aren't you?"

"Yes. It's really Shirley's hobby."

Camille laughed into the beer she'd brought to her lips, spraying foam on the table. "Seriously?"

"No," I admitted. "Merle's father did this stuff. He was so proud that he wrote it into the will. Merle got the tavern, but he had to display the carcasses."

She studied me for a minute, then inspected the decor again. "Well, it has a certain *je ne sais.*"

"It has," I said. "What would you call this school of decorating?"

"Rural rustic roadkill," she suggested.

"Potshot provincial," I countered.

"Tudor taxidermy."

"Colonial killing zone."

She laughed, a long peal of sugared notes, and I felt a certain pride at being the one who'd sparked the sound. "I believe that's a smile on your face, Sergeant Stone. Or am I mistaken?"

I fingered my lips, realizing this smile was one I hadn't had to force. "It's a distinct possibility."

She laughed again, drawing glances from Ronny, Stub, and Willie Dean. "We have an audience."

"In Hemlock Lake you always have an audience. We covered that a few weeks ago."

"Yes." She sipped her beer. "I remember." She sipped again. "I see you've cut a lot of underbrush around the lodge. It looks good. And Mary Lou tells me you're cleaning out the attic."

"Yeah." I twirled my glass slowly. "I'm getting to it a little at a time. I got the living room cleaned, too. And painted the main bathroom."

"So . . . you've moved inside?"

I hesitated. It was none of her business, but I wanted to tell her. "No. It seems . . . crowded. Like they're still there—Susanna, Nat, and my father. Especially at night."

Her eyes glistened, and she blinked. "I'm sorry. And I'm sorry for what I did a few weeks ago. I should have backed off when I saw how painful it was for you. It's the Virgo in me that makes me act that way. I got caught up in getting things organized and—"

"Here you go." Shirley set a platter of onion rings and a bowl of pink sauce down between us. "I call that my secret sauce," she said with a grin. "Tell me what you think." She waited, hands twisting in the short apron tied over her jeans and worn denim shirt, while we dipped and bit.

"Marvelous." Camille took a second bite. "The horseradish makes it."

I crammed the rest of mine into my mouth, chewed, swallowed, and reached for another one. "As good as ever."

Blushing, Shirley retreated behind the bar. Camille swallowed and ran a finger along the edge of the platter. "Anyway, I'm sorry."

"No. The blame's all mine." It felt good to claim it. "I know I'll never get over what happened, no matter what everyone says about time healing the wounds, but I ought to be able to pretend I'm doing better than I am. Or else I'll lose the few friends I have."

Her eyes brightened, the color shifting like sunlight through syrup. "So we're friends?"

I didn't stop to consider my suspicions, all the things I didn't know about her. I only knew that I liked talking with her, even when it hurt. "Yes."

She glanced toward the group at the bar. "Because we're both outsiders?"

"No. Because those cookies you left are gone. I want more."

She snagged another onion ring, a smile twitching the corners of her lips. "Is that your idea of humor?"

I widened my eyes, put a hand on my chest. "That wasn't funny?"

"No." Her lips twitched another millimeter. "Well, maybe just a little."

"Enough to get me a few more cookies? Or another piece of pie?"

"A small piece." She held her thumb and forefinger an inch apart. "Maybe I'll bring it over one of these evenings."

"Would tomorrow be too soon?"

"That's humor again, right?"

I nodded, surprised at how relaxed I felt.

"The humor needs a little work, but, okay, I'll bring the pie. If you let me clean something. That's what I'm good at, remember?"

"The blinding whiteness of my refrigerator reminds me of that daily. But would you settle for sorting, instead. There are another fifty boxes jammed in the attic. And lord knows what's under the house and in the garage."

"I'll sort," she said, "as long as it's really old stuff. Stuff from back before you were born. That's safer."

"Safer? Safer than what—cleaning out the second-story gutters?"

She dipped another onion ring, studying me. "Safer than rummaging through the more recent past. That's the way I think of it, anyway. Imagine an old picture, brown and beige and fuzzy around the edges. That's what the distant past is like. You know what happened then because somebody's told you, but it's not your past, so you never think, 'If I'd been there it would have been different,' or 'What if I'd done this,' or 'What if I'd done that.' You couldn't have changed it."

I nodded and drank the rest of my beer. She was right. All those boxes in the attic were harmless. They smelled of mothballs and held gnawed and wrinkled clothing I'd never seen anyone wear, shoes out of style for fifty years, books with yellowed pages. Those things had no connection to me. They could easily have been put there by strangers.

She seemed to hear the question I didn't ask. "It's the recent past that's dangerous." She fixed her eyes on a stuffed possum that snarled from a rafter above the jukebox. "It's waiting for you in the shadows, so close you think you could almost touch it. Change it. But you can't. So you walk faster."

I stared at my fingers, whitening against the thick beer mug as I tried not to think about Susanna and Nat. I tried to walk faster while sitting so still that I could hear the hum of the neon lights in the silent jukebox and the squeak of Merle's towel on another glass.

She sipped her beer and turned her attention to a stuffed flying squirrel, suspended on a string above the bar. "I learned the hard way that time and distance aren't enough. The only way to ease your pain is to turn around and look at what's after you."

The hum of the neon lights became the rumble of the motor on Nat's boat; the squeak of Merle's towel transformed to Susanna's strangled screams. I squeezed the mug until I expected it to shatter; I almost hoped to feel glass slice into my fingers. What could Camille know about how it felt to lose your wife and your brother on the same day? To have your father crumple like a sack of dirty laundry flung in a corner? I felt cold anger compress my chest, stiffen the back of my neck, clamp my jaws together. Look at what was after me? Hell, that's all I ever did. "You say that like it's easy." My voice was cold, bitter.

"I know it's not." She dropped her head and spoke so quietly I almost didn't hear her. "I lost my mother. And my daughter." She looked toward the quartet at the bar, then touched the corners of her eyes with her fingers, blotting tears. "My husband killed them."

I felt the muscles in my jaw go slack, my fingers slide from the glass and curl into fists. Prodding my tongue against my bottom teeth, I felt for words that weren't in my vocabulary. I felt small and mean and rotten. "I'm sorry."

She held up a hand. "He was a hitter. When things went wrong, he took it out on me. I thought he'd change, but when I was seven months pregnant he went to work drunk and got fired. It was my fault, he said. If I didn't make so many demands, he wouldn't have to drink." She paused, drew in a shuddering breath.

I wanted to get up and put my arms around her, but five sets of eyes made me a coward, kept me in my seat. "That's an abuser's logic," I said. "They blame everyone but themselves."

"I know that now. But then . . . he said he'd have to teach me a lesson. My mother tried to stop him. He beat her with the car seat she'd bought for the baby. When she didn't try to get up anymore, he beat me until I lost my daughter."

I forced myself to breathe deeply, air stabbing into my lungs. "I'm sorry," I whispered. "Tell me he got justice."

She shook her head. "Not then. Not there. He got five years. With time off for good behavior."

The travesty stunned me, and yet I felt I shouldn't be surprised. I'd seen too many domestic violence cases end in death, and too many men get off cheap. "And he came looking for you when he got out." Textbook behavior.

She nodded. "He wanted me to marry him again, forgive and forget. Like all he'd done was spill milk on the carpet." She finally looked up at me. "I said no. He slapped me. Just once. Then he apologized and said I made him crazy. But I'd had counseling by then. I knew the way he acted wasn't my fault. I ran, changed my name."

"Good."

"Yeah, for six months it was very good. And then he found me. I ran again, went to a women's shelter, got a restraining order. He violated it every day for a week."

I gripped the beer stein like it was his neck. I could almost feel the knots on his spine, the cords of his arteries. "They didn't arrest him?"

She shook her head. "He was a smooth talker, just a man who wanted his wife back. The last time he violated the order he brought a knife."

Her eyes burned into mine. "But I'd bought a gun."

I let out the breath I'd been holding. She was testing me. I wanted to ace the exam. "Tell me you killed him."

"Yes."

"You had no choice."

She shrugged. "Once I would have said I could never kill another human being, no matter what. But the hole in my heart where my mother and daughter used to be made me change." She dropped her gaze to her fingers, which had picked the breading from a large onion ring. Plucking a napkin from the metal holder at the edge of the table, she wiped her hands and motioned to Merle. He nodded and pulled two more drafts. As he started around the bar, Ronny poked a bill at him. Merle set our beers down and made the transaction. When Ronny waved off the change and started for the door, Merle picked up the beers and limped to our table.

"Anything else?"

"No," Camille blotted the corner of one eye with her napkin. "This is fine."

My mouth felt parched, my tongue shriveled. I gulped at my beer.

"You didn't finish your rings." Merle pointed at the nearly full platter. "Something wrong with them?"

"Not at all." Camille short-circuited his curiosity with a smile. "I wasn't as hungry as I thought. Could you wrap them, please?"

Merle hesitated for a few seconds. Then he lifted the platter and disappeared into the kitchen. Camille took a long swallow of beer. "I want you to know that I wasn't looking for sympathy. And I wasn't preaching, either. It's just that life goes on."

Trite words. I'd heard them a hundred times since Susanna's death. "My life is going on. I haven't killed myself, have I?"

She sipped beer and set the glass in the center of a coaster. "No, but you're an emotional hostage," she said, her voice cool and neutral. "If you got some help you could break loose, find a degree of happiness—"

"A degree?" Like happiness could be measured with a thermometer, turned up or down. "What degree does a shrink set your happiness at? Bake? Broil?"

She shrugged that off. "It's your choice. But I think you should be sure that you're actually making a choice and not wrapping misery around you because you feel that's all you deserve."

I glared at a stuffed skunk that lifted its tail from the top of a stump in the far corner of the room. I hadn't saved Susanna, hadn't stopped Nat. Misery was exactly what I deserved. Stub and Willie Dean spun off their bar stools and headed toward the door as Shirley bustled out of the kitchen with a foil-wrapped package and a green-lined page torn from her notepad. She set both down on the edge of the table.

"Sorry I couldn't eat all the onion rings," Camille told her as she flipped over the check. "I'll heat them up later on for a midnight snack." She leaned to one side and pulled a folded bill from her sock.

"Best not." Shirley took the money and made change from her pocket. "You'll have nightmares." She patted the foil. "They'll keep until lunch." She plunked coins and bills on the table, took the two dollars and a quarter Camille pushed aside, and sauntered to the jukebox.

Camille swallowed half of her beer and slid the mug to the center of the table as she stood. "I feel like we're back where we were three weeks ago. Still want me to bring over some pie?"

"I'll think about it."

Shirley turned and raised her eyebrows at me as Johnny Cash launched into "Ring of Fire." I frowned, scraped my chair back, and stood.

"Fair enough," Camille said. "You know where I am."

I trailed her to the door and nodded goodnight to Merle, who leaned against the bar and stared at a stuffed woodchuck he'd been saddled with. I wondered fleetingly if he'd ever thought about turning down his inheritance.

In the parking lot, Camille bent to touch her toes, then lunged forward on one leg to loosen the knotted muscles on her calves. I cleared my throat. "I'll give you a ride."

She slipped the foil-wrapped packet under her T-shirt and tucked the shirt into the waistband of her pants. "No need. It's only five miles."

"More like seven and a half." I looked up at a few early moths fluttering against the red neon sign that spelled out SHOVEL IT INN. The S buzzed and blinked. "And it's dark."

"We're right back where we were three weeks ago." She laughed as she started to jog away, then glanced back at me. "Why do you always say 'it's dark' like that's supposed to mean something?"

Because to me it did. I watched the darkness fold around her, then kicked the stones of the parking lot. Ramming my key into the lock, I wrenched open the door, slammed it behind me, and jabbed at the ignition. The wheels flung gravel as I spun out onto the roadway, shifting rapidly. Blind and formless anger filled my brain. Anger without a face, because I'd never seen the man she killed. Anger with her face, because she'd tried to use a scalpel on my wound to draw off the infection and drawn blood instead.

The SUV rocked onto two wheels as I took a sharp curve below Bobcat Hollow at fifty miles an hour. As I fought the wheel, I saw something shift beneath the jacket I'd flung across the passenger seat. Unconsciously I reached for it. One edge of the jacket rose. I jerked my hand back. An ugly triangular head appeared. Two eyes glittered in the green light from the dashboard. A muffled buzzing swirled around me.

CHAPTER 12

Rattler!

I jerked my right hand from the wheel, wedged my body tight against the door. The SUV heeled out of the turn and onto a straightaway. The snake's head bobbed. Its tongue flicked out, sampling the air. The roof of my mouth grew hot with the taste of nickel.

Get out! My mind screamed instructions to my body. *Take your foot off the gas. Release the seat belt. Flip back the door latch. Roll free.*

I raised my foot from the gas pedal. I drew my right hand toward the seat belt release.

The snake buzzed and shrugged off the jacket. Its head swayed inches from my hand.

I froze. Seconds drifted by like snowflakes. If I moved suddenly, the snake would strike. And then what? What would I do once the venom was in my bloodstream? My mind tobogganed through my options.

Call for help. But what if the cell phone didn't work? Drive to the nearest house. But that house was a mile away. Too far to walk if the snake hit me close to the heart. I needed wheels, couldn't take a chance on leaping out and letting my rig crash.

I shuddered. The snake drew its thick body into a tight coil. I checked the speedometer. Thirty-five and dropping. The road started downhill soon, took another sharp turn at Silver Leaf

Hollow. I'd pick up speed, have to downshift or brake to make that turn.

If I reached for the stick shift the snake would strike for sure. Brake hard without the clutch? Would that throw the snake to the floor?

The snake swayed toward the dashboard, drawn to the louvered vents spewing warm air. Good. Away from my body heat.

I pinched the bottom of the wheel, slid my left hand close to my body toward the seat belt release. Almost there. My fingers touched something slick and hard. My stomach lurched. A book. Wedged between the seat and the console. A shield. Get it loose. I hauled in a quivering breath. The snake's head swung toward me, the green glow reflecting wetly from its eyes.

The road dropped away beneath the headlights. The hill. Twenty. Then twenty-five. The wheels wobbled into a rut. A whispering buzz sent a trickle of chill sweat coursing down my spine. Get the seat belt off. My groping fingernails found the ridged surface of the belt, the buckle, the button.

Click.

The snake rattled a warning.

I hooked my thumb in the belt, moved it across my body by millimeters. Done. Left hand on the wheel. Book in the right. Watch the snake. Check the speedometer. Thirty. The road leveled out. Do it!

Left hand on the door latch. Left knee against the door. Raise the book slowly, slowly.

Now! Stomp the brake!

The SUV bucked. The snake snapped forward and then whiplashed back against the seat. I clawed at the door latch. Cool air raked my skin. The snake writhed and buzzed. The engine convulsed and died. The snake snapped toward me. I flung the book, hurled myself through the door, hit the asphalt, and rolled.

Crushed shale bit into my hands and knees as I scrabbled to my feet. *Kill it! Kill it!* I plunged into the ditch, running for the spray of light cast by the headlights, searching for a weapon. I stumbled across a rock, picked it up, then discarded it in favor of a thick dead limb. Dead, but not rotten. Clutching it in both hands, I sidestepped along the shoulder.

The dome light cast a surrealistic glow along the mottled body of the snake coiled in the driver's seat, its head resting on the steering wheel. I hefted the club. In two long strides, I could cover most of the distance. But the roof would keep me from striking hard enough.

I had to move the snake with the club, or tease him with it, hoping he'd strike and fall to the ground. I closed in. The snake raised its head and turned glittering eyes toward me. Lifting its tail, it rattled a warning. I thrust the club at it.

It struck.

I jerked the club away. Too fast. The snake twisted on the seat, buzzing like a swarm of hornets.

I stabbed at it again and it struck once more.

It tumbled to the road and writhed toward me in the pool of frosty light.

With both hands, I raised the club above my head and brought it down as hard as I could.

Pain jolted up my arms as the club connected with the roadway. The snake flopped disjointedly, striking at the air, at itself.

Half-blind with fear and anger, I hit it again and again. My hands stung and burned from the rough bark and sharp contact, my arms grew numb. Finally, out of breath, I flipped the still-twitching body into the ditch.

Casting the club aside, I unhooked the flashlight from under the dash. I probed beneath the seats with its beam, praying the snake didn't have a companion. My grandmother had sworn they always traveled in pairs. If you killed one, the mate would curl around its body to mourn and then come after you. I'd never believed that. What I did believe was that whoever put the snake under my jacket might have thought if one reptile was good, two would be better.

I straightened my shoulders, clipped the flashlight back under the dash, and tossed the book to the back seat. *Cold Mountain.* I'd meant to loan it to Mary Lou.

I climbed in and considered what the snake meant. Joke or warning? Either way, the person who put it on the seat would get no satisfaction. I intended to keep this incident to myself. Maybe he'd wonder what went wrong and give himself away. I smiled, let in the clutch, reached for the key, and saw the oozing puncture wound on the end of my middle finger.

My heart pounded in my throat. My whole arm shook as I raised my hand, thinking I must have cut myself when I broke the limb, or drove in a splinter as I pounded the snake. No. This hole was neat. A stinging pain shot up my arm. My stomach clenched and rolled. The book had shielded me from one fang, but the other had struck.

"Stay calm, Dan. Call for help."

I fumbled the key from the ignition, unlocked the glove box, and plucked the cell phone from beside my gun. For once, the self-sufficient side of my brain didn't argue that I could handle this without help. I hit the buttons. Silence. Dead zone. I flung the phone to the floor.

"It's okay. You can drive, but you've got to open the wound before you do anything," I coached myself. "Get the first aid kit."

A rattler's bite wasn't necessarily fatal. Nat had blundered across one near the garden when we were kids. It hit him below the knee and sent him screaming in circles. Dad ran the snake down and split it in two with his hoe, then went after Nat.

White with fear, Nat thrashed so hard Dad had to slap him to make him hold still. Dad made me sit on Nat's chest, pinning him to the ground. Then he'd told me to talk about Santa Claus while he drew a knife across the punctures and squeezed Nat's leg. Blood laced Dad's hand, Nat screamed louder, and I stuck my fingers in my ears and yelled out the names of the reindeer until Dad jerked me to my feet and shook me into silence.

Ordering me to call around to the neighbors and find Mom, Dad strapped his belt around Nat's leg above the wound, carried him to the truck, and drove like a bat out of hell to the hospital. The next day Nat came home with stitches and a bandage held on with wide strips of adhesive tape. Mom spoiled him with ice cream and cookies, and Dad made me do his weeding for two weeks.

With stiff fingers I unlocked the hatch, then tugged at the latches on the white metal box with the red cross. "Come on!" They popped loose and I flipped the lid and spotted the yellow plastic oblong and the black words on the side: FOR EMERGENCY USE ONLY.

"Don't panic." I could barely hear my voice over the pounding in my ears. How long had it been since the snake had struck. Five minutes? Ten? Fifteen? Was the venom already pulsing into my heart? I remembered the story of a woman who'd been struck in the face while picking blackberries in the mountains. The snake's fangs caught in her cheek. Eyeball to eyeball with her death, she'd locked her hands around the rattler's body. And that was how her husband found them, woman and snake, in a fatal embrace.

I tore at the yellow container, sending the top flying. A red-handled blade, smaller than my little finger, fell out. I dropped to my knees, fingers scrabbling across pebbles and sand, and finally touched the tiny blade. I held it between my teeth as I unwrapped a length of nylon cord from the suction device. The instructions fluttered to the ground. I didn't need them.

I threaded one end of the cord through a loop in the other end and stuck my arm through the noose. Working it above my elbow, I pulled it tight and felt the throbbing of my heart shift from my ears to my fingers. My hand seemed to swell, slick and white in the dome light's glow. Left-handed, I cut an X across the fang mark, pushed in the spring-driven plunger of the suction device, held it tight against the wound and let the plunger go. I repeated that until blood ran freely. Tearing open the foil package of antiseptic cream, I squirted it onto the bloody wound.

Knees trembling, I staggered to the door, my heart hot with poison, my field of vision narrowed to a swirling purple vortex filled with explosions of light. Red and blue and green. Ronny's fireworks. Ronny's snake?

Had he somehow popped the lock, then shoved the rattler under my jacket? Or had it been someone else? Willie Dean? Or Camille? Camille, who'd killed her ex-husband?

The tunnel around my eyes grew tighter, the exploding lights brighter and more painful. My heart battered at my eardrums. I wedged the ignition key in the slot and nudged the shift into neutral. I lifted my feet to the clutch and brake and turned the key. The engine choked and died.

"Come on!"

I turned the key again. The starter ground in frenzied agony and a green wave of nausea swept over me. I clutched the wheel, waiting for it to pass.

"Please."

A shadow moved at the edge of the headlight beams and a figure edged toward me. It was thinner than Ronny, taller than Stub, moving more gracefully than Willie Dean.

A machine-gun blast of light exploded behind my eyes, and another green wave sucked me under.

CHAPTER 13

An insistent blaring jackhammered at the edges of my consciousness. My hand burned as if I'd held it in a flame. A light seared my eyelids, and I cringed. Ronny's voice rumbled through my skull.

"Dan? What the hell is going on? Dan, are you okay?" Something heavy thudded, wood on metal, and the blaring stopped. "Goddamn horn!"

"What's wrong? Is he hurt?" Lisa's voice pinged off my ears. "Oh my god! Look at his hand, Ronny! And that tourniquet. He's been snakebit."

"Too early for snakes." A hand gripped my shoulders. My head rolled loosely on my neck, releasing a scarlet burst of nausea against the blackness in my brain. "Wake up, bud."

"Ronny! Look out! The snake's right there!"

"Son of a bitch." Ronny's hands released my shoulders. I slumped against the seat belt. Ronny let out a sharp huff of air. "It's dead."

"I'll call for an ambulance." Lisa's voice, fading into the distance.

"Tell them it's a rattler. Tell them I'll meet the ambulance on the road."

A door slammed beside me. We jolted over something, the wheels shooting gravel. I fell without moving. Hit bottom without feeling.

Susanna smiled at me as she carried her wakeboard from the garage.

"No!" *I screamed.* "Don't go!"

She didn't hear me. I didn't hear myself.

She drifted toward Nat, who waited in the boat, tinkering with the motor. Her long hair shimmered, as silvery-white in the milky moonlight as the two-piece bathing suit stretched across her hips and breasts. Nat reached out a hand to help her. She shook her head, laughing, and jumped aboard. The boat rocked like a cradle. Wavelets rippled in a slow pulse beneath the dark skin of the lake.

I fell back in the porch swing and watched them go, waiting for the dream to release me. I knew what would happen next, knew I couldn't alter it. The swing rocked. The boat sped away, the wake unfolding like a fan.

"Don't," *I whispered.*

The boat circled, idled to a stop. Susanna tossed the board into the water and leaped in behind it, holding the rope. She raised her arm.

I raised mine. The swing rocked sharply beneath me. "Look at me, Susanna! Look at me! Don't do it!"

The boat shot forward and she came upright in one smooth motion, shedding water droplets like diamonds scattered from a broken necklace. Nat carved a wide oval through the water and looked back. Susanna waved to him and mouthed a word. Faster? Frowning, Nat shook his head. Susanna raised her elbows and flapped her arms. Chicken?

"No! Nat!!" *I tried to stand. The swing lurched beneath me.* "Don't take the dare!"

Nat shrugged. He gunned the motor, rocketing along the spine of the lake. Behind him, Susanna jumped and twirled, flying out to one side of the boat and then the other, catapulting herself across the wake, changing hands on the rope. Celebrating her life. Celebrating her death.

"We're gonna get you in the ambulance now." Hands grasped my shoulders and legs, swung me smoothly onto a cool surface.

Fingers probed my wrist, unbuttoned my shirt. Something pressed against my cheeks and chin, covering my nose; something else pricked at the bend of my arm.

"They're getting an IV line in you, bud. They've got the anti-venom. Just keep breathing that oxygen. You're going to be okay."

I tried to nod, but I couldn't make my head move.

Out on the dark lake Susanna twirled and waved for me to follow.

I rocked in the swing.

She twisted, jumped the wake, and cartwheeled into oblivion.

I rocked on as Nat stumbled past me, carrying Susanna's body into the lodge.

Peering through the window, I saw him lay her on the sofa and brush wet hair from her eyes.

He knelt by her side, clutching her hands, wailing, keening, pleading for a miracle.

"His vital signs are improving." The hushed voice floated through my senses, carried on the acerbic scent of rubbing alcohol and the squeak of rubber soles on linoleum. "He blacked out. We see it a lot with snakebite."

"I should have realized that." Ronny's voice. "I should have—"

"Don't blame yourself. You got him here as fast as you could. And blacking out probably spared him some pain."

Pain, I thought. What did they know about pain? The pain no medicine could heal.

I pressed my face against the window, watching Nat. Fingers trembling, he took the rifle from the rack on the wall and stroked the stock. Now the bullet. Only one. A hollow point. He loaded the rifle and disappeared down the hallway. Empty-handed, he returned for Susanna.

"No! Let me be the one! Let me go with her!" I raised my fist to hammer on the window.

Fingers wrapped around my wrist. "You're not going anywhere. Settle down, bud." Ronny's voice, with a note I'd never heard in it before. Uncertainty? Concern?

I flexed my fingers, felt a rasping sigh grate across the tongue that had dried against the roof of my mouth like papier mache. "Water."

"Hang on, I'll get it." His hand slid beneath my head. Something pressed against my lips and I sucked, gulping cool liquid.

"Not too much," Ronny cautioned as he pulled the straw away and lowered my head to the pillow.

I tried to raise my hands for the glass and discovered only my left would move. Reluctantly, I opened my eyes and looked toward my right arm. It was strapped to some kind of board; an intravenous needle plunged into the back of my hand and held in place with tape. A clear tube snaked up from the needle to a bag of liquid suspended from a metal pole. No, two bags of liquid, two metal poles. I blinked and squinted, saw that one set was only a reflection in the dark square of a window in a yellowed wall. I blinked again and peered the other way, past the white sheet and blanket pulled up to my armpits, and toward Ronny. His hair stood up in twisted tufts, his eyes were rimmed with red lines, his beard was runneled by his groping fingers.

"You okay, bud?"

"Never been better," I croaked. "More water."

He held the flexible straw to my mouth. "Just a little at a time. If you drink too much you'll toss it."

Ignoring his advice, I clamped my left hand around the glass and sucked greedily, swishing water around my mouth, feeling parched skin tingle as it rehydrated, a cool spike driving toward my stomach.

Ronny grinned. "Don't blame me if you hurl."

I shook my head slightly, sucked harder, heard the straw

slurp at the bottom of the glass.

"That's all for now." Ronny set the glass on a mustard-brown metal table beside the bed. "Do you remember what happened?"

Yes, Susanna died. Nat died. Again. I plucked at the collar of a pale blue hospital gown decorated with tiny pink and white flowers, and stretched my legs. The movement unleashed a mild wave of nausea and an intense pounding in my skull. No, not the dream. The snake. The memory came back to me like a jet touching down on a runway, with a rush and a roar. "Someone put a snake on the passenger seat under my jacket. Big mother. I didn't see it until I was halfway home. I killed it. I think."

"Yeah. You got it. Turned it into rattler confetti." Ronny's hands gripped the metal bars on the side of the bed. "As soon as I get you out of here, I'm going to strangle Willie Dean Denton."

The nausea subsided and a vague memory shook itself like an old dog in a dark corner of my mind: Willie Dean coming into the bar several minutes after Ronny and Stub. Ronny leaving before the others. Camille waiting for me. My brain seemed to itch and burn.

"Probably went up on the ledges early one morning," Ronny said, working it out. "Found a snake just waking up. You can catch them easy when they're cold and slow."

Another memory stirred: Ronny and me, prowling the ledges. Just the two of us. "Willie Dean used to be scared of snakes, didn't he?"

"Shit, I don't remember." Ronny shoved fingers through his snarled hair. "Maybe he got over it. Who else would pull a dumb stunt like this?"

I didn't answer. The "who" depended on the "why." Stub's truck had been parked not far from my rig, and I'd bet he had a tool to pop the door lock and the good sense to wear gloves when he did it. And you probably couldn't dust a dead snake for fingerprints. Not after the beating it took. A blind alley. "How about some more water?"

Ronny glanced toward the door, then poured from a metal pitcher beaded with condensation. "It's your gut, not mine."

"It feels fine," I assured him. But I sipped at the water, letting it drizzle across my teeth and leak down my throat.

"One thing I don't understand." Ronny rocked back in the regulation hospital gray metal chair. "How'd you get to my place?"

I closed my eyes, conjuring up the battle with the snake. My heart picked up the pace, pounding blood through the arteries in my neck. I fought to draw in a slow breath. "I drove."

Ronny narrowed his eyes, shook his head. "I don't think so."

Closing my eyes again, I saw myself fumbling with the key, saw something move at the edge of the headlight beams. Had there been someone out there on the road with me? "Then who did?"

He shrugged. "You were belted into the passenger seat when I found you. The engine was running in neutral, and someone had yanked the parking brake and wedged a big old log against the horn. But you were all by your lonesome. Except for that dead snake across your lap."

I shuddered, feeling a ripple of nausea in my gut. Someone tried to kill me, and someone else had saved me. Or had killer and savior been one and the same, toying with my mind, toying with my life?

"Strange that whoever got you to my place didn't stick—"

The door swung open, banged off the stop, and rebounded. Sheriff Clement North straight-armed it again and strode to the foot of the bed. His gaze flicked over Ronny, then the IV bag, and back to my face. "You doing okay, Sergeant?"

"I'm fine," I lied as I struggled to sit up. "No need for you to come out in the middle of the night."

"Don't move, son. I can't abide phony heroism." I fell back against the pillow and saw his eyes soften. "Besides, you know I've got insomnia. I was working on one of them damn thousand-piece jigsaw puzzles when the dispatcher called to tell me what happened. Some kind of picture by one of them dead French artists. Whole bunch of water lilies all jammed together."

"Monet?" Gritting my teeth, I held back a grin.

"Yeah, that sounds like him. Knew you'd know." The sheriff focused on Ronny again.

"Ronny Miller," I told him. "Sheriff Clement North." Ronny stood and stuck out his hand. "Ronny got me to the hospital."

"What we don't know is who got him to my place." Ronny pumped the sheriff's hand. "Left him in the yard with the engine running."

The sheriff smoothed a bristling eyebrow with one thumb. "Give us a minute, will you?" He nodded toward the door.

"Sure thing." Ronny hitched at his jeans and headed toward the hall. "I'll call Lisa. Get you a cup of coffee, Sheriff?"

"No, thanks." The sheriff settled himself into the chair. "Staying awake isn't my problem." He waited until the door closed, then leaned toward me. "You really okay?"

"Yeah," I assured him. "Just shaky, pissed off."

"Normal, then. Any idea who did this?"

I shook my head. "Conventional wisdom says it was Willie Dean Denton, the local practical joker. But I seem to remember that Willie Dean would rather set his hair on fire than handle a snake."

The sheriff looked at me for a long moment, his eyes narrowing. "This isn't a joke, son. It's a warning. And it got my attention. I should never have badgered you into taking this assignment. As soon as they let you out of here, you pack up your stuff and come on back. We'll handle this another way."

I felt a flash of relief, followed by an avalanche of anger. I wasn't a quitter. I wouldn't let him make me into one. I clenched my left hand. Had I been any more in jeopardy last night than any of the empty nights since Susanna died—the nights that I patrolled the highways seeing nothing before me except her face? "No. I'll stay."

He rubbed his eyebrow again and let out a lip-vibrating sigh.

I looked away, studied the dim gray light at the window. Almost sunrise. Someone had hoped I wouldn't live to see it. I felt a malicious joy.

"Dan, think about it." His voice was low, slow and rational. "You're up there all alone. Some of these tree-huggers around the country are talking like they're in some kind of a holy war. Some of them may feel that if people have to die so they can make their point then that's the way it will be. You're a sitting duck."

"I can handle it." My mantra.

He slammed a fist on the bed. "I'm canceling your assignment. I want you out of there!"

"Then I'll resign and investigate on my own."

He slammed the mattress again, then stood and kicked the chair over. "Mule-brained SOB." He stalked to the door, yanked at the handle. "I don't want your damn resignation. But I don't want to bury you, either."

"Thanks for coming," I called after him, wondering how far I'd been manipulated and how far I'd gone on my own.

The door swung shut and opened again, a few inches at a time. Ronny peered around the corner, then strolled in, carrying a steaming cardboard cup. "Looks like you two had a pleasant conversation."

"Yeah. As relaxing as a long hot shower." I tore the tape from my right hand and tugged the needle free, laid it dripping on the pillow.

"Hey, Dan, that's not a good—"

"Where did they put my clothes?" I ripped loose the tape that secured my right arm and flung aside the blanket.

"In that locker." He nodded toward a cabinet beneath the television. "But you're—"

"Going back to Hemlock Lake. Now."

He set the coffee on the nightstand and thrust out a hand, palm up. "Now listen, bud, the doctor said you should—"

"To hell with the doctor!" I had to get back, had to show the snake handler he'd failed. I swung my legs over the side of the bed and reached behind me for the ties on the hospital gown. Cresting a wave of nausea, I wobbled to my feet. "Are you coming or do I have to break out of here alone?"

Ronny hit the horn when we reached the stop sign near the dam. When we pulled up at the post office, at least fifty people crowded the parking lot. So much for the idea of catching a look of surprise on the face of someone who hadn't expected me to return home so quickly—or at all. "Whose idea was this?"

"I only called Lisa," Ronny apologized. "You know how word gets around."

"Yeah." I opened the passenger door to a chorus of concerned voices: "Hey, Dan. How you doing? Are you okay? You look pretty darn good. Yeah. Doctors don't know shit."

Mary Lou bustled out of the building as I eased my feet to the ground, swayed against the door, and willed my knees not to buckle. Maybe the doctor who'd argued with me an hour ago did know shit. "Get back and give him some air!" Seizing my arms, she tilted her head and looked up into my face. Over her shoulder, I spotted Lou Marie peering from a dust-streaked window of the general store. Her face puckered with disdain. I wondered if she'd be fast enough and bold enough to catch a rattler. I decided she would; with so much venom of her own, she wouldn't worry about getting bit.

"Nothing wrong with you a little rest won't cure." Mary Lou's grip tightened. "What a horrible thing. Any idea who would do that?"

"None. But I'm taking applications. Got a pile in the back there. Anybody want to fill one out?" Laughter swelled through the crowd. I scanned their faces. Where was Camille? Perhaps no one had called her. Or perhaps she'd stayed away, not trusting herself to feign concern for my health.

From the corner of my eye, I saw Ronny cut Willie Dean out of the herd and back him around the corner of the building. My left hand clenched in anger. Questioning Willie Dean was my job. *If that's what he's doing,* the insidious voice in my mind countered. He might be telling Willie Dean the snake didn't do the trick, that he'd have to try again.

"Well, whoever it was, he was a yellow-spined coward." Evan Bonesteel spat the words.

"A chicken-livered sneak." Freeman Keefe nodded. "That's not the way we do things up here."

Both of them looked in the direction Ronny and Willie Dean had gone. Did I see relief in their faces? Relief that the inquisition was directed at Willie Dean and they'd skated away? I remembered the map I'd drawn. Freeman's land lay against the parcel Tom Andersen's nephew had sold.

"Is vandalism the way we do things up here?" I asked, lashing out. "Are graffiti and threatening letters the way we do things? Is refusing to help when a deputy asks—" A wave of exhaustion and nausea slammed into me, and I staggered.

Mary Lou rushed to my side. "Dan, you've got to take it easy." She glanced over her shoulder. "Where's Ronny? Dan needs to get to the lodge and get into bed."

"I'll get him." Lisa Miller shouldered through the cluster of onlookers, carrying a large paper sack. She stood on tiptoe and kissed my cheek. "I brought you some muffins and jam. I'll stick them in the back seat." She stowed the sack and hustled off around the side of the building.

"Let's get you buckled in." Mary Lou slung my arm around her shoulders as Willie Dean's wife, Priscilla, marched up with a plastic bowl of gelatin salad the same shade as the hair that had been bleached and teased so often it made her head look like a frost-bitten dandelion. She thrust the bowl toward me and locked her pale gray eyes on mine. "Willie Dean didn't do it, Dan. I swear it." She turned to face the crowd. "I know what you're thinking. You'd all like to blame him, because that's the easy way. I know he's done some stupid things in the past. That's his nature. But he can't stand to be near a snake—even a garter snake. We had one in the spring house last summer, and I was the one who had to carry it out of there." She anchored one hand on a broad hip indignantly. "I'm not going to stand by and watch you railroad my husband."

"Now Pris." Mary Lou paused in her efforts to tug me toward the passenger seat, in order to take the bowl from Priscilla. "Don't get yourself all worked up. Dan wouldn't arrest an innocent man. And as for the rest, it's just idle talk. But we all know how Willie Dean is. Why last fall he put a mouse in my cash drawer and nearly scared me out of my shoes."

"But none of his jokes ever hurt anyone," Evan Bonesteel said. "And whenever Willie Dean plays a joke, he's always right there so he can get a good look at your face. Like the time he nailed those logs in my woodpile together. I practically blew out an artery before I heard him laughing from behind the shed— far enough away to have a head start if I came after him."

"That's Willie Dean, all right." Freeman seconded his friend. "But Pris is right. He wouldn't touch a snake if he stood to make a thousand dollars."

Both men looked at me expectantly, and I nodded, thinking people could do a lot of things they never had before if there's enough at stake. Ronny and Lisa came around the corner of the building, Willie Dean a few steps behind. Lisa looked puzzled; Ronny's lips were tight. Willie Dean's face was the color of an old sweat sock. He hung back on the far side of the parking lot.

"This isn't the time to hash all this out." Mary Lou shoved me into the passenger seat. "Anyone else bring anything to help him recuperate?"

Pattie Bonesteel stepped forward, carrying a round casserole dish covered by a green and white checked towel, and Alda Keefe slid in a container of soup and a box of crackers. Ronny's mother, Rachel, supplied a plate of cookies, and two other women handed over paper sacks. Shirley McDaniel pressed a white envelope into my hand. "IOU for some chicken-fried steak and a couple of beers," she told me. "I didn't hear about what happened until a bit ago."

"Ready to go?" Ronny slid into the driver's seat and fired up the engine.

"You take it easy, Dan," Mary Lou urged as I grappled with my seat belt. The others nodded, and I heard a chorus of "take cares" and "call me if you need anything."

Ronny slapped the shift into reverse and backed out onto the road. "Lisa's gonna follow us and bring me back." He studied me sideways as we eased forward. "Unless you want me to stay for a while."

"No!" The word exploded from my lips. I did a quick verbal backpedal. "There's no need." I glanced at the stack of food in the back. "I have enough provisions for a week. I'll be fine."

Ronny shrugged and we rode in silence for a few minutes. As we passed the spot where I'd first noticed the snake, I felt the hair on the back of my neck prickle. "Did you ask Willie Dean if he did it?"

Ronny grunted. "I sure as hell didn't ask him if he wanted to host a lingerie party."

I let that pass, waited out the answer.

"He says he didn't. Says he'd sooner stick a fork in a socket than handle a rattler." Ronny downshifted on a hill. "I'd like to believe him. But if he didn't do it, who did?"

I thought of Lou Marie watching from behind that dusty window, of Camille who hadn't come to welcome me. "I don't know, but I'll find out."

CHAPTER 14

The knock on the screen door was soft but firm. Definitely not Ronny or any of the others who'd stopped in during the past few days. They'd knocked as if they believed the snakebite had affected my hearing. Or perhaps their intent had been to make enough noise to wake the dead—in case I was. I set the manicure scissors on the kitchen counter beside the bottle of alcohol and crossed the living room. Backlit by the afternoon sun, Camille lounged against the doorjamb, holding a plate swathed in aluminum foil.

She straightened and held out the plate. "You missed the Memorial Day potluck picnic at the cemetery."

"I know." I'd started for the cemetery twice this morning, but both times decided I couldn't face those graves—not with everyone watching to see how "poor Dan" handled it.

"I paddled over with some of the leftovers. Fried chicken, coleslaw, three-bean salad, corn bread, and a big fat brownie."

"You didn't have to do that."

"And you don't have to say thank you, but it would be a nice touch."

We stood there for a few seconds before I opened the door and let her pass. "Thank you. For the record, I've said the same thing to everyone who brought me food."

"You're welcome. For the record, I'm sure you did." She moved past me with a smile. "Beautiful view from that ridge. I'd never been up there before." She ambled to the kitchen, set the plate on the table, and fished in a drawer for a fork. "Just about everyone turned out."

"I expect they did."

I recalled the trips I'd made to the top of the ridge when I was a child. "Decoration Day," my grandmother had called it. Armed with clippers and trowels, scrub brushes and buckets, we'd all drive to the small cemetery above the dam at the south end of the lake. Those were the times I felt the strongest sense of the genealogical sum of who I was, and the strongest sense of wanting to somehow break the chain of DNA. But attendance was mandatory, and my grandmother would allow no slacking. We'd pull weeds, clip back bushes lanky with spring growth, scrape off moss, and scrub the mottled marble and granite monuments to members of the Stone family who'd "gone to a better rest," as she put it. I remembered, at age eight or so, wondering what "a better rest" could be. Better than a nap beside your fishing pole on a mossy bank in the middle of a July afternoon when you knew the big ones would bite any minute if you pretended to play possum? Better than the kind of sleep you fall into once a thunderstorm has passed?

Camille pulled out a chair, sat down across from me. "I thought I'd see you there now that you're back in the bosom of the community. Dig in."

I hesitated, remembering I hadn't seen her since the night I got bit, hadn't found out anything about her except the sketchy details gleaned from copies of police reports I'd requested, black and white pages listing only facts, nothing more. I peeled aside the foil, thinking she'd be too smart to poison me with food everyone knew she'd carried here. Besides, I was hungry. I stabbed up a load of slaw studded with grated carrots, slivered green onions, and poppy seeds. I recognized it from previous picnics—another recipe Lisa Miller had borrowed from Rachel and enhanced.

"All you had to do was get yourself bit by a rattler and women are stewing about the state of your health and eating habits, while the men are determined to get 'the son of a bitch who'd do a thing like that to Dan.' "

Yeah, I thought. Usually when folks consort with a snake they're booted out of the garden, not welcomed back. I chewed the tangy slaw while surveying the stack of bowls, plates, and baskets I'd need to return to their owners' kitchens. "It's been like a week of Thanksgivings." Productive, too. I'd seen most of the residents of Hemlock Lake and assessed their motives for snaking me and their abilities to follow through. I'd even seen Willie Dean, who'd handed over a six-pack and a bag of potato chips and stood in the doorway for twenty minutes, testifying to his fear of rattlers. And when Mary Lou visited, she'd volunteered that she'd been reading downstairs on the night I got bit and Lou Marie hadn't left the house. But I knew the roof of the back porch jutted under Lou Marie's window and it was a short jump to the ground. "The only ones who didn't come by were Lou Marie . . . and you."

I dropped the last two words as if they were heavy. She picked them up with care.

"I guess you have to consider that everyone's a suspect. I don't blame you. I would have been at the post office, but we left early for a round of medical appointments. It was late afternoon before we heard about it and . . . well, after the way we parted at the Shovel It Inn, I wasn't sure I'd be welcome."

I shrugged and crunched through the crisp and peppery skin of a chicken breast. Alda Keefe's recipe, I'd bet. A Memorial Day tradition, like fresh flowers on the graves, recollections of long-dead ancestors, and tracing family trees. "Looks like you're not an outsider if they invited you to the picnic."

"I drove the Brocktons over and did their weeding," she said, bristling. "That's how this hired hand got there."

Chastised, searching for something to say, I kept my gaze on my plate. Three-bean salad. Mary Lou's, I guessed. And the cornbread with chunks of red and green pepper would be Shirley McDaniel's. I turned my attention to a plump brownie, thinking it had originated in Pattie Bonesteel's kitchen. Breaking off a corner, I saw both dark and white chocolate chips and whole cashews. Way too adventurous for Pattie.

"I made that," Camille told me.

"Ah." I popped the broken corner into my mouth, and let the bittersweet chocolate melt on my tongue. "If the way to acceptance at Hemlock Lake is through its collective stomach, I'll bet you made headway today."

She laughed. "It's far less painful than letting a rattlesnake gnaw on my hand."

I took another bite of the brownie. "A lot of things are."

She glanced over at the alcohol, the scissors, a tweezers, and a tube of antiseptic cream I'd laid out beside the sink. "How's it healing?"

"Fine." I held up my hand. "See? No gangrene. No blood poisoning. No need to amputate. I was about to take the stitches out."

"Yourself?"

"Sure. Nothing to it. You just clip and pull."

She winced and turned her head. "If you don't mind, I won't watch."

"It doesn't require an audience." I fitted the foil back over the plate, wondering if she was truly squeamish or pretending. After all, she'd looked homicide in the face. It seemed unlikely that the sight of a small wound would bother her. But maybe that was the very reason it would. Maybe killing her husband hadn't hardened her heart, but softened it instead.

"You didn't eat much." Her voice carried a sharp note of concern.

"Going to report me to the women's committee?" I carried the plate to the refrigerator. "I had a big breakfast—Pattie Bonesteel's tuna noodle casserole and the rest of the cookies Rachel Miller gave me." I raised my right hand. "And that's the truth."

"Okay." She leaned back in her chair and pulled her knees up to her chest. "I won't turn you in."

"Thanks." I uncapped the alcohol, poured some over the wound. "I wouldn't want to be held down and force-fed more of Priscilla Denton's salad." I worked one blade of the scissors through a stitch and clipped.

"Me neither." She paused for a moment while I clipped another stitch. "Um. Some of them out there this morning wanted to clean your family's graves. Ronny suggested it."

My throat tightened and my shoulders drew in. An act of kindness? An act of control? A way to suggest that I was incompetent? I concentrated on the next stitch. "And?"

"And they left it unresolved. Mary Lou said she'd ask you later, and Lisa said if you didn't think you'd be able to get to it, she'd send the kids up after school lets out in a few weeks."

I swallowed, muscles constricting painfully, throat burning, stomach roiling. "If I couldn't get to it." A euphemism for "if I felt too sorry for myself to do what was required." I felt a flash of anger at Lisa, followed by a surge of gratitude for helping to prevent others from taking on the task. "Tell them I'll get to it soon." I'd do my job, just like I had when I'd filled out the reports, picked out the coffins, and dropped the soft earth on top of Susanna and Nat.

Pulling the last stitch, I poured more alcohol over my hand and thought about the graves at the southwest corner of the cemetery—the white marble cross that guarded the great uncle who'd died in the First World War, the carved granite log that sheltered the bones of my grandfather and grandmother, the marble waterfall beneath which my father would soon lie beside my mother, and the two as-yet-unmarked oblongs of earth where Nat and Susanna had been buried last fall. Where their bodies lay, I corrected myself. Not their stalking spirits. "In fact, I'll go do it right now."

Camille's voice seemed as hesitant as the breeze which barely shifted the curtains. "If you want company . . ."

I looked out the kitchen window at a mountain laurel spreading pink-tinged blossoms in a shaft of sunlight. For the Stone family record, I made a mental note that I hadn't asked for help, she'd offered.

"All right. Let's go." I wrapped gauze around my finger and secured it with a strip of tape, capped the alcohol bottle and lobbed a verbal grenade. "I'll get the tools, you check the seats for snakes."

She froze, her eyes wide. "Are you serious?"

When I didn't answer, she shook her head, laughed uncertainly. "Oh, I get it. This is an example of your emerging sense of humor." She laughed again, but her eyes narrowed. "Or is it a test?"

I liked the way she considered all the options, the way her gaze hadn't wavered from mine. "Which would you prefer?"

She studied me for a moment. "I'd prefer honesty. If you're worried that someone will put another snake in your path, I'd say a little paranoia couldn't hurt. If you're going to develop a full-fledged sense of humor, I'd be happy to feed and water it. And if you're testing, I'd say I have a healthy respect for poisonous reptiles and I *did not* touch that snake." She paused for breath, her eyes glinting in the amber light from the west window.

I nodded.

"Okay. Then how about I get the tools and you check for snakes?"

"Fair enough."

I locked up the lodge, opened the doors, and made a show of peering under the seats, knowing I'd find nothing. Whoever had put the snake under my jacket last week—and I was now certain it hadn't been Camille—wouldn't expect me to fall for the same trick twice. The snake handler would have to get to me some other way. Putting that thought aside, I helped Camille load a shovel, rake, hoe, and hedge-clippers.

The rusted gates of the cemetery hung open as they had since my earliest memories, but the hump-backed gravel road that wound among the graves looked as if someone had spread a new layer of crushed rock. Fresh flowers lay in bright bunches against the stones, and small flags fluttered here and there. I drove toward a gray granite obelisk, taller than most of the other monuments, and parked beside it.

"It doesn't look like there's too much weeding," Camille said as she pulled out the hoe. "I'll get the briers and dandelions around those small stones." She pointed to a string of shoebox-sized grave markers to the left of the obelisk.

I pried the rusted hedge-trimmers open and gazed down on the mottled stones with their terse inscriptions. First names and dates spanning pitifully short lives. "Those are my great-great aunts and uncles. Not one of them lived to be more than three."

She brought the hoe down on a clump of briers. "I guess women expected it then. No one knew much about bacteria and sanitation and there were no antibiotics. But it seems like torture. To nurse a child, love it, and be unable to keep it safe." She chopped again and again, uprooting the brier, hacking it into a dozen pieces.

I turned my back, thinking of her baby lying in some distant ground. I wanted to say something to comfort her, but my mind was empty and my throat constricted. Gulping at air, I looked at the lake gleaming like blue glass, the steeple of the tiny Methodist church glowing like polished ivory. The rhythm of the hoe slowed then stopped. She breathed roughly, rapidly, her gasps echoing my own. The hoe clattered to the ground, and I heard her blow her nose, snuffle.

"Who does the big marker belong to?"

"That's my great-grandfather's." I turned and nodded to the obelisk. "He had three wives." I pointed to three thin slabs of marble, the kind you think of when you hear the word "tombstone." They marched toward an enormous lilac bush drooping clumps of deep purple blossoms. I'd often wondered how wife number three had felt, knowing she'd one day take her place two graves away from her husband. I'd wondered if she feared she'd die before he did, that wife number four would be tucked beside her, restricting her eternal elbow room.

"Whose graves are those?" Camille pointed to the granite log, the waterfall, and the cross beyond them.

"That's where my grandmother and grandfather are, and his brother who died in the war, and my mother . . ." I heard my voice clot and coughed. "She's the reason I came back from Arizona, but I guess you've already heard that from six or seven different people."

Camille nodded and dropped to her knees to yank at a clump of crabgrass.

I gazed beyond the headstone, to the two mounded oblongs covered with thin sprigs of new grass. Closing my eyes, I saw myself standing beside Susanna next to the porch swing where my mother, shrouded in that green and blue afghan, watched over the lake through smudged and shadowed eyes. Then I attacked the new sprouts on the lilac bush viciously. From the corner of my eye, I noticed Camille watching me, but soon she returned to chopping weeds. I tossed the broken boughs behind me, working in a circle around the bush. Then I carried the cuttings into the woods and dumped them. When I was through, I cut a mountain of blooms from the top of the bush and laid them around the stones. Their sun-warmed scent reminded me of my grandmother's toilet water, of Walt Whitman's poetry. I spread more blooms on the two unmarked graves.

Camille had finished weeding and leaned against a fender, sweat dappling her forehead. "Have you ordered stones for them?"

"No." I looked down at the red-brown soil riddled with small rocks. "Markers mean they're dead. And they're not. I see them every—" I dropped the last blossoms, jerked myself back to self-awareness. "Come on. Let's go down to the Shovel It Inn. I have an IOU for some chicken-fried steak."

She didn't move. "I want to listen. If you want to talk."

I picked up the trimmer. Talking felt too much like asking for help. "I don't want to."

"Really?" Her eyebrows arched, her eyes flickered, reflecting the orange light of the sunset. "I think it's the thing you want most in the world."

I threw the trimmer at the lilac bush, heard it thud against the trunk. "No, what I want most in the world is to have Susanna back." I slammed my hands against the side of the obelisk. "What I want is to sleep without seeing her die, night after night."

Camille didn't cringe from my rage. "Tell me. Tell me what you see in your dreams. Tell me everything."

I shook my head and set my back against the obelisk, closing my eyes against her steady gaze. Darkness swirled and shifted. Then my knees sagged and I dropped to the ground, retching out words, puking up pain. I didn't try to stop myself. Perhaps I knew I couldn't. "I see them get into the boat. They look right at me, but they don't see me. I call to them but they can't hear me. I can't hear myself. And Nat starts the motor, and then I see her up on that wakeboard and the moon is so bright and she's dancing on the water. And every time I think that this time she won't make a mistake. But she goes down and I'm not fast enough and I can't get to her. I can't save her."

I pounded the sod beside the obelisk. At the edge of my awareness, Camille stepped closer, but made no move to touch me.

"And she dies," I howled. "She drowns. Over and over. And lately I don't even try to reach her. I just stand and watch."

My tears made Camille's image waver as she dropped to her knees before me. She nodded but said nothing and I went on, tearing the scabs from my soul. "And Nat brings her up. He was always a better swimmer. Always. And I'm right there, on the porch, but he doesn't let me carry her. My wife. I should carry her."

Camille nodded again. My face was wet with tears but my throat felt as dry as old newspaper. I wanted to stop but I couldn't. "And then Nat gets the rifle. He loads it with a hollow point. And he doesn't even think about my father or me, he just blows himself away." I pounded the sod again.

"Why?" Camille breathed the word.

"I don't know!" I screamed into the sky. "Because he thought he could make it even. Because he wanted to make some grand gesture. Because he couldn't face me. I don't know. But he killed my father with that bullet, too. And he cheated me. He cheated me."

Camille leaned toward me. "How did he cheat you?"

Behind my eyes I saw Nat load the gun and walk down the hallway. "Because he knew I never would have forgiven him for taking her out there. I would have hated him every moment of his life, of my life. That would have given me a reason to live. And he took that. He left me no one to hate. And no one to love."

Exhausted, I felt myself trembling in the cooling evening breeze, as empty as a man who'd walked the desert without water. Camille stretched out her hand and touched my knee.

"I think about that hollow point every day," I told her. "There are more of them in the drawer. Dozens."

"No." She grasped my hands, her warm fingers searing my skin. "Don't think that way."

I pulled my hands free and turned my head toward the unmarked graves. "I'm going to end up here anyway. What does it matter when?"

She cupped my chin in her hands, forcing me to look at her. "Forgive yourself, Dan. Please forgive yourself."

"I'll never forgive—"

Nat? She hadn't asked me to forgive Nat. She'd asked me to forgive myself. In that moment, I realized I hated all of us— Susanna who'd been so reckless with her life, Nat who'd been so thoughtless with his, and myself for being too slow, for being left behind. Wrapping my hands around her wrists, I lowered them to her sides and said, "I can't. I don't deserve it."

Tears flowed from her eyes. She blinked but didn't brush them away. "You do."

I shook my head and let my gaze drift to the sunset-stained lake beyond her shoulder. The ridge tops were bruised with purple light; the rising tide of night pooled in the hollows and lapped at higher ground. A ghostly ribbon of smoke meandered up from one of the rocky spines that hemmed in Dark Moon Hollow, rising from a spot where there was no house, where there'd been no rain for three weeks.

"Fire! On the mountain!"

CHAPTER 15

I released her wrists. "Let's go."

"What about the tools?"

"Leave them. Just get in!"

She obeyed, scanning the hills for the gossamer thread of smoke, nearly invisible against the sooty sky. I cranked the key, flipped open the glove compartment, and pointed to the cell phone. "Dial nine-one-one. Tell the dispatcher to alert the Hemlock Lake Fire Department. Fire in Dark Moon Hollow."

Her fingers punched the keys as I rammed the shift into first and popped the clutch. The wheels tore into the gravel. I heard it spatter among the gravestones. Camille relayed my words to the dispatcher as we swerved down the twisting track from the cemetery to the main road. "Where's Dark Moon Hollow? The dispatcher wants to know."

"North end of the lake. The firefighters know. The fire appears to be near the old quarries."

I skidded to a stop at the sign in front of the Shovel It Inn. Which way was fastest? Left or right? Right, I decided. There was a spur off the old logging road on the east side of the stream that led to the abandoned stone pits. I spun the wheel, laying rubber on the pavement. As we sped by Stub's garage, the fire siren sounded, a deep-throated wail. "I can't take you down to the lodge," I told Camille. "There isn't time."

"Don't worry. Just drop me at the driveway." She replaced the cell phone and shot me a grim smile. "And spare me the lecture about being out on the lake after dark. It's a waste of breath."

"So I've learned." I concentrated on taking a series of sharp turns without spinning out. We passed the turnoff to Bobcat Hollow, and I saw headlights coming down the road. Ronny. I gunned the engine, wanting to stay ahead of him, to get there first. The siren wailed again, fading behind us.

Camille braced her hands on the dashboard as I took the bend at Silver Leaf Hollow on two wheels. "How do you fight a fire in the mountains? Where will you get water?"

"We'll carry it in if we have to. If it gets to where we need a lot, they'll send a chopper with a bucket and dip it from the lake." The tires squealed out of the turn. "Or call in a slurry bomber. The trick is to stop the fire before it gets that big." I glanced at the shovel and rake in the back and wished I had time to stop for the chainsaw. "We may be able to smother it with dirt, or halt it with fire breaks." Tromping on the brake, I skidded to a stop by the driveway to the lodge. "If we're fast enough."

Camille unsnapped her seat belt. "Good luck." She leaned toward me. Reflexively, I pulled away from her lips. In another second she was out, slamming the door, waving me on.

Aware of Ronny's truck looming in the rearview mirror, I roared down the final stretch of pavement to the logging road. My headlights glinted off the chain that blocked the track and common sense overcame competitive spirit. I slewed my rig onto the shoulder, waving Ronny alongside. "How far up can we drive?"

"Half a mile, maybe more. But we don't want too many vehicles clogging the road."

I nodded, focused on what had to be done. "Got room for me?"

"Yeah. Grab your gear."

Carolyn J. Rose

Tossing the rake and shovel and the cardboard box that contained the gear I'd been issued into the bed of his pickup, I levered myself into the cab as he let out the clutch and surged forward. "No time to wait for Stub to bring the key." He angled left, bumping around the metal post that supported the chain and plowing down a small spruce that raked the undercarriage, thwanging off the oil pan.

I thought about that state land manager who had strung the chains on either side of the lake and clamped on heavy padlocks to shut off the logging roads. In the interest of firefighting, Stub held keys to those padlocks. In the interest of being a good neighbor, he often loaned those keys out to anyone who wanted to bring back the spoils of a hunting trip, stone from the quarries, or a supply of firewood. Stub would say he didn't have contempt for the law, just the idiots who made it.

Ronny muscled the truck around a stump and into ruts filled with slabs of stone that grated against each other and slid under the wheels as we climbed. "Did you see any flames?"

"No. Just smoke."

"Maybe we can knock it down quick. Before it gets into the trees."

Before it gets dangerous, I thought. Fire on the ground could be nasty, but a blaze that went into the canopy could be much worse. Burning branches could fall like fiery rain; toppling deadfalls might crush any one of us in an instant. And if the wind picked up—

"It's early in the year. We haven't had rain for three weeks, but the woods aren't that dry." I tried to reassure myself as the wheels shuddered and spun on a slick bed of pine needles.

"Lots of snags up there." Ronny reminded me of the standing deadwood that surrounded the quarry. "Lots of young hemlock. And pine."

Running with pitch, I thought. The kind of wood that made

for a vicious, spitting fire and heavy smoke. I glanced back and saw two sets of lights behind us. The truck slithered across a clearing littered with broken shale and rocked toward another set of ruts aiming straight up the side of the ridge parallel to a crumbling stone wall.

"Better leave it here," Ronny muttered, "where there's room to turn around." He trod the brake, slapped the truck into reverse, crimped the wheel, and backed up, transmission whining.

We dragged our fire gear from the back and suited up as Willie Dean roared to a stop beside us. Evan Bonesteel and Freeman Keefe were crammed next to him in the cab of Nat's truck. "The others are coming. And Stub's on the way," Willie Dean called. "He said he'll drive up as far as he can, fill the water bags, and wait to hear from us."

"He won't get far with all that water in the truck." Ronny flipped suspenders across his shoulders, shrugged into his jacket, and grabbed a helmet. "That tanker ain't an off-road vehicle." He snatched a chainsaw and long flashlight from the bed of the truck. "Let's go take a look at it. Where exactly did it appear to be, bud?" He called the question over his shoulder as he started up the ridge.

"Around the quarries." I yanked on my jacket, seized a shovel and flashlight, and stumbled after him in boots that seemed cast from cement.

"Above or below?"

"Below, I think. Hard to tell. It was nearly dark when I spotted it." I hustled to keep up, mentally adding up the extra weight I now carried. Twenty pounds? Thirty? And that was without an air tank or a bag filled with water on my back. I tried to remember how much a gallon of water weighed and how many gallons a bag held, but couldn't. The heavy pants didn't want to bend with my knees, and the jacket flapped and crackled as I moved. In a few moments, we'd left the clearing behind and those small sounds were lost in the scuffling of our feet, the crack and scrape of rocks slipping under our boots, and a whistling wheezing gasp for breath I was certain came from Willie Dean. In a few more moments I heard myself making the same sound.

Cresting the ridge, Ronny turned left and bushwhacked across a long heap of blasted and broken rock discarded by the quarrymen who'd worked beside my great-grandfather when he'd cut smooth slabs of stone for sidewalks and patios. Frost had splintered the stones, and wind and water had filled in the crevices until eventually oak and white pine set roots in moss and rotted leaves. Tumbled rocks shifted under our feet, and I heard Freeman curse and Willie Dean complain that he'd twisted an ankle. Something rustled away through the undergrowth downslope, and I thought instantly of snakes, imagined the dark mountainside crawling with them. I halted, senses heightened by fear, and felt the acrid smell of smoke sting my nose and throat.

"We're close." Ronny paused, then plunged through a thicket of scrawny oaks.

I hesitated, assuring myself that even a snake as large as the one I'd fought would have trouble striking through my boots and pants. Behind me, Evan unleashed a string of profanity at a tree branch that whipped back in his face, and at Willie Dean who'd released it. Distracted from my fear, I moved on, following the erratic bobbing of Ronny's flashlight through the leafy darkness. The pile of slag sloped downward, and I crab-walked on a diagonal trail, planting each foot with care. I didn't want to try to outrun an avalanche of stone, especially in the dark.

"It's over here!" Ronny's voice came from below and to my left.

Willie Dean yelped in surprise, and a cascade of pebbles clattered against my boots. I moved faster, running the last few yards. From behind me, I heard a heavy thud and another yelp. Evan bellowed at Willie Dean to shut up and watch where he put his feet. Freeman yelled for me to go on ahead, they'd get Willie Dean out of the hole and catch up. I forced my leaden legs into a slow trot along a narrow path between rising ledges and a sharp drop-off.

"Over here!" Ronny's voice echoed off the rock. It seemed to come from all sides.

I turned off the flashlight. Blinking, I searched for Ronny's beam or a burst of flame. Smoke clogged my nostrils, and I swallowed the raw taste of it. "Where are you?"

"A little farther along the way you're headed. You'll see a couple of big boulders. Come down between them."

Flicking the light back on, I jogged forward, swung the beam to my left, and spotted two huge weathered boulders. Their moss-covered sides looked familiar, and I had a vague memory of climbing them, of spending hours on a sultry summer morning trying to scrape my initials into the top of one, marking it for eternity. Thrusting my way through the nest of saplings that surrounded the rocks, I squeezed between the boulders and saw Ronny, hands on his hips, surveying the fire.

It smoldered in a foot-deep pit contained by a ring of stones surrounded by tamped-down earth. A pile of logs and branches had been shaped into a reclining seat padded with moss.

"We come all this way for a damn campfire," Ronny snorted.

I defended myself quickly. "I couldn't tell that from the cemetery."

Ronny gripped my shoulder. "Don't sweat it, bud. Willie Dean needed the exercise. And the rest of us can always use a little drill." He poked his light at a pile of dirt and a broken-handled shovel leaning against a young maple tree. "Looks like this scout was prepared. Want to put it out?"

"Yeah. In a minute." I surveyed a low lean-to covered with interlaced hemlock boughs, a plaid flannel shirt hanging from a branch, and a dozen empty cans and jars stacked near the fire. "I want to look around first." I moved toward the lean-to and dropped to my knees.

Freeman popped through the crevice between the rocks, spraying his light around. "Why, that's just a damn camp—Hey, that's my shirt." He strode to the tree, breath coming in ragged puffs, pulled the shirt free, and checked it for damage. "Disappeared from the clothesline a few weeks ago. How the hell did it get up here?"

Willie Dean, leaning on Evan's shoulder, limped around the side of the second boulder and let himself down on a rock, thrusting his left leg out before him. "Whooee. I'm bushed. My ankle is killing me. Anybody bring any water?"

Another childhood memory flashed through my brain. "There's a spring about twenty feet that way." I pointed up the slope past the second boulder. "If it hasn't dried up."

"I'll get it." Evan scooped up two of the empty jars, then paused. "Pattie's labels are on these." He held them up for us to see. "Look. Elderberry jelly and peach jam, both from last summer. See the dates on the labels? Now how did they get here?"

"Same way Freeman's shirt got here," Ronny said. "Same way that shovel over there with Denny Balmer's initials got here. Somebody stole them. Doesn't take much talent in a town where nobody locks their doors. I'll bet those jars came out of a pantry when nobody was home."

"Just like the cans in here." I pointed to the interior of the lean-to and a stash of provisions. Slipping on one of my heavy leather gloves, I tipped a rectangular can into my helmet. It wouldn't hurt to send it to the lab, have it printed, and see if a match turned up anywhere. Maybe whoever had camped here was responsible for the threatening letters, the fires, and the cairns. Maybe he'd been arrested elsewhere and had prints on file.

I set the helmet on the ground and surveyed the campsite. The word "primitive" leapt into my mind. That didn't mesh with the last article I'd read on eco-terrorists; it claimed they communicated with their spokesperson by e-mail. Had the guy who made this camp set up a laptop and a cell phone by the fire? It seemed pretty farfetched, but not impossible. I slid another can into the helmet and looked back at Ronny. "Who do you know around here who's got a major corned beef hash habit?"

"Willie Dean." Freeman and Evan spoke at the same time, then laughed and gave each other a high five.

"The son of a bitch stole my hash?" Willie Dean howled. "Priscilla drove all the way to that big warehouse store to get it. Three cases. On special. It was disappearing so fast she accused me of using it for bait."

I surveyed the provisions stacked along one wall of the lean-to. "You got eight cans of it in here. And a whole lot of preserves, a bag of rice, a package of spaghetti, and something that looks like venison jerky."

"That's mine, too," Willie Dean said. "The bastard's been treating my house like his own private grocery store."

"He's on a cash-and-carry basis," Ronny joked. "You pay the cash and he carries it off."

"It ain't funny." Willie Dean sulked.

"It is to us," Freeman said with a chuckle.

"I wonder if he's the guy Priscilla saw," Freeman said. "The one she thought was a carjacker. The one Stub heard rooting through his garbage."

"The one who tried to break into my cooler." Willie Dean pulled off his boot and rubbed his ankle. "And put up all those rock piles. And set my damn boat on fire."

Evan returned with two jars filled with water. "He's got a regular little boudoir set up by the spring. Soap. A piece of a mirror. An old washtub that looks like something I've seen in your garage, Ronny." He handed Willie Dean one jar and poured the other on the fire. Smoke and steam rose with a sharp hiss. "And he's got a monogrammed towel with Mary Lou's initials. He's been up here for a while."

Weeks, I thought as I examined two neatly folded blankets on a thick bed of dry pine needles. At the rear of the lean-to, wrapped in plastic bags that had once held bread, I spotted a dozen books. Crawling deeper into the shelter, I pulled a few toward me and peeled off the plastic. The first two were romances, the kind that Priscilla Denton read by the carload. Staring at the couple locked in a steamy embrace on the cover, I thought of Camille leaning toward me. Had I recoiled from the kiss because it represented intimacy and a crossing of the boundaries I'd set after Susanna's death? Or had I recoiled from the lips of that particular woman, not what she offered?

I shook off the questions and reached for another book. The title sent a cold spasm through my heart. It was a paperback anthology of Robert Frost's poems. Susanna had given it to me for my birthday three years ago. I'd spent an hour searching for it earlier this week, and now, as I stroked the slick covers, I remembered where I'd seen it last. On the passenger seat of my SUV. The morning before my run-in with the snake. I shuddered and felt my heart throb in my wounded finger. Had I found the person who'd planted the rattler?

"Who the hell is this guy?" Willie Dean put my thoughts into words. "And why is he hanging around Hemlock Lake?"

"That's what we're going to find out. We'll organize a search party. First thing in the morning." Ronny took charge. "Tell everybody to bring canteens, lunches, binoculars, and rifles."

I slid the book into my pocket and duck-walked out of the

lean-to, my mind racing. Would a massive search drive him off? Or would it force him to retreat and bide his time? Or take action quicker than he'd planned?

"We'll comb the whole area," Ronny continued. "We'll meet at the lodge at seven." He turned to me, an admission that I wore the badge. "Right, Dan?"

I hesitated, weighed my options. These men felt violated. They wanted to take action. On the positive side, they'd hunted these ridges for years and knew the terrain well. They'd spot anything out of the ordinary—another campsite, a cache of food, trails, or traces. And they'd feel like they were doing something. Besides, there wasn't much I could do to stop them. "Yeah. Seven's good. I'll dig out the topographical maps and lay down a grid."

"All right!" Willie Dean crowed. "We'll get the bastard. I can feel it."

I doubt you'll find a thing, I thought as they packed up their recovered possessions and talked excitedly about the morning's hunt. Whoever he was, he was patient, stealthy, and careful. Only the fact that he'd happened to put a damp log on his fire before darkness fell, and that he did it at the same time I'd happened to look toward Dark Moon Hollow, had led us here tonight.

I lagged behind the others as we started down the mountain. I hoped I would learn something from the fingerprints. I hoped I wasn't chasing a ghost.

CHAPTER 16

At seven the next morning, fifteen men dressed in an assortment of camouflage gear stood in the living room of the lodge, drinking coffee, checking their knapsacks, comparing theories about types of guns and brands of ammunition, and studying a topographical map and a ten-year-old aerial photograph I'd hauled from my father's room. Using an old red crayon, I'd marked off the perimeters of each search area and indicated spots of special interest—natural springs and caves, an old shelter built by quarrymen, and clearings where berries might provide food.

Now, lounging in the kitchen doorway, I sipped coffee and listened as Ronny divided the men into teams. Then he stared at my bare feet. "You want to lead a search team, right, bud?"

"No." I set my coffee cup on the bookshelf and flexed my shoulders. "I think I can be more effective if I stay down here, keep an eye on the roads, and coordinate things."

Ronny narrowed his eyes, but I continued. "I've been away a long time. All of you know the area better than I do." I pointed to a stack of plastic bags and a pile of marking pens. "Take some of those along. If you find anything our man might have left behind, get it into a bag without touching it and write down approximately where you found it."

Freeman and Evan nodded at each other, and after a moment Ronny followed suit. I moved on to the second part of what I had to say to them. "Be advised that you're out there in

an unofficial capacity—concerned citizens checking your territory. If you spot him, get word back to me immediately. Then
watch him, follow him. Don't try to take him into custody."

"Bullshit!" Willie Dean glared at me. "If we see him, we'll
take him down."

"Yeah," Evan agreed. "We know he's guilty."

"No," I said, "we don't."

"We know he stole our stuff. I bet he's the one making trouble
at the construction site." Stub pointed across the lake. "And he
probably burned Willie Dean's boat."

"Yeah. And what about the snake?" Willie Dean squeezed the
words out through a mouthful of prune Danish. "That guy tried
to kill you."

"Yeah, what about that?" Evan Bonesteel asked. "That's at-
tempted murder, isn't it?"

"I doubt it." I struggled to keep my voice patient. "But there's
no proof of anything except theft."

"We don't need proof," Willie Dean argued. "We know the
son of a bitch did it."

An affirmative rumble followed his words. The mix of
testosterone and vigilante mentality was so thick I could almost
taste it. Freeman Keefe hefted his rifle and stroked the blued
steel of the barrel. "Maybe you're overthinking this, Dan. Letting your job get in the way of justice."

Even as I searched for a reply, I realized they wouldn't listen.
In the tradition of Hemlock Lake, they intended to resolve this
themselves.

"Dan's right." Ronny's voice was quiet, but the cold edge
brought them to ragged attention. I felt relief mixed with annoyance and jealousy at his easy ability to command. "Whoever
it is up there, he's presumed innocent until we prove him guilty.
Our job is to locate him and call Dan." He tapped four areas
outlined on the map. "Stub, Evan, Freeman, and I will lead

teams through these sections of Dark Moon Hollow. Don't shoot at anything unless it draws a bead on you first. Everyone got that?"

Another affirmative rumble rippled slowly through the group. Willie Dean shook his head in disgust but said nothing.

"All right then. We'll meet at the east end of the logging road at noon and compare notes, then move further south and search some more. Grab your gear and let's get going."

I watched them go, wondering if they'd find anyone, and if they'd heed Ronny's words if they did. Would I have a suspect to take into custody or a shooting to investigate?

For the next three days, Ronny, Stub, Evan, and Freeman led squads of volunteers up and down the ridges.

They found nothing.

Pattie Bonesteel, Alda Keefe, and a few other women stationed themselves at the cemetery with long-range binoculars. Taking turns, they watched for signs of the interloper on the roads or in the open fields.

They saw nothing.

Relentlessly, I patrolled the perimeters of the lake, the side roads, and driveways. My hope was that they would flush the intruder from the woods and I would spot him and make the capture.

I found nothing except three fresh cairns—one on each day of the search.

Lee Fosmark spotted the first one near the construction site. Skeletal walls had gone up on most of the homes, roofers were at work on one, and masons laid red brick for another. Two more trailers, old models with badly rusted skins, had been set up near the center of the site. Workers had filled them with folding metal cots and rigged an outdoor kitchen under a tarp. They'd hauled in a propane stove and run an extension cord to the nearest homesite to power an aging refrigerator. They'd even rigged an outdoor shower, trucking water in fifty-five gallon drums to the top of the hill and letting gravity feed it through a hose into a can drilled full of holes atop a plywood cubicle.

"Just like a small city," Fosmark told me as we walked to the cairn.

I'd winced at the word "city," thinking about Tom Andersen's apples. The saliva that memory evoked pooled under my tongue, hot and bitter. I'd examined the rocks and noted the structure was different from what I'd come to think of as the original cairns—rounded stones carefully balanced. This one was built of flat slabs, carelessly stacked. I took several pictures. "Have you had any problems in the past day or so?"

"No, everything's been very quiet. Why?"

"We found a campsite on the mountain. Someone's been hanging around for quite a while. I don't know if he's the one building these things." I gestured toward the cairn. "Or what they mean. But it wouldn't hurt for you to take some extra precautions for the next few days. And I'll come around more often."

"That's not necessary," he said. "I don't think there's going to be any more trouble. People up here are getting used to the idea they're going to have new neighbors. In fact, you coming around keeps hard feelings alive."

I shook my head. "I have my orders."

He tried to stare me down and failed after ten seconds. "When I get a chance, I'll call the sheriff and see about changing those orders."

"Fine with me." I'd driven away, noting that Fosmark's fingernails were still bitten to the quick. It appeared he didn't believe his own words.

The next day, thinking about the new cairn and what it

meant, I turned down the driveway to the lodge and spotted nine rounded balanced stones in a shaft of sunlight. As I photographed them, I had a chill, prickling sense of being watched. I controlled the impulse to spin around, demonstrating my fear. Instead I'd turned casually, slapping my neck as if fighting off a mosquito. Except for flitting birds and a chipmunk scurrying along a fallen tree, the woods around me were still. Yet that stillness held a sense of edgy anticipation, as if at any second something would bolt from hiding and dash toward me.

I'd felt exposed without the gun I'd left in the glove box. I felt violated by the eyes I imagined studied my every movement. To control my trembling hands, I'd shoved them into my pockets and forced myself to stroll to my rig, counting a beat before I placed each foot. My nerve endings had felt like stripped wires, my mouth so dry I couldn't force a whistle through my lips. I'd driven on to the lodge, where I'd cleaned my father's rifles until the crimp in my lungs loosened.

Later that afternoon, gun in hand, I had walked back to the cairn and broken it apart, tossing the rocks as far as I could. That night I made my bed inside the lodge, in my old room in the loft. I kept the gun on the nightstand beside me and left the outside lights on. All of that was no anodyne for nameless, faceless fear.

On the third day I discovered a cairn of rounded stones beside the church. Taller than the others, it seemed to mimic the white steeple. Afterward, I'd gone by the construction site and talked with Fosmark again. He assured me that everything was fine and I wasn't needed, then hastened away to check on a delivery. I'd swung back by twice during the afternoon, unable to shake my sense of foreboding.

That night, footsore and frustrated, the searchers voted to abandon their quest after a day spent at the more populated south end of the lake, in the folded hills above Bluestone and

Bobcat Hollows. Ronny came to the lodge to inform me of their decision. "If I was some kind of a scientist," he said, "I'd probably call it a pretty good field trip." Uncapping a beer, he'd kicked back on the sofa and described three days of trekking. They'd come across a fox's den, a black bear with two cubs, and the remains of an old hunting dog of Freeman's that they guessed had gone off to die. They'd found a honey tree, a rusted axe embedded high in an ancient oak, and two sets of antlers.

"Maybe we'll go out again in a few days—unless my feet tell me no. I've got blisters on top of blisters." He drained his beer, set the bottle on the kitchen table, and got another. "If nothing else, we stirred him up, made him skittish. He won't be able to settle into any one spot. Maybe he'll just move on. Hell, maybe he's over in the next county by now."

"Could be." I didn't say anything about the fresh cairns and the feeling that I'd been watched. In my sleepless hours I'd thought steadily about the intruder, about who he was and what he wanted. He'd had his chance to harm me when he watched me at the cairn. And he'd had another chance when, sick and afraid, I'd struggled to treat my wound after killing the snake.

Perhaps he was what my grandmother would have called a hobo—someone displaced by fortune, or someone who preferred life on the road. Perhaps he was one of the mentally ill for whom the safety net had unraveled. In either case, I imagined the upheaval of the search should drive him off.

And yet, I had a crawling feeling that he had something to accomplish here, and that he would be among us until he did.

"Well, time to get on home. Nearly midnight." Ronny stretched and flexed his shoulders. "See you later, bud."

"Yeah." I turned on the outside lights for him and stood at the door, hand raised, as he limped toward his truck.

The explosion across the lake startled me. I looked around wildly, saw Ronny's feet skid in the gravel, his shadow jerking in

159

the harsh yellow light from the lamppost.

"What the hell was that?" He regained his balance and ran for the dock. Leaping from the porch, I followed. I saw it as soon as I reached the shore—a faint orange glow in the sky above Lee Fosmark's "city."

"Holy shit!" Ronny's feet thudded to a stop on the dock. "We didn't drive the son of a bitch out. We pissed him off."

CHAPTER 17

"Let's roll." I darted past Ronny, digging for my keys.

He hurtled toward his truck and, in tight formation, we roared up the driveway and thundered toward town. As we passed Bobcat Hollow, I heard the fire siren wail and saw lights pop on. A little farther along, Stub wheeled the fire engine onto the road ahead of us, lights flashing, siren throbbing. Evan pulled in line as we crossed the dam; by the time we reached the site there were three trucks crowding his rear bumper. We passed Willie Dean's dock and squealed through the turns.

"Holy Jesus!"

The air above the trailer Lee Fosmark had used as an office shimmered with heat and smoke. I stood on the brakes, slewing to a stop. As I ran toward the trailer, a window shattered and bright fingers of flame shot into the night. Then another pane of glass blasted from its frame and a smoldering figure squirmed through, fell to the ground and rolled down the slope, screaming for help. Ronny and I sprinted after him, peeling off our shirts.

"Take his legs," Ronny yelled as he dove for man's head.

The smell of singed hair and clothing clogged my nostrils as I dropped to my knees and used my bunched shirt to smother a patch of flame at his ankles. The man's piercing screams drowned out the rumble of the fire truck's engine, the thud of hose hitting the ground, the grating of metal on metal as the valve opened. The air around us shimmered with heat, glittered with sparks, twisted with the rotating lights on the fire truck.

"He's in bad shape," Ronny said.

"Is it Fosmark?" I pulled out my pocket knife and sliced the laces on a pair of smoldering canvas shoes. The acrid smell of burned rubber jabbed my sinuses. My head pounded.

"Don't know. Can't tell."

I yanked off the shoes and sliced away the socks as Willie Dean stumbled down the slope.

"Priscilla called the ambulance," he said.

"This guy can't wait that long." Ronny lifted his shirt from the victim's head, revealing tufts of scorched hair, then took a knife from the leather case on his belt and slashed the smoking shirt. I saw his jaw tighten and his chest heave. "Somebody will have to drive out to meet them. Meantime, get the burn kit from the fire truck. And some blankets. Before he goes into shock."

The man shrieked and bucked as Willie Dean scrambled off. He clawed at his face, and Ronny made a protective dome with his hands.

"What about a pain-killer? Is there any morphine in the truck?"

"I wish. We got nothing that strong."

I put my face close to the victim, willing the wild and shifting eyes to focus on me. "We're going to get you to the hospital as fast as we can. I know it hurts like hell, but you've got to stay still. Can you hear? Do you understand?"

The man nodded, took a shuddering breath, and let his hands fall to his sides, fingers scratching at the earth. Up the slope, flames spurted into the air with a sizzling hiss as the fire defied the stream of water. Shifting light played across the victim's hands and I looked hard at the torn and bleeding fingertips with their nearly invisible shards of nail. Lee Fosmark.

I leaned in close again. "We'll take care of you, Lee. You're safe now."

Willie Dean, canted to one side, staggered toward us, gripping the handle on a large case that thudded against his legs. Mary Lou, wearing a raincoat and holding a towel over her head, hustled up the slope, shading her eyes against the light from another explosion of sparks. "What can I do?"

"Talk to him. Try to keep him calm." Ronny stood quickly and handed her a set of keys. "Then get him on a backboard. Willie Dean knows how. Don't touch him where you don't have to. Get him into my truck and drive like hell until you meet the ambulance."

"Got it." Mary Lou fell to her knees.

"It's Lee Fosmark," I told her.

She nodded. "Lee, it's Mary Lou Van Valkenberg. From the post office. I'm going to take good care of you."

"Let's go, bud." Ronny spun and raced up the slope, his hair a corona of ocher light against the fire. An image of William Blake's tiger burning bright flashed into my mind and I followed, my feet digging at water-slick ground that reflected the fire and shone the color of arterial blood.

We reached the top, raced by the burning trailer and past the knot of firefighters anchoring the hose. I seized my jacket and thrust my arms into the sleeves. Jamming the helmet on my head, I turned toward the blaze, then halted, my brain registering the message my eyes had delivered five minutes earlier—not one construction worker had come to fight the fire. Wheeling up the slope, I ran toward their trailers. The fire drove my shadow ahead of me, but no flames leaped before me. Their trailers weren't burning. Yet.

Twenty yards from the trailers I heard the shouts. Ten yards more and I saw why the men hadn't come to help Fosmark. Planks braced the doors closed. One man, who'd tried to wiggle

163

through a window, hung across the ledge, legs scissoring, chest caught in the vise of the frame.

"Hang on!" I hit the first plank with my shoulder, felt pain shoot up my neck as the wood gave only an inch. I angled in under it, bent my knees and heaved. Someone had planted it firmly in the ground. As they'd pushed against the door, the workers had made their situation worse. I heaved again, blasts of dark magenta and orange lighting the back of my eyeballs. Wood ground against metal and tore free with a splintering rip. The plank fell with a hollow clatter as the door swung open, slamming into my back. I dropped to my knees as six men tumbled down the concrete block steps, their words lost in a jumble of commands as they freed their friends and raced toward the fire.

My heart hammering, I lurched to my feet, leaned against the side of the trailer, and watched them circle the blaze as an explosion rocked Fosmark's former office, tearing a hole in the side. Propane tank? Renewed, the flames leaped at the sky as the jet of water from the hose sputtered and dribbled to a stop. I saw Stub point toward the lake, and Ronny point to the vehicles behind the fire truck.

I knew what they were saying because I'd thought about it a hundred times. Only Tom's old well fed the construction camp. And Tom's pond had been graded out of existence. Until tankers from other communities arrived to back up Hemlock Lake volunteers, the only water available was in the lake. And getting it would take time.

In that time flames gutted the trailer.

"You know how I hate to use the word arson." Rich Ramseyer, the county fire investigator, squinted at the trailer through a set of round wire-rimmed glasses as he wiped his hands on a white handkerchief crackling with starch. The handkerchief reminded me that I needed a shower, needed out of the T-shirt Freeman had dug from behind the seat of his truck and handed me last night—a T-shirt that looked and smelled as if he'd used it to wipe a dipstick.

"Arson rules out too many other possibilities. Tampers with my margin of error. And you know how nervous I get without my margin of error. But when one of the first things we find looks like a homemade bomb with a timing device, well . . ." Ramseyer nodded toward the hulk of the trailer, blackened and crumpled like a tin can dug from an old campfire pit. Then he refolded the handkerchief and tucked it into the pocket of an equally starched shirt. Despite the sharp creases on the sleeves and on his pant legs, his body had all the shape and muscular definition of a sack of flour. "I think it's safe to say you've got work to do. How's the victim?"

"Better than I would have guessed. Lots of burns, but they're not too severe." I repeated the information I'd pried out of a doctor before I left the hospital an hour ago. "He'll be in intensive care for a while, though."

Ramseyer's round head bobbed, and he waved a pink and pudgy hand dismissively. "Yeah. With burns it's the pain that's the problem. And infection. He probably won't be able to tell you much, anyway. Stands to reason that if he saw or heard anything suspicious, he would have gotten out sooner."

Ramseyer glanced toward the trailers farther up the slope, then toward the knot of workers gathered in the makeshift kitchen area. "Bastard's lucky he got out at all with the door barricaded shut." He pointed toward the remains of the construction office, where wisps of smoke still uncoiled lazily into the breeze. "Lucky the window openings were large enough. Lucky he didn't die from smoke inhalation. Lucky the propane tank didn't blow sooner."

Yeah, I thought, lucky he fell asleep on the sofa instead of in the bedroom. But unlucky because someone had wanted him dead and hadn't cared that his death wouldn't be merciful or quick, hadn't cared that he'd die with full knowledge of pain, fear, and helplessness.

I thought about the bomb placed in what Ramseyer speculated was a heap of scrap lumber tossed beneath the trailer. Bombs weren't hard to make, considering that all the information you'd need was in a book or on the Internet, and you could pick up the materials without breaking a sweat. Half the men in Hemlock Lake probably had what you'd need. And most of them would have no trouble with the words "some assembly required." Given their feelings about the development site, I couldn't rule any of them out, couldn't rule out the teens, either. I sighed with frustration. The list of suspects I'd laboriously pared down had expanded again.

I thought about the primitive camp we'd found near the quarry. Could whoever had been living up there have scavenged enough tools and supplies to put an incendiary device together? I made a quick mental inventory of what we'd found and decided that if he'd constructed the device, he'd done it elsewhere or cleaned up all the evidence. But I couldn't rule him out.

"The thing about a bomb is that it usually destroys itself and most of the evidence." Ramseyer seemed to read my mind. "The lab will do what they can with the pieces, but unless we can match them to something . . ."

And how would I find that something? I couldn't get a warrant to search every home, garage, and outbuilding in Hemlock Lake. I could try asking for permission—some might give it— but odds were that while I searched elsewhere, the bomb-builder would hide the evidence. If he hadn't already.

Despite searing sun on the back of my neck, I felt a chill that made me shudder. I didn't want to think that any of the men I knew were so cold-blooded they'd wedge the trailer doors shut with subhuman murderous intent.

"Well, I'll leave you to it." Ramseyer's words brought me back to the bright sunlight. "I'll send you a copy of my preliminary report, but the lab is short-handed and six weeks behind. Or more." He retrieved the handkerchief again and blotted the row of sweat beads glistening at his thinning hairline as he ambled toward his county car. "Ten o'clock and it's already steaming out here. Time to crank that air conditioning. You know where I am if you need me, Dan. But try not to call. I'd be one happy camper if I didn't have to drive out here again this summer."

So would I, I thought as his car rattled away. I drew in a deep breath and stared at the serene blue water of the lake for a moment. Then I walked up the slope toward the workmen. Yesterday they'd waved to me as I drove up. One had told me a joke, something about a blind airline pilot. I hadn't thought it was especially funny, but I'd forced myself to laugh, feeling accepted and trusted. The fire had destroyed that. They stood as I approached, the set of their shoulders demonstrating their anger before I heard their words.

"What are you going to do now, Sergeant?"

"You going to catch the son of a bitch who tried to kill Lee?"

"We're sitting ducks up here."

"The bastard could come back tonight."

"What are you going to do to protect us?"

I held my hands up. "I'm going to do all I can."

"Sure you are." A tall man with a bristling black beard stepped forward and spat at my feet. "It was probably one of your pals who did it. One of those firefighters."

"Yeah," said a youngster with a crew cut and a diamond stud in one ear. I recognized him as the one who'd told me the joke. "Those guys can't even bring enough water. Next time they won't bother to bring the damn truck."

"They did all they could." I struggled to keep my tone rational, to ignore the bait and simply state the facts. "There's no municipal water system in Hemlock Lake. No fire hydrants. I advised your developer to put in a retention pond right away, but he put it off."

"Bullshit!" The man with the bristling beard stepped toward me, fists clenched. "You're trying to blame us. Well, we're not going to take it."

I held my ground as others growled their support. I told myself that was human nature, to shift blame elsewhere, but I still felt angry—at them and at myself. I'd seen the cairn. I should have been more vigilant. I thought about the other cairns, at the lodge and the church. Would there be another fire tonight?

Wheels crunched gravel behind me, and I glanced over my shoulder to see DeFazio's shiny red pickup truck creeping toward us. The workers' muttering subsided as they watched him slide from the truck. He wore a denim shirt tucked into the elastic waistband of crisp new jeans. A red plaid snap-brim hat covered his head and he cradled a clipboard in his arm.

"Sergeant." He acknowledged me coolly, then turned to the workers. "Good morning. First, I want to say I'm sorry for what you went through last night. I appreciate the fact that you're all still here, and I commend you on your bravery. We're not going to let this stop us."

The workers nodded to each other. The man with the bristling beard puffed his chest, basking in the praise.

"I've just come from the hospital and they tell me that Lee Fosmark will have a few scars, but he will recover and could be back with us in a month or so." DeFazio cleared his throat and glanced at his clipboard. "This was a disastrous incident, and I'm grateful that no one else was seriously hurt. As it was, we lost a lot of paperwork, but most of it can be duplicated. In a few days it will be business as usual. In the meantime, I want everyone to take a day off." He hesitated a fraction of a second, and I could almost see him wince. "With full pay."

A rumbling cheer covered his next few words, and he paused and waited for the workers to quiet down.

"Until Lee returns, I'm going to take charge of operations. The first thing I'm going to do is make sure the local firefighters have no excuses for not doing their jobs. I don't care what it costs me to get to the top of the well-drilling list around here, I'll pay it. In the meantime, we'll dig out a pond and fill it."

The workers cheered again and one gave me the finger.

A bolt of fury shot up my neck and into my brain. DeFazio had shifted the blame. I opened my mouth, but snarling rage gave way to cold recognition of futility.

DeFazio smiled. "Someone"—his gaze slewed in my direction—"wants to stop this development or scare away the folks we're building these houses for. But I'm not going to let that happen, and I don't think you are, either." He paused, making eye contact with each worker. The man had missed his calling, I decided grudgingly. He'd make a good politician, or a televangelist. "But we can't expect outside help. First thing this morning, I went to see the sheriff. He told me he'd already assigned one man." DeFazio slanted the word "man" in italicized sarcasm, and his gaze flicked in my direction again. "And he'd send others up here on regular patrols, but he couldn't commit any more. I told him that was a crock of shit!"

The men cheered. I imagined the veins in Sheriff North's head throbbing and the words he must have exchanged with DeFazio. I guessed there would be a message on my machine when I got home.

"So I told him if he couldn't protect us, we'd damn well

protect ourselves. I've got a rifle, and I'm sure some of you have guns, too."

Guns! I felt my chest compress. I flashed back to the vigilante talk Ronny had headed off three days ago. There would be no voice of reason here, no thought that anyone getting up in the middle of the night to take a piss could be mistaken for an intruder and shot.

"The first thing we'll do is to work out a rotation schedule for guarding this site at night," DeFazio continued. "Time and a half for guard duty."

The workers grinned and nodded their agreement.

"And, like I told the sheriff, the next time something happens up here, we'll retaliate. Teach these people a lesson. Fight fire with fire."

"Retaliation will only spark more violence. You can't—"

"Shut up!" DeFazio wheeled on me. "We're not listening. In fact, from now on, Sergeant, this patch of private property is off limits to you without my permission. We don't need you and we don't want you. So get the hell out."

Blood roiled in my skull, but I stared into his chilly eyes, hoping mine appeared colder. "I'll remember you said that."

As I turned away, I heard a smattering of applause behind me. I felt my neck redden and forced myself to walk with deliberate and plodding steps.

"I need to work out a schedule for guard duty." DeFazio's voice rose with a note of assurance. "Before I start, let's have a show of hands. Is there anybody who isn't familiar with how to use a rifle?"

I didn't have to glance back. I knew no one would admit ignorance and face the derision of his coworkers. Not after the way DeFazio had pumped them up.

Driving back to the lodge, I thought about Ronny, Stub, Willie Dean, and the others. Word would get around that the construction workers thought they'd botched their job. And they'd hear about threats of retaliation, too. They'd buy fresh ammunition for their guns. And Sergeant Dan Stone would be caught between two vigilante groups.

Maybe the sheriff had been right to want to jerk me out of here.

As I pulled up to the lodge, the first thing I saw was the gaping front door. Sliding my gun from the glove compartment, I crept up the steps in a crouch. But halfway across the porch, I remembered that I'd left the door open when Ronny and I bolted last night.

Smiling at my fears, I stepped into the living room. Except for the flashing red light on the answering machine, it looked exactly as I'd left it.

Then I spotted the empty brackets at the top of the gun rack.

CHAPTER 18

I ran my fingers across the brackets, confirming that my great-grandfather's double-barreled shotgun was gone. Unreliable at anything but close range, it had been one of the few heirlooms I'd intended to keep. As children, Nat and I had been allowed to shoot it only once each—to celebrate an occasion I couldn't recall. I opened the drawer in the cabinet beneath the rack and saw an empty space among the boxes of ammunition stored there.

Revolver in hand, I scanned the kitchen pantry, checked the refrigerator, and roamed through the bedrooms. I found nothing disturbed, not a blanket out of place, not a sliver of soap missing. If the thief had been the man whose camp we discovered, he'd had plenty of opportunity to scavenge enough to outfit and feed himself for a week. He could have stolen a more reliable weapon, or made off with them all.

Dropping to the sofa, I punched the "play" button on the answering machine. Sheriff Clement North's voice roared out of the tiny speaker. "Dan, damn it, that fool DeFazio is going to incite a riot up there. The stupid son of a—Well, you probably know all of that by now. Call me!"

I punched in the number, told a receptionist whose voice I didn't recognize that the call wasn't urgent, and listened to slowed-down instrumental version of a tune I couldn't quite place. Wondering who determined the playlist for hold music, I scratched my head and stared at the gun rack, thinking about

DeFazio and the sheriff, sound and fury. I decided not to mention the shotgun, just slide it into the next written report. Perhaps it had been a kid who'd walked off with it. Or someone who'd seen a chance to sell it to a collector. It was unique. My great-grandfather, who'd hunted for food, not pleasure, had whittled away at the stock while he'd waited for his prey, creating a depiction of the lake on one side and the open-jawed head of a snake on the other. A rattler. The reason the thief had picked that particular gun?

I heard a click and the sheriff roared, "Dan? Damn it. Are they all bug nuts up there? That pea-brained pig-headed asshole, DeFazio. God almighty. It's a recipe for disaster." He paused for a few seconds, and I heard his breathing, harsh and quick. "There's no way we can talk him out of it. Tell everyone they'd be smart to stay away from the site after dark. You, too. Those boys will be shooting at shadows. Understand?"

I opened my mouth to respond, but before I could, he said, "Got a meeting to get to. Call me if you need help."

Not the Stone way, was it? I wondered if the sheriff had been making a joke.

I hung up and stared some more at the rifle rack, then locked the doors, made myself a fried egg sandwich, called to arrange a platoon of mobile outhouses for the Fourth of July, took a shower, pulled the drapes, and fell asleep on the sofa.

The sun hung low in the sky when I woke up. Filtering through my grandmother's drapes, it washed the room with a hazy incandescence the color of old bloodstains. Knifepoints of sharper light sliced through the velvet where the satin lining had split with age. I walked to the window and fingered the soft fabric, releasing a cloud of dust. The motes shimmied in the red air, and I felt a sneeze itching behind my eyes. Before the summer was over I'd have to tear down these curtains and replace them with something more modern.

I felt a moment of sorrow for my grandmother's sacrifice, then shook it off and glanced around, making mental notes of other projects: worn rubber treads on the stairs, musty and fraying rag rugs, aging linoleum. Nat and my father and I had laid that linoleum when I was a sophomore in high school, one of the last things we'd done together before our interests had diverged like old logging roads in the woods.

Shaking off that memory too, I tucked in my shirt, got my wallet and gun, and locked the front door behind me. I had about an hour before dark, plenty of time for a quick sweep past the construction site to show them I was on the job, no matter what they wanted. Afterward, I'd drive up Bluestone Hollow Road and ask Freeman to keep an eye out for anything suspicious. I'd also warn him about the workers' self-defense efforts. Then I'd stop and see Willie Dean, Ronny, and the others, and tell them the same thing.

A damp wind riffled the lake and sent clouds scudding toward the sun. A storm before morning, I thought as I walked to the SUV. I was about to open the door when I noticed the glistening brown stain on the gravel behind the front wheel.

"Damn."

Kneeling, I peered at the undercarriage and saw a final few drops of oil suspended from the edge of the drain hole in the pan. Lying on my side, I stretched out my right arm, sifting gravel with my fingers, searching for the plug. I didn't find it. I knew I wouldn't. Whoever had done this had pitched it into the woods. Or taken it with him.

I drew my hand back and wiped oil-slicked fingers on my jeans. Why did someone want me sidelined? Why now? Why tonight?

Standing, I surveyed the thickening shadows among the trees. Nothing moved except a jay that taunted me from the limb of a white birch, then flew to the roof of the lodge and hurled more insults. I touched the revolver, rubbed the back of my neck, took stock of the input from my sixth sense, and decided I was alone. Whoever had drained the oil pan hadn't stayed around to check my reaction.

I kicked at the gravel. Unlike the theft of the shotgun, I couldn't keep this quiet. I'd need a new plug for the pan and fresh oil. Since I couldn't drive to his garage, I'd have to ask Stub to bring them.

"Damn." I kicked the front tire. Stub would certainly tell Ronny. They'd have a good laugh at my expense.

"Unless I lie," I told the jay. "Unless I say that someone forgot to tighten the plug when I had the oil changed." Mulling that over, I decided it was as good a plan as any. If the mystery man had drained the oil, he wouldn't step forward to set the record straight. But if someone else had done it, he might slip up.

Meanwhile, the clock was running. I had a feeling that I had to get going, had to get to the construction site, had to be there tonight. I reached for the cell phone in the glove compartment, then drew my hand back, something tingling at the base of my brain.

If I called Stub now, he would ask why I couldn't wait until morning, where I had to go that was so important. Could I trust him with the truth? I shook my head. No. He'd tell Ronny. They'd get their guns and come along. I wanted to get to the site alone, unnoticed.

I looked across the lake, calculating the distance by the road—eleven miles. Alternately jogging and walking, I might make it in two and a half hours. But if I went across the lake—

Racing to the far side of the double garage, I yanked back the bolt and flung open the door. Orange sunlight splintered off a gleaming white hull, then was blotted up by the darkness at the back of the building. The boat sat on a jerry-built trailer made of old pipe and a cast-off truck axle. I grasped the rusted pipe with both hands and lifted. I could roll the trailer down to the lake and into the water, but could I figure out how to fire up the motor?

"You're not paying attention, Danno." Nat's mocking voice echoed inside my head. I could almost see him bending over the outboard. "I swear, Susanna knows more about this boat than you do. Now put that book down and watch."

"You knew how to do everything better than I did, didn't you, Nat?" I flicked on a row of overhead fluorescent lights, revealing his woodworking equipment, stacks of leaning boards and half-finished cabinets, pyramids of cans containing stain and varnish, and piles of curling shavings and sawdust. I kicked a heap of shavings, scattering them across the paint-spattered cement floor, and glanced back at the sun, now a red half circle flattening itself against the mountain across the lake. I needed another way.

Opening the door that led to the other side of the garage, I flicked on another bank of lights and scanned nets and rods and waders, tools and sacks of fertilizer, a tiller, and rows of old coffee cans filled with nuts and bolts, nails and screws. A huge hornet's nest hung from the rafters, and beyond it, upside down on a pair of sawhorses, rested a stubby orange canoe. Nat and I had used it as children, and my mother had paddled it along the shore on her bird-watching expeditions. I turned off the lights—no point in disturbing more hornets than I had to—and scavenged a paddle from behind a stack of gardening tools. A few hornets pinged off the shell as I hoisted the canoe over my head and hustled to the lake.

The sun was a bloody fingernail raking the mountain top as I eased the canoe into the water and scrambled inside. It rocked crazily, and a small geyser of water shot up from a slit in the bow. Jerking off my left shoe, I sacrificed the sock to plug the hole, then scrambled back to shore, seized a jacket, the rifle and some ammunition from the house, locked the door again, and got under way, paddling through the choppy water.

It took a few minutes for me to remember where to hold my hands and how to draw the paddle without wasted effort. Then my muscles worked out a routine, and the canoe plowed into the darkening wind. Halfway across, I got a bearing on the light from Willie Dean's bait shop and turned south, thinking about the green light at the end of Daisy's dock and Jay Gatsby. He'd tried to buy his way back to the past, to Daisy, and died because he held onto a dream too long, died as it shattered around him. My mind leapt to Susanna, teasing death at the end of that rope.

I shuddered and dug harder until the canoe grated against crushed shale on the point of land north of the construction site. Deciding to risk the noise, I pulled it well out of the water. I had no rope to tie it to a tree and didn't want to return to find it had been sent scudding away at the mercy of the wind.

As I started up the road, I stuck to the right shoulder, ready to dive into the brush at the first sound or flicker of light. A patch of purple sky shone among the gathering clouds, ugly as a bruise. Tree branches scraped softly in the rising wind, and a thin mist slithered from the lake, sliding tentacles across the road. Just before I reached the stone wall that had once marked the north end of Tom Andersen's property, I turned west into a clump of pine.

I put each foot down with care, grateful for gusts that thrashed the limbs, covering my noise and motion. Skirting a small clearing, I saw bright lights around the trailers at the construction site, and spotted a clump of men in the makeshift kitchen. I was tempted to move faster, confident that the floodlights would make it impossible for them to see into the darkness that shrouded me. But I kept to my deliberate pace, directing my attention to the trees ahead, to the crannies in the stone wall, and to the hollows where the ground dropped away—places where someone could hide and watch.

The ground sloped upward and I climbed, one plodding step at a time, staying well inside the shelter of the woods and keeping the wall to my left. It hunched up the slope, as straight as any farmer cursing nature and clearing frost-thrust rocks by hand from a pasture on these crimped and creased hills could make it.

I reached the top of the slope and felt my way to the angle where another wall intersected, ranging south, dividing pasture from woods. Fifty feet along it I stopped. Decades ago, an acorn had sprouted between the stones. As the oak stretched upward, it shouldered rocks aside. Pressing myself against its corrugated bark, I looked over the wall and assessed my position.

The ground fell away before me, studded with stacks of lumber, piles of bricks, and the skeletons of framed-in houses. Floodlights cast stark shadows across the barren earth between the structures. Beyond them the lake lay, something more felt than seen, except where the naked yellow bulb on Willie Dean's dock cast jaundiced light. The wind shifted slightly, and I caught a sharp and sour scent—the remains of the burned-out trailer.

A glinting reflection snagged the edge of my vision, and I clamped myself to the tree. The young worker who'd confronted me that morning trudged by at the edge of the light, a silver hardhat on his head, a rifle resting carelessly on his shoulder. He glanced toward the wall once, then turned downslope.

I waited until he'd passed beyond the framed-up ribs of a house before I moved to where several spruce trees draped their boughs over the wall. Leaning my rifle against the base of the middle tree, I hauled myself slowly to the top of the stones, testing each foothold before I trusted it with my weight. I threaded myself between the branches, feeling for a flat rock I remembered, and sat, resting my back against a trunk. It was thicker and rougher than I expected, and I had to remind myself I hadn't visited this childhood retreat in nearly twenty years. I remembered the days I'd pack a book in my bike basket, snitch one of Tom Andersen's apples, and come to this spot that was mine alone.

Relaxing my muscles, I stretched my legs out before me, took the revolver from its holster, and laid it across my thighs. I drew in a deep breath, the cold air thick with the scent of the clustered needles, and zipped my jacket to my throat. The wind found my naked left ankle and chilled the points of bone. Tomorrow night I'd wear a sweater and long underwear. I'd bring coffee. Maybe some sandwiches. And a blanket. Or a tarp. Maybe both.

As I tugged the collar of the jacket up around my ears, I heard the rasp of metal on metal. Behind me, a rifle bolt clacked into place.

I didn't have to turn to know that bolt was on my own rifle.

CHAPTER 19

I froze, every muscle rigid with fear. Except my heart. It swelled into my throat, filled my mouth, battered at my ears.

The chill steel of the barrel brushed my left cheek, then rested on my shoulder. I searched the darkness for a sense of his size and shape. The fingers of my right hand moved stiffly, fitting themselves to the revolver, finding the trigger. If I threw myself to one side, could I get off a shot before he did?

I heard myself draw in a tattered breath. Overhead, the spruce swayed in a careless embrace with the wind. I drew in another breath, catching the sharp scent of my own fear. The rifle barrel lifted and I tensed, ready to somersault off the wall and come up shooting.

"You've got balls, Sergeant." The whisper hissed like steam bleeding off a radiator. "Anyone else would be pissing in his pants. Begging for mercy."

The whisper was ageless, sexless, barely audible over my hammering heart and the whipping wind. I licked dry lips, pursed them to ask "Who are you?" but felt my throat bind as the barrel touched my left ear. Now? Should I roll out now? I planted my left hand on the rock beside me. From the corner of my eye I saw the young construction worker crest the hill. If I moved, I'd draw fire from two directions.

Motionless, I counted ragged breaths as the young worker passed. The rifle barrel didn't move. My captor wasn't one of their guards; if he were, he would have called out. Was he the man who'd set the fire last night? Would he march me away from the site, or shoot me here and gamble that he'd get away? A cold, trembling nausea gripped me, and I decided he might. Risk increased the illicit thrill, upped the adrenaline ante.

The young worker picked up his pace and disappeared around a stack of plywood. The man behind me drew in several sharp breaths and huffed them out. The rifle barrel pinched my ear against the side of my head, then fell against my shoulder again. The bolt scraped back. "You thinking that fucker who set off the bomb will be back tonight?"

My fingers loosened around the revolver and I turned, giving myself time to draw in a full breath, hoping my voice wouldn't sound like the croak of a strangling frog. I couldn't show fear or anger. It was the only way to play this game to a draw. "You been up here long, Ronny?"

"Nope." He left a moment of silence before he chuckled softly. "Bird-dogged you up the ridge." Shoving branches aside, he hoisted himself up beside me, the whites of his eyes and his teeth flashing in the murky light. "You got too much city boy in you, Dan. You're about as quiet as a tank, and you leave a trail that even Willie Dean could follow."

Seething at his insults and my own ineptness, I bit down on my tongue, glad that my face was in shadow.

"But you almost got in under my radar coming across the lake instead of on the road. I'll give you major points for that." He laid my rifle and his own between us on the wall.

I planted my hand on top of the rifles. "So why were you following me, Ronny? Are you trying to finish what the snake handler started? Or are you here to set another bomb?"

He paused to the count of four. Surprised by my questions? Thinking of answers? "None of the above, bud. You and me just had the same idea—the son of a bitch would be back. I was creeping along on the other side of the road when I saw you, right when you turned into the woods."

"Well, you can go home now. This is my job."

He let the silence play out, like line sizzling through a reel when a fish goes deep and you let it run. Finally he said, "No. When there's fire involved, it's my job, too." His voice sounded thick. "You were right that first day when you told me that. I didn't want to admit it, and I still don't like what they've done to Tom's land, but you were right. I have a responsibility."

I grunted, wondering what that confession cost him and if he would have been able to make it in daylight.

We sat in silence for a full circuit of the guard, then Ronny whispered, "Another pair of eyes can't hurt, bud. Might even help."

"Sure," I whispered back. "Another pair of eyes would be good." *And I'll know right where you are if something happens.*

Ronny shifted, stretching his legs. "Comfortable spot, considering it's all rock. You used to come here and read those books of yours when we were kids. I guess you thought no one else knew about it. Truth was we all did."

I felt a deadening blow of loss strike my chest. Behind it came the raking pain of violation. I forced rigid stillness on my body. My refuge, my fortress, had been mere self-deception.

"No one else ever came here." Ronny snapped off a couple of twigs and flexed his shoulders, settling in among the boughs. "Except old Willie Dean." Ronny chuckled softly. "He brought a girl up here one night while we were in high school. Not Priscilla. Some other girl, though I don't remember which one." He chuckled again. "Willie Dean thought it would be romantic. But he forgot there are all manner of critters using this wall. Seems like she sat in something that might have been coon shit. Or possum. She didn't stick around long enough for a laboratory analysis. I told Willie Dean to stay away after that or he'd have to deal with me. Every man should have a place of his own.

This was yours."

The words felt like cool rain against my forehead, quenching the fire behind my eyes. I coughed, breaking the tightness in my throat. My mind turned over words and phrases, all of which would reveal gratitude and obligation. Ronny had understood more than I had given him credit for. Perhaps I'd been the one who built the wall between us, and all the faults I saw in him were there because I hadn't looked deeper, hadn't allowed him to be more than simply the sum of appearance and actions.

The word came hard, but it came. "Thanks."

We watched together all night, but saw nothing except a prowling fox, a low-flying owl on the hunt, and a parade of construction workers marching, then trudging, and finally dragging themselves through their rounds. Ronny had brought a small tarp in his knapsack, and we huddled under it when the rainstorm I'd expected rammed through the core of the night. The "spotty shower," as Ronny called it, brought a stiff wind that hurled drops sideways but didn't last long enough to do more than wet the ground. When it ended, Ronny opened the knapsack again and brought out a container of coffee and a plastic bag of chewy oatmeal cookies packed with walnuts and pieces of dried apricot. He gave me more than an equal share. I accepted without feeling he was trying to prove I was weak and needed more than he did.

Toward dawn we retreated back through the woods to the road and split up. The lake was calm and slick with pearly mist as I paddled home. The lodge was still and empty. I checked the locks and inventoried all the rooms. Nothing missing. After I'd slapped bacon into a pan, I called Stub and rattled off a tale of woe about rocky roads and ten-thumbed idiots at cut-rate garages. With a series of hyphenated words, he shared his own opinions, said he expected he had something that would fit, and promised he'd cruise on out after breakfast. I asked him if he'd bring whatever I'd need to get the boat going, and he muttered something about gas and oil and putting it on my tab and hung up.

Tab? The single three-letter word sounded like "Welcome back, glad to have you home again." Another wall had come down. Another wall, I realized, that I had helped erect.

Stub arrived just before seven, declined my offer of a cup of coffee, and went right to work plugging the pan and pouring in oil while I watched, wired from caffeine and lack of sleep, the muscle beneath my left eye twitching, my skin dry and prickling.

"Good thing Ronny took care of this last fall," he said as he examined the outboard motor. "You'd be surprised how many people don't winterize their boats and lawnmowers. You don't do the right thing in the fall and there's hell to pay in the spring." He rambled on as he worked, but my attention slid off his words like a pat of yellow butter sizzles across a hot skillet. Studying the glint of sunlight on the lake, I shut out the sounds of Stub's tinkering. I thought about the man on the mountain, Lee Fosmark's burned skin, the taste of Lisa's cookies, the scent of spruce, the feel of Susanna's hair between my fingers, the perfectly balanced rocks in most of the cairns, Camille's lips puckering slightly in the split second before I pulled away.

Her voice had been on my answering machine twice since that night. I hadn't returned either call. I'd barely responded to her wave the next day when I'd passed her on the road, lifting my hand awkwardly from the wheel, my brain issuing a flurry of conflicting opinions: "Her lips won't feel like Susanna's. She's only trying to distract you. You don't deserve her care."

"Hey! You listening, Dan?" Stub wiped his hands on a rag. "Let's get her into the water."

Shrugging off the collage of images, I gripped the rusting pipe framework and helped Stub maneuver the boat across the driveway to a graded area beside the dock.

"This is as far as I go." Stub dropped his side. "Too early in the season for me to put on my bathing trunks."

I laughed. From the first time I was old enough to know who he was, I couldn't remember Stub wearing anything except one-piece oil-stained green or gray coveralls. Chicken-breasted and bandy-legged, Stub seemed to regard those coveralls the way a turtle regards its shell. The heavy fabric made him seem bulkier, taller. He wore the sleeves rolled over forearms knotted with stringy muscle, and ran the zipper up barely to armpit level, revealing a permanently smudged T-shirt and a neck as thin and wobbly as a sunflower stalk. I sat on the dock to pull off my shoes.

He watched, scratching his head with a grimy index finger. "Just don't seem to enjoy getting wet like I used to. Too much trouble. Get undressed, swim, get dressed again. That's for kids. Kids and people with too much time on their hands."

He glanced across the lake toward the construction site. I stepped off the dock, lifted the end of the trailer, and waded in. Shards of shale slipped under my feet as the frigid water stung my ankles, gripped my calves, and drove a hundred needles into the soft skin behind my knees. The water reached my crotch, and my groin tightened with a cramping spasm.

Another two steps, with water lapping at my chest, I let the trailer go. The boat slid free, bobbing against the side of the dock with a series of hollow thuds. Stub hustled to tether it to a metal cleat. He stepped in, and fiddled with something I couldn't see. "Ignition's got a mind of its own, but it usually fires up after a few tries. Nat had been meaning to fix it. And don't forget you have to pump air into the gas tank."

"I won't."

He stepped back to the dock. "You can take it from here," he told me as I slogged up the bank.

Before his dust settled, I'd entered the house, stripped off my clothes, and toweled down. My skin tingled, and my muscles felt heavy with sleep, the way they used to feel when Nat and I would barter our evening baths for a skinny-dip in the lake. There was a quality in that twilight water, in the dew-rich air, that made our sheets feel like satin afterward, our mattresses as soft as the down comforter in my grandmother's hope chest. We'd slip into smooth and seamless sleep.

Hoping I could do the same now, I pulled on fresh clothes, drew the drapes, locked the door, and stretched out on the sofa. Drowsiness settled on me like a cat.

When the phone jangled me awake, the room seemed filled with fog. I blinked stiff eyelids and reached for the receiver.

"Hello?" My voice came out as a hoarse whisper.

"You still in bed at this hour?" The sheriff's voice rumbled in my ear. "Get some fresh batteries in your pager. And get your ass over to the construction site. There's more graffiti!"

CHAPTER 20

I shoved my feet into my shoes, remembering that I'd turned off the pager as I crept up the slope last night, hadn't turned it on before I tossed it on the table this morning. Another stupid mistake! I snapped it on, buckled my belt, checked the gun, and locked the door. As I drove, my mind turned as rapidly as the tires. If anything had happened last night, Ronny and I would have noticed.

DeFazio's truck wasn't there, so I gambled that my banishment wouldn't be enforced and drove up to a cluster of workers beside a three-car garage at the lower end of the development. Spray-painted foot-tall red letters slanted across the plywood walls inside: NEXT TIME SOMEBODY **DIES.** The word "dies" was twice as large as the others and twice as bold, the paint so thick it had clotted at the edges of the letters.

"Son of a bitch must be invisible," the bristly bearded worker told me. "We had guards patrolling all night, and nobody saw a goddamn thing. He must have walked right past us, maybe during that storm."

"Maybe."

He watched while I got the camera and took a couple of pictures. "Waste of film." He spat tobacco juice against the wall, punctuating the sentence. Behind him, several others watched me, one tossing a hunting knife from hand to hand. "Can't tell nothing from printed letters like that, can you?"

"No. Probably not." Printing didn't bear up to analysis like handwriting, but I was no expert. I could compare it to earlier graffiti, but then what? I still had no idea who the author might be. I wondered if one of the workers had sprayed this message to drive a wedge further between us. Maybe the one glaring at me right now.

"Just going through the motions, huh?" He smeared the words with a light layer of sarcasm and smiled, his thick lips wet and red against his beard, his nose large-pored, like an enormous strawberry.

I chalked his attitude up to fear. After all, he'd called the sheriff's office. That told me he was hedging DeFazio's bet. "Not much else I can do."

He turned his voice up a notch. "What are we gonna do about somebody who walks right in here anytime and does what he damn well pleases?"

I didn't answer.

I didn't know.

"I hear there was more graffiti over at the construction site last night." Mary Lou's inflection turned the statement of fact into a question.

"Yeah." I rested an elbow on the counter. "How did you hear about it?"

"Willie Dean. He says you can see it from his dock." She plucked a bill from the power company out of my box and laid it on the counter. "Of course, he couldn't read what it says until he got his binoculars out." She narrowed her eyes. "I thought they had guards up there. I heard that from one of the workers who came in for some stamps," she told me before I could ask. "So whoever had that spray can walked right past them, huh?"

"Looks like."

"Think they did it themselves?"

"Why would they?"

She shrugged. "That's what some are saying. I doubt it myself."

The bell jingled and the door grated open. Cool air eddied around me.

"Hi, Mary Lou." Camille's voice, gritty as sandpaper, smooth as honey. "Hey, Dan, how's it going?" She closed the door and bellied up to the counter beside me, laying down a pile of letters and a five-dollar bill. "I need some first-class stamps, please."

I moved a half step away as Mary Lou swept the five into a drawer beneath the counter. "How many?"

Camille scoped me from the edges of her eyes and moved a half step of her own, her lips tightening and her chin drawing into the high neck of her lavender T-shirt as she widened the gap. "Oh, enough for these letters and however many more I can afford."

Mary Lou riffled the pile of envelopes. I kept my eyes on her hands as she opened the drawer beneath the counter, counted stamps and tore them off a sheet, then pushed a few coins back to Camille. "Don't spend that all in one place. Spread it around so it does some good for the economy."

Camille laughed, the rising and falling notes stroking the whorls of my ears like fingertips. I felt something in my chest quiver and forced myself to take another half step away as she stuck a stamp to the corner of an envelope addressed to someone in Atlanta, someone named Mercy. She peeled off a second stamp and the quiver in my chest increased, sending a flurry of chills down my spine.

Mary Lou coughed. "You need any stamps, Dan? While I've got them out?"

I shook my head hard. "No. Thanks. See you later." Clutching the power bill, I turned toward the door, peeling my shoes from the floor. I felt as awkward as the day my voice began to change. "Good-bye, Camille."

" 'Bye, Sergeant Stone." She laughed again, and I heard Mary Lou snigger. "Nice almost talking to you."

I walked stiffly to my rig and hauled myself inside. Seething with embarrassment, I stabbed the key into the ignition and cranked it until the starter grated. What the hell was wrong with me? Grinding the shift into reverse, I squealed out of the slot beside the Brocktons' car, arcing around until I faced the highway. I smacked the shift into first. Camille stepped in front of me. I hit the brake.

Trailing a hand along the fender, she ambled to my window, lips curved into a lazy smile. "I'm not pursuing you, Sergeant Stone, so there's no need for you to go out of your way to avoid me."

The protest was mechanical. "I . . ."

She raised a hand, her eyes darkening. "I know a brush-off when I see one. I overstepped my bounds the other night. I'm sorry. You know I'm—"

"There's nothing to be—"

"—from the South." She raised her voice, the honey drying to a coarse-grained sugar. "Where people are more demonstrative. I was just saying 'Thanks for the ride, take care of yourself.' Nothing more."

She smacked her hand, opened palmed, against the door. "We're adults, Sergeant. If there's a problem, we should talk about it. We can be friends. Or not. It's your choice."

Her running shoes squeaked on the asphalt as she turned aside. Before I could speak, she'd slammed the door and fired up the engine. I saw Mary Lou peering from the post office window, fingers against the glass. I popped the clutch and blasted onto the highway. Living under so many eyes was getting old. And there were only two ways out—catch the arsonist, or quit.

I drove up to the cemetery and parked where I could look out over the lake while I examined Camille's words. Where did she get off dissecting my thoughts? Chastising me?

I flung open the door and strode to Susanna's grave. The lilac blooms I'd spread had withered, the blossoms turning a rusty brown, the stalks curling in upon themselves like question marks. "I miss you," I told the silky grass. "I miss holding you. I miss your eyes. I miss your lips." Susanna's mouth had been wide, her lips thin and soft. When I kissed them, I could feel her teeth, each one distinct, beneath the flesh. Not like Camille's would be, I imagined. Her lips were thicker, cushioned.

I shook my head, angry at myself for having noticed so much about Camille's mouth, feeling I'd betrayed Susanna. Exhausted, I sat at the foot of the grave. A shifting breeze combed the grass like fingers through fine hair—Susanna's hair, blond and straight, dropping over her shoulders like mist. Not like Camille's tangled curls, which framed her face like a tarnished copper halo. I swept my hand across the grass, feeling the blades tickle my palms. "I thought we'd always be together."

The breeze faded, and I glanced at the cloudless sky, then across the lake toward the development site. Sunlight flashed off a trailer window and a bright red truck, the size of my thumb at that distance, rolled up beside the black smudge that had been Lee Fosmark's trailer. I couldn't see the spray-painted warning but I knew it was still there, a reminder that I hadn't done my job.

"But I will," I told Susanna's grave. "I will."

I found Ronny at Stub's service station, his feet sticking out from under the fire truck, cursing all things with moving parts made on an assembly line. I squatted beside his legs. "Something wrong with the truck?"

"Nah. Just the usual shit." His voice echoed tinnily through the radiator. "Thing's old enough to be in a retirement home. And all the places that need grease you can't reach unless you're double-jointed and have arms like a baboon. Heard you had some trouble with your rig."

"Yeah. I tried to save a few bucks and got sabotaged. Lucky the plug didn't go out on the highway."

"Ain't that a fact." His tone told me he'd accept my story until he had more evidence. "So what's up, bud?"

"I didn't fall asleep last night, did I?"

"Not that I noticed." He grunted and turned onto his side.

"You didn't see anything, did you? Anyone besides the guards?"

"If I had, don't you think I'd have stuck my elbow in your ribs?"

"Yeah. I was just checking."

He shoved a can of grease across the floor, then wiggled out from under the truck, sat up, and wiped his hands on a strip of old pillowcase. Beneath the grease, I could see that someone had spent hours embroidering "Hers" with purple thread, and trimming the edge with elaborately looped tatting like my grandmother used to create. And now it was a rag. I felt a burst of stinging sorrow for the woman who'd plied the needle and worked the shuttle between her fingers.

"You thinking about the graffiti they found up there this morning, bud?"

I nodded.

"Stub told me about it. He heard from Willie Dean." Ronny chewed his lower lip. "Wonder if he hit before we got in place. Or after. There were some spots we couldn't see from up there."

"Yeah, but the construction workers passed that garage a few hundred times during the night." I stood, pressing my hand against the insignia on the truck's door. "Of course, it could have been one of them."

"You think?" Ronny ran his fingers though his beard.

"No." I heard a note of confidence in my voice and realized that on some deep level my mind must have been examining the idea since it came to me. "I can't see what they'd have to gain by it. When I broke them out of that trailer they were scared. Hard to believe one of them would do anything to frighten the others more. So it was someone else. And he took a real chance."

"Well, I think we've already established that he don't mind a little risk. Gets his rocks off on it." Ronny hauled himself to his feet, pitching the pillowcase scrap into a barrel in the corner. "The guy's got big ones. Setting the fire and coming right back to rub our noses in it. If you'd asked me, I'd a bet the farm that he'd have moved on after we took apart his camp and tore up the ridges looking for him."

"You think it's the man on the mountain?"

I'd aimed for casual, but my voice held a sharp note of surprise. Ronny picked up on it right away. "Well who else? It ain't me. And it ain't you. Willie Dean's right close and could sneak over there the easiest, but he don't have the brains or the nerve. Plus, he's as clumsy as a hog on ice. And the rest of them, well . . ." He paused, eyes strafing a twenty-year collection of calendars on the walls. "Nah. It ain't none of them. There's some might have sent those letters, and some might get out there with a can of spray paint, but that thing the other night, that was something else."

I'd come to the same conclusion. I suspected that whoever had started the game with the anonymous letters had dropped out. There was another hand moving the pieces around the board now and another brain controlling that hand. But did that hand and brain belong to a stranger? I played devil's advocate. "I'd hate to think it was anyone I knew either, but you've got to admit that most of the guys up here could build a bomb from stuff they've got laying around. And you hear all the time that some mass murderer gets caught and neighbors swear he was always pitching in to help haul out the garbage."

Ronny frowned. "That's city neighbors, not country. It's different up here. Except for Camille Chancellor and that kid Freeman's daughter married, I've known everyone here a good long time. I'm in and out of their houses. I know their wives and kids and the names of their dogs and cats. I'd feel it if one of them started that fire." He thumped his chest. "I'd know."

I stared out at the road and didn't argue, didn't tell him that a year ago I would have said I felt sure that Nat never would have taken his own life.

"What are you going to do, bud? You going back up there again tonight?"

"Yeah." Tonight, tomorrow night, the night after. It was the only way I knew to go. By being there, I might prevent this guy from doing more than wielding a spray can.

Ronny clamped a hand on my shoulder. "You want company?"

Two days ago I would have said no, but last night on the wall I'd felt closer to Ronny than to anyone since Susanna died. I'd felt that I wasn't alone—and more than that, I'd felt that I didn't have to be alone. "Yeah, but there's no point in both of us going without sleep."

He nodded slowly. "Okay. Fair enough. I don't mean to get in your way, bud. That's just the way I am." He gazed at a stack of aging tires. "It's Dad's old habit, one I can't break. But you call me if you need a hand." His eyes narrowed with thought. "I haven't told anyone we were up there, and I won't tell anyone you're going back. Except Lisa. But she won't say a word."

"Thanks. I'm thinking I'll get some timer switches for the lodge so it will appear that I'm there when I'm not."

Ronny grinned. "I like it." He snapped his fingers. "Tell you what. Let's keep that man on the mountain off balance. I'll round up a few of the guys, and we'll go out every evening for the next week or so and scout around the woods. Hit some spots at random, stir him up, keep him moving."

I felt a pang of jealousy—not because this was Ronny's idea, but because I wanted to tramp the ridges with him. I wanted not to be alone. But the construction site was a magnet for violence. Sooner or later the arsonist would return. And I'd be waiting.

CHAPTER 21

The next three weeks passed in a noxious blur of daylight patrols and nightly stakeouts. Early each morning, I'd drive to the site, make myself seen, and search for new cairns or signs of vandalism. I was careful to follow DeFazio's renewed orders and stay off the property, but toward the end of the first week I flagged him down as he drove in one morning and, pretending ignorance, tried to advise him about the patrols.

"I don't know if you're using stationary guards or walking a perimeter but it would be a good idea to vary your—"

"It's none of your business what we're doing or how we're doing it." He gunned the engine and a belt whined under the hood. "There hasn't been any major trouble since we started doing your job." He roared off, and a minute later I'd seen him talking to a few of the workers and pointing my way. Poisoning the well.

I also tried to persuade Ronny to call off his forays. "No point in wearing yourself out."

He had rubbed red-rimmed eyes and glowered at the ridges around the lake. "He's still up there somewhere. I can feel it. But he's next to invisible."

"Yeah. I hate to see you spinning your wheels."

"Well, see, bud, that's the thing about spinning your wheels. The dumb guy goes on churning mud until he's in up to the axles. The smart guy tosses a few branches under there and drives on out." He'd fixed steely eyes on me, making it clear

196

that he was the smart guy. "There are a few places we haven't covered yet."

I'd felt the rift between us opening again. "It's your call."

"Damn right it is." He'd taken a step back, as if he'd felt himself teeter at the edge of the rift. "It's a free country."

We'd left it at that, and I'd driven off to get groceries, pick up the mail, and catalog new cairns—all similar to the originals, built with eight or more smoothed and rounded rocks, exquisitely balanced and stacked in order of size. Only two, the one at Willie Dean's dock and the one near Lee Fosmark's trailer, had been built from flatter and rougher rocks heaped up almost indifferently.

Studying the pictures, I got the same feeling I'd had about the threatening letters and the arson attempts. There were two people at work here, two minds directing the action. One, the careless builder, seemed to have copied the other's idea without art and skill. Those copies had both appeared before fires. The others seemed to have no links to threatening letters or graffiti except for the cairn I'd dismantled near the lodge. That could be connected to the missing shotgun and drained oil pan.

I thought about Stonehenge, the pyramids, and the enormous carved heads looking out over Easter Island, about cemetery monuments and memorials on battlefields. If those smooth-stone cairns weren't warnings, if they were simply artistic endeavors, it seemed that the creator, wanting to be admired for his work, might have come forward, or at least dropped hints to his identity. I wished my whirling mind could get some traction.

On alternate days, with increasing dread, I'd call my father. Our one-sided conversations were bracketed by what I couldn't mention: the things I'd hauled to the dump or boxed up for charities, the repairs that might infringe on his sense of owner-ship. I couldn't tell him I'd planned to paint his room, covering the chilly gray-white walls with a warm beige. If he could, he would argue that the walls had always been white, that white was good enough for him and for his father. I felt like I was betraying him, denying him his rights.

In the afternoons I'd sleep for a few hours, then take the boat out and cruise the edge of the lake, or halt opposite the development and drop a line. Sometimes I'd actually catch something—a lake trout or bass—and grill it for dinner. I'd found a half-dozen cookbooks in the pantry and surprised myself by marking a few recipes and hunting out the necessary ingredients. Lou Marie didn't carry many of them and her bitterness took the edge off my appetite, so I'd journeyed farther and I'd picked up jars of herbs, spices, and canned specialty items. I found the process of cooking both soothing and satisfying. If I was still here when Labor Day arrived, I'd be ready for the town picnic with a bowl of dilled potato salad and a platter of trout crusted with crushed almonds.

I made a conscious effort to keep my mind off Camille. I told myself she was a suspect and should be kept at arm's length. I told myself I didn't have to talk with her because there was nothing to talk about. I didn't have to try to resolve a problem because there was none.

When darkness fell I'd load a few supplies in the boat and head across the lake, motor throttled back to just above an idle. That was the toughest part of the routine. I'd slide my hands over the gunwale, wondering if this place or that was where Susanna had set her foot the last time. Some nights I'd reach the construction site weighed down by depression, and other nights I'd be consumed with rage. On those angry nights, I plunged more recklessly through the woods. The workers didn't hear me. Their fear had abated as the days passed without incident. They often sat outside, cracking beers and listening to music or a ball game.

Two weeks before the Fourth of July, Lisa called the planning committees together for an early-evening meeting at the Shovel It Inn. I'd spoken with her only briefly to tell her my assignment had been taken care of, but Mary Lou had given me regular updates on everyone's progress and reported that Lisa was doing a "bang up" job. But Lisa didn't seem to share that confidence; she twisted a button on her blouse as she walked to the front of the room and her left hand clutched her notes so tightly her whole arm trembled, making the sheaf of curling yellow paper flutter and crackle. Clearing her throat twice, she pushed a strand of caramel-colored hair out of her eyes and looked around at the three dozen faces turned toward her.

"Thank you all for coming," she began, her voice sounding wispy, fragile.

Willie Dean cupped his ears. "Louder. We can't hear you."

Lisa stiffened, her gaze flickering across the audience. I smiled and gave her a thumbs-up. She cleared her throat once more and tried again. "Thank you for coming. And thank you for all the hard work you've put in over the past few weeks. Especially all of you who've been picking up litter and fish line and hooks. The shoreline looks great!" She offered a split-second smile, then looked down at her papers. "Willie Dean and Evan," she said, nodding toward them, "will be coming around to collect your barbecue grills next week, so clean them up and write your names on them with waterproof marker. Don't worry about filling the tanks; they'll take care of that."

She paused to breathe and the fluttering pages grew still. "If you've got any card tables or folding chairs or lawn chairs, let them know." She held up a red, white, and blue flyer. "This is our notice. It says bring your own, but you know how people are. It would be nice to have a few extras for the older crowd."

"Like Freeman." Willie Dean chortled and looked around with a grin.

His remark earned him a slight ripple of laughter. Even I chuckled.

Lisa waited a moment before she said, "Speaking of Freeman, he found a great deal on bunting and paper plates and napkins and plastic utensils." Lisa beamed at him. "And he got the supplier to give us credit so we don't have to pay until August."

"Way to go!" Evan applauded his friend.

"Merle and Shirley are going to take care of the beer garden," Lisa continued. "They'll absorb the up-front cost and split the profits with us, and Willie Dean's going to get the soda through his supplier, so we can run a tab on that, too."

Willie Dean clasped his hands over his head like a boxer claiming a win.

Lisa nodded toward Ronny. "The fireworks people are also giving us credit as long as we pay within a week. And Dan," she said, pointing to me, "has taken care of our potty problem and it's not going to cost us a dime."

"You can't say old Dan doesn't give a shit about Hemlock Lake," Willie Dean roared.

Ronny, lounging in the back row by the wall, opened his eyes, blinked, and gave me a nod. Mary Lou turned to smile at me, while others tittered and a few clapped. I felt a warm wave of acceptance, followed by a cold spray of uneasiness. I'd lied to Lisa when I told her there would be no charge for the herd of mobile outhouses. The truth was that I hadn't solicited a donation to the cause like the others. I had agreed to pay the bill myself. That decision was based partly on a desire to help Lisa, but more to avoid asking for help, even help for a good cause.

Lisa flashed me a smile, shuffled her papers, and cleared her throat again. "Almost everyone in town has agreed to supply a dessert or a salad, or both, so there will be plenty of great food. But we do have to pay up front for the chicken and hot dogs, the buns, the charcoal, propane, ice, and things like relish and barbecue sauce." She paused, and I saw her take a deep breath and lift her chin. "And, unfortunately, I seem to have painted us into a corner. I discovered yesterday that you can't just throw a party like this without special insurance."

Her shoulders slumped. "I feel like I've let you all down by not doing my homework and finding that out before we got this far along. But there's no way around it. We've already advertised. If we cancel the fireworks, we'll disappoint a lot of people who might not find out it's called off until they drive up here."

"So go ahead and get the insurance," Willie Dean said.

"Yeah. We can't cancel now," Stub chimed in. "We'd look like idiots. Get Ronny to cut a check."

Lisa cleared her throat. "I wish it were that simple. But it's expensive, and as some of you know far better than I do, there isn't enough in the account to cover it."

"We gotta have fireworks," Willie Dean whined. "What are we gonna do?"

"Well, I've been thinking about that almost nonstop since yesterday." Lisa brushed her hair back from her forehead. "I know most of you don't have much you could spare. Ronny and I don't, either. But I'm hoping each of you could put in a little to see us through. Maybe fifty from each family?"

Around me, husbands looked at wives and both shook their heads. Denny Balmer turned his pockets inside out, spilling two nickels and a penny onto the floor. Willie Dean laughed.

Lisa's lips tightened, her eyes darkened. "If everything goes well, you'd get it all back right after we sort out the finances."

I thought of my checkbook in the glove compartment. I started to rise, but hesitated, glancing at Ronny. It would undermine his role of community caretaker.

"I don't know, Lisa." Evan Bonesteel scratched his head. "I mean, what if it rains? Seems like we could take it in the shorts.

And then we—"

"I'll loan you three thousand dollars. Will that be enough?"

Like everyone else, I swiveled in my chair. Camille leaned in the doorway from the bar, a green vinyl-covered checkbook in one hand, a pen in the other. She caught me looking and turned away.

Lisa's open-mouthed surprise transformed to a sparkling grin. "Wow. That should be more than enough." She bolted to the back of the room, stuck out her hand, then flung her arms around Camille. "Thank you. Thank you so much."

Camille returned the hug. "You're welcome. It's no big—"

"We can't take your money." Louisa Marie stood, fists clenched, her chin mottled and quivering. As heads jerked toward her, I wondered why she'd come. Surely she hadn't volunteered to serve on a committee. And surely no committee chairperson had asked for her help. "You can't buy your way into this town. Put your checkbook away and get out."

Lisa turned, chewing at her lower lip. She kept one arm around Camille's waist. "I know you don't mean that, Louisa Marie."

"Yes I do. I mean every word of it." She glanced at Ronny, then at Freeman and Evan. "We don't know anything about this woman. She could be the one starting the fires." She paused in a hiss of whispered reactions. No one backed her, but no one told her to sit down. "She's an outsider. It's not the way we do things. If we can't raise the money ourselves from here in town, then we just won't—"

"Oh, fiddle-faddle." Mary Lou bounded to her feet, addressing the crowd, not her sister. "Camille had nothing to do with those fires. I say if we let her come to the Memorial Day picnic, and we did, and if we ate her brownies, and we did, then she's practically one of us. Her money's just as green and it spends just as well as everyone else's. Doesn't it?" She paused, gauging the undercurrent of whispered comments, then shrugged and smiled. "Besides, like Evan says, we could get rained out. We could lose our shirts. And if we do, wouldn't you rather that she gets stuck holding the bag?" She walked to the back of her room, stood on tiptoes, and laid her arm across Camille's shoulders. "I say let's take this woman to the cleaners."

Camille laughed. "We're going to have a sunny day and a horde of people. I'll have the money back in my account before the bank knows it's gone."

"Let her do it!" Willie Dean stood, clapped, and chanted. "Write that check. Write that check!"

Others took it up. Lou Marie stalked out, shouldering past Camille as the chant filled the room. "This calls for a round of beer on the house!" Merle called over the din. Chairs scraped linoleum, and the crowd surged toward the door.

"Where'd Camille get money to burn?" Ronny tugged at his beard.

I shrugged. Did it come from a life insurance policy or a victim's reparation fund? Had she saved it? Or was it payment for arson? If so, who was the paymaster?

"Well hell, she ain't got a mortgage. She's living and eating for free at the Brocktons' and getting paid for it, too. Easy work if you can get it."

Lisa weighed in before I could respond to Ronny's comments. "There's nothing 'easy' about cleaning a huge house, cooking, and keeping up a yard. Just because you think it's woman's work doesn't mean it isn't hard."

Ronny's face turned the color of raw steak. Lisa's blanched. Turning on her heel, she brushed past me and left the room. I looked away, studying the pattern of lines in the linoleum, avoiding Ronny's eyes and his furious embarrassment, wondering how Lisa would pay for her criticism.

In a moment Ronny broke the silence. "She must be reading

another one of those stupid books. You know, the ones for people who just can't be happy with all that they've got. Who writes that shit, anyway?"

I shrugged, wanting to take her side but knowing that would make things worse.

"So, you going back up there tonight, bud?"

Having witnessed the scene with Lisa, I felt as if I owed him. "Yeah. You, uh, thinking you might come along?"

"Nah." He yawned. "I'm going to get a beer and hit the hay early. Been milling oak all day. That's wood with an attitude." He squeezed my shoulder, digging the point of his thumb into the soft tissue below my collar bone. Payback for my glimpse of the holes in his castle walls. I didn't flinch, didn't give him any satisfaction. He removed his hand and slapped my back "You be careful, bud. You saw that new rock heap this morning, didn't you?"

"Yeah. I saw it."

The cairn had appeared after a four-day hiatus. Made of flat and chipped stones, it leaned against a tree beside the road not far from the construction site. Clearly the work of the careless builder, it resembled the one I'd seen near Lee Fosmark's trailer before the fire.

CHAPTER 22

Despite the broiling western sun, the interior of the lodge was dim behind drawn curtains. I'd locked all the windows before I left, and now I reversed the process and flicked on a box fan in the living room. It drew in air as sticky as fresh cotton candy. Peeling off my shirt and scraping my shoes from my feet, I dropped onto the sofa, massaging the spot under my left shoulder blade where a muscle knotted and jumped. My anxious brain clicked words together like rosary beads. "Fire. Fire. Tonight. Tonight." I closed my eyes just for a moment.

Nat picked up the receiver and punched in ten numbers. I knew the call was to me, knew he'd get my machine. I even knew the message he'd leave: "It's Nat. Susanna's dead. Forgive me." Six words. No explanation. No comfort.

I watched as he set the receiver back in the cradle and stared at the picture of my mother on the mantel, fully aware that I was dreaming, that I couldn't change what would happen next. For the first time though, I was conscious of something else—a tingle of impatience. He moved down the hall. Feet heavy with disloyalty and guilt, I trailed him.

Nat entered the bedroom and bent over Susanna. A tear fell onto the ragged welt that circled her neck, and he straightened, wiping his eyes with the heels of his hands. Leaning heavily against the bureau, he tore the final page from a paperback thriller, scrawled a few sentences and anchored it under his wallet. He plucked a snarled

205

blanket from the foot of the bed, shook it out, and laid it over Susanna, drawing it up to her chin. With his fingers, he combed her damp hair out across the pillow, closed her sightless eyes, and lay down beside her, the rifle between them. He stretched his arm, fitted his finger to the trigger and opened his mouth to take communion with death.

The rifle recoiled in grim and unholy silence. Nat's body bucked. Blood, brain, and bone sprayed across the carved headboard. His arms reached out to me, then fell.

I awoke, hot and angry, to the call of a whippoorwill and the whine of a mosquito beside my left ear. I slapped at it, knowing it would elude me. The windows framed squares of deep gray lit by small strobing lights. Fireflies. I sat up among the damp and sagging cushions, pinching my watch to make it glow green. Nearly ten. I'd slept too long.

I shrugged into my shirt, stepped into my shoes, strapped on my gun, and made my way to the kitchen to brew a pot of coffee and piece together a sandwich: ham and Swiss cheese on rye, with lots of brown mustard. I put it into a plastic bag and tossed in a handful of malted milk balls in case coffee didn't give me enough of a charge.

Closing the windows again, I turned off the kitchen light, took my rifle from the rack, locked the door behind me, and picked my way slowly across the porch and down the steps, letting my eyes adjust to the night. On the ridge above the lodge a fox yipped, and nearby some small creature scurried for shelter, rustling leaves crisped by the early summer drought.

Untying the rope, I jumped into the boat, set the knapsack down, and hunkered over the motor. As I braced my left hand against the gunwale, I smelled it. Gasoline.

I ran my right hand over the motor, searching for a leak. I touched a severed hose. "Son of a bitch!"

Grabbing the knapsack, I vaulted to the dock and ran for the

SUV. I had no time to take the canoe, no time for stealth. The engine ground for what seemed like hours, then caught, and I slammed the shift into first and plowed through the gravel toward the road, rolling down the windows as I went, checking the oil light, wondering why he hadn't sabotaged my rig as well as the boat. The wheels shimmied and slewed, then struck the asphalt. I shifted and jammed the gas pedal against the floor. Trees raced toward me at the edges of my headlights. The engine whined, and I toed the clutch and gripped the shift again when I reached the straightaway beyond Silver Leaf Hollow.

A ragged figure hurtled from the woods at the muzzy edge of the headlights. He semaphored his arms once, and then flung them wide.

I braked, my hand drifting to my gun. "Who are you?" A long coat, buttoned to the neck, flapped around stringy legs and bare feet; gray hair straggled from beneath the ski mask that covered his face. Was this the man who'd been camped on the mountain? A hobo who'd happened by and saved my life the night the snake bit me? Or was this the arsonist, trying to distract me, keep me from getting to the construction site?

"Damn!" My head pounded with possibilities. Drawing my revolver, I braked harder, skidding. I wanted this man. I wanted the answers he could give me.

The tires locked against the asphalt with a rending squeal, and I stopped thirty feet from him. I yanked the shift into neutral, leaned out the window, and aimed the gun at his head. His dirty hands were open and empty. No weapon. Unless he had one under the coat. "You're under arrest. Lie down and put your hands above your head."

In the span of a second, the man shook his head, pointed up the road, drew a forefinger across his throat, and plunged into the woods.

"Stop!" My finger tightened on the trigger, but I didn't fire.

Limbs swung back into place behind him. I heard a few twigs snap over the rumble of the idling engine, and then the woods were silent.

"It won't work," I told the silent woods. "You'll have to do more than that to keep me away." I nudged the shift into first and fed gas, easing over to the right shoulder. I wanted to leave any footprints he'd made undisturbed. In the morning I'd return with the camera and photograph them. And I'd ask around about that coat—gray-blue and studded with silver buttons, it had hung to his ankles. People would remember a coat like that, even if it had been stashed away in an attic for years. It shouldn't take long to find where it had been stolen from, and maybe I could lift some fresh fingerprints.

I jerked the shift into second, then braked. If I marked this spot tonight, I wouldn't have to search for it in the morning. Turning in the seat, I snapped on the dome light and surveyed the heap on the back seat. Snatching up an empty water bottle, I tossed it out the window and followed it with a couple of cola cans. They clinked off the asphalt and bounced into the grass on the shoulder. Satisfied, I clicked off the dome light and reached for the shift. That's when I saw a knee-high glitter at the boundary of the headlights.

Frigid teeth champed my neck, sending blades of ice slicing across my back and shoulders. Gun in hand, I eased forward a few feet and peered into the funnel of light. There!

I braked and slipped the shift into neutral. Still holding my gun, I kept one eye on the woods where the stranger had disappeared and crept toward the wire stretched across the road. No, not a wire. A thin strand of fishing line. Transparent. Except where it twisted and threw back the light.

I followed it to the right and found it had been wrapped twice around a young white birch tree and tied off. On the opposite side and a little farther up the road, the line made a half turn around a young maple, then looped into a halter for a stick lodged against the triggers of a shotgun. I didn't have to look at the stock to know it had a rattlesnake carved on one side. I didn't have to turn my head and trace the trajectory to know the shot would have struck the SUV as I passed.

Nausea knotted my stomach, bile surged into my throat. If the timing had been right and the aim solid, the shot would have caught me in the face and neck.

Shivering, cold sweat trickling down my spine, I grabbed a T-shirt from the back seat. Digging my knife from my pocket, I pulled the line taut at the birch on the right side of the road and sliced through it. Using the T-shirt as a glove, I removed the rocks that anchored the shotgun in place and carried it to my rig, coiling up the fishing line as I went. I doubted crime lab technicians would find any fingerprints on it. But I had to try.

I stowed the gun in the back, then leaned against the rear door, willing myself to stop trembling. Someone had channeled me toward this spot, tampering with the boat to force me to drive, betting I'd be angry and distracted, moving too fast to notice the trap. And the ragged intruder had warned me. But hadn't removed the trap. Had he wanted me to find it intact? Had he thought I would learn something from it?

A sharp crack echoed across the lake. My head snapped toward the construction site. A second percussion shattered the night. I lunged behind the wheel and took off.

CHAPTER 23

Above the shrieking growl of the engine, I heard a series of sharp reports from across the lake. Gunfire. The siren gasped into a sobbing wail, and I rocketed past Stub's garage just as he rolled up the door to release the fire engine. I tore across the dam, past the store and post office and Willie Dean's dock. I swayed through the final turn, and the gunfire grew louder—a mix of calibers, a deadly drumming that thickened the stagnant air.

Shafts of harsh light illuminated the construction site, casting razor-edged shadows. In the makeshift kitchen area a group of men stood in a rough circle, aiming their guns toward the dark perimeter of the site. I leaned on the horn as I turned off the main road. Ahead of me, halfway to the first house, Willie Dean's truck sat canted in a ditch. He hunkered behind it.

"Stay down," I yelled as I roared past, blasting the horn, hoping the workers would recognize my SUV and respect my badge even if they didn't respect me. Behind me the fire truck's siren let loose a throbbing howl.

The young worker with the earring leveled his rifle in my direction. I flinched, hunching behind the wheel. The man with the bristling beard clamped a huge hand on the kid's rifle barrel and levered it toward the ground. I braked hard, defining an arc in dry earth that would someday be a landscaped lawn or garden.

"Everyone okay?" I vaulted to the ground.

"Yeah. We're just fucking fine!" Diamond Stud jerked the rifle from his friend's hand and glared. "We enjoy having some kamikaze lob grenades at us."

"Grenades?"

"You think we don't know grenades?"

This wasn't the time to argue. "How close did they hit?"

"Can't tell." The man with the beard pointed toward the top of the slope. "Up there somewhere. In the dark, with everyone yelling and shooting, I don't know exactly how near they were."

"How long since the last explosion?"

"Five minutes. Maybe ten."

Siren bawling, the fire truck lumbered into the turn below me, with Ronny close behind. From the corner of my eye I saw Willie Dean creep out from behind his truck and flag them down, pointing in my direction. I motioned for them to stay back and scanned the site for flames or rising smoke. The odor of gunpowder stung my nose and clotted in my throat, but I smelled no burning wood, spotted no flickering fire.

"He's probably gone. But we'll need to make sure." I directed my words to the men who'd been the most vocal, betting they were ready to take some action. "Split up into teams of two or three, turn on every light you've got, and aim the ones you can toward the perimeter. Make a lot of noise. Let him see your guns, but don't fire unless he shoots first."

Several of the men nodded and began tapping partners and checking their guns.

"I'm going to bring the firefighters up," I told the workers, making quick eye contact with each one, "and let them check over the buildings, make sure nothing is smoldering that might ignite later. And I'll need someone to come with me to find where the grenades landed."

Diamond Stud's eyes narrowed, but his bearded friend nodded. "Yeah. I'll get everyone going on the lights." He turned to the others and gave directions.

As they moved off among the houses, I strode down to the fire truck. Stub sat at the wheel; Ronny leaned against the door, Willie Dean beside him. "There's no sign of a fire," I told them. I nodded at Willie Dean. "You were here first. Did you see anything unusual?"

"Besides twenty guys shooting at me?" He laughed and looked to Ronny and Stub for approval. "That unusual enough for you?"

I brushed it aside. "Anything else? Anyone driving away from the site? Running along the road?"

He scratched his head, then shook it. "Nope."

"What happened?" Stub pointed toward the workers. "Were they setting off fireworks?"

"No, they say someone lobbed in grenades."

"Grenades!" Willie Dean's eyes widened. "Where would you get grenades?"

"Shit, almost anywhere," Stub said.

"Yeah," Ronny agreed, rubbing his eyes. "If you've got the dough, you can get hold of all kinds of military stuff like that."

"Really?" Willie Dean stared at him. His amazement seemed false. An act?

"Sure," Stub said. "Maybe you should get some and give them to the tourists who can't get a fish on the line. They can just pull the pin and lob the grenade into the lake and kablam, they've got their limit. Fish might fall right into the boat, too."

"Wow!" Willie Dean rubbed his chin and the others laughed the way men do when pressure is suddenly lifted.

"Shit, Stub," Ronny said, "now you're giving him ideas." He turned to me. "We ought to go up there and check things out."

"I know. That's what I told them you'd do."

"Think you can get them to hold their fire?" Stub pointed

toward a group of men marching toward one of the most distant houses.

"They're checking the perimeter. They won't shoot unless someone fires at them. Start at the lower end here and stick close together."

"You got it." Stub climbed out of the truck and plunked his helmet on his head. "Grab a flashlight, Willie Dean."

I left them, plucked my own flashlight from the SUV, and returned to the makeshift kitchen. Diamond Stud still cradled his rifle. "Ready to go take a look?" I asked.

"Yeah." The man with the bristly beard shoved out a hand. "Name's Carl, by the way. That's Troy." He nodded at the man with the earring.

I shook Carl's hand. Troy didn't offer to shake. "How many explosions were there?"

"I don't know." Carl rubbed his beard. "It seemed like they were all around us, like they went on forever. But now that things have calmed down, I don't guess there could have been more than half a dozen, maybe even less."

"It wasn't like we could take time out to get an accurate count," Troy sneered.

I directed my questions to him. "Did you see or hear anyone running away?"

"No."

"See any of the grenades coming in?"

"No."

"Me neither," Carl told me. "With the way the noise echoed off the mountains and the houses, it was hard to tell exactly where the attack was coming from." He turned and headed up the hillside, the beam from his flashlight poking into the darkness. "Sounded like most of them hit up here."

Troy leveled his rifle at the darkness. "What if he's still out there?"

"Then you'll wise him up," Carl said. "Raise his IQ by about thirty caliber. My money's on you, Troy boy."

Troy grinned and puffed out his chest in a way that told me he didn't understand sarcasm, then hurried to take the lead. I followed along a roughly graded road, playing my flashlight into the heavy shadows beside stacks of bricks and piles of lumber.

"Here's one crater," Troy called, circling his flashlight beam around the ragged hole gouged in the side of a foundation.

"And here's another." Carl pointed to the twisted metal frame and broken sill of what had once been a sliding glass door, the fractured boards of a makeshift set of steps.

I peered into the house, saw pieces of glass strewn like popcorn across the subflooring and countertops, embedded in the insulation.

"What a damn mess." Carl touched the warped metal. "We'll have to tear all this out. Order another door. Guess it could have been worse."

"Look over here!" Troy signaled with his light. "Son of a bitch blew up the whole master bathroom."

"Tell me that's not the one with the custom tub," Carl pleaded.

"Wish I could," Troy called back. "It took out the skylights, too. And that fancy chandelier."

"That'll set us back six weeks. Maybe more. One-way glass, chandelier imported from someplace in Europe, marble floor, mirrored tile. That bathroom was gonna be a regular work of art."

I listened to the reverence in his voice and realized that if one of the workers was behind the attack, it wasn't Carl.

"Here's another one." Troy's voice echoed from inside a house off to our left, sadness wrapped around his words. "Got the kitchen. Blasted the oak cabinets to bits."

"Bastard knew where to hit us to hurt us the most."

I nodded, making a note of that as I drew a mental map and considered how I would have executed the attack. "I'm guessing he watched the site from the tree line over there." I pointed toward the edge of what had been Tom Andersen's apple orchard and the wall where Freeman's property began. "When your patrol reached the bottom of the development, he ran in. He got the kitchen and bathroom, threw one up against the sliding door, and maybe lobbed a couple at random. Probably took him less than a minute."

"Seemed like an hour at the time," Carl said. "I've never been in combat, but I've heard people say time seems to stand still. Tonight I knew what they meant. Even caught myself praying. I'm not the kind who does that every day."

I understood. Prayer was pretty much off-limits to men in the Stone family. After all, prayer too often involved asking for help.

"I guess you're not worth what they're paying you to stay up here, Sergeant." Troy strode down the slope, rifle over his shoulder, and halted two feet in front of me. "You're not stopping this guy."

I recognized that this was a time for reassurances, not recriminations, so I didn't mention that DeFazio had barred me from the property. "If someone is really determined, it's almost impossible to stop him. Just ask the guys who guard the president." Troy's eyes remained hard. "It seems like you had a pretty good security system in place," I said, stroking his ego, "but he must have watched long enough to find a weak spot." The spot I'd tried to tell DeFazio about weeks ago. "Were you walking a regular circuit?"

"Yeah," Troy said with pride. "Every ten minutes."

"You could set your watch by him," Carl assured me.

And that's just what the person who threw the grenades did, I thought, as I grappled for a less accusatory way to point out the problem. "Well, if DeFazio won't hire a professional security company after this, you might want to think about a double sentry system. Or mix it up, speed up, slow down, double back. That might keep him off balance, make him think twice."

Troy said nothing. His lips compressed to an angry white line.

"Good idea." Carl laid a hand on Troy's shoulder, and I guessed this wasn't the first time he'd had to redirect the younger man's fury. "Troy, how about you work out a system and brief the others." Troy nodded and Carl turned back to me. "Meanwhile, what about the rest of the night?"

"The firefighters will be here for a while, and I'll put in a call to the fire investigator. I'll patrol until dawn, and as soon as it's light, we'll search for evidence. You might want to get some sleep."

"I don't think I'll ever sleep again. I was down for the count, dreaming about hitting the slot machines in Las Vegas for a big payoff, when that first grenade blew." Carl grinned, teeth flashing against the wiry black beard. "But maybe if I sucked down a beer I could relax."

"I'm staying awake." Troy squinted at me. "To make sure the sergeant does his job."

I shrugged. "Suit yourself. Just don't pick up any fragments, and keep away from this area." I moved my hand in a rough half circle, defining the path I suspected the grenade-thrower had taken. "He might have left footprints." *Might* being the operative word, I thought. The drought had baked the ground, and construction crews would have made many prints, but a running man's shoes could have left their marks. We could get lucky.

"I don't take orders from you." Troy got in a parting shot and headed for the far side of the site.

"He'll do what you ask," Carl told me. "He's just a little hotheaded. Always has to make a show of going his own way." He lowered his voice. "And to tell you the truth, I think he was more scared than the rest of us." He stretched and yawned. "Well, if you don't need me, I'm gonna get a brewski. We'll be dealing with one freaked-out developer in the morning. Not that I blame him. Stuff like this can lower the livability quotient, if you know what I mean."

Rolling his head and flexing his shoulders, Carl started down the road.

"See any fire, Dan?" Stub called from beside the sprawling skeleton of a detached garage.

"No." I walked toward him. "There's a lot of damage, but nothing caught."

"Yeah," Ronny's voice called from off to my left. "Lucky the propane tanks aren't in yet."

"Or the oil tanks for the furnaces," Stub said.

We converged above the kitchen area, where Carl spoke to half a dozen others, pointing to us and to the area I'd warned them away from.

"You sure got here fast," Stub said. "I saw you pass the garage."

"I was out on the road when I heard the explosion. I'd been up at the cemetery." No one would question that. "Who called it in?"

"No one," Stub said. "When I heard that first explosion, I bolted out of bed and hit the siren. No point in waiting for the call."

Willie Dean ambled up, trailed by Evan, Freeman, and Denny. "Where do you think he got the grenades? Think he stole them somewhere and cached them where we couldn't find them when we searched?"

"Huh?" Ronny took off his helmet and scratched his head. "Who?"

"The guy up there on the mountain." Willie Dean gestured

over his shoulder. "Think he brought the grenades when he came here?"

"Could have," Freeman said. "He didn't get them through the mail. And you can't pick them up at Lou Marie's store. Maybe he 'borrowed' somebody's car and drove up to Albany."

I scrutinized Freeman. Did he have a reason for saying Albany? I vowed to check with cops up there and see what they knew about grenades for sale.

"I think we'd know if he stole a car." Ronny squelched that line of thinking.

"Yeah, it's not like we have vehicles to spare." Stub nodded at the four-car garage. "Not like these folks will."

Evan curled his lip at the garage. "A few more bays and this guy can set himself up a dealership."

I let them talk, keeping silent about the shotgun and the man who'd warned me. He was the one person who couldn't have lobbed the grenades. I frowned in disgust. That meant I was back to square one. Again.

Rich Ramseyer puffed his pudgy cheeks and blew out a "pffwah" of disgust as he looked at the remains of the oversized bathtub. "Nothing. I'll bet that's what they're going to find at the lab. Nothing to tell us who did this." The fire investigator yanked a perfectly pressed handkerchief from his rear pocket and blotted his forehead. "But don't worry. I'll go through the motions. That's why they pay me the big bucks." He snorted a laugh and laid a soggy hand on my shoulder. "At least you don't have to check on black market military supplies. These weren't grenades. Just some garden-variety pipe bombs. And my best guess right now is he used fuses instead of timing devices, but I'll know more when I get a look at all the pieces they turn up." He pointed to the team of technicians and deputies combing the ground between the houses and the woods.

"This guy's smart. Bides his time. Picks his moment."

Knows the woods, I thought. *Doesn't make a sound or leave a trace.* That took me right back to some of the men who'd come when the fire siren sounded. Ronny treaded softly enough to come up on me unnoticed a few weeks ago. Evan always got his deer. So did most of the other men. Freeman, so the story went, once walked up behind a berry-eating bear and her cubs and walked away undetected. Willie Dean seemed dumb and clumsy, but he'd been acting the fool for years. I couldn't count anyone out.

"Well, I'll get back to my air-conditioned office and write up my report. Such as it is." Ramseyer mopped the back of his neck, waddled to his car, and rolled down the hill.

I watched him go, exhaustion beating on my shoulders with the morning sun. It would be pointless to check alibis. A man smart enough not to be seen would be smart enough to make it appear he'd been somewhere else. But I'd have to ask. And put myself back on the outside.

I slammed my hand against the fender. I needed one shred of hard evidence. One link in a chain that would lead me to the arsonist. Then I remembered the shotgun I'd handed off to Ramseyer to deliver for me. Maybe the man who'd warned me off had seen the person who set it up.

All I had to do was find him and ask.

The markers I'd left along the road the night before were gone. The dust between clumps of grass on the shoulder had been swept with a pine branch that brushed away his footprints. The fishing line had been untied from the white birch—only a thin brown bruise marked the delicate bark.

After ten minutes of searching, I discovered a small branch that might have been broken when the man plunged into the woods. I cast back and forth, working my way up the ridge, but he'd left no further signs and no tracks. At least none that I could detect.

I thought of calling for a tracking dog, but remembered the last time there'd been a search the department had had to hire the dogs and their civilian handler. That meant money. That meant no way.

I leaned against the fender, drinking an overpriced can of lime pop that Louisa Marie had condescended to sell me, asking myself questions I couldn't answer.

I finished the soft drink and crumpled the can between my palms, then tossed it onto the floor in the back. I'd been at Hemlock Lake for two months and I didn't know any more than when I'd arrived.

When I got back to the lodge, I called the sheriff.

"Bombs. Sabotage. Ambushes." North's voice rumbled down the phone line. "It sounds like you're in someone's way and he wants you out of there." He paused and I heard a tapping noise, imagined him knocking his pipe against the arm of his chair. "I guess, in a twisted way, we can call those signs of progress. But we still know next to nothing."

I told myself not to get angry; he was only echoing my own thoughts. "We might if the guys at the lab got to the evidence I've sent in. I've had stuff sitting down there for weeks."

The sheriff sighed. "They're overworked and they've had two guys quit. There are a lot of cases piled up." He sucked in air, inflating his voice. "Look, Dan, sending you up there was my idea and I thought it was a good one at the time." I heard the scratch of a match, and then he sucked at his pipe. "But you're a sitting duck. I thought I was helping you, but I was wrong."

"That doesn't matter. I'm not leaving."

"All right." His voice sounded old, exhausted. "It's still your call."

CHAPTER 24

On the morning of the Fourth of July, having stood my solitary watch at the construction site, I lay back in the canoe at the center of the lake and watched a carmine sun claw its way over the mountains. It rose higher, color fading to a white blaze that leeched the blue from the sky around it. Patriotic, I thought. And the sign of another scorching day.

Prodded by the sheriff, DeFazio had hired a security firm, but still I'd stuck to my schedule—keeping watch by night like some demented shepherd guarding an indifferent flock, waiting for revelation and fearing it at the same time.

On the positive side, I'd crossed all the youngsters off my suspect list—by questioning their peers I'd found that all had been elsewhere when the bombs were tossed. But no one admitted to knowing anything about that long coat the stranger on the road had been wearing. And neither the sheriff nor the media received a letter claiming credit. If eco-terrorists were behind the attack, they weren't acting the way they usually did. Was the arsonist an outsider or one of us? My mind chased itself in circles trying to decide.

When I reached the lodge, I dragged the canoe out of the water and carried it to the garage, where I turned it over and checked the patches on the bottom. I'd found the holes— eighteen of them—when I returned after the bomb attack. I let on to Willie Dean that I believed the holes were due to age and said I'd keep patching material handy and check the bottom every day. I'd replaced the sliced gas hose on the powerboat but never mentioned it to anyone but the sheriff. With stubborn and twisted logic, I didn't lock up the SUV or get the alarm I'd considered. That would be admitting I knew the oil spill hadn't been an accident, and I'd be damned if I'd give the vandal that satisfaction. I was beginning to wonder about my sanity.

The air inside the lodge was dense, the walls and floor and furniture radiating steamy heat. I opened the windows and turned on the fan, then poured myself a glass of orange juice and cooked a high-cholesterol breakfast. Greasy bacon and buttered toast put me to sleep quicker than bourbon ever had. But without alcohol, the dream's sharp edges cut deeper into my brain.

They lay on the bed, unmoving. Blood congealed on the headboard, clotted on the pillow, dried black against Susanna's golden hair.

I dragged my gaze away, pushed Nat's wallet aside, and studied the slanting letters of the note he'd left behind. The pencil point had dug into the flimsy paper, ripping through it. "She got tangled in the tow rope. I couldn't save her. My fault. I should have been stronger. Forgive me."

A fly circled the lamp beside the bed, then dropped to Nat's bare shoulder. It rubbed its front legs together, like a man sharpening a carving knife before dissecting the Thanksgiving turkey. The fly took off again, circled Susanna's head, lit on the bridge of her nose. I lunged for it, brushing it off with one hand, catching it against the other, crushing it. As if it meant something to protect her from a fly. As if it meant I hadn't failed her.

Another fly buzzed near the window and I drew the blanket over her face. But not Nat's. Let the flies have him. I studied his ravaged face, committing the horror to memory. Dry sobs convulsed my chest.

I woke up knowing the image burned into my brain was memory, not dream.

"About time you got here, Uncle Dan." Ronny's daughter Julie, wearing a bright orange swimsuit and a striped towel tied around her waist emerged from a crowd of teenagers, grinned, and handed me a red, white, and blue helium balloon. "I was hoping you'd show up before supper so that Mom will be busy talking to you when I fill my plate." She pointed to a string of tables, covered with red paper, laden with covered dishes, and surrounded by women setting out utensils. Beyond the tables, Willie Dean poured ice into sweating washtubs filled with canned soft drinks while Freeman, Evan, and Ronny stood at attention beside a row of sizzling barbecue grills. The aroma of searing beef and chicken swirled through the heavy air, mixing with the scents of warm beer, perfume, and perspiration.

"Why's that?"

"So she won't make me eat any bean salad to be polite to Mary Lou. Or so you can eat it if she makes me put it on my plate."

"Oh yeah?" I accepted the balloon, pushed a strand of hair off her sticky forehead, then rested my forefinger on the tip of her nose. "What do I get in return?"

Cocking her head, she gave me a broad smile. For a second I saw Lisa at that age, teasing me into letting her ride on the handlebars of my bike, or buy her a soda. I wondered how things might have turned out if she hadn't been Ronny's girl. "I'll steal you an extra one of Camille's brownies." Julie ran her tongue over her lips. "They're yummy."

I spotted Camille at the end of the table, closest to me. She peeled crinkled plastic wrap from a platter, glanced at me, then half-turned away, making it clear she was the one doing the ignoring.

"Two brownies," I bargained, thinking I'd cut out of line before I reached the desserts. I wasn't sure how Camille and I had reached this place, and I didn't want to think about what I'd have to do to turn things around. But it was for the best. She was still a suspect. The Brocktons retired early each evening; Camille had no one to vouch for her on the night of the bombing.

"Deal!" Julie seized my hand and shook it. "Let's go get plates."

"Not so fast, young lady." Lisa put her hand on Julie's arm. "Our guests eat first, you know that."

"Ah, Mom." She tossed her head. "There are hundreds of them. And I'm really hungry. I've been swimming all afternoon. I can't wait."

"Go get a soda from Willie Dean." Lisa slipped something into Julie's hand. "And nibble on this." She put a finger to her lips. "Don't tell the others."

Julie and I glanced down at the napkin and the thick hunk of carrot cake it contained. "Oh boy." She sprinted away.

"It won't spoil her appetite," Lisa told me. "At that age nothing does."

I grinned, remembering some of the snacks I'd put away before dinner during my teenage years. "How's it going?"

"Terrific." She grinned back. "Better than I ever dreamed. Look at this crowd." She swung her arm, taking in knots of people lounging in chairs and on blankets clustered in the growing shadows under the trees, swimmers bobbing in the sunset-tinged lake, and kids and dogs racing along Willie Dean's dock. "Even some of the construction workers came."

"You did a good job getting the word out and drawing people in. Cars and trucks are crammed in all the way back through town. I parked up near the road to the cemetery."

"You should have brought the boat over."

"Yeah, I should have. Guess I wasn't thinking clearly."

"And no wonder. You look like you're dead on your feet." She lowered her voice, took a half step toward me. "Ronny says you've been at the construction site every night for a month." She put her finger to her lips again. "Don't worry. I haven't told anyone."

She gestured toward Troy and Carl and some of their buddies, who were placing a piece of plywood across two sawhorses. "It's nice of them to help, isn't it? I mean, they could have just stayed away, considering the kind of welcome they got, and the fire and bombs and all. Ronny says they hadn't been all that friendly themselves, and they'd get a free show whether we liked it or not. Well, all that's true, but Mary Lou said it was time we cleared the air. So she went up this morning and invited them. Told them we weren't against them personally, just against having so much development so fast." Lisa lowered her voice to a whisper. "She bought their tickets."

I shifted my gaze to Mary Lou, who held a jar of relish out to Ronny and made a turning gesture with her right hand. He laid aside his barbecue fork, twisted the lid without effort, and handed it back. I wondered if he knew about her generosity and had accepted it, or whether Lisa had kept that secret, too.

"But it's more than just growth, isn't it?" Lisa's brow furrowed, casting a shadow across her eyes. "Ronny says that once people around here see those houses, the furniture and cars, none of us will be happy with what we have. He says our houses will look cobbled together and our furniture worn out. Ratty. Not even good enough to give to charity."

I half agreed with that, but leaped to the defense. "Nobody's going to toss out their family heirlooms to keep up with new-comers."

She punched me lightly on the shoulder. "You know what I mean. Ronny's scared more people will sell their land to make quick money. And he could be right." She chewed at her lower lip.

I avoided her eyes, telling myself selling wouldn't be about money for me. It would be about unshackling myself from the past.

"Nobody up here is rich," she went on. "We're all about the same. We see nice things in magazines and on television, but that's not real, not next door."

"Lisa!"

We turned to see Mary Lou pointing at her watch. "Time to get dinner underway if we're going to get finished by dark."

"Gotta go." Lisa squeezed my arm. "I'll save some slaw for you."

The first rocket rose screaming into the night, burst with a boom that shook the ground, and sent a shower of green sparks drifting down the sky.

The crowd clustered on the shore gasped with delight.

The children on the dock squealed and jumped, rocking the floats and sending bright ripples out into the lake.

Unbidden, a sigh of delight escaped my lips, as it had the first time my father set off a small rocket over the lake. I could almost hear the scrape of the kitchen match, the hiss and bang, could almost see colored sparks drifting to earth like bright snow. Clutching that memory, I edged back to the road, distancing myself from the crowd.

Another rocket flared. Then two more.

Ronny strolled up the slope and stood beside me at the edge of the road. "Makes you feel like a kid again, don't it?" He glugged down beer and craned his neck as a second rocket exploded into a dozen white flares that detonated into glittering blue stars.

"It does."

"You leaving?"

"Thought I would. But I want to check on the construction site first."

"Don't they have security guards there now?"

"Yeah, but I'm still keeping watch."

"Don't blame you. I'll walk with you."

He finished the beer and crumpled the can against his forehead, a sign it was the sole survivor of a six pack. Two rockets went up together, red and blue. We ambled down the road into the shadows, Ronny humming "Hotel California." In front of us, a light from the development sparkled through the trees.

"This turned out pretty good," Ronny said. "Made us some real money."

I knew that was all I'd ever get in the way of thanks for my part in it. I could take it or leave it. "I'm glad."

"Yeah. We'll have enough to—"

A loud explosion sounded behind us. I hit the asphalt and rolled into the ditch on the lake side of the road. Ronny did the same.

A firecracker arced from behind the stone wall that bordered the road and hit in front of us, its fuse sizzling.

I heard a second explosion.

"Son of a bitch!" Ronny leaped from the ditch, hurdled the wall. I heard rocks scrape against each other, tree limbs snap. "Come back here!"

Someone crashed to the ground with a howl of pain.

"Serves you right, you bastard!"

Springing to my feet, I vaulted the wall and dropped into a well of shadow. A rocket exploded above the lake. By the wavering light I saw two figures wrestling in the underbrush. A fist drew back, connected with bone.

"Oowww. Stop. It's me." Willie Dean's voice. "It was a joke."

The fist connected again with a damp, sick crunch.

I stumbled through the brush, gripped the collar of Ronny's shirt. "That's enough."

He drew his fist back again, and I trapped it with both hands. "Ronny, you've hit him enough."

"Stay out of this, bud." He tore his fist loose.

By the light of another aerial explosion I saw Willie Dean's slack and bloody face. I jerked hard on Ronny's shirt, rolling him toward me. He turned dead weight and took me over with him, slamming me into a stump. A burning pain shot across my back, and I curled into a ball, writhing in agony.

"I told you to stay out of this. I'm sick of that sorry little son of a bitch and his jokes." Another rocket lit the sky and I saw Ronny's face, the color of a fresh scab. "I'll bet he tossed those bombs. Probably laughed himself sick over that one. I'm going to beat him to a bloody pulp. I don't care if he never gets up."

"You'll have to beat me first." I struggled to my knees, crawled toward Ronny and Willie Dean.

"If that's the way you want it." Ronny grabbed my belt and threw me to the ground. Another bolt of pain sliced my back from kidney to kidney. Green nausea cramped my stomach. "He's not worth it, Dan. It's time he learned a lesson."

Ronny drew back one leg, cocked the knee, preparing to kick Willie Dean in the groin. I clawed for my gun. A rocket burst like thunder overhead, releasing a downpour of silver sparks.

No. A gun's the last resort.

Ronny paused for half a second, and I caught his foot and heaved. Propelled forward, he flailed his arms, snatched at the branch of a young oak, and fell. I flung myself on top of him. Ronny bucked, tore one arm free, and whipped it against the side of my head.

"Don't expect any mercy, bud." His breath reeked of beer and barbecue.

I rolled away again. He lurched to his feet and came at me.

"Daddy?" Julie's voice. Ronny halted. "Daddy? I saw you go down the road. Where are you?"

"Over here," I yelled. "In the woods. Behind the wall."

"What are you doing?" The next rocket revealed her, straddling the wall. "And what's wrong with Willie Dean? Why is he all bloody?"

Grasping a tree trunk, I reeled to my feet and stared at Ronny's bulk. The flaring light showed him combing leaves from his beard with his fingers.

"Willie Dean's all right, honey," Ronny said, panting. "He fell down. He'll be okay in a minute."

"It doesn't look like he just fell down." She swung the other leg over the wall as Willie Dean twitched and moaned.

"He did," I said, supporting Ronny's story. The easy path. "Willie Dean thought he saw somebody prowling up on the hill." I gasped for air. "When he went to check it out, he tripped and rolled. Knocked himself stupid." Dragging myself to Willie Dean's side, I put my fingers on the pulse point in his neck. "He'll be okay in a few minutes. Why don't you take your dad back to the lake?"

"No." Ronny took a step toward me, breath huffing from his mouth.

Julie looked up as a rocket burst in a cloud of red and white. "Come on, Dad, you'll miss the ending."

"No. You go on back. Now."

"I don't want to walk back alone." She jumped from the wall, then hesitated. "I'll stay here and help you and Uncle Dan." It was both statement and question.

"Let it go, Ronny," I whispered.

"Stay out of it, Dan," he whispered back. But in the fading light I saw his fists uncurl slowly. In a moment he turned toward his daughter. "Get back over that wall. You'll get into this poison ivy and itch for a week."

"But Uncle Dan's in it," she whined.

"Uncle Dan don't have the brains God gave a brick." Ronny clambered over the wall, towing Julie behind him. "I'll find you later," he told me.

I didn't doubt that he would.

I helped Willie Dean to his feet, hoisted him over the wall, and slung his arm across my shoulder, half walking, half dragging him. Fireworks sent our shadows lurching around us in a crazed dance.

"I was just fooling around, Dan," he mumbled from between swollen lips. "Trying to get a rise out of you, that's all."

"It wasn't funny, Willie Dean."

He rubbed his bleeding nose on his sleeve. "I saw you two start down the road and remembered I'd bought a few of those big blasters and thought, 'Hey, I'll see how high old Dan can jump.'" He coughed and spit. "I don't know why Ronny got so mad," he said, his voice an insistent whine. "I was just having some fun, that's all. Just playing a little joke."

"Sometimes you go too far."

I helped him to the recliner in his living room and left him for Priscilla to patch up. I'd had all I could take of his sense of humor.

When I got home, the lodge was stifling and the red light on the answering machine blinked like a glowing ember. I punched the "play" button as I hurried toward the kitchen to scrub off poison ivy oil with the brown laundry soap stowed under the sink.

The halting words from the machine stopped me in the doorway: "Mr. Stone. This is Jessica Bolton. At the nursing home." As I turned and walked back to the machine, she said, "Your father's had another stroke. It was quite severe. He's in the hospital."

I laid my hand over the message light, as if I could feel my father's fading pulse.

Jessica took a breath and said, "The doctors think he doesn't have much time left."

I'd waited for this call since October.

I'd thought it would bring relief.

It didn't.

CHAPTER 25

My father seemed to wither as I watched. "Haven't had any rain for a month. Lake's down about a foot and I've been running the hose on Mom's rosebushes." I pried the words from my raw throat, scraping them across dry lips. I'd been talking most of the night.

My father's right hand plucked at the sheet that covered his shriveled legs and shrunken chest. His left eye remained shut, the lid sagging, the eyeball beneath it compressed into the socket. His right eye, yellowed and cloudy, twitched back and forth. Not encouraging signs, a nurse had admitted.

A thin bead of spittle rolled from the corner of his drooping lips. I blotted it with a tissue. His skin felt slack under my fingers; it seemed to draw away from the white whiskers covering his cheeks and chin. His breath carried the scent of the damp underlayer of the forest floor—the sweet and musty odor of warm decay.

"We had a big Fourth of July celebration." I tossed the tissue into a wastebasket and took a long swallow of water. It burned the back of my throat. "Had a company put on a fireworks show over by Willie Dean's dock. Lots of noise and color. Blue, green, red, white. Looked real pretty reflected in the water. Like the flowers in Mom's garden. She would have loved it."

I'd talked about my mother a lot during the night. I'd related incidents from my childhood, recalled my long-dead grandparents, verbally replayed football games I'd suited out for,

World Series contests we'd watched, fishing trips we'd taken. But I hadn't spoken a word about Nat or Susanna, although they'd crowded my brain. I wondered if he remembered that Nat was dead, or if the stroke had wiped that horror away. Was his roving gaze searching for the son he loved best? If he could talk, would he ask me if Nat was on the way? Would I lie and tell him Nat would be here any minute?

I rubbed my tired eyes. There were no rules in this emotional wasteland. I'd have to make my own. I cast back into my childhood, looking for a memory I hadn't already dissected. Hours ago, when I'd found myself repeating a story for the third time, I'd begun to mix in the present, mentioning people he knew, describing some events in excruciating detail, editing others out completely.

I hadn't uttered a syllable about the future, but it loomed ever larger on the landscape of my mind, the way the Rockies tilt out of the plains.

His right eye closed and then opened. I reached for a bottle of saline solution and dribbled some onto his eyeball, blotting the drops that ran down the side of his face, along the edge of his ear, mingling with his waxy hair. The eye winked again, mesmerizing. Could he see the door? Was he watching for Nat?

"We had a great supper, too. Mary Lou brought her bean salad. Lisa made that coleslaw you like. There were hamburgers, hot dogs, and chicken. Ronny and Evan and Freeman cooked. And there must have been two dozen desserts. Cakes and pies and cobblers and cookies." And Camille's brownies, I thought. I hadn't mentioned her, either. They would never meet. The doctor didn't expect him to live until noon.

My father's mouth moved as if he were trying to form a word. I leaned closer, but heard only the soft grunt of each breath.

"Everybody pitched in." I heard my voice falter, the words fracture. Raising the glass, I swallowed the remainder of the water. "Except Louisa Marie, of course. She hasn't allowed herself to have any fun since the day she decided Jefferson was never coming back. Doesn't like others to have much fun, either, but there was nothing she could do to stop us." Not that she didn't try. I thought about her refusing Camille's check and wondered again if there had been something behind Camille's gesture other than simple generosity. Did she care more about being an outsider than she admitted? Or was she trying to buy acceptance and divert suspicion? I put the thought aside and went on, telling the husk that was my father about kids frolicking in the lake, about how Ronny and Stub would overhaul the fire truck.

A nurse cracked the door open and raised an eyebrow at me. I nodded and mouthed the words "I'm okay." She nodded back and crossed the floor on silent shoes, fingered my father's wrist, counting off his dwindling heartbeats. Her lips rolled into a tight line. She tapped the IV bag, nodded again and left, the door swishing behind her.

I took another sip of water and told my father about the jay that perched on the roof and how it felt to let the canoe glide across twilight water. Outside the window, the sky lightened. The eye flicked toward me and away, hypnotically. The fingers plucked at the sheet. The second hand on the bedside clock stutter-swept around the dial. My father and I waited, one long second at a time, for death to stop for him, for the doors of Emily Dickinson's dark coach to open, for him to take his seat and glimpse eternity. I could almost hear the wheels rolling toward us. I had that empty feeling of being left behind I'd get as a child, the certainty of being excluded, cheated out of an adventure that Nat would have—even if that adventure was only a trip to the store while I was at school.

My father's eye flicked faster, the fingers scrabbled at the light blanket, the horny nails and rough skin catching on the fabric with a dry scratching sound. I sat at attention, fingering the call button, knowing I wouldn't push it until the coach had long departed.

A rattling sigh leaked from between my father's lips and lies burst from my own, lies I thought would ease his way. "I've been cleaning out the lodge, Dad. Nothing major, just tossing some old clothes the mice got into, painting the trim. It's looking good. I'm thinking I'll move in permanently. It's peaceful there. And I know everybody in town."

The eye snapped left, right, left, right. Had I reached him? The knot in my chest tightened. I summoned the ghosts.

"Nat's on his way. He got hung up, um, down at the hardware store, and he, uh, had to stop and pick up Susanna." I nearly choked on her name. "They'll be here soon. Susanna . . . Susanna and I are going to start a family. It would be good to have kids running across that porch again, wouldn't it?"

A bubble of spit appeared at the corner of his mouth.

"If we have a boy, we'll name him after you. If we have a girl, we'll name her after Mom. They'll grow up swimming and fishing and running through the woods, just like Nat and I did."

The fingers tightened on the sheet.

"Maybe Nat will get married, too."

The eye flicked right, left, right. The fingers relaxed. A last slow exhale passed my father's lips. His ghost joined the others.

I sat with my lies for a quarter of an hour, then pushed the call button. The nurse steered me from the room, got me a cup of acidic coffee, and turned me over to a self-important little man with pointed shoes. He presented forms and I signed them. He made suggestions and I ignored them. I called the funeral director who'd taken care of Mom, Nat, and Susanna, and told him he had more work. I called the sheriff and disregarded his advice to get a motel room, get some rest, talk with the chaplain.

I drove to the lodge, threw open the windows, and dragged

clothing from my father's closets. I up-ended dresser drawers, emptied the bookcase, ripped papers from cubbyholes in the old secretary in the corner. Opening the cedar chest under the window, I tossed wool shirts and sweaters behind me, digging like a dog through the remnants of my father's life. "You never saw that I had to be who I am, had to be someone besides your son, besides Nat's brother." I pummeled a jacket, threw it to the bed. "No matter what I did, it was never good enough."

I kicked a hairbrush under the bed, booted a wristwatch into the corner. I had given it to my father one Christmas when I'd come home from college. Waterproof and shockproof, it had a tiny compass and an alarm. I'd thought it was the perfect gift for a man who loved to hunt, who sat up late with his friends but needed to rise before dawn. He'd thanked me when he opened the box, but he'd kept another strapped to his wrist, one that Nat had bought. It had a picture of a baseball player on it. The arms, one holding the bat, marked out the hours. It gained an hour a week and the crystal fogged over in the center on damp days. When it finally stopped, he'd slipped it over one of the decorative posts on the dresser.

"Well you're with Nat now." I retrieved my gift from the corner, dropped it on a bare patch of floor, and set my heel on it. The crystal shattered with a sharp crunch. "You're with the son you loved."

Love. Even as I'd lied about Nat and what would happen to the lodge, I'd withheld that word, just as he always had. Gripping the doorknob, I wondered if that had been intentional or merely force of habit. Had I loved him? Had I felt something more than a sense of obligation and place? Had I, in spite of all my vows, become like him?

The phone rang as I crossed the living room and walked down the steps to the lake. The water lay so still it seemed as if it were locked beneath a skin of new ice. I stared into it, looking past my face and into the mud on the bottom. A frog pushed toward the sky, raising a cloud of silt. It broke the surface, sending a half circle of ripples across the reflection of trees and mountains. One eye swiveled in my direction before he blinked and dove for deeper water. I shivered, reminded of my father's eye, wondering again what he'd seen, what he'd known, at the end.

Scuffing along the shoreline, I searched for flat, oval stones that fit comfortably into the V between my thumb and forefinger. When I'd collected an even dozen, I walked to the end of the dock and flung them, my arm cocked. The first two bit into the surface and sank. The third hopped once. Then the angle and release came back to me, and the next few skipped as they should, like they had when I was eight and perfected my technique. I counted ten hops on the eleventh throw, and the final stone literally floated the last few feet, slicing in without a splash. Nat had never been able to skip a stone.

A flash of light, sun on a windshield, caught my eye, and I watched a battered silver car creep hesitantly down the driveway. The engine idled for a few seconds, then gurgled to a halt, and I heard the ratcheting of the emergency brake. Camille stepped out, smoothed a white T-shirt over a pair of green shorts, took a few steps toward me through the gravel, and paused, shading her eyes against the sun.

"I'm sorry about your father," she said. "Mary Lou's worried. She's been trying to call you all morning but you don't answer. She asked me to come by and check on you. See if you need anything."

"Nothing." I turned away, watching ripples slide across the lake, spreading the way talk would about my father's death and how I was taking it.

For a minute there was no sound except the clamoring jay. Then I heard the slap of water on wood and felt the dock bobble beneath me. I didn't turn. "I don't need anything, Camille."

"I know you don't. But sometimes it isn't only about you. Sometimes it's about other people, too."

People who should mind their own business. "I want to be alone."

"All right." Her voice was patient, calm. "I'll tell Mary Lou you said that. But don't think for one minute that will stop her from coming to see you, or stop Alda or Pattie from bringing over cakes and casseroles. Don't think they won't call, whether you answer the phone or not. Don't think you won't get a stack of sympathy cards."

"I won't open them. I don't want sympathy." My skin crawled at the idea of their pity, their mistaken assumptions about my bond to my father.

I heard her sigh. "People here knew your father all their lives. They feel a loss. They need comfort, too."

"Then let them 'comfort' each other. Have one of their potlucks and hug the living shit out of each other. Just tell them to leave me the hell alone."

After a moment the dock jounced. My shoulders relaxed. Then it shifted again, and I realized she'd moved toward me, not away. "It's okay to be angry, Dan. It's a normal phase of grief."

"Who the hell cares?" I screamed at the lake. I spun on her, my jaw tight, blood pounding in my neck and temples, fingernails digging into my palms. I wanted her pity least of all. "Take your goddamn smug amateur psychology and get the hell off my dock." I took a step toward her, an orange roar of rage filling my head.

She straightened her shoulders, tipped her chin back. Tears formed at the corners of her eyes, and I heard the breath catch in her throat. Raising one hand, she spread the fingers slightly and placed them against my chest.

Her hand burned like a brand, scorching the skin beneath my shirt, searing through bone to my heart. I heard myself grunt. My arms dropped and my knees buckled. I fell to the dock, tears burning like acid in my eyes and on my face. I cried for the shell of a man who had been my father. I cried for that flickering eye, the plucking fingers, the words neither of us would say. I cried because I knew the past was immutable, because I was left not with a sense of losing something, but with a sense of never having had it.

Camille knelt and touched my hair. I seized her arm, pulling her tight against me. She gasped. Then her hungry lips rose to meet my own.

CHAPTER 26

The living room was bathed in a wine-red light that made Camille's skin glow like polished copper. Wiping sweat from my forehead with the back of my hand, I sat up and looked away from her nakedness. "I never meant for that to happen."

She stretched, her chest arching. "I could say the same, but I'd be lying." She ran a fingernail down my spine, making me shiver despite the heat, making my groin tighten. A wrenching spasm tore through my gut. I'd betrayed Susanna.

"You're thinking about Susanna, aren't you?" Camille rolled over and snagged the T-shirt she'd shed. "You're human, Dan. You have needs."

"But I should be able to—"

Control myself. Like skipping rocks, control was something I used to think I'd perfected.

I heard the whisper of cloth as Camille shrugged into the shirt, felt the couch shift as she sat up beside me, felt her hand on my thigh, her fingers hot on my skin. "Listen to me, Dan. Nothing you and I do can touch what you had with Susanna. You'll have that forever." She brushed a hand across my hair. "I don't expect to be allowed into those places in your mind or in your heart."

Looking at her sidelong, I felt guilt seep away, leaving exhaustion and an oily, grimy feeling. Her words had created a convenient loophole I could slither through. For the first time, I asked myself what Susanna would have done if I had been the one who died. Would she have cloistered herself? I watched Camille as she buttoned her shorts. My groin tightened again. "What do we do now?"

She shrugged and glanced at my rumpled jeans and shirt. "It's been a while since I've been with a man." Her voice sounded soft, wistful. "Well, I guess you could use the word lonely. Longing." She flushed. "It felt good. It would feel good to be with you again."

I studied her face, weighing her words.

She spread her hands. Her eyes flared like embers fanned by a downdraft. "No strings, no promises. I don't let myself get attached. I intend to drive away at the end of the summer." She ran a fingernail down my back again, circling it slowly at the base of my spine. I felt my breath quicken. She leaned into me, ran the tip of her tongue along the outer whorl of my ear. "I'd like to drive away with a smile on my face."

"I—"

The phone rang. Our heads snapped toward it.

"Mary Lou?" Camille laughed.

I shrugged. It rang again.

"She won't give up. Sooner or later you'll have to answer."

"Later." It rang once more and the machine picked up. I heard my own voice telling the caller to try again. Then the dial tone droned out a message more impersonal than my own. I thought about the person who'd hung up and all the others who would call and drop by before my father was settled in the ground. Having bawled like a baby in front of Camille, and then having made love to her, I felt transparent, vulnerable. Everyone so much as shaking my hand or looking into my eyes would recognize that and, like wolves, sink their teeth into my neck.

"Do you want me to leave?" She hooked a toe on one of the sandals she'd kicked off.

"No." I placed my hand on her arm, feeling the muscle and bone beneath her moist skin.

"But if you don't answer the phone, they'll drive over. Like I did. If they find me here they'll say—"

"They'll say my father is barely cold and I'm between the sheets with a woman." I laughed, the sound harsh and metallic. "I know exactly what they'll say." I put my hands on either side of her face and pressed my lips against hers. Let the wolves tear me apart. "I don't give a damn. They don't make our rules."

My father had gone to church fewer than a dozen times in his life—when he married my mother, the day Nat and I were baptized, and whenever duty called him to a funeral. Still, Mary Lou felt that a religious ceremony was necessary. "If not for you, then for the rest of us," she'd begged.

I'd come to realize that it was easier to give in than to argue. And so, three days after my father's last breath, we clustered beside Nat and Susanna's graves. The fine grass had withered to yellow and lay slack like my father's hair. The descending sun turned the marble monuments the color of wild roses, and a thin sheen of moisture stood out along the jutting ridge of Reverend James Balforth's nose. In a dry and singsong monotone he'd labored for fifteen minutes to resurrect Matthew Stone's memory, praising him as a loving son, a husband and father. He'd called upon Freeman and Evan and others to recount anecdotes from the past. Finally, he'd opened his Bible and asked us to bow our heads in prayer. Beside me Lisa and Ronny bent their necks, but I kept mine stiff, my eyes on the darkening woods beyond the graves.

I let my gaze drift to the lake, lying shadowed by the mountains, then focused on the hole where my father would soon lie. Then I looked at Camille, who stood with one hand gripping Angela Brockton's elbow. On her other side, William

Brockton leaned on a pair of canes. Close to ninety, both of them. I wondered what they thought, what they feared, as they stared into the gaping grave. Thankfully, none of us would recite anything about dust and ashes, or hear a shovel bite into the mound of soil nearby, or flinch from the soft rattling thud of dry earth hitting the coffin. By my request, we'd walk away, leaving Matthew alone on the hill. I'd seen him into the dark coach. Someone else would see him into the ground. Someone would fill the grave tonight, mound the soil, pat it smooth, and sow seeds. But no grass would grow until the drought broke.

"Amen." The minister signaled Mary Lou, who came forward and laid a bouquet of red roses on the coffin lid. One by one, others followed suit, covering the box with a blanket of blossoms. I watched, my jaws locked, waiting for the last blooms to be placed, for the last pair of pitying eyes to slide over me. Reverend Balforth cleared his throat. "Just a reminder. Ronny and Lisa Miller will be hosting a dinner for Matthew's friends and, uh, his family." His gaze flicked to me, then to the grave. "Please drive safely. I hope to see you all in church on Sunday."

"When pigs fly," Ronny whispered.

"Sshhh." Lisa put a finger to her lips.

"You'd have to nail me to the pew." He nudged me with his elbow. "I'd sooner listen to a politician gassing about the deficit or some such shit."

"Well, you don't have to tell the whole world how you feel," Lisa whispered. "And you don't have to be so insensitive. We're not at the Shovel It Inn, Ronny. That's Dan's father in that box."

"It's okay, Lisa." I glanced toward Camille, who baby-stepped beside Angela Brockton, inching toward their car. We'd agreed to meet at the lodge in a few hours. I felt a warm tingle at the back of my neck.

"You holding up okay?" Mary Lou seized my hand. She wore

a gray dress and a black hat that looked like a teacup with a veil. I suspected it had belonged to her mother.

I tore my thoughts from Camille. "I'm doing okay, Mary Lou. Thanks for sending over that casserole."

"Oh, that was no trouble, Dan, you're—"

"Poison." Louisa Marie spat the word into my face and leveled a gnarled finger at my chest. "You killed your father." I heard Lisa draw in a sharp breath, saw Mary Lou's mouth tighten. "Always acting like you were better than the rest of us. Moving away." Louisa Marie looked around at the circle of faces, smiled smugly, and raised her voice. "Then coming back to take sides with those interlopers." She pointed across the lake toward the development site, the sleeve of a faded black blouse sagging from her skinny arm. "Don't think Matthew didn't know what was going on, how you practically accused your friends. Some of us told him the truth."

I opened my mouth, but decided not to give her the satisfaction of argument. Behind her, Ronny ignored Lisa, who tugged at his sleeve, signaling with her eyes that he should do something.

"And now . . ." Lou Marie paused for dramatic effect, making sure all ears strained for the next words. "Now you're sleeping with that mixed-breed slut."

Several people gasped as Lou Marie swung her finger to point across the cemetery at Camille, who'd half-turned to see what was happening. A worried crease appeared between her eyes, then smoothed as she raised her chin, preparing to take what came. Beside her, Angela Brockton tilted her head, puzzled. I wondered if the elderly woman could hear. I tried to cue Camille with my eyes—get into the car and go. One of us should be spared.

"Matthew will be spinning in that grave. And your mother. And Susanna. She's not even gone a year and you take up with some tramp."

The circle of faces seemed to revolve around me. I felt as if I'd been stripped and locked into the stocks on the village green so I could be taunted for my sins.

"That's enough, Louisa Marie." Mary Lou shouldered her way between us, taking my hand and squeezing the fingers. "Dan loved Susanna. He adored her. Everyone knew that. He loved her until the day she died. But life goes on."

"You don't know anything about love!" Lou Marie screamed. She pointed the finger between her sister's eyes. "Death isn't some punctuation mark at the end of your vows. If you love someone, you love him forever. For all eternity."

I heard another quick intake of breath from the crowd around me. Lisa's fingers released Ronny's sleeve and her hands went to her mouth to contain a sound of surprise. For the first time in more than two decades, Lou Marie hadn't directed her remarks through someone else. She'd spoken directly to her sister.

Mary Lou squeezed my hand again. "Not everyone can do that, Louisa Marie. Some of us aren't as strong as you are. We can't tell time by eternity. We need comfort while we're on this earth."

"Comfort!" Lou Marie snorted. She glared toward Camille and then at me, her eyes narrowing, her lips curling with scorn. "Yes, you're getting comfort all right. You think no one saw her car in your driveway? You think we don't know what you did when you drew your grandmother's drapes."

My sense of being caught in a transgression was as strong as it had been when, as a seven-year-old, I'd taken a dollar from my father's wallet, only to have Lou Marie snatch the candy bars from my hand and order me to return the dollar, saying she knew it was stolen because my father always paid my allowance in coins. Now she shot me a look of supreme satisfaction and pointed at the brown graves. "You're the one who should be in the ground. You're poison, Dan Stone. You're poisoning this whole community."

Turning, she strode into the gathering gloom, a twitching shadow among the gravestones.

Mary Lou's fingers crushed my hand, her short nails pinching the skin.

"Well." Ronny looked around, then winked at me. "That was an interesting change of pace. Anyone else ready for a beer?"

A shallow ripple of nervous laughter moved the crowd. Gaping faces turned away from me, Camille herded William and Angela Brockton toward their car, and Mary Lou's fingers relaxed. "Never mind her, Dan. You know how she is, how she's been since Jefferson . . ." She cleared her throat, raised her voice so that everyone could hear. "All of us know you loved Susanna. You would have given her the moon." She peered up at me, her scrap of veil fluttering, and lowered her voice. "Camille is a fine woman, Dan. You've had a rough time of it. You have a right to some happiness."

I wondered about her words later as I stood in Ronny's living room, a beer turning warm in my hand. One by one, my neighbors had come up to me, shifting their feet, gazes wandering quickly from my own. They'd expressed sorrow for my loss, told me how much they'd miss Matthew, and studiously avoided any mention of Louisa Marie's outburst. I decided they felt ashamed of the way she'd ruptured the decorum of the funeral, but they agreed with what she'd said.

Probably every one of them had known about Camille before Louisa Marie broadcast the information. But now it was in the public domain, and they could dissect every facet of our lives and our relationship. I squirmed inside the suit I'd put on for the funeral, wanting to bolt from the house. Control, I told myself. Pride. It only hurts if you care. I lifted my chin, forced myself to remain by the dining room door, and reviewed the reasons I'd checked Louisa Marie off my list of suspects. Living close against her sister, she couldn't have made the bombs, or planted them. But she certainly could have goaded someone else into action.

Lisa, her voice bright and sharp, did all she could to make me feel at home, piling roast beef and potato salad on my plate, standing by me while I forked it into my mouth, chewed, and swallowed without tasting. Mary Lou guarded my other flank, commenting on the berry cobblers, Lisa's crafts, the drought, and a hundred other small things.

Willie Dean, grinning and winking broadly despite his bruised and swollen face, sauntered up after I set my plate aside and gave me a dummy punch to the ribs. "Old Lou Marie sure got riled up. Hee, hee, hee." He laughed out an eruption of scents— garlic, beer, and bratwurst. I focused on the clock on the mantel. *Just get through this.*

"Thought she was gonna pop an artery when she lit into you up at the cemetery. Hee, hee. I'd pay to have a videotape replay of that." Dumping half a bottle of beer down his throat, Willie Dean directed his attention to Mary Lou. "Pay to have a tape of her talking to you after all these years. Kinda scary, though, that part. Kinda of like an omen, maybe. A sign, you know."

"You've had too much to drink, Willie Dean." Ronny seized his arm and towed him toward the porch. "You're a damn fool."

Sometimes fools are the wise ones, I thought as I watched them go. Shakespeare made good use of fools. Sometimes the jester is the only one who can see the truth—or admit it.

Camille's voice was on the answering machine when I got home. "I'd better not come over tonight, Dan. Angela Brockton slipped and fell on the porch steps. She's okay, but she's going to need my help to get out of bed during the night. And I feel like we're under a microscope right now. Probably the way you felt when you were a kid. Anyway, if you need . . . if there's . . . call me if you want to talk."

I replayed the message twice, dialed the first four digits of her number, and glanced at the clock. Eleven-fifty. The Brocktons would be asleep. The ringing would startle them, make them worry the way phone calls in the night can. I set the receiver down, then grasped it again, my palm sweaty, my hand shaking. I wanted to talk to her, to apologize for Louisa Marie.

But what was there to say? Camille and I had agreed our relationship was both physical and temporary. Lou Marie had recognized that from a seat of harsh judgment. I set the receiver back in its cradle.

I walked to the SUV and hauled in stacks of plastic containers, jars of jams and relishes, bags of bread and rolls. Lisa and Mary Lou had packaged up everything left on the table, instructing me which items would freeze and which I'd need to eat right away. I stuffed it all into the refrigerator.

When I was done, I poured three fingers of bourbon into a glass and sat in the porch swing. Through the trees on the far shore I saw a pinpoint of light—perhaps the lamp in Camille's bedroom. I took a long swallow and thought I'd get the canoe out and paddle across the lake.

"And then what? Toss pebbles at her window? Climb up the rainspout?" I laughed at the image and took another swallow.

A barrage of gunfire shattered the air. Dropping the glass, I ran.

Would this never end?

Chapter 27

As I approached the construction site, Willie Dean leaped into the road, aiming a rifle at me. I braked hard, vaulted out, and tore the gun from his hands. "What the hell is going on?"

"I saw somebody sneaking around!"

Three shots blasted from the construction site, and a bullet pinged off of a rock nearby. I raced back and leaned on the horn for a few seconds. "Stop shooting!" I blew the horn three more times. "It's Dan Stone. Stop shooting!"

Footsteps pounded toward us, and headlights swooped in from both sides. Willie Dean squinted into a set of high beams and raised his right hand as Ronny approached.

Willie Dean said, "Get me a Bible and I'll swear on my mother's grave. He had a gas can and he was heading for that first house there." He pointed to a massive two-story home, its huge window frames gaping, still empty of glass.

"And like the idiot you are, you just took a shot at him," Ronny said. "You didn't stop to think that as edgy as everyone is, you'd be touching off a firefight?" He surveyed the rifle-clutching construction workers surrounding us.

"All I thought was I needed to stop him! Before he torched something!"

"Okay, okay." I got between them, put a hand on his sweaty shoulder. "Let's start at the beginning, Willie Dean. Where were you when you saw this person?"

"Down there on the road." He pointed south, over the heads

of Freeman, Evan, and others just arriving. "By the parking lot above my dock."

"What were you doing out there?"

"Couldn't go to bed. Guess I had a little too much to drink over at Ronny's. The room was spinning and all, and Priscilla told me I'd be in deep shit if I hurled on the carpet. So I went out to get some air."

The perfect witness. Drunk. Disoriented. Half-asleep. "And you had your gun with you?" I tapped the barrel of the rifle I'd taken from him.

"Not the first time," he muttered. "The first time I just went out to take a whiz off the porch. But I thought I heard something, so I went back and got the rifle and loaded it, and then snuck out to the road. I heard the noise again, kind of a sloshy-tinny sound, and I went a little farther and sure enough, there he was, kind of scooching along by the wall with a big old can of gas. I could even smell it."

"Could you tell who it was?"

Evan leaned forward. "It was the man on the mountain wasn't it?"

"Oh, hell," Ronny said. "It wasn't him. That son-of-a-bitch is practically invisible. If he's still around. And he don't make any more sound than a ghost. Plus, he's smart. He's not gonna be sashaying along in front of Willie Dean's house, swinging a can of gasoline."

Those were valid points. The others nodded. Stoked by their approval, Ronny said, "And if anybody's going to spot him, it sure ain't gonna be a dumbass like you, Willie Dean." He threw back his head and laughed. "Admit it, you were shooting at a possum, weren't you? Or maybe a raccoon trying to get into your garbage?"

"I saw somebody," Willie Dean protested.

"Sure you did." Ronny winked broadly at the construction

workers. They guffawed.

"I did. I'm sick of eating your shit, Ronny."

Willie Dean drew back a fist and let fly at Ronny. He ducked easily, then raised his own fists. "You going to fight me? You'll be an even bigger fool if you try. Everybody knows that. Everybody but you."

"That's enough." I angled between them again. "Go on home now, Willie Dean. I'll talk to you tomorrow."

"I'm gonna fight him, Dan."

"No. He'll hurt you. Worse than the other night. It's not a fair fight."

"Then give me my gun and I'll make it one." He lunged for the rifle.

I held it over my head. "Freeman. Evan, take Willie Dean home." They hesitated, looking to Ronny for an okay. I raised my voice. "Do the right thing. Get him out of here."

"Okay." Freeman nodded and stepped forward to grasp Willie Dean's elbow. "Come on, Evan."

Evan hesitated again, then followed Freeman's lead. I felt the breath I'd been holding explode from my chest as they moved away. Turning, I studied Ronny, still bouncing on his toes, his fists curled at his belt. Twice now I'd stood between him and Willie Dean. Ronny had always enjoyed a good fight, but it wasn't like him to pick it. Ronny's style was to stand his ground and let the fight pick him. And where was the satisfaction in fighting Willie Dean?

"Want me to get you a puppy to kick?"

Ronny glared at me for a second, then threw back his head and laughed, his chest convulsing. "You're not buying into his shit, are you Dan? You don't believe he actually saw somebody sneaking around with a gas can, do you?" He laughed again, doubling over and gasping for air. "Because if you believe that, I've got some swampland in Florida to sell you. Like I told you the other night, I bet Willie Dean tossed those bombs. Hell, he lives right down the way. It would be the easiest thing in the world."

"Except there isn't any proof."

And not enough evidence to get a search warrant for Willie Dean's house. I'd run that idea past the sheriff, who'd laughed almost as hard as Ronny. "You know those things don't grow on trees," he'd told me. Catching Priscilla alone, I'd taken the long way around the barn to ask her about that night, saying she must have been scared out of her wits when the explosions started. She'd giggled. "Slept through them," she'd told me, tapping the side of her head. "Earplugs. Every night. Willie Dean snores so loud you'd swear someone was taking a chainsaw to the bed. I didn't wake up until he turned on the light and started looking for his pants." I believed her. I doubted Priscilla could lie so convincingly.

"Hell, we caught him with the fireworks, didn't we? Doesn't that tell you he's guilty?"

I shook my head. "No."

"Keeerrrrisst." Ronny punched the air above his head. "He tried to run you down your first day in town. He burns his own boat—at least I'll bet he did—and then he pulls the stunt with the fireworks. He's probably the one who put that snake in your rig. But every time you let him off." He looked around at the circle of men. "The rest of us have had it with him, bud. The next time he does something stupid, don't get between us or you'll be sorry."

Nat smiled at Susanna's reflection in the mirror. She smiled back, eyes sparkling, raised her right hand, swept her hair from the back of her neck, and gathered it on top of her head, a mound of glittering gold. With her left hand, she offered the slender strings to her halter top. Nat fastened them in a neat bow. She picked up a hairbrush and ran it through her hair, tossing her head so the feathery strands brushed his face, showered his shoulders with light.

Nat laughed, then turned toward the door, walked across the living room, down the porch steps and out to the dock. In a moment she followed. In a few more moments she'd be dead.

I woke, hands knotted into fists, arms and legs twitching. The anger was as intense as any I'd ever felt, an anger that drew heat toward itself, toward a black hole at the core of my soul. Nat had shared her final moments, her final smiles. Guilt overlapped the anger. If I'd been there, her smiles would have been mine, wouldn't have been the last.

The anger didn't ebb as I shook off sleep. I quivered with rage as I made coffee and toast, carried breakfast out the kitchen door, and perched on a rock in a puddle of sunlight. The fury felt the same as it had last October when I'd entered the lodge and found their bodies.

I breathed deeply and slowly, trying to refocus the anger into the present, into where I was now, not where I hadn't been then. I thought about Ronny's actions last night. Did he truly feel Willie Dean was responsible and that I was denying the evidence against him? Was that the cause of some of the anger gnawing at my gut?

The jay sailed down from the ridgepole and landed ten feet away, head cocked, eyeing the toast I hadn't touched. Was I shielding Willie Dean? Was I doing that to thwart Ronny, to assert myself? I tossed a corner of toast to the jay. It hopped back a foot, cocked its head again, then swooped on the offering and carried it away to its nest. A few months ago I might have done that, but I'd changed. I still wore pride like a favorite shirt, but I didn't button it tight to my throat each morning, didn't secure the cuffs. I had begun to realize how it allowed others to define and manipulate me; that knowledge made me feel soiled.

The jay returned and I stood, shredded the toast, and tossed it to him. Then I headed to the construction site to look for footprints I knew I wouldn't find. The anger went with me, coiling through my intestines like a snake.

As the week passed, examining my anger and trying to determine its source became my routine, as normal as making coffee, as ordinary as the feel of the toothbrush against my palm. I told Camille about it one evening as we lounged on a barely submerged boulder that, before the drought, had been six feet beneath the surface.

She listened to all my explanations, then smiled and stroked my forehead. "The well of the unconscious is a vast and uncharted place. Maybe Louisa Marie touched on something you won't admit—feelings about the color of my skin, or my past."

I answered without thinking. "That's bullshit. I'd know it if I felt that way."

She'd chuckled, a sound I found both sexy and mocking. "Not necessarily. The mind is like the ocean on those old maps, back when people still thought the earth was flat. Cartographers drew in sea serpents and whirlpools and mountains shrouded in mist. It's the same way inside your head. You can see a little bit of that ocean. But you can't see what's beneath the waves or beyond the line of the horizon."

I'd responded by ducking her, and vowing not to bring up the subject again. I'd channeled the anger into work, patrolling extra miles, going over everything I knew about what had happened that summer, haranguing the sheriff about lab work yet undone. In between, I made a study of Willie Dean, watching the way he spent his days, often standing outside his house at night as he sprawled in his recliner. He seldom drew his drapes. I imagined a man guilty of arson would take greater efforts to shield himself from other's eyes, but decided a guilty man could just as well live a public life to proclaim his innocence.

The one thing I did notice was that Willie Dean avoided Ronny after the night of my father's funeral. He skipped the regular volunteer firefighter meeting, sent Priscilla to get the mail, and stayed out of the Shovel It Inn. Had he asked, I would have advised him to do the same.

Rock cairns were now appearing at the rate of one a night. Each was a work of art—rounded rocks perched atop each other with exquisite patience and care—and clearly the design of one mind, the work of one pair of hands. I got out the geologic survey maps, sectioned off the ridges, and searched alone for traces of the mysterious man.

Once I found a place where he'd slept on a bed of moss and cooked fish over a fire he'd built in the bottom of a neat hole dug with a sharpened stick. The camp was old. I knew he'd been gone for many weeks, but I lay on the moss beside the impression of his body and, like a dog, sniffed for his scent. I smelled only the rustiness of dry, curling moss.

Every night, for three and a half weeks, I expected to hear the fire siren, or gunshots, or my pager. As each dawn came, I felt a surge of relief. I told myself the arsonist had given up.

And then he struck again.

CHAPTER 28

A dusty haze hung in the warm August air. It dyed the setting sun a soft magenta and gave the twilight sky depth and sheen like velvet. Camille and I had made love, then sprawled on the dock, eating ice cream cones, counting fireflies, and gossiping about our neighbors the same way we imagined they speculated about us. Some time after eight she left, and I fell into a restless sleep, setting the alarm for ten and knowing I would wake with my body knotted around that core of molten anger.

The fire siren's wail cut the dream short. Bolting from the couch, I jerked on my jeans and a shirt, stepped into a pair of running shoes, and hurried to the porch. The siren howled again. I scanned the sky, searching for a glow. Nothing. I cupped my ear, listening for shots. Nothing. I ran back to the living room, seized my gun, pager, and keys, and sprinted for my rig. All the time the siren keened like a chained dog.

I spun out of the driveway, gravel flying, and hit the asphalt with a rending squeal, racing toward town, betting the fire was in that direction, not on the mountain. Second gear, third, fourth. A vision of the shotgun trap flitted across my mind, and my right foot twitched toward the brake.

"Not tonight." I forced my foot back down on the gas and rocketed into the next turn. I'd outrun the pellets—if there were any. My pager went off, and the sharp tones activated the one-way radio clipped to the sun visor. The dispatcher's raspy voice called out the codes and unit number and then gave the location—Bobcat Hollow.

"Holy shit!" I stomped the gas pedal to the floor. A dozen houses lay scattered along the road that ran deep between ridges. "So far up you have to truck in daylight," my grandfather used to say. A long way to truck in water. After weeks of drought, only a few slimy pools remained in Bobcat Creek and ponds were low. We had to knock this fire down fast.

I took the turn on two wheels and saw taillights shimmying erratically as the fire truck jounced along the potholed road ahead of me, whipping up a choking cloud of dust. The rotating lights on top turned the trunks of the birches into slashes of garish red and lit the dusty leaves from beneath, creating a canopy of colliding colors, the roof of some satanic circus tent.

I braked, staying ten feet off the truck's bumper. Now I could smell the smoke, taste it at the back of my throat, feel it burn like bile on the soft tissue at the roof of my mouth and leave a sour aftertaste that couldn't be swallowed. The truck lumbered through a turn, the trees opened to the meadow, and I saw a ghastly glow through the evergreens beyond it. Ronny's house!

Reflexively, I trod on the gas, then backed off as the fire truck's rear lights bloomed in my windshield. "Faster!" I hammered the wheel with the palms of my hands even as I told myself that was pointless. Stub would drive the truck as fast as he could, given the condition of the road and the tons of water in the tank.

I looked to the right, gauging the distance across the meadow, the depth of the ditch at the side of the road. Could I get there quicker if I drove cross-country? I remembered the old barbed wire fence that bordered the meadow, the stone wall, tall hummocks of grass and deep depressions where water collected in the wet seasons. My heart churned in my chest.

Headlights appeared in my rearview mirror—three sets. Someone leaned on a horn. Ahead of me, wicked orange light seemed to swallow the horizon. A tornado of sparks whirled into the air as we turned up Ronny's driveway. From that angle, the flames seemed to disappear. I realized the front of the house was untouched. Maybe we could save it!

The fire truck trundled closer, headlights playing across the house. I saw smoke swirling from open windows and rope ladders dangling from the second floor.

Stub powered the truck across a row of rose bushes, crunched aluminum lawn furniture beneath the wheels, and halted. An arm-waving figure ran toward him as I yanked the wheel, skidding up against a hydrangea bush. I leaped out and raced for the truck as Freeman, Evan, and Willie Dean blasted into the driveway.

"Get your gear on!" Freeman yelled to me.

I didn't listen. I ran toward the child in the green nightgown who'd thrown her arms around Stub.

"Take her," he ordered.

I swept Julie against my chest. "Where are the others?"

"Uncle Dan," she sobbed, clutching at my shirt. "Justin and Dad are in the back. But Mom's still inside."

I slid an arm under her legs, lifted her easily, and ran again, turning the rear corner of the house. A bright tongue of flame shot from a shattered window, slicing through the thin stream of water Justin sprayed from a garden house. Ash smudged his arms and T-shirt, his hair stood up in tufts, and the yellow-red light from the fire made his face a mask of horror.

Behind me I heard grunts and shouts and a soft clatter. Julie sobbed against my neck. Inside the house something cracked sharply. Glass splintered.

"Get back!" I yelled to Justin.

The tongue of flame withdrew, sputtered, then shot out again, licking at the paltry stream of water. "No! Dad's in there,"

Justin yelled. "He went to find Mom. We have to hold back the fire."

"No!" I juggled Julie across my shoulder, grabbed his shirt, and hauled him to the edge of the lawn. "Stay back. This is where he'd want you to be."

"I've got to help Dad." He lowered his head and tried to charge past me.

I seized his shirt again. "Help him by staying alive."

"Mom. I want Mom." Julie wailed.

"It'll be okay. He'll get her out," I told her. "If anyone can do it, it's your dad."

"I'm so scared," Julie whimpered. I could barely hear her over the shouts of the firefighters and the rolling crash of the fire. "There's so much smoke inside. What if he doesn't find her?"

"He'll find her," Justin insisted. "He's the best."

"What if he doesn't? We heard him yelling. Justin and I did. Yelling 'Fire!' and 'Get up and get out as fast as you can!' The smoke made my eyes sting, and I got down on the floor and crawled to the window and tossed down the ladder."

I remembered the kids' rooms were at the front of the house, in the original part of the structure. The bedroom Ronny and Lisa shared was at the rear. When he'd added the den, he'd expanded that room.

"We didn't think about Mom," she said with a sob. "We thought she was out already. And then Dad had the hose and the fire was getting bigger and Justin said, 'Where's Mom?' and I ran around and around the house and she wasn't there. And Dad went in. And now he's gone, too."

I felt Justin sag, so I released his shirt. "Your dad will get her out," I insisted. "And your mom knows what to do." But I felt a numbing chill in my gut. Ronny should have found her by now. They should be out. I set Julie on her feet and kissed the top of her head. "Your dad could find a diamond in a hailstorm. But I'm going in, too. Stay here and stay together."

Justin nodded and slung his arms around Julie. I raced to my rig, popped the hatch, and yanked my gear from the back. The stiff pants fought me as I ran, boots thudding against the baked ground. "I'm going inside," I yelled to Evan. I ripped the breathing apparatus from its rack and struggled into it. I stumbled up the steps toward the front door, raising my knees high. Smoke roiled through the door, clotted the entryway. Inside the living room, dim shapes of furniture hulked in the lethal fog, backlit by a hellish glow from the den. Following the yelp of the smoke detector, I groped my way toward the stairs.

Ronny staggered down. Lisa lay limp in his arms. "I didn't get to her in time," he gasped. "I tried to revive her, but I think she's gone."

"No! Not Lisa!" Heartsick, I shoved him outside, tore her from his arms, laid her on the dead grass, and ripped off my breathing apparatus. I tipped her head back, pinched her nose, and pressed my mouth against hers, forcing air into her lungs.

Coughing, Ronny knelt beside me and compressed her chest.

"Breathe, Lisa, breathe," I ordered, hoping to prove Ronny wrong.

"Mom," Julie howled. She broke away from Justin and threw herself across her mother's legs. "Mom, wake up."

Justin knelt beside his sister. From the corner of my eye I saw him exchange glances with his father, then put his hand on Julie's shoulder. The sounds of the fire seemed to fade as Ronny and I worked. Lisa's sightless eyes grew dull and dry. Helplessly, I watched Julie cry as I breathed for the woman I knew I couldn't save.

Ronny began to sob, great rasping heaves of his chest that matched the artificial beat he imposed on Lisa's heart. "I was asleep in the recliner and I heard a noise and saw a bright flash and then the fire was all around me. My shirt was burning. I ran to the living room. Rolled on the rug. Called to Lisa and the kids. Got outside and got the hose. I saw Julie and Justin. I thought she got out, too."

He paused and I felt he was waiting for validation. "You did all you could."

He shook it off. "No. No, I didn't do enough." He stopped pumping and rocked back on his heels. "It's too late, Dan. She's gone."

I forced another breath into her lungs. "No."

Ronny laid a heavy hand on my shoulder and repeated the words I'd said to him. "You did all you could."

"No." I hadn't. I hadn't been smart enough to catch the arsonist. It was my fault. Always my fault.

Ronny rose to his feet and staggered past Freeman and Evan. He grasped Willie Dean by the front of his jacket, lifted him up, then knocked him to the ground with a single punch. "You bastard," he bellowed. "You came after me, but you got her. You murdering bastard."

I leapt to pull Ronny away, but he turned aside, dropped to his knees, and flung himself sobbing against the parched earth.

A relentless sun cast stark shadows across the withered grass of the cemetery. Clutching her grandmother's hand, Julie stared at her father as Ronny released a handful of soil into the open grave. Pebbles rattled against the coffin lid. Julie cringed and buried her face in the lacy sleeve of Rachel's black dress. Beside me, Mary Lou stifled a sob as Justin followed Ronny's lead. The clod of earth pressed in his fist fell with a hollow thud and spattered across the lid.

I felt tears swell beneath my eyelids, felt my tongue thicken and my throat close around my windpipe. I wanted to howl in pain but held my breath instead, struggling for the emotional control I used to find so easy. Mary Lou gripped my hand and offered a woeful smile as Reverend Balforth asked us to bow our heads and launched into the Twenty-eighth Psalm, the part about the wicked who speak peace with their neighbors while evil is in their hearts.

Ronny's face contorted with anger, and he half turned from the grave to glower at Willie Dean, who stood, shoulders slumped, fifty feet away. I rose onto my toes, leg muscles tightening, ready to get between them again. Willie Dean had been a fool to come to the funeral in the stuffy little church, an even bigger fool to follow the procession to the cemetery. But as Mary Lou had observed, Willie Dean felt he was damned either way. Staying away signified guilt. Coming made Ronny even angrier.

"He didn't do it," she'd assured me. "He couldn't have. Willie Dean may have been on the outs with Ronny lately, but he adored Lisa. He would never have done anything that would hurt her. You've got to find proof."

I'd nodded and refrained from saying what we both knew: that finding proof was easier said than done. Priscilla had told me Willie Dean was in bed with her when the siren went off. But Priscilla had been exhausted from a day of canning raspberry jam and she'd had her earplugs in, as usual. When I'd questioned her further, she admitted she'd never heard the siren.

Stub was certain he'd seen headlights beam across the lake when he pulled the truck out of the garage, but just assumed that since the lights were near Willie Dean's house, they belonged to his truck. Freeman thought Willie Dean had been right behind him all the way from the stop sign by the dam, but later allowed that, in the stress of the moment, he might have been mistaken and that Willie Dean might not have fallen in behind him until he started up Bobcat Hollow Road. Ronny persisted in believing Willie Dean had tossed an incendiary device, driven out of Bobcat Hollow, waited for the others, and then tagged along.

Willie Dean had let me search his house and the bait shop. I'd found nothing to link him to any of the fires. Ruling him out left me back at square one, looking for other motives and theories. Had the arsonist hoped to take Ronny out of the equation, to ensure that firefighters would be frightened and confused, to ensure that the next fire at the construction site did major damage?

Rich Ramseyer had surveyed the smoking rubble, mouth pressed into a thin line that puckered the blob of fat on his chin. "Miller was in here when it started?"

I'd pointed toward the blackened skeleton of Ronny's recliner in the charred remains of the den. "Asleep. In that chair."

Ramseyer shook his head. "He drink a lot?"

"Some," I temporized, realizing I'd seldom seen Ronny without a beer on a hot evening. He consumed it like others drank water or lemonade, as if he were simply replacing bodily fluids. I'd never seen him reel or stagger, never considered him to be drunk.

Ramseyer nodded. "That explains why the smell didn't wake him up right away." He pointed to the place where the window had been. "Your friendly neighborhood arsonist probably poured accelerant through the window. Camper stove fuel, maybe. Let it soak into the carpet. Let the fumes spread. Then tossed in something to ignite it. Flare, maybe. You can depend on those to burn long and hot. We'll dig through the ash and see what we uncover. It's a good thing this part of the house was built recently and to code. That slowed the fire, contained it. But the vents over that woodstove sent the smoke into the bedroom above." He shook his head sadly. "You find any fuel containers?"

I'd searched as soon as it was light enough to see, covering every inch of the house and yard. "Just the ones Ronny used to fill his mower and chainsaw. Both full to the brim."

"He must have taken it with him." Ramseyer shook his head again and waddled toward his car. "This guy knows his stuff. But his timing was off last night. Your pal was lucky. If the fumes had built up a few more minutes before they ignited, he would have been one crispy critter." Ramseyer wedged himself behind the wheel. "Shame about his wife. Was she a heavy drinker, too?"

I'd felt a flash of anger and rushed to defend Lisa's memory. "I never saw her drink more than a glass of wine."

He'd sucked on his lower lip for a moment, and I could tell he didn't believe me, or thought my knowledge was sketchy at best.

"Well, maybe she was a sound sleeper, didn't hear him yelling. Didn't hear the smoke alarm. It happens. Not often, but it does." Ramseyer had glanced again at the upper storey. "I expect they'll find smoke inhalation killed her. They'll run tests for drugs and alcohol, though. That's routine."

"And maybe we'll have the results from the lab by next Easter!"

He'd shrugged. "They're doing the best they can."

But am I? I wondered as Reverend Balforth cast his eyes dramatically toward the sky and finished his sermon.

"Amen." I heard relief in the word as I uttered it. Willie Dean scuttled away with Priscilla close behind.

The minister shook Ronny's hand, clapped Justin on the shoulder, and touched his palm to Julie's head. Beside me, Mary Lou sighed. Then she gasped and nudged me as her sister stalked to the open grave and tossed a bouquet of limp roses onto the casket. Lou Marie squared her narrow shoulders inside a black dress two sizes too big for her, and fixed her gaze on

Justin and Julie. "Your mother always dreamed of getting away from here. Well, now she has."

The crowd echoed Mary Lou's gasp as they stared at Lou Marie, then at the children. Justin's solemn expression didn't change and his eyes didn't flicker, but Julie's face crumpled. Bawling, she charged around the grave and head-butted Lou Marie, shoving her over onto a pile of dirt and falling on top of her, fists flailing. "Don't you dare say anything about my mother, you old witch. Don't you dare!"

"Julie, you stop that!" Ronny stepped toward his daughter, but I darted ahead of him, letting Julie get in a few more punches before I lifted her off.

"It's okay, Julie. It's okay." I cradled her against my chest. "No one can hurt your mom now. It doesn't matter what anyone says."

Julie sobbed against my starched shirt as Mary Lou stroked her hair and pressed a tissue into her hand. "Your mom's probably sitting on the edge of a cloud with a bunch of other angels and having a good laugh over this." She nodded over her shoulder toward Lou Marie, who was brushing dirt from her dress.

Lou Marie shot me a Medusa-like glare and stomped off.

I rocked Julie as I walked toward Rachel's car. "Let's get you to your grandmother's house, okay?"

She snuffled into the tissue and hugged me, her face against my neck. "You'll find the person who killed my mom, won't you, Uncle Dan?"

"You bet I will," I told her.

But I wondered whether I'd made a promise I couldn't keep.

CHAPTER 29

Julie ran to a bedroom the minute we reached Rachel's house. Justin drew his father aside, got a nod of approval, changed his clothes, made a sandwich, and drifted out the back door and into the woods. Mary Lou, Pattie, Alda, and the other women kept up a barrage of bright comments as they brought out bowls and platters of food. They talked about Lisa's artistic talent, recalled the Fourth of July festivities, and wondered how she'd found time to get everything done. The men, hands clutched around glasses of whiskey, gravitated toward the den, where Ronny made conversation with the anxious inward concentration of a man trying to pass a kidney stone.

I edged to a corner and pretended to study a faded photograph of one of Buck's ancestors as I scanned the men reflected in a small mirror beside the photograph. I couldn't imagine any of them setting a fire that might injure children, kill a woman.

"You okay, Dan?" Freeman whispered as he held out a square bottle half-full of brown liquid. "Need another drink?"

I gazed around the stifling room where the sluggish pendulum of a grandfather clock opposite the fireplace counted the cadence of mourning. Seconds settled like dust in the spaces between the threads of lacy antimacassars clinging to armchairs in the seldom-used formal living room. Minutes congealed with gravy ladled atop the pot roast arranged on the "good" dishes set on the thickly embroidered tablecloth in the dining room. I nodded. "Make it a double."

Disoriented, nauseated, clumsy, and stiff—partly from the liquor, and partly from having confined myself within the conventions of the afternoon—I drove back to the lodge. The setting sun made the logs glow orange, but inside it seemed almost chilly.

"Might as well do a little work." I hung my suit in the closet of my room in the loft and slipped on a pair of jeans and a T-shirt. Meandering down to the kitchen, I crossed to the bulletin board and surveyed the array of photographs I'd taken at the fire scenes. Blackened rubble and yellow crime scene tape. Nothing I hadn't seen before.

I moved on to the next bulletin board, the one on which I'd pinned the pictures of the cairns. I had divided them into two groups—flat rocks and round stones. I'd pinned the most recent photo in the center of the board—a shot of a stack of pancake-like rocks I'd discovered on Bobcat Hollow Road just below Ronny's house the morning after the fire. Thirteen of them and so flat they could have been stacked up in a minute or less. After I'd snapped the picture, I'd kicked the rocks into the ditch.

Now I examined the picture, hoping I'd see something more. The cairn resembled only three others, all related to arson. I decided again that there were two people at work here, people with different agendas. Then I second-guessed. Could there be just one person making it appear that there were two?

I banged ice cubes from a tray and jammed them into a glass, covering them with bourbon. I knocked back half the liquor, splashed more on the ice, and confronted my fish-eyed reflection in the polished curve of the kettle on the stove. "Why don't you admit you're worthless? Why don't you quit? Finish cleaning out the place, stick up the 'for sale' sign, and watch Hemlock

Lake disappear in your rearview mirror?"

I swilled down more liquor, walked to the front door, and peered at the lake that continued to draw in on itself, revealing an ever-widening stretch of sun-baked mud and rock. We'd had no rain since the night Ronny and I passed long hours on the wall above the construction site. The dock sat high on the fifty-five gallon drums that a month ago had floated it but now rested on the lake bottom.

I let my gaze follow the line of the dock across the lake toward the one gable of the Brocktons' home visible through the trees. "And quit that, too. Stop using her and get out of here."

Alcohol fueled my angry resolve. I seized a handful of garbage bags from the pantry, hauled empty cardboard boxes from beneath the porch, collected a broom, rags, and window cleaner, and opened the door to the one space I hadn't entered since Ronny and I opened the lodge—Nat's room.

Sunlight slanted through dark blue curtains, staining the blank spot on the floor the way Nat's blood had stained the headboard. I dumped boxes and bags, opened the curtains wide, and flung up the window sash. An apathetic breeze caught the dust on the windowsill, lofting motes into a shaft of sunlight. I watched them flutter for a few moments. Nat and Susanna were turning to dust, and the bed on which they'd lain had been reduced to ash. And I remained. To sweep up after them.

I went to work, taking down framed photographs of Nat and his friends, of Nat and my father, my mother, and my grand-parents. There were three shots of Susanna—one taken as she rode the wakeboard behind the boat, one of her unpacking a picnic basket in a golden meadow, and one from our wedding, a shot I didn't remember ever seeing before. She smiled directly into the camera while I, distracted as we cut the cake, had turned to look over my shoulder. There were no other pictures of me. I hadn't expected there would be. I piled the photographs in a box, thinking I'd give them to Mary Lou. Perhaps she could recycle the frames for her historical displays.

When I'd cleared the walls, I made myself another drink and tackled the bookcase that lined one wall. Legal thrillers, action novels, and espionage tales crammed the shelves. I packed them into boxes, wrote "library" on the lids, and lugged them into the living room.

Nat had been scrupulous about caring for his tools and equipment, but careless about his clothing. Jeans and sweatshirts lay in a heap on the floor of his closet, shirts dangled by their sleeves from hangers, and sweaters had been wedged onto the shelves above. Sweating from my exertions, I gulped my drink and considered sorting and washing the garments, then donating them to a church rummage sale. My mother would have done that.

But as I pulled a wad of sweaters from the top shelf, anger roiled in my brain. The one left behind to clean up made his own rules. I crammed Nat's clothing into garbage sacks and dragged them onto the porch. The sun had fitted itself into a notch in the mountains like a salamander seeking a crevice among the rocks. Cobalt shadows avalanched down the mountainsides and spilled onto the lake. I flicked on the porch light and the lamps in the living room and retrieved more ice for my glass and more liquor to float it on.

Nat's tall dresser, crafted from bird's eye maple, had once belonged to my great-grandmother. Elaborately carved and topped by a beveled mirror, it had matched the bed frame I'd burned last fall. I ran my fingers over the satiny wood. "Is it still an heirloom if there are no heirs to leave it to?"

My reflection didn't hazard an answer. Snapping a garbage bag, I opened the deep bottom drawer and dug out yellowing long underwear and knitted wool caps. The next drawer held T-shirts and sweat pants, a study in white and gray. The one above contained athletic socks—some nearly new and paired off, rolled up against each other like lovers, others sprawling alone at the back of the drawer as if the search for a mate had exhausted them. I swept them all into the bag and opened the fourth drawer. Thrusting my left hand inside, I snatched at the contents. My fingers released a rainbow of colors into the bag.

My eyes struggled to focus on the wispy fabrics. My mind struggled to sustain the lie I'd lived with for nearly a year.

It failed.

"You bastard!"

Trembling with fury, I yanked Susanna's lacy underwear and gossamer nightgowns from the drawer and scattered them across the floor where the bed had stood. I saw Nat and Susanna in that bed, saw them as I'd found them—together in death as they must have been a hundred times, a thousand times, in life.

"You rotten bastard!"

I'd had one thing in my whole life that trumped anything in Nat's hand. I'd had a wife. "Did you take her because she was mine? Or did you take her just because you could, because you knew I was too trusting to see?"

I fell to the floor, pounding my fists against the planks, remembering a hundred times I'd seen them glance at each other. Had I lied to myself about Susanna, too? Had Nat taken her, or had she taken him? Who else knew? My father? How could he not? And my neighbors? Had they been laughing behind their hands while they offered what I didn't know was double sympathy? *Poor Dan, he lost his wife. Twice.*

I crawled toward the door, crying, shuddering as a fresh jolt of pain stabbed at my brain. How long had Nat and Susanna intended to lie to me? How long had I intended to lie to myself?

I staggered to my feet and reeled toward the gun rack. The room wavered, light flaring around the lamps, shadows ballooning in the corners. Susanna, swimsuit pasted to her body, her wakeboard under her arm, strolled toward the porch where Nat waited, grinning.

"I'm coming to get you, Nat!"

I fumbled a shotgun from the rack, yanked open the drawer, and scrabbled among the boxes of ammunition. Hand-in-hand, the ghosts trailed out the front door and crossed the porch.

"I'm coming all the way to hell to get you!"

I wedged a shell in on the third try. Stumbling to the couch, I fell among the cushions, clutching the shotgun to my chest, squinting into the barrel where death waited for me to pull the trigger.

"Look back, Nat. I'm right behind you."

CHAPTER 30

"Dan! Don't!" Camille's scream sliced the air.

I stared down the narrow black tunnel past the end of my life.

"Put the gun down, Dan."

"No." I opened my mouth, touched the barrel with the point of my tongue, tasting gun oil. From the corner of my eye I watched her edge toward me. I wondered if she'd passed Nat and Susanna as she climbed the steps.

"Dan. Please look at me."

Her voice sounded as if it would shatter at any second, like the antique Christmas ornament I'd dropped the year I was four. "Stupid clumsy kid," my father had cursed. He'd ordered me to my room, where I'd cried myself to sleep. I pondered the memory, the clarity and texture of it. I became aware of the vast depths of my mind, its ability to process thought, to call up pictures, to recognize ongoing reality while conjuring the past. Amazing. And in a minute I would shut it all down. Fry the circuits, short out the nerve synapses. I wondered how my thoughts would appear when the shot tore through the roof of my mouth and into my brain.

"Please put the gun down."

"Susanna didn't love me. She loved Nat. She slept with him."

She drew in a sharp breath. "How do you know that?"

"I remembered, that's how. I remembered everything I told myself I didn't see or hear or sense, everything I told myself was just my imagination. And now I'm going to kill him." I slid the barrel into my mouth. Metal grated against my teeth. Would I hear the blast? Would I smell gunpowder before my senses shut down? Would I hear the shotgun hit the floor?

She came closer. "He's dead, Dan. You can't kill him again. You'll only kill yourself."

"Right." I fumbled for the trigger and slid the barrel from my mouth to explain. That was important. She needed to know. I stabbed the skin between my eyes with my forefinger. "I have to get him out of here. That's the only way I can get her back."

"I understand." She took another few steps and lowered herself to the couch beside me so carefully I couldn't feel it sag. I marveled at that observation too, wondering if my senses, dulled by alcohol, had been heightened by proximity to death. I turned my mind to her comment, decided it wasn't accurate. I peered into the barrel, seeking confirmation.

"No," I said. "No one understands."

She nodded. "You want her back. You want things to be the way they were. Or the way you thought they were."

She didn't get it. "That's not what I said. Aren't you listening? I love her!"

"Yes. I'm listening." She chewed at her lower lip. "But you just said she didn't love you. So how is this going to work? Let's say you get to . . . to wherever you're going, and you kill your brother. Will that make Susanna love you? Or will she still love him the way you love her?"

"No. The way she . . . I . . ." I slammed the stock against the floor. "Stop trying to confuse me!"

"Okay." She held up her hands, palms out. "But, for the record, does this mean you're giving up?"

"Giving up on what?"

"Well, on everything. Catching the arsonist. It's a murder case now, isn't it? So I guess if you kill yourself, you're saying you can't solve it."

"That has nothing to do with this!" I slammed the stock against the floor again.

Camille didn't flinch. "It does, actually." Her voice was cool, controlled. She smoothed her hair with her right hand and leaned back against the cushions, as casually as if I'd just offered to make her a cup of coffee. "I'm just trying to get it all straight. People will ask me what you said and did before you pulled the trigger." She craned her neck, peering around the room. "Did you leave a note?"

"No."

"Why not?"

"Because I don't have time," I snarled, bracing the barrel under my chin, fingering the trigger. "I have to go after Nat."

She shrugged, turned her palms up. "Okay. But you know how people are, how they gossip and pick through facts like they're sorting bad apples out of a box before they buy. They'll want to have every last detail or they won't be satisfied."

She stiffened, eyes darkening, and put one hand to her throat. "Oh my god, they'll blame me! They'll say it's my fault you killed yourself!"

I lowered the gun. "Why the hell would they do that?"

"I don't know." She leaped to her feet and paced in a tight circle. The motion made me dizzy. I closed my eyes. "Why would Louisa Marie accuse you of killing your father?"

"Because she's a miserable withered old bitch," I yelled. The sound made my head pound, and I lowered my voice. "Because if she can't be happy, she doesn't want anyone else to have a chance at it." I opened my eyes, stroked the barrel of the shotgun. "No one listens to her, anyway."

"Yes they do, Dan. They don't always seem to, but what she says is like a cut you don't keep clean. It festers, the infection spreads, and then—" Her eyes widened. "What if they say I killed you? I could be charged with murder."

I threw my head back and laughed. "That's the stupidest thing I've ever heard, Camille. That's not the way a criminal investigation works. They'd see that your fingerprints aren't on this gun. And look at me, look how I'm doing this." I hunched forward and slid the barrel into my mouth again, gagging as it depressed my tongue. Nodding toward my hands, I wiggled my fingers, showed her how they touched the trigger. I yanked the barrel from my mouth, hearing it scrape my teeth, tasting blood like an old penny on my tongue. "See that? When they process the evidence and see where my fingerprints are, they'll know I pulled the trigger myself."

"And when will that be? I've heard you complain about the crime lab. It could be months before they sort this out. Well, no thanks. I went to jail once while they took their time looking for the truth, and I promised myself I'd never go again! I'm getting out of here." She started for the door. "Give me time to get back to the Brocktons'. Write a note while you're waiting." Pausing in the doorway, she looked at me and shook her head. "You're going to make a hell of a mess in here."

"That won't be my problem."

"No. I guess it won't. But it would be neater if you did it outside. Of course, the flies will get there faster," she said matter-of-factly. "So when I hear the shot, I'll call Stub right away and ask him to come over and check on you. Flies are disgusting. I hate the way they buzz around dead things." She placed her index finger on her chin. "Maybe you could do it down on the dock. That way you'll fall into the water. If the shot doesn't kill you, you'll drown."

She leaned on the last word. Susanna had drowned. My heart pounded behind my eyes, blurring my vision. "Don't tell me how to kill myself." My voice sounded as petulant as a child's. "I can do this without your micromanaging."

"I know you can," she jeered. "You've been committing emotional suicide every day since Susanna died. You're a damn expert, a whining, sniveling, wallowing, depressing expert on self-inflicted misery. You know what? I'm sick of hearing about how perfect she was, how beautiful she was, how much you loved her. I bet she's laughing her ass off!"

I threw the shotgun to the floor, leapt from the couch, and stalked toward her. "Don't talk about her!"

Camille laughed bitterly, backing away across the porch. "Or you'll do what? Hit me for telling the truth? That's as stupid as killing yourself because she cheated on you."

"She was my wife. I loved her." I ripped the words from my chest.

"She slept with your brother!" Camille backed down the steps.

"I don't want to live if I can't have her." I snatched at the railing, caught it on the second try.

"You didn't have her, Dan. Nat did. You can't change that." Camille edged toward the lake, sliding into shadows beyond the range of the porch light.

"I loved her." I let go of the railing, threw my head back, and howled into the night. "I loved her!"

Darkness surged around me like a riptide. I rode it down.

CHAPTER 31

Warmth lifted from my forehead and cool took its place, wet against my eyelids. My head throbbed, my lips seemed glued together, and nausea twisted my gut. I groaned, hearing it as a rasping hum deep in my throat.

"How are you feeling?"

I swallowed, the spasm grinding my throat like broken glass.

"Want some aspirin? Orange juice?" Cool peeled away and I saw Camille. Her skin had a gray tinge and her hair looked limp and greasy. "Coffee? I just started a pot."

I blinked. "Where am I?"

Her eyes narrowed. "In your front yard."

"Oh." I surveyed the sunlight reflecting off the lake, saw the jay swoop from a birch tree and land on the dock. I fingered the blanket tucked around me and the pillow stuffed beneath my head. I flexed my legs and arms, feeling stiff muscles tighten further in protest. I felt under my right hip, removed a jagged rock, and tossed it aside. Probing my mind for a shard of memory, I found the image of Freeman offering the bottle. "Did I have too much to drink at Lisa's wake?"

She frowned. "Is that the last thing you remember?"

I saw worry in her eyes and knew there was more, felt cold fear rise into my throat. "Yeah. Freeman had a bottle. Evan had one, too. What happened after that?"

She took a deep breath. "You put a gun in your mouth. You

said you were going to hell to kill your brother and get Susanna back."

"What? Why would I say that?"

"You don't remember?"

"No." I staggered to my feet. "I drank too much at the wake. I don't remember anything after that." Grasping the railing, I started hauling myself up the stairs. "I'm going to take a shower."

She ran ahead of me, braced her arms against the doorframe and blocked my way. "Don't go into the house."

"Why? Because there are guns in there?" My words were slow and patient. "I must have been joking last night."

"You weren't. But your mind has buried it. That scares the hell out of me." Tears welled in her eyes. "The next time you glimpse the truth, I might not be around to stop you."

Something dark twisted in my gut. Dank sweat broke out on my back and forehead. "I don't want to talk about this. I want coffee. I want a shower."

I tried to move her left arm, push past her into the lodge. She gritted her teeth and locked her knees. "I could call the sheriff."

The dark thing twisted again. "Don't do that." I shuffled to the swing and collapsed into it. "Tell me everything."

She did.

Half an hour later, I watched Camille refill my coffee mug and hand it to me. I saw my fingers close around the bright green mug, but couldn't feel the heat, couldn't raise the mug to my mouth. I felt as if my nervous system had decided no messages should be sent to my brain again because it couldn't be trusted. My hands trembled and I set the mug on the porch railing. "What am I supposed to do now?"

"Drink your coffee."

I raised the mug and slurped the hot liquid.

"You're not 'supposed' to do anything," she said. "Your mind built a barrier to try to protect you. Then you recognized something you couldn't deny, and that barrier was breached. The pain was so intense you weren't rational." She chewed at her lower lip. "You may never get over this if you don't get professional help."

I flinched at the word "help," and she put her hand on my shoulder. "It's like losing an arm or a leg. You get therapy so you can learn how to work with the injury and go on."

I shrugged her hand away. "If I want to go on."

She sat on the railing and looked out across the glassy blue water. "There's that, too. The gun's still loaded."

I shook my head. "No. That was the way Nat took." Maybe not so much because he felt guilty about Susanna's death or how it would hurt me, I realized, but because he loved her so intensely he couldn't continue. I recalled the words he'd scrawled before he'd shot himself, "I should have been stronger." I'd thought he meant he should have been a stronger swimmer, should have reached her sooner. But now I wondered if he had been referring to strength of will, saying he should have been strong enough to resist her. He'd asked me to forgive him. But could I? Was I strong enough for that?

"They were a lot alike, you know," I said. "Susanna was like a meteor. A flash of light and heat. Spontaneous combustion. Nat was, too." More emotionally accessible than I'd ever been. Nat didn't hold himself back, didn't just read about other's feelings. I gulped down half the remaining coffee, feeling warmth spread through my chest and across my shoulders. Once they'd met, what followed was inevitable. The only puzzle was why they'd hidden the affair from me. Had it been because they both loved me, tried to shield me? I swallowed the rest of the coffee with the grim realization that I would never know, never have that bitter consolation.

Camille cleared her throat and pursed her lips. I could tell she had a hundred things she wanted to say but wouldn't.

I stretched out my hand and she grasped it. "I'll be okay," I told her. "I've got you to help me, don't I?" I forced a smile, trying to coax one from her. "Until the end of the summer, right? You're not going to break that promise, are you?"

Tears glistened in her eyes. "No. I won't break that promise."

I wondered if she cried because she pitied me—a man who'd been cheated on, lied to. Then I wondered if she was lying to me. Just like Susanna had when she'd promised to forsake all others.

Leaning against the ladder, I struggled to hold the plasterboard above my head. My arms ached from the strain, a muscle in my back twitched. "Have you got it?"

"Yeah." Ronny lifted it from my hands and flung it into the room behind him—the room that he and Lisa had shared before the fire. I heard it smack onto a growing stack as I lowered myself to the ground. "Is that the last one?"

I glanced at the empty pickup truck, felt relief relax my muscles. "Yes. You need anything else from down here?"

"There's a bag of screws on the seat." His voice faded into the recesses of the house. "Bring 'em on up."

I retrieved the bulging paper bag and stepped between the studs defining the wall of what had once been Ronny's den— and would be again when he finished rebuilding. After several weeks of red tape, the insurance company had cut him a check, and he'd started ripping out fried carpeting and charred floor- ing, tearing off blackened knotty pine paneling, and hauling burned furniture to the dump. Each morning, when I drove up Bobcat Hollow Road, the sight of the house hit me like a sucker punch to the gut. My mind replayed images of Ronny carrying Lisa down the stairs, Julie falling on her mother's body, the casket sliding into its slot in the earth.

For three weeks after my realization about Nat and Susanna, I'd done little more than sleep or rock in the swing on the porch. Around me, summer grew stale. Grasshoppers thwanged among clumps of dead grass; katydids began their grating whispers as the nights closed in. Camille came every day, fixed lunch or dinner, puttered in the kitchen, urged me to shower or walk to the dock, chatted about our neighbors or simply sat beside me. We didn't make love, didn't kiss when she left. I'd called the sheriff and told him I wanted unpaid leave. I was no good to anyone. He hadn't argued.

While I'd clutched my loss to me in brooding silence, Ronny had become a wild man, sharing his anguish with the whole valley. Roaring drunk, he'd gone to Willie Dean's house, night after night, calling him out, daring him to fight. Willie Dean, sensible for once, had remained behind locked doors, until Stub, Evan, or Freeman prodded Ronny back to his mother's house, where he'd drink himself to sleep.

After a week, Ronny transferred the blame from Willie Dean to the man on the mountain. He told Stub he realized Willie Dean couldn't have started the fire without screwing something up, leaving a stack of evidence behind. It had to be the man no one had been able to find. As fresh cairns appeared, he kicked them over. He spent his days prowling the ridges. Often, I heard gunshots echoing from the mountains. Stub, Camille told me, worried that those shots would spark a blaze in the tinder-dry woods and finally confronted Ronny and demanded he stop. Surprisingly, Ronny agreed. He abandoned the search in favor of nursing a succession of beers at the Shovel It Inn, throwing darts, and playing heart-wrenching tunes on the jukebox.

It had been Camille who'd suggested I lend Ronny a hand with the rebuilding, pointing out that I wasn't busy doing anything else, nudging at me until I'd collected some tools and headed over there. Just below the meadow, I'd stopped, shifted to reverse, and nearly returned to the lodge. Examining that impulse, however, I'd been able to recognize it as the more depressing of my options, and I'd gone on.

The first day I worked beside Ronny, my slack muscles had protested every effort. My tongue had fumbled simple words. But now I felt as if the rebuilding was a lifeline and that Ronny had clutched at it, pulled himself to some uncertain shore, and tossed it back to me.

I climbed the stairs to the second floor, stepping onto the plywood floor we'd put down yesterday, and offering the bag to Ronny.

"Thanks, bud." Tossing it aside, he yanked a wadded handkerchief from his back pocket and wiped his face. He'd lost weight since Lisa died—twenty pounds or more—and the skin on his cheeks had fallen in. His beard seemed bleached, a theater prop pasted on carelessly. He glanced at the stack of plasterboard. "Want to tackle this now, or tomorrow?"

I shrugged. "Doesn't matter to me. Work is work."

"I heard that." He flexed his shoulders. "Let's start on the ceiling, then. I'll hold 'em up and you screw 'em in place."

"Okay." I filled my tool belt with screws, hefted the power screwdriver, and quickly fell into a rhythm. As I worked, I wondered how Ronny would finish off the room, what color he'd paint it, whether he'd put up curtains or blinds, replace the king-size bed—or choose something smaller, so the empty side where Lisa would have slept wouldn't appear so large a barrier between himself and the rest of his life. How long would it take him to heal? *Less time than it took you,* I told myself. Ronny wouldn't spend ten months lying to himself. But then, Ronny's wife hadn't been having an affair with his brother.

"They're letting the security guards go at the end of the week. Some of the owners are moving in over there."

"Huh?"

Ronny nodded toward the west. "At the development. They've finished four of the homes. All except the landscaping."

"Oh."

He dropped his chin and squinted at me. "Haven't you been checking on the place?"

"No." I drove in a screw, the bit chattering, metal on metal, as it jumped from the groove.

"Thought that was your job." Ronny braced the plasterboard with one hand and scratched his chin with the other as I set another screw.

"Used to be. But I wasn't much good at it."

He said nothing, changed hands, and rubbed the back of his neck.

"Maybe I'll stay on up here, work with you," I said and laughed.

He squinted again. "That what you're thinking?"

"No." I drove in another screw. "I'm thinking of going back out west."

"Arizona again?"

"No. New Mexico, maybe." Someplace Susanna and I hadn't lived. A place with enormous flat vistas and raw jagged mountains that stood out against the sky and didn't confine me like the slopes around Hemlock Lake. I'd find a simple job with no responsibility.

He stared at me. "What about the lodge?"

I grappled for a lie. "Maybe you know someone who'd want to rent it for a time."

"Not offhand. But I'll ask around. Mary Lou might have an idea. Hate to see someone I don't know in there, but I guess that's what it's coming to up here. Everything's changing. And not for the better." He flexed his shoulders again and walked over to look out of the space where a window would go. "It started the day they bulldozed Tom Andersen's orchard."

Or the night Susanna died on the lake, I thought. Pick any date on the calendar, start a cycle from that point, and make it mean whatever you want.

"But there ain't nothing we can do about it," Ronny continued. "And like you said, there's money over there, and some of it might as well find its way into my pockets. Hell, Willie Dean's already getting his share." He hefted another piece of plasterboard and fitted it into place as I fished a screw from my tool belt. "I heard he's gonna be a caretaker for a couple of them. You know, water their plants, adjust the heat so the pipes don't freeze. And Priscilla, she's going to be like a, what do you call it, a personal shopper. Fill their refrigerators before they come up on the weekends. Maybe do some cooking." He laughed. "That'll work until they taste it. But between that and taking care of their boats, Willie Dean's set for life."

I nodded and drove in another screw. Set for life. The words rang against each other like new coins.

CHAPTER 32

Six days later, after sawing boards beside Ronny late into the evening, I crawled into my narrow bed in the loft. I fell asleep immediately, but woke deep in the night, my body twitching with exhaustion, my mind whirling around the black space where the dream used to unfold, where Susanna and Nat used to die. I stumbled out of bed, arranged a drop cloth, and got to work rolling primer onto the walls of Nat's empty room.

I thought I'd imagined the first ring, but when the phone jangled again, I placed the roller on the edge of the pan and wiped my hands on my jeans. As I walked to the living room, I checked the clock on the mantel. Two twenty-four A.M. Good news seldom arrived at that hour. I snatched the receiver to my ear and grunted a hello.

"Dan?" The sheriff's voice was grim.

"Yeah."

"I know you're on leave but you're the closest. I need you to go to Ronny Miller's house and hold the fort until I get a detective out there." He paused and sighed. "That's not an order. It's a favor."

An order could be refused. But a favor . . . "I'm on the way." I strapped on my gun and headed out, cocking my head, listening for the fire siren but hearing nothing except the slow lap of water against rock and the scuffle of some small creature alarmed by my movements. Sniffing the air, I caught only the dusty scent of dry leaves.

I turned onto Bobcat Hollow Road, my tires raising a thick plume of dust. My taillights dyed the dust crimson as I towed it behind me into the bend below the meadow. The house appeared, one side blazing with white light, the other sealed in the night. Nothing moved.

A favor. The words rang in my head. No mention of danger, no words of caution. I let off the gas, downshifted to second, studied the house.

I parked at the far corner of the driveway, wedged into a deep shadow, and drew my gun.

"Around here, bud." Ronny's voice sounded hollow, colorless. "We're around back."

We? I clutched the gun and slipped along the side of the house. "Are you okay?"

"Yeah. I am. I'm okay. It's over."

I paused at the corner of the house, squinting into the beams of the work lights he'd rigged in the den. Ronny sat on the ground, legs splayed, rifle across his knees, face haggard in the harsh light. He nodded toward the meadow. "He's dead."

I peered into the shadows, spotted a man stretched face-down at the edge of the blighted lawn, a man who seemed to be trying to drag himself into the light.

"It's Willie Dean," Ronny said.

Willie Dean? The most reasonable thing in the world and the most illogical. I felt no surprise that Ronny had killed him. But why would Willie Dean, who'd feared and avoided Ronny, come here in the middle of the night? I holstered my gun and walked to the dead man's side. His fingers had torn deep gouges in the powdery dirt, gouges filled with the blood that spilled from his chest. I knelt and put two fingers against his neck, knowing I'd feel nothing except the throb of my own pulse, but needing to touch him, like a child might stroke a dead pet to confirm the loss. "What's he doing up here?"

"He came to finish what he started." Ronny pointed beyond me. I squinted into the dark, spotting a rifle and a blue plastic container a few feet away. "I couldn't sleep." Ronny hauled himself to his feet and leaned the rifle against the house. "So I walked down here from Mom's place. Thought I'd get some sanding done on the paneling we cut today. Nothing much. Something to pass the time of night. You know how that is."

He said it as if he'd been inside my skin during the dark hours and knew exactly how it felt. I nodded and stood, my eyes on the rifle only a yard from Willie Dean's hand.

"If I hadn't stopped to get a beer, I never would have heard a thing. He would have shot me and then torched the place." Ronny pointed to the container. "But I heard the rifle bolt snap. You know that sound, don't you, bud? There's nothing like it in the world."

I remembered the night he'd surprised me on the wall, remembered how my heart had clenched with fear, squeezing a burst of blood to my brain.

"I didn't stop to think, just hit the floor. I heard the bullet smack into the wall, and I crawled down the hallway and got that rifle." He jerked his chin toward the gun he'd set down. "All of mine went in the fire. That's my dad's. Don't know why, but I brought it down here a few days ago. Good thing, too." He nodded at Willie Dean's body.

I held my silence, dumb with disbelief. Willie Dean? I'd never thought him capable of murder.

"Maybe I rode him too hard," Ronny said, his voice mournful. "But I told him I was sorry. Night before last. I told him I'd been out of my head about Lisa, didn't know what I was saying. Willie Dean thought she hung the moon. He'd cut off his arm before he'd hurt her. When I sobered up, I saw that. I paid for him and Priscilla to have steak dinners at the Shovel It Inn."

I stared at Willie Dean's hands and imagined them gripping a knife and fork, cutting into a slab of rare beef. I looked down at the puddle of blood and felt the ground lurch under me.

"I was sure he wasn't the one who started the fire. I would have bet my life on it." Ronny pointed with his right foot to the rifle. "Hell, I nearly did."

My nod was automatic but all the while a voice in my brain kept asking questions I couldn't answer. Why, after all these years, and after an apology, would Willie Dean strike out at Ronny? And why would he think he'd succeed?

The rain, forecast for a week, arrived just as Reverend Balforth closed his Bible. The first thick drops struck the ground like BBs, raising spurts of dust, then flattening into dark circles like tarnished coins. The parched soil wouldn't accept the moisture. Within moments, rivulets of gritty water coursed among the tombstones. Willie Dean's mourners cupped their hands above their heads and hustled toward their cars. Priscilla lingered for a minute, peering into the grave, watching water bead up on the slick black lid of the casket.

Finally she turned away and clutched my arm. "He didn't do it, Dan. I know it looks that way, but Willie Dean didn't do it. Not any of it." Her dandelion-fluff hair lay plastered to her forehead; mascara ran in dark streams toward the corners of her mouth. "You'll prove he didn't, won't you Dan?"

I patted her hand, peeled off my jacket, and placed it across her shoulders. I didn't remind her this wasn't my case, didn't tell her I hadn't returned to duty, didn't point out that I was a failure. She wanted something to believe in. Even if that something was a lie. "I'll try, Priscilla. I'll do all I can."

But without his help in his own defense, proving Willie Dean innocent could be next to impossible. If he hadn't gone to Ronny's house with arson and murder on his mind, then he'd been set up—either by Ronny, or by somebody else who used Ronny as executioner.

"If you could just find that man who's hiding in the mountains." Priscilla's eyes, gray as the rain, shifted to the casket again. I stared off at the ridges across the lake. When the rain let up, I'd search once more. The damp ground would hold his tracks if he still walked the hills. "Oh God," she wailed, "I wish I'd heard him get out of bed. I wish I knew why he went up there." She sobbed, her shoulders heaving. Then she bolted toward the truck that had once been Nat's.

For a few minutes I remained, watching rainwater leach through the mound of earth beside the grave and emerge in rusty trickles. I thought of the questions that Willie Dean's death answered and the crimes it solved. And I thought of the blanks I couldn't fill in, no matter how hard I twisted and forced the evidence.

But despite their reservations, almost everyone else in Hemlock Lake had, with a sense of relief, decided Willie Dean was responsible for everything. They'd admitted it was a sad situation, they said they hated to think one of their own would do such things, but they agreed that justice had been done.

It was simpler that way. As Camille said, blaming him removed the unknown, gave them a place from which to move on. Even the sheriff seemed satisfied. He'd cut short my arguments, reminded me I wasn't assigned to Willie Dean's shooting, and told me to call him back in a week or so and let him know whether I planned to return to duty or resign. I'd seethed for a while, but then understood that, like almost everyone else, he'd grown bone-weary of the situation.

Wiping rain from my eyes, I walked to the SUV and drove back to the lodge. The road was awash, slick with a long summer's residue of dust and oil. The tires hydroplaned in the straightaway below Bobcat Hollow, and I took my foot off the gas and rode out the skid. Dead leaves, brought down by the pelting drops, clogged the windshield wipers, leaving dark streaks on the glass. I turned down the drive to the lodge and saw the lake, like molten lead at the bottom of a clay bowl. How long would it take to fill again?

Camille knocked on the door as I was drying my hair, then bustled in, carrying a paper sack, rain glistening on her head like a diamond tiara. "Did Louisa Marie show up?"

"No. So Freeman lost a five-dollar bet to Evan."

She grimaced. "They were betting at the funeral?"

"Not in the church," I said, defending them. "Outside."

She didn't smile. "And what about Ronny? Was he there?"

"No. Until there's a ruling of self-defense, he's keeping a low profile."

"Anybody betting on that ruling?" Her voice vibrated with sarcasm.

"No. No one wants to bet on a sure thing."

"And *is* it a sure thing?"

I shrugged. "Seems that way."

She frowned, then shook it off. "I brought you some hot soup." She walked to the kitchen, talking over her shoulder. "When I saw the clouds building up, I got to work. It's cream of mushroom and potato. With crumbled bacon and sour cream to put on top. Comfort food." She laughed. "Funny how all comfort food is high in fat and calories and cholesterol."

I leaned in the doorway, rubbing my head with the towel, listening as she pulled a bowl from the cabinet and set it on the counter. "I don't think I've ever heard of anyone in need of comfort sitting down to a big salad with low-calorie raspberry vinaigrette dressing. Or to a bowl of braised tofu." Silverware clattered. "Or a dish of steamed broccoli with a little lemon juice." She laughed again.

"You don't have to be so cheerful," I told her as I slung the towel around my shoulders. "Not on my account. I'm okay.

This funeral didn't—I'm okay, that's all. Getting better every day."

She nodded, put the soup bowl into the microwave, and turned to me, her eyes the burnished red-brown of oak leaves in autumn. "I know." She chewed at her lower lip. "It isn't your spirit I'm trying to lift, it's my own."

I held out my arms and she stepped into them, fitting her head against my neck. "What's wrong?"

"Nothing. I mean, it's not wrong." She lifted her head, and I kissed her for the first time in a month, tasting the vanilla in her lip gloss, smelling the sweet flowery scent of her shampoo. "It's just timing, I guess."

I tipped her head and looked into her eyes, seeing doubt and pain. I kissed her again, marveling at the soft give of her mouth, marveling that I was able to lose myself in kissing her without feeling I'd committed an act of betrayal against Susanna. Perhaps I hadn't been lying when I'd said I was okay. Perhaps I had crossed an emotional boundary. Or perhaps, on a more childish level, I'd decided that I wouldn't be faithful to someone who hadn't been faithful to me. "What is it? What's the problem? You know if I can do anything about it, I will."

She looked into my eyes, checking my resolve. "I know." The microwave bell dinged, and she turned with a sigh. "But we made a bargain, remember?"

"No."

She set the soup on the table, pulled out a chair, and gestured for me to sit. "That I'd leave at the end of the summer." She pointed out the window at the slate-colored rain. "And it's over. The Brocktons leave in three days."

I shook my head. Things were just starting to feel right again. I wanted to be with her as a whole person. "A bargain can be renegotiated."

"Sometimes," she admitted as she opened small containers of

sour cream and crumbled bacon. "But one of us might feel cheated."

I took her arm and turned her toward me. "You?" I ran my hands down her back, slid them under her sweatshirt, and pulled her against me. "Do you feel cheated?" I kissed her, feeling myself stiffen as I unhooked her bra.

"No." Her fingers fumbled at my belt buckle as I pulled off her shirt. She shrugged out of her bra, raised my T-shirt, and pressed her bare flesh against mine. "Not right now."

A week later I helped Camille drain the Brocktons' water pipes, close up their house, and pack her car. The night before, we'd fallen on each other like wolves and made love until we ached. Now we treated each other with formality and care, as if the slightest touch would bruise, a word spoken too far above a whisper would slice skin and draw blood.

The rain had continued since the funeral—as pelting showers, as a persistent drizzle, and lately as a penetrating mist. Like a sodden shroud, it lay over everything in the valley. Trees sloughed off moisture with each gust of wind, flinging drops to the ground in disgust.

"After a summer of drought, I thought I'd be glad to see rain, but I'm tired of it already. I can feel winter on my shoulders." Camille hugged herself, but moved no closer to me. "It will be good to see the sun again."

I clung to the words. A clue to where she'd be? "So, you're going south?"

She gave me an enigmatic smile. "I don't know where I'm going yet, Dan. And even if I did, I think it's better that we break clean."

I didn't argue. That would feel too much like begging; and I didn't want her to stay with me out of pity. Like Susanna had? I shrugged, staring at the pewter lake. It reflected only smoky mist.

"You'll be leaving yourself in a little bit," she said, consoling me.

"Not for weeks, maybe a month. The lodge isn't ready to sell yet."

"It would be ready if you were ready," she said softly.

I turned to look at her. "What does that mean?"

She opened her mouth as if to speak, then shut it. "Nothing."

"Are you saying I don't want to leave Hemlock Lake?"

She didn't answer.

"Because I will," I insisted. "As soon as I clean out the garage and get the rest of the painting done and replace the old faucets and make some repairs in the kitchen . . ." I stopped, realizing that everything on that list was unnecessary, that the lodge could be sold as it stood. Was I saying a long good-bye? Or was I like a mother who plans her daughter's wedding in exquisite detail because it will be the last thing under her control?

"I'll miss you, Dan." Camille stretched a hand toward my arm, then drew it back, as if she might burn herself.

"I'll miss you, too." The words were inadequate. I sucked in a breath, wanting to tell her about what had been in my mind when I kissed her after Willie Dean's funeral, how I'd felt whole, free. Would she believe me? Or would she think a man afraid to be alone would say anything he thought might change her mind?

"It couldn't last. You see that, don't you?" She avoided my eyes, peering across the lake toward the lodge. "Eventually it would fall of its own weight. I'd be a constant reminder of when you . . ." She shivered. "That's no basis for a relationship."

"No relationship will last if one of the people involved won't stay in one place long enough to take a risk."

She whiplashed toward me, stung by the words I'd intended to offer only as a statement of fact. Her eyes flashed, and she struck back. "Or if the other person leans on the past like a crutch and refuses to allow himself a future."

And now it was too late to tell her what was in my heart, too late to do anything but let her leave. Stone family pride stiffened my spine. Gritting my teeth, I stalked to the SUV and wrenched open the door. As I slid in, I spotted a coil of rope I'd bought to repair broken window-sash cords.

"Here." I slung the rope at her. "Take that. When you find a place where you want to stay, a person you can stay with, then tie yourself down so you don't walk away out of habit."

I heard a strangled cry, but I didn't look back.

CHAPTER 33

Four days later, Ronny and I wrestled a roll of linoleum through the back door of the lodge and dumped it on the kitchen floor. "Could have gone with them squares with the sticky stuff on the back," he said. "But no. You like a challenge." He rubbed his hands together. "Getting cold out there, bud. Might get frost tonight."

Taking my cue, I retrieved the bourbon from a cabinet above the sink and got two bottles of ale from the refrigerator we'd maneuvered into the living room along with the table and chairs. The stove had been relegated to the back porch. That gave us the room we'd needed to tear up three layers of old linoleum and put down a new one—a muzzy blue and white swirling pattern that would go with the countertops. "We could leave the rest for morning."

Ronny took a slug of bourbon, then twisted the cap off a bottle of ale, drained half of it, and wiped his mouth with the back of his hand. He took two more swallows and set the empty bottle beside the sink. "Nope, I'm refueled. And the night's still young. Let's get it cut."

I set my untouched bottle aside, and together we grappled with the rolled linoleum, lining it up against the wall. "We make a good team." Ronny clicked out the blade of a utility knife and cut the string. The linoleum unrolled with a series of dull slaps. "Come November, if you haven't taken off, we'll do some deer hunting."

I kept my gaze on the floor, my lips tight. I didn't want to antagonize him with honesty—not about hunting, and not about the paper I'd signed agreeing to list the lodge for sale on October first, three days from now. Silence widened between us, like a fault line ripping through the earth. I searched for words to toss across the chasm. "You and Lisa were a good team, too. I sure miss her."

"Yeah." He clicked the blade in and out. "Where'd you put that bucket of glue?"

"In the living room."

"Find it while I get the trowels. And turn on more light. It's dark as a tax man's heart with just that bulb over the sink." He strode across the kitchen and out the back.

I moved to the switches by the door to the living room, the ones that controlled the overhead fluorescents in the kitchen, the ox-bow chandelier that hung from the living room ceiling, and the lamps that bracketed the mantel. The phone rang as I searched for the glue among the clutter of boxes and bags hauled from the pantry floor. Snatching up the receiver, I grunted a hello.

"Dan? How are you doing?" Sheriff North's voice was thin and edgy.

I carried the phone to the length of its cord and peered behind the refrigerator. "I'm okay. Getting better every day."

"Good. Good." I heard his sigh, almost heard his thoughts: *Dan won't give me any trouble, he'll resign like a man.* "Good," he said once more. "Have you given any thought to coming back?"

"No." I'd been consumed with priming and painting, ordering linoleum, buying caulk and varnish, consumed with trying not to think about where Camille might be and wishing I'd been strong enough to be weak enough to beg her to stay.

"Does that mean you haven't thought about it, or you're not coming back?"

"It means I haven't—" Something pinged at the back of my mind, like sonar picking up a distant shape. I glanced at my watch. Nearly eight. Why would the sheriff call to discuss this now? "What's happened?"

"You've got good instincts, son. I've always said that. The lab finally sent back the analysis on some of your evidence. But if you're not on the job, I'll turn it over to someone else."

"What did they find?" My mind projected images behind my eyes: the fires, the bombs, the camp on the mountain, Lisa and Willie Dean. Ronny opened the front door, waved the trowels, and raised an eyebrow. I shrugged and motioned for him to get another bottle of ale from the refrigerator. He shrugged back and set the trowels on the couch.

"So you're back with us." The sheriff made it a statement, not a question.

I hedged my bet. "For right now, yeah. What have you got?"

Ronny twisted the top from the bottle and shied it into the fireplace. It tinked off an andiron and skittered across the hearth.

"I thought that's the way you'd try to play it." The sheriff chuckled. I heard paper rustle and his chair creak. "Okay. No matches on the fingerprints on those cans of food. At least no matches to what's in the system." He paused and I heard the flare of a match and the soft sound of him sucking on his pipe. Paper rustled again. "No fingerprints on that shotgun. None on the fragments of the pipe bombs from the construction site."

"If what you've got is nothing, then why did—"

"Hold your fire until I'm finished, son. I haven't told you about the toxicology report on Lisa Miller."

I glanced at Ronny, who'd sauntered over to the fireplace, set his bottle of ale on the mantel, and toed the twist-top back into the fireplace.

"And?"

The sheriff cleared his throat. "Was she in the habit of taking a lot of pills? Antidepressants? Sleeping pills?"

Ronny strolled toward the open front door.

"I don't know." I thought about Lisa, her energy, the projects she took on. "She didn't seem like the type to take sleeping pills. But—"

All the pieces I'd puzzled over for months collided at the center of my brain and fell into place. My jaw dropped. I stared at Ronny.

He pivoted and lunged for the rifle rack.

I dropped the phone, rolled behind the couch, and scrabbled for the gun I'd set on the bookcase weeks ago. I was three feet away when I heard the rifle bolt clack home.

"That's far enough, bud." Ronny's whisper was as cold as a January wind.

My muscles sagged on my bones, and the skin between my shoulder blades twitched as if it could feel the bullet coming.

"I tried to warn you off, bud, but you just hung in."

Why hadn't I seen it? Because he had once been my friend? Because I'd been distracted by personal demons? Because I refused to believe he could kill his own wife?

"Get over there and hang up that damn phone. Then pull the cord out of the wall."

I hoisted myself upright, tottered to the phone, and tore it from the jack, telling myself to keep cool. The sheriff knew I was in trouble. In half an hour he'd have a team at the top of the driveway. They'd secure a perimeter, scout the situation, and advance to the lodge. I glanced at Ronny and knew we'd figured our way to the same answer: they'd arrive too late.

"Sit down on the couch for a bit," he said.

I lowered myself to the cushions and set the phone beside me. Only a few weeks ago I'd sat in this same spot, intent on killing myself. Now every cell in my body was determined to live, to find Camille, to tell her it wasn't about her helping me or me needing her, it was about whatever came next. I bargained for time, hoping Ronny would want me to take his confession to my grave. "Why did you kill Lisa?"

Ronny sighed. He hooked a kitchen chair from a stack in the corner, turned it upright, and settled into it, the rifle across his knees. "I didn't want to, bud, believe me. But I didn't have a choice. It was all getting away from me. When those guys at the construction site didn't leave after the letters and the graffiti, they forced me to escalate."

Forced? Cold queasiness filled my gut. Ronny was beyond reason.

"I thought I could lay it all off on the man on the mountain," he said. "But then Lisa found the makings for the bombs. She told me to turn myself in. She said you'd understand and see that they went easy on me." He laughed, a nasty sound, more a feral growl. "Lisa always thought you were the smart one, Dan. Too bad you weren't smart enough to save her."

He raised the pitch of his voice, sing-songed the words. "She wanted me to confess to everything. Make restitution. Get help for my problem!" His voice rose to a roar. "What happened was her own damn fault. I told her a thousand times to stay out of my den." His voice dropped to a matter-of-fact tone. "She should have stood by me, backed me up."

The set of his mouth and the intensity of his eyes told me he had no doubt he'd done what was right. I shuddered. "And Willie Dean?"

"Hell!" Ronny stood and snagged the bottle of ale he'd set on the mantel. I took in his every move while my brain manufactured a dozen worthless plans for escape. "I'd wanted to do that for a long time. Twenty, twenty-five years. It was getting so I couldn't look at his stupid face without feeling my blood pressure shoot up. Then he started pandering to those new folks. It made me sick. I decided he could take the blame for everything."

And that plan almost worked. "How'd you get him to come to your house in the middle of the night? I'd have thought he'd be suspicious."

Ronny tipped his head back, drank deeply. "Not after I bought him that steak dinner. The condemned man ate hearty." He laughed again, the sound raising the hair along my arms. "I called him at the bait shop, told him I'd spotted a campsite when I was tearing up the mountains a few weeks ago." He sucked ale. "I told Willie Dean to keep it between the two of us so we'd get all the credit for creeping up on the guy in the middle of the night. Shit! Willie Dean was so dumb he believed I'd pass by Freeman, who could surprise his own shadow, and pick a moron with two left feet to tag along. It was like shooting fish in a barrel."

And you always liked an easy win.

He drained the ale and sprawled in the chair, studying me. "What's the sheriff got? What'd he say about Lisa?"

I spread my fingers. "Nothing much."

"Don't lie to me, bud. You suck at it. Your eyes twitch and your voice squeaks." He pointed the rifle at my chest. "What's he got?"

My throat tightened. I coughed to clear it. "He said something about sleeping pills."

"And you said you didn't think she was the type." Ronny chortled. "Well, there's a whole world about precious, perfect Lisa you just flat didn't know, bud. Lisa took pills, oh yeah, she took pills. She said I made her nervous." He squinted, gave me a crafty look. "Probably got so nervous that night, she took a shitload of them and didn't wake up when I yelled." He laughed, smug and mean. "Yeah, that's exactly what happened. And no one can prove it didn't go down that way."

He could be right. If he could get rid of me, and if he got a sharp lawyer, he just might argue his way out of a murder charge. Two murder charges, I corrected myself, thinking of Willie Dean. No, three. I'd forgotten to count myself.

He smiled. "It's a shame you won't be at the trial. You'd be the star witness." He got to his feet. "But you'll be next to sweet little Susanna by then."

I stiffened, thinking about the unmarked plots in the cemetery. I'd never ordered stones for Nat and Susanna. Or for my father. Would my grave remain unmarked, too? Would Camille learn of my death, visit the cemetery, clear the weeds?

"Here's what we're going to do, bud. Pick up that bucket of glue—it's there behind those chairs—and head to the kitchen. You're going to have an unfortunate little accident. Seems you needed more light. So you got this old kerosene lamp." He stepped to the mantel and lifted the red-glass-globed lamp that had been my great-grandmother's. "And it seems it tipped over somehow and caught the place on fire." He sloshed the liquid inside. "Go on, get going."

"The sheriff will know it wasn't an accident."

He prodded me again. "Shut up and get up, bud."

I struggled to my feet, my body numb with fear, my mind racing. I crossed to the stack of chairs, bent and fumbled for the bucket, thinking that I could throw it as a diversion. Then I could dive at Ronny's knees, knock him to the floor, wrestle the rifle away. I tensed.

"Don't even think about it, bud. You were the quarterback, remember? You never made a tackle in your life. Now get going."

Grasping the heavy bucket, I stumbled toward the kitchen. The floor seemed to buck and wobble beneath my feet. I didn't want to die. Not when my life was about to start again.

"Jesus, bud," Ronny laughed. "You're a sorry excuse for a man." He jabbed the barrel into my right kidney. "Suck it up, boy. Show me some of that Stone family pride."

I jerked away from the rifle, flung out a hand to steady myself. My fingers touched the edge of the switch plate. How much time did I have? "The sheriff's on the way."

He threw back his head and laughed wildly. "On the way ain't the same as on the spot, is it?"

I inched my fingers along the plate until the edge of my hand rested on the switches.

"And he's got to prove I was here when your accident happened."

I flailed at the light switches and wheeled to my right, hurling the bucket at his chest as I hurtled toward the door he hadn't closed.

Ronny grunted. The bucket crashed to the floor. I whacked my knee against the end of the couch and stumbled.

A bullet cut the air above my head. I dove and scrabbled across the threshold. A second bullet shattered a window as I belly-crawled across the porch.

"You son of a bitch!" Ronny's feet thudded behind me.

I somersaulted down the stone steps and scrambled for the SUV, digging the keys from my pocket.

The outside lights blazed on. I dodged for the corner of the house.

Ronny shot again, and a searing pain arced through my left shoulder. I heard myself scream and felt my arm go numb. The keys dropped from my fingers as I clamped my right hand to the wound. I ran past the back porch, past my mother's roses and the path to the spring, then crumpled beneath a lilac bush.

CHAPTER 34

"Get back here and die, you pathetic fuck!" Ronny thundered down the steps.

A warm wetness welled through my fingers.

"Where are you, bud? I know I hit you. Come out now, and I'll make it quick."

I crept uphill away from the house, thankful for the sodden ground that muffled my movements, but cursing the brush-clearing that left me little cover. I had to reach the road, link up with my rescuers. When I was out of earshot, I'd swing up the ridge, double back, find a sheltered spot, and wait for help. It was only three hundred yards. The length of three football fields. But Ronny wasn't on my team.

The lights on the back porch flared. A bullet sliced through the leaves a few feet ahead of me. "I know what you're thinking, bud. But you won't get to the road. There's a lot of ammo in the lodge, and I'll use it to lay down a blanket of fire." He shot again. "I'll get you. You can bank on it."

Another bullet pinged off a rock, and I flattened myself behind a tree. *Fire enough,* I told myself, *and someone will come to see what's going on—Stub or Freeman or Evan. Or maybe not.* With their windows closed against the raw air, they might not hear the shots, or might not be curious enough to leave their warm houses to see what was going on.

"Too bad Nat and your father didn't believe in night scopes. It would save us both a lot of time." He pounded two more shots into the woods. A bullet hit my tree and I flinched, my shoulder tightening with a spasm of pain that doubled me over.

I straightened by inches, peered around the tree, and saw him set the rifle down and fit a shotgun to his shoulder. Pellets rattled the brush around me. One gouged my right ankle. I bit down on a scream.

"I know I hit you, bud. You're losing blood, dying an inch at a time." He turned and fired toward the driveway. "Come out and let me get a clean shot."

Move toward the water, I told myself. *He won't expect that. Get around him in the lak*e.

The lake. The lake. A voice deep in my brain repeated. I staggered, struggled to recall the line that began Robert Frost's poem. I wanted to sit. Lie down. Sleep. My knees buckled.

A load of buckshot spattered the water. I stiffened. Had he anticipated me again? I held my breath and heard the next pellets dance off the garage roof. No. He was drawing a circle of fire. Under cover of the next blast I hobbled faster, my left arm thudding against my side. Four steps. Six. Ten. I slipped on stones slick with icy dew, fell to my knees, and rolled down the muddy slope. The cold water hit like a hammer against my chest, pounding air from my lungs. I lay on my back for a moment, drawing in shallow whistling breaths, praying Ronny hadn't heard the splash.

"You still with us, bud? You haven't died on me, have you?" Ronny fired two more shots toward the road. "You should be advising me to give myself up and shit like that, shouldn't you? Reading me my rights? Or have you figured out that would be a waste of time? They're not going to take me out alive, bud. But they won't get you out alive, either." He fired again. "I can't let you win."

Trembling, I clamped my hand tighter to my shoulder, rolled onto my side, got my feet under me, and duck-walked into the lake, shoes sticking in the muddy bottom. Just a little farther. Waist level. Then I'd move parallel to the shore, get around the tongue of land on which the lodge sat. Then back into the woods and up to the road. One step at a time.

He fired two more shots, and in the silence that followed I heard his feet crunching in gravel, coming toward me. "You're not in the lake, are you? That would be a bad mistake. You could never swim worth shit."

I shoved myself toward deeper water, remembering my dream, the way I'd fought the lake. Water rose to my waist, my chest, closed around my neck. It burned the wound like a brand. Risking a look back, I saw Ronny pulling something from my rig.

"I got your official flashlight, bud. If you're in the lake, I'll spot you."

He strode to the dock, the narrow beam playing across the planks, strafing the lake. I lay back, settling my head into inky water, breathing through shivering lips.

"Ha. You're dead meat!"

The first bullet sizzled a few feet from my nose. I sucked in a breath and went under. When I came up, the flashlight beam found me in an instant but his shot went wild.

"Son of a bitch. You're making this hard." Ronny fired two more shots; one struck so close I could have grabbed it. He set the flashlight on the dock. "I need more light. A lot more light." He laughed viciously. "Don't rush off."

I pushed away from the bottom, paddling with my right arm. My feet felt like anvils chained to my ankles. My spine felt like a rod of ice driven through my gut. The water widened between me and the dock.

"I'm gonna build a bonfire, bud," Ronny bellowed. Gasping, I peered back at the lodge and saw him set fire to a twisted torch of newspaper. "Old as this place is, it'll be gone inside twenty minutes. You want to stop me, you come back. Now!"

I hesitated, thinking of my grandfather's knotty pine panel-ing, my grandmother's drapes, my mother's curtains, family photograph albums, the glass-eyed stag above the fireplace, and that brand new linoleum. Then I thought of Camille. I paddled farther into the lake.

"All right then. Don't say I didn't give you a choice." He stepped through the door. In a minute I saw flames flickering, knew they were chewing at those velvet drapes. I felt a stabbing loss and managed only a few limp strokes before the flashlight beam slid across the rippling water and found me. Ronny stood at the edge of the dock. Behind him, the windows blazed with crimson light.

"You're one gutty dude. I gotta give you that." He raised the shotgun to his shoulder. "It's too bad you—"

A shot sounded.

The shotgun clattered to the dock. Ronny crumpled beside it.

I raised my right arm, signaling to whomever had taken Ronny out. "I'm in the lake!" I floundered toward shore. A wild-haired figure in a long coat emerged from the night and stood silhouetted against the flames, rifle at his side. He shaded his eyes and scanned the lake.

I slapped the water. "Over here!"

Tossing the rifle aside, he stripped off the coat and ran. His gray hair, stained by the rising flames, streamed behind him like the tail of a comet. He smacked the water in the kind of racing dive Nat had been so good at. In a few strokes he was beside me. "Corporal Jefferson Longyear, reporting for duty, sir."

Jefferson Longyear? Louisa Marie's Jefferson Longyear? It couldn't be. He'd been missing for years. No one had been able to find him. Everyone had thought him dead.

I tried to tell him that, but he wedged one bony arm under

my chin and the pressure cut off my words. Anchoring a hand in my right armpit, he towed me toward shore, his legs scissoring beneath me. "We'll get you out of here, Sergeant."

I struggled to hold my eyelids open. Jefferson Longyear must be dead, so I must be dying. His ghost had saved me from the snake and warned me about the shotgun because my time hadn't come yet. But now it had, and he'd come for me.

I tried to break the ghost's hold. "I want to live."

"I know. Let me do the work, sir." His voice was confident, controlled. "Don't fight."

I struggled on, shoulder and ankle throbbing. Flopping my head to the side, I tried to gauge the distance to the end of the dock, to the next world. Only a few more yards.

Glass shattered, and I jerked my head toward the lodge. Pennants of flame fluttered from the broken window. The pulsing light touched Ronny. He twitched, struggled to his knees.

"Ronny's getting up," I marveled. "He must be going with us."

"Motherf'er." Jefferson's arm dug at the water, turning us away from the dock. His legs scissored harder. "Keep your head down, Sergeant."

Ronny coughed and spat a stream of dark liquid onto the dock. He reached for the shotgun. "So you've got a friend, huh, bud?" He fumbled a shell from his pocket, fed it in, and raised the gun to his shoulder. "Well, you're both going to die."

"Take a deep breath, Sergeant." I heard Jefferson gulp air. His arm tightened across my neck, and we dropped beneath the surface. Pellets, their force broken by the water, stung my legs. *We're not dead,* I thought, *or it wouldn't matter whether Ronny shoots us. We're alive!*

I kicked along with Jefferson, and we broke the surface, gasping. Far down the lake, a siren wailed. I couldn't feel my legs, couldn't feel my left arm. But my teeth no longer chattered.

Fire chewed at the walls of the lodge, streaked the lake with scarlet. Ronny lurched to his feet, staggered to the end of the dock.

"This time for sure, bud." Ronny brought the gun to his shoulder again, then cocked his head and turned toward the lodge. He took aim at a dark figure that stood, legs braced in a shooter's stance, at the edge of the driveway.

A shot sounded. The shotgun dropped from Ronny's hands, bounced off the dock, and splashed into the lake. He bent at the waist, seemed to stretch and reach for it, then collapsed into the water.

The dark figure raced toward us.

"Who's that, Sergeant?" Jefferson gasped in my ear. "Friend or foe?"

I tried to tell him I didn't know, but my mouth wouldn't work. My eyelids drooped. I felt my feet dragging me down, warmth spreading through my icy chest.

Jefferson's legs thrust against the water, but it crept higher, around my neck, over my chin. Flames stampeded across the roof of the lodge.

"Help me, Sergeant. You've got to help me. Kick!"

I tried. I couldn't. Water reached my eyes. The flames wavered and blurred.

Jefferson worked his legs like pistons. My head rose, and I choked down a breath. The dark figure reached the end of the dock. It swung its arms and hurled something toward us, something that snaked out over the water and slapped the surface a few feet away.

"The rope!" Camille yelled. "Grab the rope!"

Epilogue

Camille braked at the top of the driveway and gazed at me, doubt clouding her eyes. "You're sure you want to see the lodge again?"

I reached across my body with my good arm and touched her cheek. "I have to."

"I know." Her foot left the brake, hovered over the gas. "But it's such a dismal day. Maybe we should come back when—"

"No." I wiped the side window with my sleeve and looked out at the gray November sky. I'd lost October to transfusions, surgeries, and rehabilitation, to dreamless sleep and exhausted hours in one chair or another. "Sunlight would be more cruel."

She nodded and let out the clutch. The tires crunched down the gravel driveway, and I saw the charred remnants of the lodge. Two blackened walls still stood, the logs cross-hatched where flames had gnawed at them before Hemlock Lake firefighters and crews from three other towns had subdued the blaze. The roof had fallen in, and the front porch had burned away, leaving only the stone pillars and chimney, grim sentinels guarding the wreckage. "Total loss," my insurance agent had told me. "And don't count on seeing any money until your father's estate is settled. The way the legal system moves, that could be months, maybe a year."

"What a waste." Camille turned off the engine. "What a horrible waste."

I heard tears behind her voice, and I knew she wasn't talking about the lodge, but about Ronny and Lisa and Willie Dean, about Julie and Justin and Priscilla, about the betrayal of trust and love.

I opened the door and eased out. Camille stood by, not offering to help, just being there. It felt good to know I could stretch out my hand and touch hers, lean on her if I needed to, wanted to. She'd come back to me. But how long would she stay?

Staring at the rubble, a kaleidoscope of memories played across my mind. I saw my grandparents, my parents, Nat, and Susanna on the porch as it had once been. I saw Ronny light the torch, the blaze erupt behind him. I tracked my flight into the brush, then to the lake. Water the color of ash lapped at the dock where a length of rope lay. I moved toward it.

"We can stop and see Jefferson later if you'd like." Camille kept pace with me. "You'll be amazed at what Lou Marie and Mary Lou have done to fix up that old school building for him." She shook her head. "It seems so strange to hear them talking to each other. And I still can't believe he was able to hide in there, right in the middle of town, without anybody knowing."

"He was a sniper. He learned how to be a ghost. It was the one thing he never forgot." I threaded my fingers through hers, thinking about the man who'd walked away from a hospital and spent years in an endless maze of lonely streets, piling up rocks, building grave markers for enemies he'd killed, friends he'd lost. A year ago, a picture in a magazine had triggered a recollection of the life he'd had before the war, and he'd made his way to Hemlock Lake.

"Mary Lou will never forgive me if I don't take you by the post office," Camille said. "She saw us drive into town, and she's probably organizing an impromptu welcome back celebration."

I winced, but acknowledged it was a rite I'd submit to. "All right."

I released her hand and stepped onto the dock. Picking up the rope, I coiled it into my weak hand as I looked across the lake. The leaves had browned and dropped around the Brocktons' house. Two weeks ago they'd offered to let me stay there through the winter. They'd made Camille the same offer. We'd both said we'd think about it. Neither of us had raised the subject since.

I turned to the lodge, putting my back to Camille so I wouldn't see the answer in her eyes before I said all the words I'd practiced. "I love you, Camille, but I can understand if you've stayed with me only because I was hurt."

She didn't answer, and I plunged on, my gaze fixed on the ruins. "And I can understand if you're planning to leave now that I'm better. But I wish it could be different between us. I want you to love me. And I want to go with you."

She plucked the rope from my fingers and strode toward the lodge. "You can't go with me, Dan." She uncoiled the rope and slung it around a soot-blackened pillar. "Remember what you told me when I drove away?" She knotted the rope around her waist. "To tie myself down when I found a place I wanted to stay?" She cinched a second knot. "Well, this is it." She opened her arms. "You can't go with me because I'm not leaving. I'm staying here with you."

With a whoop of joy I bounded toward her.

ABOUT THE AUTHOR

Carolyn J. Rose was born and raised in the Catskill Mountains of New York. After graduating from the University of Arizona, she joined Volunteers in Service to America and worked with food and medical programs in and around Little Rock, Arkansas. There she began a career in television news that took her to Albuquerque, New Mexico; Eugene, Oregon; and Vancouver, Washington, where she lives with her husband, radio personality Mike Phillips, and a motley collection of pets. Visit her at www.deadlyduomysteries.com.